In the Shadow of Versailles

Max Anderson Mysteries, Volume 1

Hayden Trenholm

Published by House of Straw Press, 2021.

IN THE SHADOW OF VERSAILLES

First edition. September 15, 2021.

Copyright © 2021 Hayden Trenholm.

ISBN: 978-1927881613

Written by Hayden Trenholm.

This book is dedicated to my wife and writing partner, Liz Westbrook-Trenholm for all her advice and support over the years.

One – Saturday, November 30, 1918

Every evening Max walked from his hotel, past Gare du Nord, toward the Basilica de Sacre Coeur, now in the final stages of construction at the top of Montmartre. When the pain in his leg grew too great, he would stop in the first bar for a croquette and a glass of beer. After his exertion, he was thirsty and would drink half the beer in a single gulp, the liquid cold and crisp in his mouth, and then sip the rest while he slowly ate the fried cake. He had only been in Paris a week but already, his leg felt stronger and, each day, he made it a little farther up the hill. By Christmas, he thought, I'll be strong enough to go to midnight Mass. He thought of his Uncle George, deacon in the First Baptist Church, turned red with rage at the very thought, perhaps finally succumbing to that long-promised stroke. It was almost worth climbing all those stairs.

Max knew he could not stay at L'Aquilon forever. It was a warm refuge against the night and Jean Marc had proved a generous and trustworthy host. The food in the restaurant was simple but hearty but, soon, he would have to find a flat where he could cook his own food. His income was steady but small and, until his confidence in his French improved, he would have no chance to increase it. When his discharge pay was spent, he would have to move to a cheaper neighbourhood on the far side of the river. Perhaps the railway porter who had been so kind to him on his arrival in Paris would have a suggestion.

He finished his beer and dropped a few sou on the table for the barman. From here he could go right and take Clichy to Rue Fontaine before turning back to the hotel. Those streets were lined with cafés and bars and there might be music. He could flirt with the

1

girls who worked in the dance halls though he was not fit enough to dance and had no interest in the other services they offered. Paris had been asleep since 1914 but now that the war was over, the city was packed with strangers and full of enthusiasms. Its citizens seemed determined to prove that the City of Light was still the brightest beacon in all of Europe. Sometimes, it seemed to be trying too hard.

Instead, Max turned to the left and took a quieter route past shuttered shops and houses, the dark broken only by an occasional street lamp and the thin lines of light that showed beneath the curtained second floor windows. The few people he passed seemed absorbed in their own thoughts, haunted by memories the rest of Paris wanted to forget.

He was passing a stone church opposite Square St. Bernard when he heard the cry. It was faint and echoed against the stone walls of the old buildings so that, at first, he couldn't tell where it had come from or even if it was a man or a woman.

The cry came again, clearer and more desperate.

"Aux secours! On me tue."

They are killing me. The voice was coming from the far side of the church. The streets were now deserted. Max was weaponless save for a small pocketknife and his cane. He thought of the Webley service revolver he had kept for reasons he did not understand, hidden in a box at the bottom of his suitcase. He might as well wish for the moon.

A third cry, a harsh inchoate groan of pain. A familiar tremor ran along his legs and he had to force himself to turn toward the sound. After the first step it was easier and Max hurried along the wrought iron fence that surrounded the church, each painful stride threatening to tumble him to the ground. His only asset was surprise. He stepped through a narrow gate, bellowing with his best parade ground voice. Three men, their faces covered in scarves, were punching and kicking a fourth, who was slumped in an archway against a blue door trying to shield his face with his upraised arms. At Max's shout the gang froze in a violent tableau, lit by a single dim streetlight opposite the church's rear entrance.

Before they could react, Max took two quick steps and struck the closest gangster, a short thick-set man in a striped shirt, across the neck with the head of his cane. The man staggered and almost fell. The second, taller but as heavily built, leapt toward Max, hands outstretched. He recoiled in pain as Max's small blade cut a gash across the back of his hand and up his arm.

The victim was not helpless, either. He took quick advantage of Max's interruption, stepped close to his third assailant and shot a hard right into the man's broad belly. He followed with a short chopping left to the man's ear. The gangster turned and fled, the other two fast behind.

They had barely disappeared in the darkness before a policeman came flying around the corner, his white stick raised and his cape billowing behind him.

"Almost when we needed one," muttered the short dark man Max had rescued, picking up his hat.

The gendarme, puffing and red faced, looked from Max to the other man, who was now dabbing at the blood on his face with a white silk handkerchief. He said something fast that Max didn't catch. He shook his head. "Pardon, ne comprend pas."

"Is this wog bothering you, monsieur?" he repeated in barely comprehensible English.

Max shook his head more emphatically and switched back to French. "No, he was being attacked by three men. They went that way." Max gestured with his cane along the street. The officer, a sergeant by the markings on his sleeve, nodded but gave no indication that he intended a pursuit. He took out a notebook and took their names, addresses and the few bits of description they could provide.

"Monsieur Barzani," he said at last, "Do you know why you were attacked?"

"Perhaps they wanted to rob me of my wallet," Barzani shrugged, speaking such precise French that Max felt envious. "Or perhaps it is because I'm a wog."

The gendarme glared and snapped his notebook shut. With a promise to find them should he require anything further, he turned on his heel and strode into the gathering gloom.

"We have heard each other's names but we have not formally met," said Barzani, in English as flawless as his French. He extended his hand. "Hevel Mohammed Barzani, late of Tehran, freelance diplomat and currently a man about town."

Max took the hand and shook it warmly, slightly embarrassed by the policeman's words and behaviour. He tried to match the precision of Barzani's French. "Maxwell Michael Anderson, late of Truro and the Nova Scotia Highlanders. Currently between drinks."

"Then we must remedy that. Drinks and a cigar, too. I have some imported directly from Cuba that you simply must try."

"I wasn't trying to cadge..."

"Of course not, my friend" said Barzani, taking Max by the arm. "I owe you a great debt. I think those men intended more than a simple beating. I would be a poor son of Allah if I did not offer some token of my gratitude. Now come. I know a charming little bistro a few blocks from here where we can be refreshed and build upon what I am sure will become a great friendship."

§

Le Coq Bleu redefined the meaning of charming in Max's reckoning. On the corner of Rue Gabrielle and Drevet, half way up Montmartre, the bar was small and, except for the garish neon rooster in blue and red that hung in the window, dimly lit. There were a dozen square tables covered in faded checkerboard cloths in the L-shaped room and a zinc covered bar along one wall. There were stubby candles stuck on small blue plates on every table but only a few were lit.

Max recognized the old porter, Henri, perched on a stool at one end of the bar. He nodded and Max thought he should speak to him, thank him for saving him from robbery, or worse, at the Gare du Nord. But Barzani was crossing the room so Max merely tipped his cap before following his new friend to a table by the window.

Barzani shrugged apologetically at the flickering sign. "Quite the remarkable piece, is it not? They say the owner won it in dice game with the designer, George Claude. Despite the glare, I prefer this table to the rest."

He must be very particular, thought Max, as he looked around the bar. Fewer than half the tables were in use. Most of the customers were men, sitting in groups of three or four, muttering in low voices and hunching over their glasses of beer or thin red wine. They had the look of workmen from the factories that filled the area on the far side of Montmartre. At one table, two women, their faces flushed and voices loud from drink laughed shrilly at some remark one of their companions had made. Their dresses draped loosely over their shoulders but were cut low in the back. One wore a flamboyant hat of lace and feathers, the other had her hair cut short in the new style. Both their lips were smeared with bright red lipstick.

"It is charming," said Max.

Barzani laughed. "It has its charms," he said, gesturing with his head to the far end of the bar, opposite from where Henri sat. A girl sat alone, sipping from a glass of white wine. Her face was pale, an oval beacon shining out of the shadows, framed by straight black hair. Max didn't realize he was staring until she caught his eyes with her own wide grey ones. She smiled softly and Max felt the heat rise in his face. An answering hint of colour flushed her cheeks but she didn't break her gaze, searching for something Max was sure his face didn't hold.

Max dropped his eyes to the table. The girl laughed, not unkindly, and said something to the bartender. He rushed to refill her glass.

"Don't worry, Max, she is his spoiled niece not his girlfriend," said Barzani. "Minette is available although unattainable."

The bartender sauntered to their table.

"You'll want your usual," he said.

"What else, Yesim, what else? But for my friend a glass of your finest cognac." Yesim nodded. "The finest, mind you, and in a clean glass. And some ice if you have any in that chest of yours."

Barzani smiled broadly, his teeth slightly crooked and yellow from tobacco. "One must be precise, don't you think?" He winced and put his fingers to the left side of his mouth. The bleeding had stopped but it was beginning to swell. His left eye, too, had begun to discolour and puff closed.

"Maybe you should see a doctor," said Max.

"Nonsense. Nothing a little ice and a night's sleep won't cure."

"It looks bad."

"I've collected worse bruises on my college's rugby fields – not to mention the back alleys of Jerusalem."

Max nodded. There was no doubt that Barzani could take a punch and throw one, too. "Who were those men? What did they want from you?"

"Nothing more than my wallet, I'm sure. It will teach me to take poorly-lit shortcuts."

Good advice. Still, there was something odd about the assault. Robbers get what they want and go; these men seemed intent on inflicting a beating. *Not my business, it's enough they didn't succeed.*

Yesim returned with their drinks and a plate of olives. He handed Barzani the ice wrapped in a bar cloth. Max tasted his cognac. The musk aroma filled his nose and mouth but the liquor burned his throat and filled his belly with warmth. Barzani watched him drink, then took a small sip of steaming darkness.

"Not as good as the coffee shops of Tehran but the best you will find in Paris. Yesim, as his name implies, was not born here. Now about those cigars."

He reached inside his jacket and withdrew a silver case like five tubes welded together. He extracted two cigars.

"These are called Panatelas – average in length but a little thinner than most. Good for a casual smoke in a place like this. Not something you would smoke in the finer men's clubs."

He passed one of the cigars to Max, who took it gingerly. He had never been a real smoker; an occasional shared cigarette in the trenches between attacks, when boredom fought with tension and any relief, a joke, a drink or a cheap smoke, was welcome.

Barzani clipped the end of the cigar with a pair of small rounded scissors then handed the instrument to Max who tried to copy him.

"Careful not to cut too much," said Barzani, gesturing for Max to move the scissors closer to the end. "That's better. Now the taste."

He slid the cigar under his nose and smelled along its length. Then he put the cut end in his mouth and drew on it in short sharp puffs. Taking out a pair of long matches, he passed one to Max and lit the other, waiting until the sulphur burned off before applying it to the end of the cigar. He took several slow pulls, half rotating the tube as he did so, until the entire end glowed red. He held the smoke in his mouth for a moment before exhaling it through his nose. The smoke was pungent but not entirely unpleasant, almost like the smell of burning cedar.

Max watched him carefully, for some reason not wanting to embarrass himself in front of Barzani. He was not a large man, four or five inches shorter than Max, himself not quite six feet tall, and quite slim. Yet he had already proven himself agile and quick in a fight and, even now, the left side of his face bruised and swollen, he had an air of calm elegance. *Dapper, this is what they mean by dapper.*

His face was swarthy, almost dark brown, but he was clearly not a Negro. Max had grown up with Negroes and there had been some in the trenches, especially after the Americans arrived. His middle name was Mohammed so he must be a Moor or an Arab of some kind. His beard and moustache were black and had recently been barbered. His eyes were lively and so dark they seemed like reflecting pools, glinting with light from the candle and the neon rooster. His age was indeterminate, though Max supposed he was at least thirty though not more than thirty-five. He was well dressed in a white shirt with a high detachable collar, now flecked with drops of red, and a dark wool jacket with thin lapels over a patterned waistcoat. The silk handkerchief was back in his breast pocket, carefully folded to hide the bloodstains. He wore a broad tie, printed in a geometric pattern that hurt to look at too long in the flickering light.

Max ran the cigar under his nose. The smell of tobacco was strong but there was an underlying sweetness that surprised him. He lit the cigar the way he had seen Barzani do it and took a cautious puff. It was different, not as harsh as the cigarettes he had tried before.

Before he could draw deeper, Barzani said, "Don't inhale. Hold it in your mouth and nose. That's where all the pleasure is."

It was alright though Max didn't think he would make a habit of it – if for no other reason than it looked expensive.

"What brought a Canadian soldier to the back streets of Paris on a cold December evening? Surely you were not looking for a foreigner who needed rescuing? Not that I'm complaining."

"Ex-soldier," said Max. "I've had my fill of fighting. Paris seems like a good place to be."

"There is no better place than Paris. If you have money."

"It's not bad even if you don't," said Max.

"But surely, after four years in Europe, you must long to see your home and family again."

Max took another draft on the cigar but didn't reply.

"Ah," said Barzani, "my father has passed, too. Last year. But your mother?"

This man is a stranger, someone I will never see again. Maybe if I tell him, he will take away the bitterness when he goes.

"My mother died when I was twelve – she had been ill for years. My father, two years later, in an accident in his factory. So they say."

"You disagreed?"

Max shrugged. "The opinions of boys don't count for a lot. My uncle George said it was an accident and the coroner agreed. I have no proof to the contrary. Doesn't matter now. I got my inheritance – what was left of it – when I was twenty-one. My Uncle could no longer forbid it so I quit university and signed up. No one seemed unhappy to see me go. Now, I'm happy to stay away." Even his brother, Ben, too young to really remember their parents, hadn't come to see him off.

Barzani took several puffs on his cigar while he gazed at Max thoughtfully. Max felt his face flush under that steady appraisal. "The past doesn't exist, my friend," he said at last. "The last four years put an end to it. People think they can put it all back together but they can't. The future is waiting and it will be men like you and I who will build it."

"That's quite a speech from a man who doesn't drink."

Barzani laughed. "You are quick. Nonetheless, what I say is true. Next month, the leaders of the world will arrive in Paris. All our troubles will be discussed and analyzed and every past wrong will be set right. We are all here for our own reasons – even if some of us don't know what they are yet. There was a purpose to our meeting tonight – of that I am sure."

Max smiled. He doubted that anything had a reason anymore. But he had tasted good cognac and smoked his first cigar so he supposed that was purpose enough.

Barzani took an expensive-looking watch from his vest pocket. "I have a late engagement that I really can't miss. I am staying at the Grand, near the Opera House. If you would like to share another smoke, drop by and ask for me there." He handed Max a small gilt embossed card. "In the meantime, I have an account here. Feel free to have another drink and try your luck with Minette."

With that, he picked up his slightly battered fedora and strode out of the bar. Max watched him march purposefully down the street. *What a strange man. I don't suppose I'll ever see him again.* He felt an odd pang of regret as he slipped the card into his pocket and ordered another cognac.

Two – Sunday, December 1 to Thursday December 12, 1918

The next morning, Max walked along the Quai on the right bank of the Seine. He was moving slowly after the exertions of the night before, stopping every few dozen steps to look at the river or the grand buildings that lined it.

He heard his name called and when he looked up, Barzani was dashing across the street, dodging through the welter of horses, cars and bicycles. The only sign of the previous night's encounter was a slight discoloration around his left eye.

"You're a fast healer," said Max, wishing he could say the same for himself.

"I try to wear my bruises on the inside," said Barzani, smiling. "Soaking up some history?"

"Mostly soaking up this rain," said Max, looking up at lowering skies.

"This isn't rain," said Barzani. "You haven't seen a Parisian rain. But if a little mist bothers you, we can find a coffee house."

"No," said Max. "I need to walk off some of this soreness."

"Why not?" Barzani moderated his usual brisk pace to match Max's slower gait. He paused frequently to describe some point of interest.

"Do you see this bridge?" said Barzani, "It was built with stones taken from the Bastille. And that statue, it's a copy; the original was melted down by the revolutionaries. And, look up, see that window – it is said that Madame Duplessis, the famous courtesan, would lower a rope to allow her lovers to climb up to her, while she was under house arrest."

They walked for an hour as Barzani recounted in lurid detail what bloody crime or juicy scandal lurked behind each shuttered window or down every narrow street. Max learned more of the secret history of Paris in that hour than from all the books he had read in England.

When they approached La Louvre, Barzani rested his hand on the low parapet wall. The rain was heavier now and Max was reconsidering Barzani's offer of a coffee shop.

"In 1910," said Barzani, "the whole city flooded in the winter rains. It was a miracle that the museum wasn't destroyed – a miracle made from the sweat of men. They piled sandbags here, even tore up the cobble stones to build a wall, higher than a man could reach. It is an inspiration to me. That men will risk everything to preserve what is best. It is a lesson we should never stop learning."

Max ran his hand across the smooth cement on the top of the wall. After all he had seen in the war, it was hard to believe that the sacrifice of men could actually count for something.

When they had passed the Louvre, Barzani glanced at his watch.

"I'll have to leave you now, Max," he said. "I have business nearby. I enjoyed our walk."

"Me, too," said Max. "I... hope to see you again."

"Look for me at Le Coq Bleu. I often stop there when I'm in Montmartre. For Yesim's coffee, of course." Barzani smiled and winked.

And a glimpse of the fair Minette. He watched the little man walk briskly away from the river, past the Louvre, until he lost sight of him in a small park that separated the museum from a large church.

The Seine was swollen with winter rains and water foamed white against the footings of the Pont Neuf, though it was in no danger of overflowing its banks. Max's emotions matched the turbulence of the river below. *Did he feel betrayed because of Barzani's interest in a girl*

*to whom he had never even spoken? No, not that but still something felt
oddly treasonous. But who was betraying whom?*

They had spoken again for a few minutes on the street two days
later and then on Thursday, Max had found Barzani at his favorite
table in Le Coq Bleu and they had talked away the afternoon over
brioche and soup. For the first time, since he had left the hospital,
Max found himself talking about the war, about the things he had
seen and the friends he had lost. It had ended with an invitation to
the opera. Hevel, Max decided that day, was the older brother he had
never had.

§

The Grand Hotel was well named, occupying half a city block
across the street from the ornate stone and gilt Opera de Paris. The
entrance was on a quiet side street and two liveried doormen vied
for the honour of pulling open the heavy metal and glass doors. Max
dropped a few sou in the hand of the successful bidder and stepped
into the foyer. The concierge stared at him disdainfully. Max knew
his demob suit, though the best he had, was none too good for all
that.

Barzani, on the other hand, was impeccable in a black wool suit
highlighted by even darker silk trim. His shirt, in the new style with
collar attached, was crisp and white, set off by a tie of red silk and
matching pocket square. Max raised his hand in greeting. Barzani
smiled in response and waved Max across the lobby to the entrance
of the gentleman's club.

The foyer was dominated by a chandelier that hung from the
ceiling like a cluster of crystal grapes and Max paused beneath it and
gazed upward. The intricate pattern of glass formed a maze of light
and shadow and, for a moment, it reminded Max of the tumbling
chaos of the trenches of northern France. His stomach lurched and
he had to lean on his cane to keep from falling.

Barzani was at his side, his hand on Max's elbow. The warm smell of tobacco and musk enveloped him and Max was back in Paris again.

"Are you all right, my friend?" asked Barzani. "You look pale. That flu that's going around—"

"No. It's... It's all a bit overwhelming."

"When Paris stops surprising you, you should check your pulse. You might be dead."

"Should we go across the street?" asked Max.

"The Opera is more than an hour away," said Barzani. "I thought a drink and an h'ors d'ouerve before would be in order."

"I don't know if I'd fit in."

"If I worried about such things, I wouldn't go anywhere. Act like you belong."

"It's just..." Max dropped his voice to a whisper. "I don't think I can afford it."

Barzani smiled and put his hand on Max's shoulder. "My idea, my treat. Besides, I'm still in your debt. You bought lunch the last time."

"At Le Coq Bleu."

"Lunch is lunch. They have a very nice cellar here. And an excellent selection of beers. Or so I'm told."

"What should I have?" asked Max, as he gazed at the extensive list of drinks the waiter had presented them.

"On that, I can be of little help," Barzani shrugged. "Ask Henri the next time you're at Le Coq Bleu. He'll talk your ear off about *terroir* and vintage. But I highly recommend the foie gras and the snails." Barzani himself didn't drink on religious grounds but took pleasure in watching others enjoy themselves.

Max settled for a Belgian beer – the only thing he recognized – and tried the escargots. The chewy texture was a surprise but the salty butter and garlic they were soaked in was a perfect match for the crispness of the lager.

After, Barzani led him across to the main entrance to the opera, pointing out the busts of composers interspersed among the angelic muses that ringed the front of the building. In the foyer, he bought Max a glass of sparkling wine, then took him by the arm.

"Follow my lead," said Barzani, as he took him across the hall to a cluster of men, attentive to the pronouncements of an elderly gentleman with an impressive white mustache. Barzani waited until the man paused and nodded in his direction.

"Max, may I present the Count Auguste de la Boix? Count, Lieutenant Max Anderson, late of the Canadian Expeditionary Force. A decorated hero of the battle of Amiens."

The Count peered at Max, his dark eyes sharp despite his advanced years, and then nodded. "Do you speak French?" he asked.

"I try," said Max. "I don't always succeed."

"Good response," said the Count. "I like my heroes with a dash of humility. Leave him with me Barzani. I have interests in Amiens. I'd like to see how well he looked after them."

Barzani nodded and drifted away and was soon in intense conversation with one of the Count's former audience.

"I'm afraid the Germans left much of it in a sad state." Max had seen little of the countryside, other than the inside of a trench, but nothing much could have survived the weeks and months of constant shelling.

"I suppose I'll have to go and see for myself. Perhaps, you'd care to come along, revisit the site of your former glory."

Max's voice froze in his throat. He wasn't sure he would ever be ready to return to northern France. All his memories were of horror, not glory. The Count leaned in, as if he couldn't wait for Max's response. He was saved from making one when Barzani reappeared at his side.

"There are so many important people that Max should meet if you will excuse us, Count."

"Of course, I'm sure we'll have a chance to discuss this further, Max." *Not if I have anything to say about it*, thought Max.

Barzani steered him away from a large man standing to one side who seemed to be intensely studying the faces of everyone who passed.

"Who's that?" Max asked.

"Captain Alphonse Gereau of the Prefecture," said Barzani, taking Max's elbow. "Not someone you want to take too great an interest in you. These gentlemen, on the other hand..."

This time it was a general – not a senior one – but Max had to resist the urge to salute. Again, Barzani spoke to one of the entourage. And so it continued until the chime sounded to call them into the theatre for the opening curtain. Each time, it seemed to Max that Barzani spoke to the most dangerous-looking person in the group.

The opera itself was everything Barzani had promised and more. The richness of the costumes and the elaborate sets that drifted on and off stage like fragments of a dream enchanted Max. But the music of Saint-Saens, and especially the voices, carried him away. He understood not a word but he understood everything. As the climax approached, Max felt overwhelmed. Tears stood on his cheeks and he tried to wipe them away without being noticed, until he saw other men openly weeping. *Paris truly is a different country.*

In the next seat, Barzani slept, his faint snoring a gentle counterpoint to the singers on stage.

§

The following Thursday, they met again at Le Coq Bleu. Barzani was in the midst of a discourse on the benefits of a scientific education to hone one's logical instincts, when they were interrupted by a messenger from the Grand. Barzani tipped the boy and sent him on his way before opening the envelope and briefly scanning the enclosed note.

"I'm afraid I've been called away. It's rather important."

"Is there anything I can do to help?" asked Max. Barzani had spoken little of his work but what little he had said intrigued Max. "Freelance diplomat" sounded exciting and it certainly paid well if Barzani's generosity was any indication.

"I appreciate the offer," said Barzani. He peered thoughtfully at Max. "The people I'm dealing with are averse to surprises. I couldn't bring someone unannounced. But... there may be something you can do for me. We'll discuss it next time we meet."

"I can at least walk with you," said Max, reluctant to cut their argument short, especially now he had thought of several telling points to make in defense of the law, which he had spent two years studying before the war.

"I'm only going as far as the first cab stand," said Barzani. "Stay, finish lunch." He raised his voice slightly. "I am sure Monsieur Henri Compte will be glad to keep you company and teach you about wine."

Henri looked up from his usual place at the end of the bar. "Nothing could give me greater pleasure."

Max shrugged. It would give him a chance to practice French slang with a master. In any case, he had wanted to thank him for the rescue from the crooked porter and for steering him to the L'Aquilon and away from "the gaudy flops on the main drag."

Barzani gave up his seat with a slight bow of his head. He dropped a few francs on the table, then, in a seeming afterthought, took out another twenty and pressed it into Henri's hand.

"A student cannot learn from poor materials," Barzani said, smiling.

"With this," said Henri, "he'll learn so much it will make his head hurt. Now, tell me, in your best French, how you are enjoying your hotel."

"My room is surprisingly large and well lit both with electric lamps and natural light in the afternoon. There is even a balcony. The food is even better than you described it and Jean-Marc is an excellent host." Henri nodded approval and then asked him to repeat it in the past tense.

They were well into a bottle of Yesim's best, which Henri declared adequate for beginners when Minette came through the door behind the bar. She was dressed for outdoors in a long dark coat.

"Wear a hat," said Yesim, "it might rain."

"Yes, mama," said Minette. She patted her uncle's cheek. "You worry too much. It's sweet."

Yesim actually blushed. "And don't—"

"—talk to strange men. Though that's what they want mostly. To talk to someone. And see a friendly face."

A pretty face, more likely, thought Max.

Where are you off to, Minette?" asked Henri. "I don't like the sound of you talking to strange men, either."

I just wish she'd talk to me. Maybe I'm not strange enough.

"Father asked me to help the sisters at St. Anne's mission."

Father? Oh, of course, a priest.

Henri crossed himself. "Talk to them all you want. Those poor bastards gave everything for mother France. They deserve a pretty face and a soft voice.

Minette's smile faded. She nodded somberly. "It's the least I can do."

"You're a good girl, Minette," said Henri.

"Thank you, grandfather, I try." She winked at Max. "Even though it's more fun to be bad." She blew a kiss to the room.

"Be in by ten," said Yesim to her parting back.

"You do worry too much, Yesim," said Henri. "What trouble can she get into with nuns and cripples?"

Yesim merely frowned and went back behind the bar.

Three – Tuesday, December 17, 1918

No matter how far he walked each evening, his journey always seemed to end at Le Coq Bleu. He told himself that he came to see the girl, though after four days he had still not spoken to her, but he always felt vaguely disappointed that Barzani had yet to make another appearance. He had gone to the Grand but Barzani had been out both times he called. He asked Yesim but the bartender would usually shrug and say – "he hasn't been in today" or "you just missed him." Max would have a beer or an *eau de vie* and chat with Henri, who had offered to help him become a real Parisian, before heading back to L'Aquilon.

On the fifth day, he arrived determined that this time he would speak to Minette. She wasn't there but he did see a familiar face, although it took him a moment to place it. It was the gendarme from the church. He was sitting by himself at a table near the door, the remains of a substantial meal scattered on the table.

"Did you have any luck finding those gangsters?" he asked.

"This city is full of apaches."

"Bonnet couldn't find his ass with both hands," said Henri.

"I'll find your ass with my boot in a minute, old man," said Bonnet. "I remember you now. The American who hangs around with wogs."

Max didn't correct him about his nationality. Americans were popular these days and, anyway, most Parisians didn't know where Canada was, even though it had one of the largest groups of French speakers outside France. He repeated his question.

"I've been wrestling with bigger matters," said Bonnet.

"You mean that fat whore you fancy at Labelle's, François?" said Henri, snorting. Henri thought he was very funny after his third brandy.

Bonnet flushed and stood up. Max rested his hand on his shoulder. Bonnet slapped it aside but turned back to his drink.

"Nothing was stolen. And no one was hurt. No one important, in any case. And, as I say, I have other cats to whip." He glared at Henri.

France, at its best, truly believed in its revolutionary slogans – liberty, equality and fraternity. At its worst, it was still more open to strangers than most places in the world, a lot more than America or Canada. But there were still lines drawn between Frenchmen and foreigners. Some drew the lines thicker than others.

"I won't keep you from your busy schedule," said Max. Bonnet grunted and pushed away from the table. He walked out without bothering to pay.

§

The bar had almost emptied. Even Henri had finally left and Yesim was noisily washing glasses and checking his inventory. Max had been nursing his second beer for more than an hour when Minette finally walked in. She wasn't alone. She was with an older man although, from the way he had his hand draped around her waist, Max doubted he was another uncle.

"You need to keep a better eye on your niece, Yesim," the man said. "She's been keeping questionable company."

"I can see that, Lachance," growled Yesim. "Go up to bed, Minette."

"I'm not tired," said Minette. She was more than a little drunk. "Open some champagne. The good stuff."

"I said to go to bed," said Yesim.

"You're not my father."

Max finished his beer. There was no point in staying. But he couldn't bring himself to go.

"Go ahead, Yesim, open a bottle," said Lachance. "I'll pay."

"With money or promises?"

Lachance smiled sourly but took out his billfold and laid two crisp notes on the bar. Yesim held them up to the light before tucking them into his shirt pocket. He rooted through the ice chest and brought out a magnum. Lachance looked at it critically.

"It's not Mumm's but it will do." He glanced around the bar at the two remaining clients.

"There's plenty to go around. Drinks for everyone."

"Yes," said Minette, "when Minette celebrates, everybody celebrates. Come have a drink with us, Max."

He was surprised she knew his name; Yesim must have mentioned it. He stood carefully, leaving his cane leaning against his chair, and joined Minette and Lachance at their table. The other man was too drunk to get up. Yesim grabbed him by the arm and escorted him to the street, locking the door behind him. He turned off the neon rooster and closed the shutters.

"A private party," said Lachance. "Excellent!"

Yesim put four tumblers on the table and joined them.

"Come now, Yesim," said Lachance, "even this stuff deserves flutes." Yesim grumbled but fetched better glasses.

Lachance turned to Max and studied him thoughtfully for a moment before extending a hand. "Eduard Lachance. From Minette's stories, Captain Anderson, I expected someone a little larger, a little more dashing. Did you really rescue our friend, Barzani, from a carload of thugs?"

Minette tells stories about me, barely hearing Lachance's other comments. Lachance was watching expectantly.

"I was a lieutenant. And there were only three and they were on foot," said Max, "but, yes, I did give Hevel a helping hand."

"Saved his life don't you mean," said Yesim. "Barzani told me so himself."

"Maybe," said Max, "though Bonnet would have been there in a few moments if I hadn't intervened." He felt slightly uneasy that people were talking about him behind his back but flattered, too.

"Bonnet," Lachance spat on the floor. "Three against one are too stiff odds for him. Drink up, drink up, we have a bottle to finish."

Max regarded Lachance over the rim of his glass. The man wasn't as old as he had first appeared. He had been a bruiser at one time, evident in the shape of his shoulders and thickness of his neck, although he had gotten soft and fat as he aged. His hands, too, were large with thin lines of scars around the knuckles. The hands of a fighter. But not a professional or even a street brawler; his nose was unbroken and there was no sign of damage around his deepset eyes or his large ears. He was a man who hit people while others held them. Or who only hit those who couldn't hit back. He looked at Minette but she merely smiled and sipped her drink.

"You have me at a disadvantage, Monsieur Lachance. You seem to know all about me but I know nothing of you but your name."

"Who ever knows anyone? Isn't that what the philosophers say? But I am Lachance, owner of La Coquette over on Caulaincourt. And part-owner of this dump, as well."

"This dump makes more money for you in a week than La Coquette makes you in a month," growled Yesim. "When I don't let you drink for free."

"True but you have a much lower overhead," said Lachance, "and the clientele is so... déclassé. Present company excluded, of course. Have you seen a lot of Hevel since you saved his life, Lieutenant Anderson?"

"I'm done with the army. Call me Max. Or Anderson if you prefer. I haven't seen Barzani at all."

"Really, how peculiar. Well, I must be off. La Coquette is still open and I need to get back to make sure the manager isn't stealing all the proceeds." He crossed to the bar and extracted a half dozen notes from the cash box. "Goodnight, Max, and Minette, my dear. Do come and see me again. I'll take my cut tonight, Yesim. Save you a trip tomorrow." Lachance smiled at Max. "Such a funny game, isn't it? I give him money and then I take it back."

After he had gone, Yesim jerked his head angrily at Minette. She pouted but said nothing before heading up the backstairs to the flat she shared with her uncle. Yesim glanced meaningfully at the front door.

"Take the bottle with you," said Yesim, "it's no good once it's been opened."

Max grabbed the magnum by the neck, retrieved his cane and began the long slow walk back to his hotel.

Four – Wednesday, December 18, 1918

He awoke to the sound of church bells pouring into his room from the church that loomed over Place Franz Liszt. Answering chimes echoed in his head. He rolled over with a groan, knocking the empty champagne bottle off the bed onto the floor where it landed with a hollow thump.

He rang the buzzer over his bed but it was ten minutes before a rap sounded on the bedroom door. It was Jean-Marc, carrying a tray with a steaming cup of coffee and a basket of sugared rolls.

"From the way you sounded last night I figured you'd want coffee."

"Where's Marie?" Max mumbled. The cook's wife usually delivered his breakfast, an arrangement for which he paid a few extra sou. Well worth it on most mornings.

"Marie's sick – that damn flu, you know. As for everybody else? Don't you hear the bells? It's like a holiday."

"What?" Max felt confused. "I can't have slept through until Christmas."

"That's next week," said Jean-Marc. "This is bigger than Christmas. The President is arriving."

"What President? Arriving where?"

"President Wilson from America. His train from Brest arrives at the Gare Saint Lazare in an hour. If you hurry, you'll be in time for the parade."

Jean-Marc set the tray on the writing desk and hurried off, presumably to see the president.

Max had seen a Prime Minister – Laurier during his 1911 whistlestop campaign – but never a president so he pulled on some clothes and headed for the station.

It *was* like a holiday. The broad boulevard leading to Lazare was full, entire families, many in their Sunday best, streaming toward the Right Bank station where all the boat trains from Atlantic ports arrived. There were soldiers, too, or veterans back in uniform, too many with a sleeve or a pant leg pinned up, but otherwise impeccable as if prepared for inspection. Max tried hailing a cab but the few he saw winding their way through the crowded streets were all full to overflowing. The entrances to the Metro were equally jammed and, in the end, it was easier to walk. Paris was a city of three million but its central core was surprisingly compact and Max let himself be carried along by the festive crowd.

The weather, too, seemed in a celebratory mood. The sun was low this close to the solstice but the sky was clear and the watery light sparkled off the rooftops and gilt facade of the Palais Garnier that housed the Opera. Even the public pissoirs that dotted the streets of Paris like monuments seemed to have caught the mood. The men jostling together to relieve themselves told jokes and shared stories of the war—humourous now that it was over.

Lazare was even more crowded than usual and Max checked that the button flap on his inside jacket pocket was done up, a guard against all but the most skilled of pickpockets. The city was not as full of thieves as the guide books and ever-present signs in the underground suggested but there was no need to tempt fate.

Two bands – one in the uniform of the French Foreign Legion and the other draped in sashes of red white and blue – the tri-color that both republics shared – competed in Lazare Boulevard outside the station proper, while another – the official welcoming party – practiced the Star-Spangled Banner in the broad entry hall separated from the platform by a series of high arches. The cacophony of melodies and themes rising and falling as each band achieved momentary ascendency seemed to Max strangely pleasing. It was as if the bands were conversing, joking, arguing, reaching momentary accord before disagreement set in again.

Max worked his way through the crowd, slipping along walls or through gaps that appeared and disappeared in the milling throng, until he was able to gain access to the cavernous hall where twenty-seven tracks converged from all over the west and south of France. The platform was nearly five hundred feet wide and more than sixty deep beneath four peaked rooves in steel and glass. One end was cordoned off by a line of Paris police, called `swallows` because of their billowing capes and their habit of swooping down on miscreants with a bludgeon now, ask questions later approach to civic order that did nothing to reduce Parisians` simultaneous respect and distrust of them. Attached to the far end of the terminal, an office building overlooked the station and Max could see soldiers behind the large glass windows with sniper rifles at the ready.

Max knew almost no one in this part of the city – he avoided all parts of the city frequented by Americans so he would not be tempted to speak English – so he was surprised to see not one but two of his acquaintances standing on the edge of the platform. Henri, the porter who had recently become his French teacher, had wrangled a place far from his usual haunts at the Gare du Nord and waited, his blue coat brushed and his buttons polished, for his opportunity to carry the bags of the president, or, at least one of his party. At the next archway but one, some forty feet away, Hevel Barzani was engaged in an animated conversation with a tall heavy-set man in a long grey coat. The man`s collar was turned up and his hat was pulled low over his face but he seemed oddly familiar to Max.

Barzani was gesticulating with his left hand, stabbing his finger repeatedly into the bigger man's chest. The conversation seemed one-sided; Barzani hardly paused to take a breath although the other man occasionally shrugged or shook his head. After a few moments, the bigger man stiffened and gestured with a twitch of his head. Barzani glanced over his shoulder and spotted the pair of swallows who were moving deliberately in their direction.

He reached into his jacket and withdrew an envelope or folded piece of paper and offered it to his companion. The hand that reached to take it was heavily bandaged and Max jerked in sudden recognition. It was the gangster he had cut with his pocketknife. But why, wondered Max, would Barzani be talking to one of his assailants and what could he possibly be giving him? A train whistle sounded in the distance and the crowd surged in response. When it parted again, both Barzani and the gangster had disappeared from the station.

§

The arrival of President Wilson was everything Jean-Marc promised it would be. The train whistle blasted as the locomotive pulled into the station, each blast followed by an answering cheer. The train rumbled forward amid great billows of steam. The police line solidified as the President's car rolled to a stop near the centre of the platform. Even from a distance, Max could see that its sides had been reinforced with steel plates and its windows heavily shuttered. An American President – McKinley in 1901 – had already died by an anarchist's hand on American soil and the government, ever concerned about the undercurrents of rebellion in the Paris streets, was determined not to allow a recurrence in France.

The security did nothing to dampen the crowd's enthusiasm. Before the train had rolled to a stop, cries of "Vive l'Amérique!, Vive le président!" rung out all along the platform. Hundreds of small flags, some French but mostly American, filled hands and painted the crowd red, white and blue.

The Prefect of Paris, decked out in his sash of office and with a chestful of medals, led a delegation to the edge of the tracks. As the train hissed to a stop, the Prefect stepped aside, his place at the head of the welcoming party taken by an elderly man of stocky build and sporting a bushy white moustache, compensation perhaps for his nearly bald head. A murmur rustled through the crowd. "Clemenceau. Le tigre!"

The French Prime Minister had come to greet his American counterpart, an honour that was probably lost on the American entourage. Max raised a small pair of field glasses he had bought from a street vendor to his eyes to get a closer look.

The band broke into a lively, if slightly jumbled version of the American anthem, as the railcar door opened and Wilson, followed by two burly men in dark suits, disembarked. The contrast between the two world leaders was dramatic. Wilson, fifteen years younger than the French Prime Minister, was tall and slender with a thin ascetic face behind wire-rim glasses. He was clean shaven and the hair on his head was thick and wavy above his high intelligent forehead.

Clemenceau grasped the American's proffered hand and then pulled him down for the more traditional French greeting. Wilson looked bemused and slightly embarrassed as Clemenceau kissed him on each cheek but he had apparently been well briefed and endured similar greetings from other members of the official party.

Soon the platform was full of disembarking Americains, wrestling with suitcases and trunks. At a signal from the concierge, Henri and his fellow porters rushed forward and, despite the throngs of gawkers and hangers on, quickly began to impart a sense of order. The President, his wife and a half dozen of his closest advisors were bundled through the station to waiting limousines while the others were organized into groups for transport to their lodgings.

Max followed as closely as the police escort permitted, morbidly curious about the men who had, in a way, sent millions to their deaths on the battlefields of Europe and who would, now, determine the future of many millions more in the coming treaty negotiations. Did they bear a special mark of greatness that set them apart from other men, that signified their special ability to make such momentous decisions? If they did, Max couldn't see it.

The two marching bands seemed to have come to some accord for when they spotted the President, emerging through the main doors onto Rue Interieur, they both launched into the same lively processional so the music seemed to come from everywhere and nowhere at the same time.

Wilson seemed surprised by the size of the crowd waiting in the streets outside the station. He paused, to the chagrin of the burly men who tried to edge him toward the security of the waiting cars. But whatever else he might be, the president was still a politician. He made a slow half turn, his hand raised in greeting, while his body guards scanned the crowd and rooftops for possible danger. Finally, Clemenceau himself took Wilson's arm and guided him gently into the back seat of one of the large black touring cars before sliding in beside him.

When the three cars carrying the main party were loaded, the drivers revved their engines in warning and, with few blasts of the lead car's klaxon to scatter those slow to move off the street, roared away from the curb, south toward the Palais du Justice on L'Île de la Cité, where the official reception would be held.

The cars were soon swallowed up in a sea of flag-waving onlookers. The crowd, in no mood for the party to end, swirled about the station under the watchful glare of bicycle-mounted swallows. Parisians were known for both their passion and their unpredictability. Celebrating throngs could transform into rampaging mobs at the slightest provocation, whether provided by extremists of the left or right or even triggered by agents planted by competing branches of the government, eager to rouse the City for their own obscure motives.

Max didn't understand Parisian politics, formed by over a hundred years of revolution and repression but he was fast learning that things were never as they appeared in the *City of Light* where even secret plots had hidden meanings. Henri's French lessons did not confine themselves to the intricacies of the subjunctive or to the "false friends" that could so easily lead a Canadian in Paris astray.

The police had closed the Metro station at Lazare with no indication it would open again soon. Max wasn't ready to tramp from station to station looking for a ride back to Gare du Nord. His leg had improved over the last weeks but the half-hour walk from his hotel to Lazare had started his knee throbbing.

If I'm to suffer for my sins, I might as well enjoy them first. Why not enjoy the festive mood? With Christmas only a week away, many of the stores were festooned with lights and tinsel decorations. Bars and restaurants offered "plats de fête" and a few had posted small signs in their windows, "English Spoken Here," in honour of the arriving American delegation. Max avoided these – it was too easy to backslide – and sought out a brasserie on one of the side streets.

The area around Gare Saint Lazare catered to the English, American and Canadian visitors who had drifted into Paris ever since Thomas Cook and Baedecker had begun to extol the virtues of the "La Belle Vie" forty years before. The station was the final stop for the Channel trains, which only paused in Gare du Nord, as well as those from the Atlantic ports. But Max knew from his war-time leaves that beyond the main boulevards, old Paris still thrived in the small cafés and artisans' shops, even here where Baron Hausmann's renovations, the broad boulevards and rows of uniform apartments that had ripped through Paris neighbourhoods during the reign of Napolean III, were most obvious.

He walked southeast toward the Louvre, planning to stop for lunch at Chez Tom-Tom or Les Cochons Vrais – two of his old watering holes. After, he would browse the stalls at the huge Les Halles market, for a belated Christmas gift for his brother, Ben, back in Nova Scotia, before catching the Metro back to Gare du Nord and his hotel.

Max reached Chez Tom-Tom in a few minutes. He glanced at the menu du jour, debating whether to stop here or continue on to Les Couchons Vrais when, across the Boulevard de l'Opera, he spotted Barzani, visible through the window of Le Café de la Paix, a large and popular restaurant. He was sitting at a table with two men. One, a tall red-head in a brown suit, was talking, leaning toward the other two and punctuating his words with swift chopping motions of his right hand into his left palm. Barzani and his companion, a shorter dark-haired man with sharp features, listened intently.

The second man, dressed in a collarless white shirt and dark beret – the style affected by residents of the student quarter on the left bank of the Seine, shook his head and said something that caused the other two to throw back their heads in sudden laughter.

Max was still curious about Barzani's behaviour in the station. He had been weaned on deception and there was something about Barzani's continued interest in him that caused suspicion to stir in his breast. Despite that, he felt a closeness to the man, a feeling he hadn't had for anyone since the early blood-soaked years of the war. Perhaps that was it – the heat of battle formed fast bonds. He waited for a break in the traffic and then hurried across the street as quickly as his damaged knee would allow.

Yet, by the time he entered the restaurant, Barzani had again disappeared, though his two companions were still at the table, finishing their coffee. He hesitated before approaching them.

"Pardon" he said. "Êtes-vous les amis d'Hevel Barzani?

"What's he saying about Hevel, Joseph?" the red-head asked his companion in a low southern drawl.

"He wants to know if we're his friends," said Joseph.

"Damned if I know. Have a seat. Sittez-vous."

"It's okay, Ginger, I think he's an American."

"Then he should speak American," grumbled Ginger. "It won't be long before everyone else is."

"I'm Canadian actually," Max said as he slid onto the chair, Barzani had lately vacated. "Max Anderson."

"All the same to me, Max," said the American, holding out his hand. "Peter Buchan. Though most folks call me Ginger. And this is Joseph Asper. Joe is from Serbia..."

"Croatia," interjected Asper.

"... and is studying at the Sorbonne. He's the one who knows Hevel."

Asper shrugged expansively. "I am acquainted with him but I hardly know him. I'm not sure if anyone really does. He comes and goes. He always has some little plan in the works. More importantly, he always has money."

That's true though where it comes from is yet another mystery.

"And what brings you to Paris, Mr. Buchan?" asked Max.

"I'm with the American delegation," said Buchan. "I work for Colonel House. And he has the ear of the President."

"So, you're one step from the President himself?" Max had his doubts. Buchan looked younger than most of men he had commanded after his field promotion in the dying months of the war.

Buchan's freckles darkened and he grinned sheepishly.

"You're a sharp one, Max," said Buchan without rancour. "More like four steps. If I was any lower in the scheme of things, I'd be carrying the First Lady's luggage."

Max doubted that too but kept silent.

Asper glanced at his watch. "Is the station at Lazare open yet?"

"It wasn't when I left ten minutes ago," said Max.

"Damn! I have to run, Ginger. I have a meeting with – well, never mind. Perhaps we could have lunch again next week. Without Barzani, I think."

"Sure, sure," said Buchan. "You have my card. I'm staying at the Hotel Vendome – the only place on the Square that isn't the Ritz. I don't have my schedule yet but drop me a line and we'll try to set something up."

It was an obvious evasion and Asper clearly knew it but he nodded and smiled tightly with just his mouth. He shook Buchan's hand and bowed slightly in Max's direction before hurrying from the restaurant and heading toward the station at Auber.

"They warned us about this on the boat over. Everybody has a case to plead – the Arabs, the Jews, the Poles, none more than the Croats. They'd like their own country but at the very least they want autonomy in Greater Serbia. I knew Asper slightly when he was at Princeton but he greeted me at the train like a long-lost brother." Buchan gazed thoughtfully out the window. "Someone must have tipped him I was coming." He chuckled. "Wheels within wheels, right? We met this Hevel on the street and he brought us here to... chat."

But you did most of the talking. "I should be going, too."

Buchan laid his hand on Max's forearm. "How do you know Barzani?"

Max slid his wrist free. Ginger Buchan was looking at him intently, suddenly appearing older than his years. Max didn't know who Colonel House was but he knew about Colonels and the men who worked for them. The less said the better.

"We go to the same bars in Montmartre. You know how it is. As Asper said, Hevel always has money."

Buchan laughed. "You were looking to hit him up for a loan? Well, if you're short, I could fix you up."

"Why would you do that?"

"You were in the war, right?"

Max nodded and absently touched the small scar on his left cheek.

"Then you know about pressure. And about patience. And you speak French," said Buchan. "I've got some German and a little Russian but I don't 'parley vous.' You could do a little work for me. Translating, looking into things and such."

"My French is only fair," said Max. "Paris is full of translators."

"Sure. And the official delegation will use them. But you ain't one of them. You're one of us. And you're unofficial, like. Not everything needs to go through channels, right?"

Max wasn't sure which them and us Buchan was talking about. And he was less sure he wanted to get involved in the younger man's petty espionages. But he did want to protect Hevel.

"Why not? I need to start making some money. It might as well be in American dollars."

"Now that's the spirit." Buchan slipped a billfold out of his jacket and separated two tens from a stack of bills. He passed them and a business card to Max. "Call on me Monday at four."

"At the Hotel Vendome. Is the entire American delegation there or are they in the Ritz?"

Buchan looked sour, then grinned. "Neither. They're at the Hotel Crillon on Place de Concorde. Colonel House values my... independence."

Max sat looking at the bills for several seconds after Buchan's departure. *What have you got yourself into, Max? This isn't why you came to Paris.* Although perhaps it was. He had wanted a complete break from the past – his family and the farm, university and war. Here, he was in Paris, being paid for speaking French and engaged

by not one but two men to practice the most Parisian of activities –
intrigue. He shoved the money into his jacket and signalled to the
waiter for lunch.

Five – Thursday, December 19, 1918

Despite the unexpected influx of cash, Max knew he had to make plans to leave L'Aquilon. Buchan's dollars could dry up as quickly as they had started flowing and, even at the favourable rates Jean-Marc was giving him, the hotel and restaurant were too big a drain on his dwindling resources.

But L'Aquilon would always be his first home in Paris and he had loved it from the moment Henri had brought him to its doors.

§

The windows of Hotel L'Aquilon had been grey with soot and the double oak door, its finish stained and its fixtures in desperate need of polish, had been lit by a single flickering bulb.

"It isn't pretty but it's cheap and clean, the concierge speaks a little English and won't go through your things when you are out of your room. The menu is limited but the food is plentiful and well prepared," Henri said when Max hesitated.

Jean-Marc, whose English was comparable to Max's Nova Scotian French, carried his two bags up the narrow winding stairs to the third floor. Max followed slowly, leaning heavily on the sturdy banister, polished by years of passing hands. The carpet on the third floor was worn and the once-elegant wallpaper, faded, but the hall was spotlessly clean and smelled faintly of lavender.

"You are a veteran." A statement rather than a question. "I lost a brother and a son to the Boche on the Marne," Jean-Marc said.

"It was a bad time."

Jean-Marc didn't say anything more about the war or ask about Max's wounded leg.

"Henri said we should look after you," Jean-Marc said, stopping in front of a set of double doors of dark wood. The room beyond was flooded with light from the setting sun. "Best room in the house."

"I can't afford more than we discussed."

"All rooms cost the same," Jean-Marc smiled and handed Max the key. "Some are better value. There is a sink with cold water in the corner there. The bath and toilet are one door down but across the hall. If you want hot water, get up early. A small breakfast is served on the second floor from seven to ten."

The room was large by Parisian standards, although few North Americans would describe it that way. A single bed with a gleaming brass frame and a solid wooden headboard stood against one wall and a small armoire along the one opposite. A thick Persian rug covered most of the worn wooden floor. The only other furniture was a round-topped trunk at the foot of the bed and a narrow oak writing desk and straight-backed chair in front of the west-facing window. A small landscape painting hung over the bed; a framed photograph of the Eiffel Tower to one side of the desk was the only other decoration.

The aroma of fresh baking filled the air and, for a moment, Max was transported to his boyhood, sitting at the kitchen table watching his mother making pies while bread baked in the oven for their evening meal.

"The room is nice," said Jean-Marc, apologetically, "but it is right above the kitchen."

"It's fine," said Max. He had pressed a franc into the concierge's hand.

Max dug in his rucksack for the bottle of brandy he had bought when the boat-train paused in Calais. He poured two inches into the water glass he found on the sink. The window slid upwards, the counterweights perfectly balanced and noiseless in their operation. He swallowed the brandy in a single gulp to ease the pain in his leg, refilled his glass and set the bottle on the writing table within easy reach. The

balcony was barely wider than his body. One end was filled with a
ceramic planter, still crammed with dead plants from the summer.

The hotel looked over a small park, a triangle of fading green,
named, the porter had told him, for a famous composer. A gravel path
circled a fountain and cut between several flowerbeds, mere patches of
brown dirt at the advent of winter. A young couple, their arms linked,
strolled across the park as Max watched; the man had the familiar
rolling gait of an amputee. The remains of the war lingered everywhere.

§

Finding quarters that fit both his budget and his needs would
be a challenge. Finding one as well matched to his nature would be
even harder. Montmartre suited him, at least for now. Everything
he had read, everything he had learned since coming here told him
so. This arrondissement was home to thousands of immigrants from
across war-torn Europe – Russians, Slavs and Poles – and the French
colonies in Africa and Asia. Yet it remained, at its core, French.
Families had lived and worked on the same twisted streets for
generations, even centuries. A deep sense of tradition fuelled strong
resistance to and resentment of change. At the same time, Paris, more
than any other part of France, more than any place Max had ever
been or heard of, embraced the founding principles of the revolution
– and most of all brotherhood. Paris embraced the exotic, for it
saw itself as the most exotic place of all. And no quarter was more
Parisian than Montmartre.

Change was coming. It was inevitable. The terrible losses of the
war had scarred the nations of Europe, none more so than France
on whose land most of the battles had been fought. Eight million
Frenchmen had died or been wounded. The signs were everywhere:
in the faces of too-young widows; in the bent backs of men forced
to work beyond their years; in the streets and shops filled with
strangers. Change was coming and Max wanted to be part of it, not
as a stranger but as a Parisian.

No, he thought, *I will stay here on this hill, looking over the city of my re-birth. I will stay here as long as I can, embracing and resisting the new with my fellow Parisians.*

Max caught a glimpse of himself in the mirror over the sink – his square jaw clenched, his blue eyes narrowed and flashing, the thin scar on his cheek livid with passion. It was all he could do not to laugh. *So serious, Max. How did you get that old?*

§

Jean-Marc offered to cut the rent by twenty percent, provided Max paid in advance on the first of every month. It was a tempting offer and Max told the concierge he would think about it although he knew it still wasn't sufficient.

"Fair enough," said Jean-Marc, nodding. "I know what it is like to live on a budget. If you like I can ask around. I know a few places that might suit you. A little off the beaten track but still close enough to walk to your favourite haunts."

He already had "haunts."

§

Max stopped by Le Coq Bleu that evening looking for Hevel Barzani, though in fact it was Minette he hoped to find. The electricity was off again and Yesim had placed several kerosene lanterns on the bar and lit all the candles on the tables. It lent a cozy, if somewhat smoky, air to the place. The girl was nowhere in sight.

Sitting in his usual place under the now dark neon sign, Hevel looked up from his newspaper when Max entered. He waved to Max, who, after picking up a sandwich and a beer at the bar, joined him. Hevel was drinking one of the small dark cups of what he called espresso.

"Where have you been, my friend?" asked Hevel. "I haven't seen you in days."

"We seem to keep missing each other," said Max.

"Exactly so," said Hevel. "I dropped by L'Aquilon earlier today but..." He shrugged. "Jean-Marc tells me you are leaving."

"Thinking of leaving. I haven't finalized my plans." Max felt reluctant talking about money in front of Hevel, who seemed to have so much of it.

"Well, there are lots of better hotels than L'Aquilon," offered Hevel. "I can recommend one if you like. Name the neighbourhood and I'm sure I can help you."

"The neighbourhood is fine," said Max. "It's just.... I'm planning on going to Spain in the spring, maybe Italy too. I need to—"

"Say no more. It isn't cheap to travel."

"Yes," said Max.

"If money is an issue, I could –"

"No," said Max, flushing. "I've always made my own way. Thanks, but I can take care of myself."

"I understand. But remember, pride goeth before the fall."

Max bit into his sandwich to keep the sharp retort from leaving his mouth. All his life, men had spouted scripture at him when they wanted to make him do as they wished instead of what he knew was right. He knew Hevel meant no harm by it. *He's nothing like my uncle.* In fact, thought Max, *he's more like my father than any man I've ever met.*

"There's plenty of money to be earned in town," said Hevel after a few minutes of silence. "The Americans are always looking for 'ears in the street.' The British, too, though they are a bit more tight-fisted."

Max wondered if Hevel somehow knew of Ginger Buchan's offer. It seemed doubtful that the American would have let it slip. Hevel was probably one of the things Buchan wanted him to "look into."

"Why are you so interested in my well-being?" asked Max. *Why am I being so cautious, Hevel has shown me nothing but kindness.*

"You did save my life," said Hevel. "If nothing else I owe you a debt of honour."

Then Max remembered the scene in the train station. Hevel had a relationship with one of the men who had attacked him. Had the whole thing been an act, a show to draw him in? *Don't be foolish, what interest could an ex-Lieutenant hold for these men?* But part of it had been show – even though the blood on Hevel's face had been real.

"I suppose," Max said. He wondered why he didn't confront Hevel about his suspicions. The time didn't seem right, somehow.

"Look," said Hevel, "you've shown yourself to be a man who can be counted on in a pinch. And, I find your company – refreshing. You can't imagine the kinds of people I have to deal with every day in my line of work."

"And what is your line of work?"

"Let's just say, I make arrangements for other people. Transmit messages, set up meetings, gather information. I don't think you quite grasp what is happening now, and the possible futures that these events could bring. Imagine – all the leaders of the great powers, the winners of this brutal war, gathered together in one place for weeks, maybe months. People will come from around the world as delegates to the great peace conference – but really as supplicants to these four men: Wilson, Clemenceau, Lloyd George and Orlando. My people, too, will come. My job is to prepare the way."

"A freelance diplomat, you said. And you can make a living doing that?"

Hevel laughed. He circled his finger in the air to call for another round. They sat in silence until Yesim brought another coffee for Hevel and a second beer for Max.

When Yesim had retreated back behind the bar, Hevel leaned over the table and spoke in a low voice to Max.

"Not everyone is looking for the same peace. A few would even return us to war. Some will achieve their peace; others will remain in danger. President Wilson has his fourteen points – and they are very fine indeed – but it may be more difficult to enact them than to draft them. I need someone I can trust. Someone I can call on at a moment's notice. A man of action. A man who owes no allegiance except to his own sense of justice."

"And you think I'm that man?"

"Aren't you, Max?"

"I don't know. Maybe I'm not the person who would know."

Hevel laughed and clapped Max on the arm. "Just the answer I was looking for. Stay at L'Aquilon. It's out of the way but close to the action. They have a phone, so I can reach you if need be. I'll pay the rent. No, wait, it's not a hand-out." Hevel glanced around the bar before extracting a bundle of papers, tied together with a green ribbon, from inside his suit jacket. He held them between his body and the edge of the table so only Max could possibly see them.

"I need to put these someplace secure," he said.

"Even L'Aquilon has a safe for valuables. Surely your hotel could keep them for you." Max wondered if he would trust his valuables, if he had any, to a hotel safe. He trusted Jean-Marc but others worked behind the desk. Others who had lost much in the war, including their honour.

Hevel took another sip of his coffee. When he replaced the cup, it rattled against the saucer. He sat still for a long moment, his face expressionless, his eyes never leaving Max's face. Then he shrugged and slipped the papers inside his jacket.

Nearly four years in the army and I still don't know not to volunteer, thought Max. He held out his hand. Hevel folded the documents into his newspaper and passed it to him.

Max resisted the urge to look over his shoulder to see if any one had witnessed the transaction, the way he had witnessed the transaction in the train station, a matter he still couldn't raise. At least, he now understood why Hevel always took this seat under the window. The glare of the neon bird hid him from observers in the street. Even dark, its bulk blocked his movements. And from his vantage, facing into the bar, Hevel could see both entrances and every other table. Only the space behind the bar was hidden from him and no one went there except Yesim and, occasionally, Minette.

"What are they?" asked Max, smiling. "War bonds or the plans for a new submarine? Perhaps love letters from the Prime Minister's mistress?"

"Nothing so interesting or important. Or so valuable," laughed Hevel. "Still there are a number of people who would pay to know their contents or, even, of their existence. Still more who would be happy if they never came to light."

"Men like the ones who assaulted you?"

Hevel shrugged. "Men like that are minnows but they lead to bigger fish. There is one shark in particular you should watch for. Have you heard of André Bucard?"

Max shook his head. "Should I have?"

"Probably not, though his name appears in certain journals from time to time. Still, it is a name to be wary of. I wouldn't want those to fall into his hands." He nodded at the papers hidden inside the newspaper.

Max knew without it being said that Hevel wasn't worried if he knew their contents. Perhaps they were in code or a foreign language. Perhaps they dealt with things that a "man of action" would never understand. Or, perhaps, Hevel trusted him. The paper felt suddenly heavy and he set it on the table, resting his hand protectively on top.

"How long do you need me to keep them?" asked Max.

"Perhaps a few days," said Hevel. "Possibly as long as a month. Certainly not beyond the end of January."

"That long?"

"That's why I want you to stay in L'Aquilon for at least six more weeks. It's why I'm willing to pay to have you do it. When I need these back, I will need to contact you as quickly as possible, either directly or through men I trust more than most, Jean-Marc or Yesim. The fewer places I need to look for you, the better."

"Alright," said Max. "But I'll deal with Jean-Marc. Four years of the army paying my bills was enough."

"Of course. A man needs to look after himself." Hevel scanned the bar again and took out his billfold. He extracted most of the bills inside and pressed them into Max's hand.

"Put it away," Hevel said, when Max hesitated.

"It's too much," said Max but he shoved the money into his jacket pocket.

"Spend what you need and give the rest back if you like."

"I said I would do it," said Max, "for the price of my room. I don't renege on my deals."

"We wouldn't be having this conversation if I thought you did," said Hevel. "But enough. Look who has graced us with the gift of her presence."

Max swivelled in his chair. Minette stood in the door. A man loitered outside but he didn't follow her in.

"Will you join us, Mademoiselle?" asked Hevel.

"Why not?" said Minette. Her face was slightly flushed, and her dark hair clung in damp ringlets to her pale forehead. Max supposed she had been drinking again, perhaps with the man who still lingered outside the café, smoking. *It's none of your business*, thought Max. But, still, he felt a tightness in his chest when he thought of it.

"Buy me a drink, Max. My uncle knows what I like."

"Another coffee, Hevel?"

"I won't sleep. But you go ahead. I love to watch people drink."

Max held up two fingers to Yesim, indicating Minette with the tilt of his head. He seemed to understand for he quickly brought another beer for Max and a glass of white wine for his niece. He frowned at Minette but said nothing.

"My uncle thinks I take too many risks," said Minette, after Yesim returned to the bar.

"Do you?" asked Hevel.

"Of course," she said. "It makes me feel alive. But I'm not stupid about it."

The man outside the bar finished his cigarette. He threw the butt on the cobbles and crushed it with his boot. It seemed for a moment that he was going to come in the bar but instead, after glaring at Max and Hevel for several long seconds, stalked away into the darkness.

Hevel shivered slightly, although as near as Max could tell he hadn't turned to look. "Why do I feel like I have made another enemy?"

"Oh, Roget's all right," said Minette. "Lachance told him to take me home. I think he misunderstood his mission."

"And how is my old friend, Eduard?" asked Hevel.

"I think you use that word too lightly. I'm not sure Lachance has any friends. None that he hasn't paid for at least." Minette had already finished her glass and waved at Yesim for another. Her uncle ignored her. Minette took a drink of Max's beer and put the glass in front of her. Yesim shrugged and poured another glass of wine.

"Have you considered my offer?" asked Hevel, smiling softly at Minette.

"To go back to Istanbul and become part of your harem?" She reached out and circled his wrist with her fingers.

A shadow passed over Hevel's face. He glanced at her hand still encircling his wrist, then looked down at his now cold coffee. When he looked up, he was smiling more broadly but his eyes were hard and hurt.

"I live in Tehran and I don't have another wife, although at my age, I should have two. But even if I had as many brides as the Caliph himself – you would shine among the multitude."

"I like you, Hevel," said Minette. "You make me laugh."

"We all have our roles to perform." He withdrew his hand from Minette's grasp and made a show of looking at his watch. "I must run. Be careful Max. It's a dangerous world." Max wasn't sure what Hevel was warning him against, but he'd glimpsed four red crescents gouged into the skin on Hevel's inner wrist.

Hevel stood carefully as though it pained him to rise. Max wondered if he had underestimated the man's age. He suddenly seemed much older than the thirty-five Max had previously guessed. Hevel bowed slightly to Minette and adjusted his hat – a new bowler – with the careful motions of a man who had been drinking cognac instead of coffee. With a final nod to Max and a soft word to Yesim, he left the bar without looking back.

"You hurt him," said Max.

"I know," said Minette, not meeting Max's eyes. "Hevel is not what he seems."

"No," said Max. "I can tell that he isn't."

"I'm not talking about the deals and counter deals. All that spy stuff. That's what he does, not who he is."

"Then who is he?"

Minette laughed and shook her head. She traced a figure eight into the moisture on the table top with a long white finger. "I don't have the answer to that," she said. "I don't think anyone really knows who Hevel is – not even Hevel."

That seems to be the general consensus, thought Max.

"I'll tell you this though," she said, her voice hard, contemptuous. "Hevel wants to rescue people. From the war. From the peace. From themselves."

She looked up then and glared at Max. "But not everyone deserves to be rescued and not everyone wants to be rescued."

"Not everyone needs to be rescued," said Max stiffly.

"Everyone needs rescuing, Max, but some would rather drown." She shook her head and giggled, her mood shifting in an instant. She ran her fingers across his hand where it still lay on the folded newspaper. A tingle ran up Max's arm. Trepidation, and it had been a long time since a woman had touched him. "Listen to me, you'd think I was as old as my uncle. How old do you think I am, Max?"

"A gentleman never asks."

"That's you. An officer and a gentleman."

"Just a man, really."

She leaned over and kissed him on the cheek. Her breath was sweet and warm against his face. "It's late," she said. "And I have been drinking, too much perhaps for a girl who won't turn twenty-three for..." she thought for a moment and laughed, "twenty-three more days."

"I'll have to remember to wish you a happy birthday," Max said. He dropped some coins beside his beer glass and stood up. "Good night, Minette."

"Don't forget your newspaper."

Max carefully tucked the paper – and its hidden documents – under his arm and followed Barzani into the night.

§

The money spread out in front of him on the small desk in his room made an impressive display. There were French francs, American dollars, British pounds and even Italian lira. It was not lost on Max that these were the currencies of the big four powers at the peace conference. Delegations had already begun to gather although the conference itself was not scheduled to start for another month.

He already had Buchan's twenty dollars tucked in his money belt behind the headboard of the bed. Now he could add another hundred from Barzani. Changing money was often complicated and time-consuming, though he had read that several American banks were opening branches along the Boulevard de l'Opera. He supposed he could go to one of them if he needed. The British twenty pounds – in four crisp five-pound notes – would be easier to spend. His own bank, the Guaranty Trust on Rue d'Italiens, had operated in Paris for decades and would take them and the dollars on deposit. Jean-Marc might take them in payment as well. Max wasn't sure if the better exchange rate at the bank would justify the time and bother.

There were nearly two thousand lira, too, useful he supposed, if he actually did go down to Italy. He really had no idea how much it was in real terms.

It was the francs that surprised him. Eight thousand seven hundred francs was a lot of money. It was far more than he would spend over the next six weeks, although he supposed he could find ways if he were so inclined. He set aside what he would need to pay Jean-Marc for the next few months and then put the remaining smaller bills in his wallet before adding the larger ones to the pile destined for his money belt.

That raised another issue. His hiding place felt secure when only a few hundred francs were at risk. He trusted Jean-Marc to an extent but he didn't know everyone who had access to his room – chamber maids and waiters and the like. The headboard was heavy and he doubted the belt could be found by accident or even by a casual search but the documents – still wrapped in the newspaper beside the pile of cash – created new problems.

Max had no doubt they had something to do with the machinations at the conference. Much was at stake – men had died by the millions to conduct a war, might not a few more die to forge the peace they wanted? Hevel had implied there were people who wanted to get their hands on them. If they – whoever they were – found out that Hevel no longer had them, would any of them know or even suspect he might have passed them to Max? A determined searcher would certainly find the money belt or anything else Max chose to hide in the room.

He had taken on an obligation, a foolish one perhaps, taken on out of pride, but an obligation nonetheless. He had promised Barzani he would keep the documents safe. The money didn't matter. To hell with the money, he thought, I won't spend a dime more than the cost of the room. That was the deal. He shoved the cash into the belt and shoved it behind the headboard. He felt better then, even though he knew it wasn't secure. He would find another place to hide it in the morning.

It was late, already Friday, but he didn't feel tired despite the beer he had drunk at Le Coq Bleu. He took the bottle of brandy from the desk drawer and poured a couple of fingers in the tumbler from beside the sink. If it didn't help him sleep it might at least get rid of the headache that pounded behind his eyes. He would only have one, he told himself. Only one and then he would go to bed even if he couldn't sleep. He would lie there and try not to think of the things that would make him want to drink another.

And he would try not to think of Minette, her red mouth and the pale skin of her neck and shoulders, the swell of her breasts beneath her blouse. He had been with women before, twice during the war here in Paris and once in London after he had been able to walk again. He had exchanged money for a release from the loneliness that seemed to haunt him even in the company of others. They had seemed willing or at least he was willing to persuade himself that they were. They had done things to overcome his reluctance and then whispered sweet words in his ear as he entered them. Each time it had been the same. A fierce merging of bodies on a thin mattress in the dark. A moment when for once he didn't feel alone and then it had passed. And he returned to his world and she to hers with no names exchanged but only money.

Minette was different. She wasn't like those women. Not like any woman he had ever known. What had Hevel called her – available but unattainable. What had she said herself: I like taking risks but I'm not stupid about it?

Maybe she was a new kind of woman. One who could be good and bad at the same time. He thought briefly of the marks she had made on Havel's wrist. But he also thought of his visit to St. Anne's mission, watching her from the shadows as she cared for the broken men there. The gentleness in her face had broken his heart. But he had also seen her with Lachance. He didn't know. All he knew was that he was thinking about her when he had promised himself that he wouldn't.

The brandy was almost gone and, despite, his early vow, he poured himself another finger and went to sit on the iron balcony. The air was cold and smelled of damp earth but the brandy warmed him. To the east, the lights of Paris glowed but to the west, the streets and houses were mostly dark and stars glittered against the velvet blackness. The money, the documents and what to do with them could wait until morning. For now, he had the city and the night sky and he had his memories and the brandy to help him forget them.

Six – Friday, December 20, 1918

In the end, he decided to take the money belt to his bank and place it in a safety deposit box, another expense he felt he could fairly charge to Hevel's account. After paying Jean-Marc for the room he still had plenty of cash on hand which he could keep in his wallet or in an envelope stuck under the heavy trunk at the foot of his bed. It wouldn't be difficult to find but its loss could be borne now.

The documents were another, more difficult matter. They had to be available at a moment's notice. Banking hours would hardly do. He carried them with him while he dealt with the money and then returned to his room where he examined them in detail for the first time.

Hevel hadn't explicitly asked him not to look at the papers. His lack of concern became obvious when Max had them spread out on his desk. They might be meaningful to Hevel's enemies but they meant little to him.

A few were plain enough. There was a large fold-out map, wrapped in a piece of oil cloth, of the lands that comprised or abutted the Ottoman Empire. Max had seen a similar map during a briefing he had attended for his commanding officer, Colonel McCallister, in the days after he had earned his commission in the field. This map had been overdrawn with thin lines in red, blue and green ink. In places they paralleled each other so closely they almost merged. In others, one colour would veer away from the other two and, in still others, all three lines took different paths before returning to some point of commonality. Hevel had said the great powers would make decisions that would affect people far outside the boundaries of Europe. Perhaps these were different proposals to divide up the Ottoman lands – although whose proposal each colour represented was impossible to tell.

Only slightly more revealing were bundles of letters, some original, some clearly copies that discussed, in the vaguest terms, an agreement – they called it – between the two signatories, identified by the single initials F and W. Although two of the letters were written by hand – a broad flowing script that slanted down the page – the rest were typewritten and in English. They talked of presenting a common front, focussing on their shared objectives and of using an American mandate to thwart the ambitions of England and France. One letter from W to F asked if a man called Lawrence could be counted on to intervene with his countrymen. The response assured W that he could be relied on "if he can be made to remember who his countrymen are." In another, F warned W that "certain men, you know of whom I speak, are trying to poison the waters by circulating the Protocols. Some who should know better give them credence, but they carry no weight in my camp."

For the most part, the letters, there were nearly thirty of them, were frustratingly vague. They referred to other documents or to meetings and events without providing any details as to time or place let alone the identities of the participants. A reference to "the letter from H on September 12" or "the matter regarding C discussed last month" hinted at great things but explained nothing. These were letters between intimates. Not friends perhaps but allies who knew how to remind each other of their obligations without revealing much if the letters were read by strangers.

In any case, they mean nothing to me. He felt like a pawn in a game he didn't understand although he supposed, Hevel would explain it all to him if he thought Max needed to know.

Of the other eight documents – all typed and ranging in length from a single page unsigned letter to a more formal document running nearly eight pages of dense text – six were written in languages other than English or French. Max thought the longest one might be Italian and two of the others were written in what might be Greek; at least the script looked similar to symbols Max had learned in mathematics. The one French document was either in code or came from the hand of a lunatic – incomprehensible in any case.

The lone English text consisted of Wilson's fourteen points – the basis for the American position at the negotiations. They had been printed in both English and French in many of the Paris newspapers the day after the president's arrival and Max had read them with interest. Some sections of this copy were underlined and notes, in a cursive lettering Max couldn't identify, littered the edges of the paper. It was these notes, undoubtedly, that rendered the document valuable.

Folded together, the documents were over four inches thick, too large to carry comfortably inside a jacket for any length of time. Besides, the obvious bulge in his coat made him a target for pickpockets or worse. It had been nerve-wracking to carry them to and from the bank. It was out of the question to do it on a daily basis. Hevel had seemed to have no such difficulty, thought Max, he must have had a special pocket sewn into the lining of his coat, something you might expect of a spy rather than a simple diplomat.

Any other option, carrying them in an attaché case or a knapsack, seemed equally fraught. He had dismissed the idea of hiding them in his room but perhaps he had been too hasty.

The bed was metal and the mattress thin. Other than the space behind the headboard, where he had kept his store of cash, it offered few possibilities. The trunk, though large, had only a single compartment, topped by a removable tray. He might risk a few hundred francs but he couldn't hide something more valuable under it.

That left the armoire, the small sink and the writing desk. The sink was a simple affair, fastened to the wall and supported by a thin ceramic pedastal that hid the drain. He might be able to slip a few of the papers into the opening at the back of the podium but then there was the risk of water damage.

The desk was small but its construction was sturdy. Made of heavy oak reinforced with brass fittings, it was a solid piece of furniture, made more so by being bolted to the floor. The three small drawers were well-built and could not be easily removed without tools. A thief might be reluctant to rip them from their fittings if only because of the risk of the noise alerting the hotel staff – another reason, perhaps, why Heval preferred him at L'Aquilon rather than a rooming house. He couldn't keep the papers in the drawers but perhaps he could fix them to their undersides.

With some difficulty, Max lowered himself to the floor and peered under the drawers. The lower one was too close to the floor to be of much use but the other two provided a space, perhaps a quarter inch deep, where a document or two might be hidden without interfering with the movement of the drawer.

Of course, he realized, there is no need to keep everything together. If he used a number of hiding places, it reduced the chance of an intruder finding all the papers, especially if he didn't know the sum total of what he was looking for.

Within the hour, Max had found three more caches. The most secure wasn't even in the room but rather on the cast iron balcony that overlooked the park. A small planter still held the dead remains of the summer's growth. Carefully peeling back the matted vegetation he was able to scoop a small hollow in the earth beneath, dropping the soil onto the sidewalk below, where it would be swept away by Jean-Marc in the morning. He refolded the map and wrapped it and the bundle of letters in the oilskin. The cloth was large enough to go around the resulting package more than twice so

Max decided to add his service revolver. If his room was going to be searched, he preferred to keep his revolver in the safest possible place, rather than beneath his undergarments in the armoire. He tucked the small box of .445 cartridges into a pocket in his shaving kit.

He was able to slide two of the thinner documents under a loose floorboard behind the radiator. Two more found a home in the armoire where a hole in the back panel had been shoddily repaired. With a document affixed to the bottom of the two desk drawers, he was left with Wilson's fourteen points and the unsigned letter. The solution was in plain sight. Max took down the framed picture from beside the desk and replaced the photo of the Eiffel Tower with the Fourteen Points. The frame hid most of the notations and the letter could be hidden between it and the replaced photograph which held everything in place. Placed back on the wall, it simply appeared as if Max were a proponent of Wilson's plan.

Satisfied with his morning's work, Max headed to Le Coq Bleu for lunch and another chance to see Minette.

§

She was working behind the bar when Max arrived, serving drinks and sandwiches to the mostly male lunchtime crowd while her uncle carried supplies up from the cellar. She smiled when she saw Max and gestured him over to the bar. A few of the other patrons grumbled at the preferential service and one offered a lewd suggestion that made Max bristle. Thanks to Henri's patient coaching, Max could carry out most of his daily business in French but the finer points of the vernacular still escaped him. Still, he caught enough to know he should hit the man. Minette simply arched an eyebrow at the offender and uttered an even more obscure epithet that caused him to blush and slink away from the bar amidst the hoots and catcalls of the other customers.

"I'll have to remember that one," said Max.

"It wouldn't mean the same if you said it," said Minette. "And my uncle wouldn't appreciate it if you started a brawl. Beer and a brioche?"

"Why not? The day is young and you're so beautiful."

"Is that a Canadian expression or are you getting fresh, too?" Minette's smile suggested she wouldn't mind if he did. Before he could reply, Minette turned back to serve the other men who were crowded against the zinc. By the time she returned, the moment had passed.

"Hevel was here looking for you about an hour ago. He asked me to give you this if you came in." She passed him a folded sheet of paper and Max wondered if it was yet another secret he would have to find a place to hide. But it was simply a hand scrawled note asking him to meet Hevel at the corner of Richelieu and Montpenser at 19h. 'Bring the map and enough money for a night out.'

"You shouldn't get mixed up in his business, Max," said Minette. "It won't come to any good."

Max shrugged, drained his beer and wrapped the remains of his brioche in wax paper. He was already mixed up, had been mixed up with Hevel since the day he saved him from a beating. He wondered if he would do it again if he had the chance. *You do what you have to do*, thought Max, *whatever it takes to let you keep looking in the mirror every morning*. He shoved the note and the sandwich in his pocket and headed back to L'Aquilon for the map.

Seven – Friday, December 20, 1918

The intersection of Richelieu and Montpenser formed one corner of a square bordered on one side by building that housed the Comédie Française, one of the oldest theatre troupes in Paris with roots all the way back to Molière. It was almost all the way to the Louvre but Max decided to walk even though he now had money to spare for cabs. The doctors had told him that regular exercise would keep the joint from stiffening and would strengthen the muscles around it. They had also told him that the pain would eventually subside but that hadn't happened yet, so he sometimes wondered how good their other advice was.

Still, he supposed he was lucky to have the leg at all, even one that relied on a cane for walks of more than a dozen blocks. It had been bad in the last days of the war; the number of wounded overwhelming the skills of the doctors and medics who were left. A philosophy of "lose the limb to save the life" prevailed and field amputations were more common than not. Max had the good luck to be treated by a doctor fresh from his training and not yet crushed by the futility of healing wounded men simply so they could go back in the trenches and die. Luck. His uncle would have claimed that God was watching over him but where had God been looking when half the men in his command died?

Max shook his head to clear away the unwanted thoughts. The air was cold but the Christmas lights in the storefronts and cafés lent a warm glow to the streets. There were stalls along the sidewalk, farmers selling winter vegetables or fresh baked bread, other vendors hawking knitted hats and scarves in grey or brown or hand-carved wooden toys for Christmas. The smell from the charcoal braziers they used to keep warm was heavy but not unpleasant.

Max stopped at one stand on l'Opera and bought three wrinkled apples. The young girl, who served the customers while her father or grandfather sat on a stool and smoked, was pretty until she smiled, revealing blackened teeth. Max smiled back and bit into one of the apples. The flesh was firm and dry but the taste was sweet, all the flavour of the fruit concentrated in a few mouthfuls. He finished the apple and shoved the other two in his pockets until later.

He was early so he bought a newspaper and a small leather-bound journal to keep notes in. He took a table at a café near the corner and ordered an espresso and a small *eau de vie*. The front page had a long piece about the upcoming conference but it didn't say much that Max hadn't already heard from Hevel or Henri.

The view from the café window was more interesting in any case. Couples and families strolled or lingered around the two large, nearly identical, fountains that flanked Boulevard de l'Opera before it passed through a great arch to join Rue de Rivoli. In the largest of the three parks, a string quartet, the players wrapped in scarves and wearing fingerless gloves were playing to a small but appreciative audience. The music was just audible through the thin glass of the café windows and to Max it seemed to capture the essence of winter in its sweeping notes.

At ten past the hour, Hevel still hadn't arrived. That was unusual. The man was sometimes hard to track down but he was punctual with appointments. Max folded the paper and considered having a second brandy but decided to wait to see what Hevel had in mind. His instincts told him he might need to have his wits about him before it was all done.

After a few minutes, he paid his bill and walked slowly around the edges of the square. Perhaps his friend had decided to do the same thing and was sitting in a bistro watching for him to arrive.

Every neighbourhood in Paris had its own distinct character formed by history and circumstance. Nearly three million people lived within the remains of the old city walls and more packed the villages and slums beyond its boundaries. Even before the war, huge numbers of people had flocked to the city from the rural provinces, seeking work in the workshops and warehouses in the city centre, the factories on the outskirts or the docks along the Seine. Many simply settled near the train station where they arrived; those from the Alsace around Gare L'Est, for example, or from Breton near Gare du Nord. That was changing, too, as immigrants from the French colonies or those escaping persecution – White Russians fleeing the Bolsheviks and Jews running from pogroms in eastern Europe – flooded the city.

The immigrants, old or new, lived in tenements that lacked even the basic amenities. According to Henri, fewer than half had electricity or even running water; some lacked heat. Max had seen the honey wagons roaming through city streets in the early hours emptying the cess pits that served as sanitation in many of the poorer neighbourhoods. The smell had been overwhelming in December. He couldn't imagine what it would be like in summer.

Most Parisians spent half their budget on food and had little left over for rent even if decent apartments had been available. There was much talk – and several stories in the newspaper – of tearing down the city walls and building more housing, but for now most people did the best they could, raising their families in small apartments and turning a weekly visit to the public baths into an outing. Hevel's money at least spared him that fate for another few weeks.

Not that the *flaneurs* and shopkeepers here in the heart of the city faced such difficult choices. The five- and six-story apartments that lined the grand boulevards of Baron Haussmann might be small but they were warm and dry and, mostly, equipped with all the modern conveniences.

Max had circled the block and was starting to get worried when he spotted Hevel picking his way toward him through the traffic on St. Honoré. He was flushed and winded but greeted Max with a wave and a broad smile.

"My apologies," he said, "Everything takes longer than you think. You have it?"

Max nodded and reached inside his coat for the map.

"No," said Hevel, "you keep hold of it for now. I'll let you know when and if I need it. Now, have you eaten lunch?"

"A brioche a few hours ago," said Max, "and an apple on the walk here."

"I've had nothing since breakfast," said Hevel. "Let's have some soup now and a real meal at a more civilized time."

Max was still not used to eating at civilized times – ten o'clock was considered barely humane – but he nodded his agreement.

When the food was ordered, Hevel leaned forward and asked in a low voice. "Everything is secure?"

"As safe as I could make them and still have them available when you wanted them."

Hevel frowned. "There are always compromises to be made. In this as in most things in life."

Some things should never be compromised, thought Max, though at the moment he wasn't sure how long that list was or what was and wasn't on it.

"You brought some money?" asked Hevel. When Max nodded, he said, "You probably won't need it unless we should become separated."

"Is that likely?" asked Max.

"Not likely," said Hevel, "but possible. We aren't going far but it will be late when we're done. You'll want to be able to hire a car."

There was something Hevel wasn't saying, but Max didn't press him on it. Taxis, both horsedrawn and motorized, were common in the streets of Paris and the latter competed both on fare and on the speed by which they delivered their passengers. Cost was not the main reason you didn't want to risk taking them.

A waiter laid a platter in front of him. Max felt suddenly famished and gave no further thought to conversation. The rich tomato broth was thick and spicy, filled with chunks of root vegetables and shreds of chicken. The rye bread was almost black. Softened with the broth, it was still chewy and had a spicy, nut-like flavour. Max washed his food down with a crisp beer, so pale it was almost white. Hevel drank seltzer.

Max finished first, wiping the bottom of the bowl with the last of his bread. He wiped a bit of broth from his chin and looked across the table at his friend.

Hevel was half through his own soup and had barely touched the bread. Not a crumb or drop of broth stained the cloth around his plate. He touched his napkin to the corner of his mouth and smiled. "Would you like some more?" Hevel asked. "Or perhaps a pastry?"

"No, thanks. Sorry," said Max, slightly embarrassed by the other man's careful manners. "In the army, you get in the habit of eating fast."

"It is a habit you should strive to reform. Food should be tasted, not merely swallowed. But you are young, plenty of time to learn to enjoy the finer things in life."

Once again, Max wondered at Hevel's age. Not that it mattered. He had always been more comfortable with older men than those his own age or younger.

"I am meeting a man at ten o'clock," said Hevel. "Can you stay with me until then?"

"I came prepared to stay the whole night."

"I doubt that will be necessary." Hevel paused. "The man I am meeting is a rough sort. Did you bring your knife?"

Max nodded. He had thought to bring his revolver but when he held it in his hand, he felt the old feelings. He hoped it wouldn't come to that. "It's not much of a knife."

"The fact that you have it and are willing to show it at the right time should suffice to keep the peace."

Hevel pushed his plate away and signalled for the bill.

"You've hardly eaten," said Max.

"Nerves. I'll have more later, when our business is done. But before business, pleasure." He dropped a few coins on the plate with the bill and stood up. "Do you like music?"

"It's alright, I suppose." He had enjoyed the music in the park, but he wasn't in the habit of seeking it out. After his mother died, the piano had sat untouched in the parlour. The only real music he knew were the sombre hymns of the First Baptist church and military marching bands. The Opera had been a special case, not simply music but an *event*.

"You don't seem enthusiastic."

"I agreed to come with you tonight. If that includes music, that's fine by me."

Hevel shook his head. "So serious. Well, come along."

At the curb, Hevel hailed one of the motor cars that were slowly circling the square. Two almost collided in the rush to get the fare. Hevel jumped in the back seat. Max followed gingerly. He had only taken a motorcab twice before and one of those journeys had ended abruptly in a collision with another car. Hevel gave an address in Saint Denis, the small village on the far side of Montmartre.

The driver shook his head. "I don't go up there. The roads are poor and, even if I don't get robbed, there's no chance of a fare back," he said.

"What if I double the regular fare?"

"Triple it and you have a deal."

"Why don't we meet halfway?" said Hevel.

"But I want half of it up front. And you're on your own for getting back."

"It's not so far that we couldn't walk," said Max. That was true of much of central Paris.

The driver scowled and pulled away from the curb. The Renault jerked and backfired once but then accelerated smoothly and headed west to Fontaine before turning on Cliancourt. With one hand on the wheel and the other on the horn, the driver wove through traffic at what, to Max, seemed an alarming speed. Only when he turned off the main street onto a narrow, cobbled street did he slow to a more reasonable pace. The car turned twice more, each time onto a street narrower and rougher than the one before. At last, he pulled over beside a nondescript door. The only light came from the car's headlamps.

"Are you sure this is the address you wanted?" he asked.

"Quite sure," said Hevel, handing the driver the remainder of the fare. As soon as they had descended, the car drove off at the best speed the driver could muster, leaving them standing in the dark.

Except it wasn't completely dark. The large windows on either side of the door had been painted black and where the paint had chipped, pinpoints of light shone through. Faintly, he heard a steady throbbing rhythm like the heartbeat of a great beast. Max shuddered and looked over his shoulder but saw no sign of life anywhere in the darkened street.

"Your instincts are good," said Hevel. "These doors are often watched by members of the Sûreté or their agents. But I have some assurances that they won't be here tonight."

Hevel rapped three times on the door. There was an answering triplet and Hevel knocked twice more, paused and then twice again. A small window snapped open, spilling a square of light onto the street. It was quickly blocked by a dark-skinned face.

"Why, Mr. Barzani," the Negro drawled. "Long time no see."

"Good evening, Jake," said Hevel. "Who's playing tonight?"

The door opened wide and Jake ushered them in, closing it quickly after them, as if afraid all the light and warmth would seep out. The interior was a single long room with a bar running along one wall, the remaining space packed with tables and people. The light came from a dozen large kerosene lanterns and scores of candles scattered around the room. The faint rhythm had resolved itself into music, though nothing like Max had ever heard before. Some of the clientele were sitting at the tables snacking from trays of bread and olives or drinking wine out of tumblers, but many of them were packed onto the tiny dance floor. Max tried not to stare but he couldn't help it. He had never seen a Negro dancing with a white woman before.

"Just some boys from the neighbourhood ragging around right now but we got a trumpet player from New York dropping by later tonight," said Jake, as he ushered them to one of the few vacant tables. "Rumour has it he'll be bringing a new singer along with him."

A half-dozen musicians, all Negros, crowded on a small stage at the far end of the room. The drummer laid down a steady beat, echoed and reinforced by the stand-up bass, while the piano filled in the gaps between the beats. The melody – almost familiar – was carried by a saxophone and trombone. The sixth band member had his back to the audience, his head bobbing and finger snapping in time. He faced the crowd and began to sing.

> How 'ya gonna keep 'em down on the farm
> After they've seen Paree?
> How 'ya gonna keep them away from Broadway,
> Jazzin' around,
> And paintin' the town?

The voice was surprisingly high and sweet. It took a moment for Max to realize the singer was a woman, dressed in a man's suit. He leaned across the table and whispered to Hevel. "Is there something illegal going on? Is that music against the law?"

Hevel shook his head but didn't answer until the song was finished and the band left the stage with a promise to return "when our whistles are wet."

"Only barbarians would make music against the law. We haven't come to that yet. Some men, even French men, would object to the mixing of races but the world is full of fools. But that isn't illegal either, not in Paris anyway."

Jake returned to their table with a tray of olives, a carafe of red wine and a single glass. "We're trying to find someone out back who can run that crazy French coffee maker."

"What happened to André?"

"Didn't you hear? He just got sick and died. I sent him home about ten o'clock three nights ago and he didn't make it through to morning, it was that fast."

Max shuddered. In the days before he was wounded, the influenza had swept through the trenches. More men died in a week than the Germans had killed in months. It had seemed to pass with the coming of fall but there had been a resurgence in recent weeks.

"Terrible news. Don't worry about the coffee; some seltzer would be fine," said Hevel.

"You're the boss, boss." Jake nodded and winked as if they were sharing a secret.

"If nothing's illegal, why are the windows blacked out?" asked Max after Jake had left for the second time.

"Most of the men on that stage served in the 369th regiment. They weren't good enough to fight alongside other Americans but were assigned to the French Army, where they became one of the most decorated units in the war. The Harlem Hellfighters they called them. They left the army with honourable discharges. Not everyone in this room can say the same."

"Deserters." Max looked at the men around him, staring from face to face to see if the marks of cowardice were written on them. It was rumoured that more than fifty thousand deserters – from all sides of the war – had flocked to Paris, trying to lose themselves in the cobbled streets and the sea of faces. He looked at the men, but he could see nothing but practiced cheer and the same haunted eyes that stared at him so often from the mirror over his sink. He looked down at his hands, resting in his lap. His left one was shaking slightly and he grasped it with his right to halt the tremor.

"I know what you're thinking Max.," said Hevel, gently. "But not everyone ran away from the war. Some walked away – no longer convinced, if they ever had been, that any justice could be found in battle, any greater honour in fighting than in refusing to fight. If the mutineers on both sides had had their way, the war might have ended a year earlier. They never talk about that in the official records. In any case, the war is over now. We have to focus on peace. That's where honour lies."

"If you say so," said Max. "Forgive and forget."

"Forgive, yes," said Hevel. "But we must never forget."

The music started again although the band had lost three members and gained two new ones. The music was mostly fast, made for dancing, but a few of the songs were slower, the songs about lost loves or homesickness. Max sipped at his wine, being careful not to get drunk, and oserved Hevel watching the players, or, more often, not watching, sitting with his eyes closed and his head swaying to the rhythm.

They spoke only in short bursts between the numbers and then only of trivial things. A few minutes past ten, Hevel gestured as a short white man, dressed in a heavy grey overcoat and fedora, entered the bar. The man glanced in their direction then cut across the room and went through a small door, half hidden by a wrought iron screen. A few seconds later, Hevel led Max after him.

The door opened onto a narrow hall. A flight of stairs took them down to another heavier door. A beefy white man with a thick neck and a shining bald pate nodded at Hevel and ushered them into a dimly lit low-ceiling room. The room was partitioned with cloth screens into a number of small chambers. The air was redolent with sweet-smelling smoke. Max's eyes burned and his head felt suddenly light and far away. Hevel took a pair of damp cloths from an attendant, placed one over his mouth and nose and handed the other to Max.

"Take shallow breaths," he said and led the way into the warren. Men, and a few women, lounged on mats, mostly alone but sometimes in groups of two or three. Each mat had a pipe beside it and the residents took occasional languid sips from the long flexible stems. Most seemed unaware of their presence though a few turned and followed them with unfocused gazes.

The man they had followed was on the far side of the room in low conversation with a thin Chinaman.

"Guten Abend, Herr Doktor Schmidt," said Hevel.

Schmidt jerked around at Hevel's voice. His face seemed stretched and flattened as if it had been ironed – with a broad box-like jaw and high flat cheekbones. His nose was small and his eyes deep-set. He was clean-shaven but his hair, the colour of ripened wheat, fell in lank bangs over his ears and across his forehead.

"Perhaps some other language would be better," said Schmidt, in English. "The French seem to hold a grudge against my people and, even in their present condition, some here might feel the urge to act on it."

The Chinaman had left but now returned with a small package wrapped in dark paper and twine. He handed it to Schmidt in exchange for a handful of bills. Schmidt put the package in his overcoat pocket and led the way to a yet another door.

The room was a storage area, boxes and crates stacked haphazardly against two of the walls. A barred window high up on the wall opposite the door let in fresh air through a broken pane. Max stood under it and took several deep breaths of the cold night air to clear his head. He had never been in an opium den but he recognized it from lurid stories in detective magazines. The habitual pain in his leg had faded but it did not tempt him.

"I came alone," said Schmidt, indicating Max with a desultory wave of his hand.

"You did not," said Hevel, switching to French. "I saw your man in the bar upstairs. He couldn't keep time to the music."

"That was not music," said Schmidt. "Bach is music. Wagner is music. That was—"

"My mistake," said Hevel. "And. then there is the man guarding the door, so you brought two to my one. Although you had best fetch him before he succumbs to the fumes next door. You know how easy it is to dream away a night, when you only meant to stay an hour."

Schmidt shrugged and smiled, showing several gold teeth. He returned after a few moments with the beefy man. He swayed slightly as he stood by the door but his eyes were alert and Max knew he was only feigning. Max slipped his hand in his pocket and worked his clasp knife open. He wouldn't use it against an unarmed man but, as Hevel had said, simply showing it might be enough to keep the peace. He wouldn't worry about the other man unless he came downstairs. The crowd would not support a German in a fight.

"You have what you promised?" said Schmidt.

Hevel nodded to Max and he took the map out of his pocket and handed it to Schmidt. He eagerly unfolded it, then snorted in disgust.

"What do I care about this?" he said, shoving the map back at Hevel, who refolded it and gave it back to Max. "We don't care what happens to Kanaken or Kikes. What about our colonies?"

"This is a sample – to show you that I have access. A map of your colonies is irrelevant, unless you care whether it is the French or the English that take them. What should worry you is the map of Germany."

"We know we will lose territory. The Alsace is even mentioned in Wilson's fourteen points and the French will settle for nothing less."

"The French," said Hevel, "would eliminate Germany as a nation if they could."

Schmidt flushed but the other German didn't react. "It will never happen," said Schmidt.

"No," said Hevel, "But only because the Americans won't let it. Self-determination cuts many ways."

"What do you want from me?" asked Schmidt. "More importantly, what do you have to offer?"

"The Poles and the Czechs each have grievances. Their demands will be substantial and some of them must be met. But a word in the right place could limit the damage. It is in no one's interest to see Germany humiliated."

"Tell that to Clemenceau," said Schmidt.

"Granted," said Hevel. "But he is only one of four."

"And what do you want from me?"

"Certain documents are being circulated. I... we would like it to stop."

"The truth must come out," said Schmidt, grinning again.

"There is nothing true about them," said Hevel. "We both know that."

"Perhaps we should let history decide," said Schmidt. "But I understand your concern. I'm not the author of these things, not the publisher nor the distributor."

"But a word in the right place."

They were like two men sparring with each other. Even their gestures reminded Max of boxers, trying out each other's defences, careful not to leave an opening in their own. Neither would name the documents – perhaps the other man would recognize it even in French – although Max supposed they were the Protocols mentioned in the letters.

Schmidt shrugged. "It's not as easy as that. It is not simply factions in the German army who believe these things. You should concern yourself with French who believe it. And Germans have no influence over the French."

"And Arabs have no influence over the Americans – but we know people who do."

"Very well," said Schmidt. "You will speak your words and I will speak mine. Perhaps they can have the effects you say."

Hevel nodded and stretched out his hand. Schmidt stared at it, a vague look of disgust across his features. Hevel nodded again and withdrew his hand.

"I will be watching you, Barzani," said Schmidt. "Any hint of betrayal will be paid in blood."

Hevel waited until Schmidt and the other had departed. "I wonder if that was a line from Wagner," he said, chuckling. "It certainly had that air about it."

Max hesitated then said. "I'm not sure... I'm not comfortable dealing with the enemy."

"But the war is over."

"No," said Max. "There is an armistice."

"Max. You hardly seem the type to argue over semantics."

"The Germans are still the enemy."

"Someone is always the enemy, Max. Today it is the Germans, tomorrow, who knows? My job... our job is to do what we can to forestall the inevitable. Make tomorrow next month or next year."

It would be good to have no enemies, thought Max. *Or at least to be at peace for a little while.*

"Let's go see what that New York trumpeter and his singer have to say for themselves," said Hevel.

The bar had filled in their absence but Jake found them a table near the back. They ate smoked trout followed by lamb stew spiced with cinnamon. The band now consisted of the drummer and bassist, along with the New York trumpeter and the singer. She was dressed in an evening gown with narrow straps that emphasized her alabaster shoulders, and, for a moment, her pale oval face and short dark hair reminded him of Minette. Her voice seemed too big for her slim figure and echoed the trumpet as if they were conversing in some strange new language. Max liked it when the musicians sped up at the end of a song. It made his heart throb and his mind blank.

At some point, he realized that Hevel had left, though there was money tucked under his plate for the bill along with a note telling him the quickest way to get back to his hotel. Max listened until the band took another break and then made his way to the exit.

With no public urinal in sight, he stopped in a shadowed nook to relieve himself. As he did up his trousers, a hand was laid across his left shoulder.

"Don't turn." A man's voice, deep, raspy from too much smoke or whiskey. Or perhaps a survivor of a gas attack during the war. "It's better you don't see me."

Max didn't move. The knife lay open in his pocket but it might as well be back in the hotel. There was no threat in the voice, just the calm assurance of a man who knew he was in control. He might have a knife of his own or even a gun. Perhaps all he had was his voice.

"What do you want?" asked Max.

"Don't talk, listen." The man said. His voice was strangely familiar. Not one he had heard before but similar somehow. "You're a friend of Barzani?"

Max nodded. It was the dialect. He spoke French the way Yesim and Minette did, slightly nasal and fast.

"You were with him tonight. We saw you." Was there more than one man behind him? Max couldn't tell. He had heard no one approach. He heard nothing now but the voice, almost in his ear. If there was anyone besides the man with his hand on his shoulder, they were being absolutely still. "He met with a German. What did he call himself this time – Gruber? Bratwaldt? Schmidt?"

"Schmidt." Max saw no point in not confirming what the man already knew. He was surprised when a forearm across the back of his neck shoved him hard against the wall. The point of a blade was pressed below his left ear.

"When I want you to talk, I'll tell you."

The man was using his right arm to press Max against the wall, while he held the knife in his left hand. The angle of the arm against his neck was slightly from above so the man was tall; the pressure he exerted suggested he was heavy as well.

"Barzani had something to sell," the man said.

"That Jew tinker always has something to sell," said a different voice, soft, slightly sibilant, three or four feet away and to Max's left.

Max wasn't sure what God Hevel worshiped but he was pretty sure He wasn't Jewish. Neither of the Jews he met in the war drank heavily but they weren't abstainers either. Hevel had told him his religion prohibited the drinking of alcohol.

"We have an interest in Barzani's merchandise too, though we have no intention of paying him for it" said the first voice. Max could feel the map weighing heavily in his jacket pocket. "Maybe you could tell your friend that for us."

They didn't mean to kill him then, though he didn't suppose it would take much to change their minds. And they didn't know that he was holding Hevel's papers for him – maybe didn't know him at all, except that he had come in with Barzani and left alone.

"You'll do that, won't you?" He pushed Max again pressing his face to the rough brickwork so he had to turn his head to keep his nose from breaking. The moon had risen above the edge of the buildings and, although it wasn't full, the street was no longer dark. He still couldn't see the men behind him, but he could see the hand on his shoulder. It was large and pale with thick stubby fingers and tufts of black hair between the knuckles. He was wearing a silver ring with a kind of cross on it. "Tell him to stop working against the interests of France if he ever wants to see his home again."

Whatever other skills Hevel might have, he is a very easy hand at making enemies.

The knife was gone from Max's neck. A few seconds later, the man punched him hard in the kidneys, banged his head against the wall and then punched him twice more. Max felt his legs go. The last thing he heard was a shrill whistle. He wondered if it was the air escaping from a punctured lung.

When he swirled up out of darkness, he was on his hands and knees, throwing up lamb and red wine. Someone was kneeling beside him, offering him water out of canteen. Max rolled away and fumbled for the knife in his pocket.

"It's okay," said Bonnet. "They ran off when I blew my whistle."

Bonnet helped Max back to his feet. He leaned him against the alley wall and waited until he was able to breathe without gasping.

"You should be more careful of the company you keep."

"They were trying to rob me," said Max. "I don't know who they were."

"Hmmm," said Bonnet. "Why were you in this neighbourhood?"

Why were you? This is a long way from your usual beat, thought Max. "There is a music club near here. A friend suggested I try it out."

"Barzani?" asked Bonnet.

"No. Minette." Max wasn't sure why he lied. Maybe Hevel had enough people looking into his affairs already.

"Really," said Bonnet, "Let's drop by Le Coq Bleu on our way home and you can tell her all about it."

"It's late. They're probably closed. And as you can see, I've had a long night."

"Nonsense. Yesim is always open for an old friend. And there is nothing like a brandy to ease the pain of a beating. Trust me. I've administered enough to know."

Eight – Saturday, December 21ˢᵗ, 1918, early morning

Yesim was cleaning up when the cab deposited Max and Bonnet in front of the café. Henri was perched at his familiar location at the end of the bar, nursing a final glass of wine. Yesim scowled but poured them both a glass of brandy. At Bonnet's insistence, he locked the door and turned off most of the lights. Yesim poured himself a small Dubonnet and joined them at a table well away from the bar. He brought the brandy bottle with him. Henri stayed at the bar, but his gaze never left them.

Max swallowed half his drink in a single gulp. His sides and back still ached from the beating and the ugly welt across his cheek was starting to sting. He was still queasy from vomiting, but the brandy seemed to help so he finished it. Yesim poured him another.

"Where's that pretty niece of yours?" asked Bonnet. He topped up his own glass without asking.

"She's up at Lachance's place. He's paying her now."

"Oh?" said Bonnet. "And what's the going price?"

Yesim clenched his fists and started to stand. Max put a hand on the smaller man's arm. Bonnet had been jittery in the cab, all the way across the mountain, tense like he wanted to hit something. Or someone. Yesim would be as good a target as any and in his present condition, Max wasn't sure he could do much to stop him.

"She dresses pretty and greets his clients at the door," said Yesim, settling back in his chair. "The Americans find her accent charming."

"It's too bad," said Bonnet. "Lieutenant Anderson wanted to tell her all about his adventures at the night club she recommended. What was its name?"

"It didn't have a name that I know of," said Max. Only Bonnet still called him by his old rank.

Yesim cocked an eyebrow in Max's direction and nodded. "I think I know the one you mean. No names. No signs. Music, dancing, a little something extra for the discerning gentleman. Minette raves about it all the time. I think she gets a commission if they mention her name. Enterprising girl, my niece."

Yesim is clearly a more accomplished liar than I am, thought Max.

"Bah, you could be describing half the illegal dives in the district," said Bonnet. "Speaking of which, are your licenses still in order?"

"Of course," said Yesim. "I paid my bribes down at HQ just last week. Didn't you get your cut?"

"Someday I'll close this place down and send you back to Marseille where you came from."

"Could you do it next month?" said Yesim. "The weather is beautiful in the south at this time of year. Really, Bonnet, I know everyone else has to give you free drinks too but where else will you find a bar where they joke with you like a real human being?"

"Do you have any food behind that bar of yours?" asked Bonnet.

"Sure, why not?" said Yesim. "There are a few things left from lunch hour. I'd have only wasted them by eating them myself."

"And bring some beer, too. I can't wash down stale sandwiches with brandy."

Yesim went behind the bar and brought back a basket of food and a couple of bottles of cold beer. He let Henri have his choice before bringing the rest to the table. Bonnet picked out a pain bagnat, sniffed it and then put it back and took a brioche stuffed with ham instead. He shoved the basket across to Max.

Max glanced at Yesim, who shrugged. Max took the tuna sandwich Bonnet had rejected.

"How much do I owe you?" Max asked.

"It's on me," said Bonnet. Yesim rolled his eyes.

"No," said Max, putting five francs on the table. "I don't like to be in debt to anyone."

"Suit yourself," said Bonnet. "Though an attitude like that can get pretty expensive. How does a fellow like you support himself anyway?"

"I get by." Max wondered how much Bonnet knew about his business. The man was crude but cunning in a rough way. You couldn't rise to sergeant in the Sûreté on corruption alone. Everyone in the neighbourhood seemed afraid of him, to one degree or another, except perhaps old Henri who didn't seem afraid of anything. Even Yesim for all his sarcasm knew better than to push too far. It couldn't be a good thing that a man like Bonnet was taking an interest in his affairs.

"There are lots of opportunities for a smart young man like yourself to get rich," said Bonnet.

"I don't see you living in a palace yet, Bonnet," said Yesim.

"Why don't you go talk to Henri? He looks lonely."

Yesim grunted but did what he was told. Bonnet shifted his chair so his back was to the two men at the bar. He leaned into Max and spoke in a low voice.

"Those two idiots think they're smart. HQ has got files on both of them, thick as my thumb. I could tell you everything they do from hour to hour, right down to how often Henri farts in his sleep. But you're different. As a foreigner, all we know about you is what you included on your registration card – where and when you landed and the hotel you're staying in."

"There's not much else to know."

"There are ways I could test that theory," said Bonnet, showing his teeth. "And of course, there is what we officially know and what we actually know."

"Why doesn't that surprise me?"

"See, just as I said, you're a smart young man. Listen. I've got connections. Things are underway. Big things – bigger than this goddamn conference they're holding next month. There are people working behind the scenes – it might surprise you how high up some of them are placed."

"There are always people in high places working behind the scenes. Isn't that what caused the war?"

"The war was caused by bankers and Bolsheviks," said Bonnet. "Everybody knows that. There was an article in La Croix by Bucard that lays it all out."

Bucard. Hevel had mentioned him. Max was surprised Bonnet hadn't blamed the Jews. Everyone else he had met today seemed to. Maybe it was implied. He was getting tired of this. His back still ached despite the brandy and his face had gone from stinging to throbbing. *Why was he of such interest to so many people?* Of course, he knew the answer to that. It wasn't Max Anderson they were interested in; it was Hevel Barzani.

"It's late," Max said.

"It's later than you think," said Bonnet. "I work for the Tenth division – not that anyone will admit it exists. We work within the prefecture to keep an eye on people who otherwise can't be watched. Like that American spy, Buchan."

"Why tell me?" A cool shiver traced its way up Max's spine. *They do know things,* he thought.

"We're stretched thin. Someone like you – well, you could play a useful role. You speak English and your French is more than passable. You can – and do – mix with all sorts of people who would never talk to me. If you heard anything unusual, you could pass it on to me."

"And what would I get out of this?"

"The honour of serving a greater cause."

"Then there's no money involved."

"There could be – there's always money involved. Right now, people hate the Germans. Clemenceau and the rest think they're still a threat. But I tell you, they are nothing compared to that gang that have stolen Russia. The Bolsheviks were minor players in starting the last war but they'll be the leaders of the next one. That's who we all have to guard against."

"Isn't the mayor of Bobigny a Bolshevik?" asked Max.

"Don't rub it in. That's my hometown. What do you say? Do you want to work for me?"

"Is he trying to recruit you to his mythical division X?" Bonnet jumped. Henri had crept across the bar until he was standing right behind them. "Don't listen to his bull – there's no such thing. He's a blackmailer who wants you to dig up dirt on potential victims."

"I'll dig up dirt and bury you under it, old man." Bonnet leapt to his feet and slapped Henri across the face. Henri slapped him back. Max jumped between them as Yesim came from behind the bar, a lead pipe gripped in his hand.

"Enough, enough," Yesim bellowed.

Bonnet shook himself loose and straightened his uniform. "Don't forget what I told you, Lieutenant. These fools have no idea what's happening right under their eyes. Thanks for the sandwich, Yesim. But if I catch you serving drinks after hours again, I'll shut you down." He turned on his heel and strode to the door.

Bonnet's exit would have been dramatic if he hadn't forgotten the door was locked. He cursed and fumbled with the latch and then slammed the door behind him so hard it made the glass rattle all along the front of the café.

"And he calls us fools," muttered Henri.

"Aren't you worried?" asked Max. "Hitting a policeman—"

"And I'm still standing –do you think he's going to brag about that."

"And it's his word against ours," added Yesim. "Do you want another sandwich?"

"I should go, too," said Max. "It's been a long day."

"Don't be stupid," said Henri. "That face of yours needs some tending to. What did you do to it anyway?"

Max gave Henri and Yesim a highly edited version of the evening's events – leaving out the meeting with Schmidt and the interest of his attackers in Barzani's business.

"This city is going to hell when a man can't even take a leak against a wall without being robbed," said Henri. He had washed the scrape on Max's face with warm water and was now working with a pair of tweezers to remove flakes of brick from the wound. "This will be sore for a few days – but if we can get it clean, it shouldn't scar. Much."

"I heard that women like scars," said Max.

"Sure," said Henri. "If they are discreet and come with a heroic story. Not if they cover half your face and were the result of a back-alley mugging."

"So, you don't think there's anything to Bonnet's secret division?"

"I wouldn't say nothing," said Henri, plucking a stone chip from Max's face. "They'd have files on us all if they could. As it is, they know something about most of us – some more than others. They keep a lot of information in the vaults of the Hotel de Ville."

"Maybe someone needs to burn it down again," said Yesim, laughing. He put a large brown bottle of hydrogen peroxide and a box of gauze on the table.

"Don't joke about that," said Henri. "You weren't there." He soaked a cloth in the antiseptic and dabbed it against Max's cheek.

"Someone burned down City Hall?" asked Max. The smell of peroxide stung his nose but Henri was gentle so there was little pain.

"It was a long time ago," said Henri. "Before you were born. Hell, before Yesim was born, I bet."

"I was two," said Yesim. "Bouncing on my father's knee on the docks of Marseille."

"Ever since the revolution, the men who rule France have been afraid of Paris," said Henri. "That's why we don't have our own Mayor – only a Prefect appointed by the Minister of the Interior."

"And why the Prefect of Police – also appointed directly by the Minister – has twice as many cops under his command than the head of the National force," added Yesim, from behind the bar.

"But I thought there was a city council," said Max.

"There is and they elect their own president but he has no real power – the Prefect and, especially, the Prefect of Police, are really in control," said Henri. "I said that the government doesn't really trust Parisians but that's not exactly true. It is not those who were born in the City they fear – they're mostly bourgeois shopkeepers who are happy to maintain the status quo. It is all the people who come to Paris – to work, to try to make a better life for themselves, or just to get away from troubles at home – that's who they are afraid of. It used to be men from the provinces they watched the most –"

"When I first came here from the south, I had to report to the police every time I changed rooming houses or got a new job," said Yesim. He had finished tidying the bar and come to join them at the table. "There were too many of us to really enforce it but if they caught you with out-of-date papers, they could put you on the train home if the mood struck them."

"Or if the bribe wasn't big enough," added Henri. "Now it's the foreigners they watch and there are more of them every day. It's not so bad for the Poles or the Italians. If things get too rough, they can always run to their embassy – the cops don't want to start another war. But the poor bastards from Algeria or from our Asian colonies have nowhere to turn. Technically citizens, but without the right to vote – who can they turn to?"

"Those poor bastards are taking our jobs and stealing our women," said Yesim.

"They used to say the same thing about you, Yesim," said Henri, frowning.

Yesim laughed. "You have to know I'm only joking, right? I haven't become a follower of the Action Francaise or that Bucard fellow Bonnet is always talking about."

Henri nodded. He finished dabbing at the wound and pressed a thin gauze bandage against it, which he attached with sticking plasters.

"You came from Marseille?" said Max.

"My family lived in Marseille long before it was part of France," said Yesim, a hint of pride in his voice.

"But..."

"The name, I know. You cannot imagine the grief it has given me, especially with my complexion. My father, despite spending his life on the docks, never learned to swim. When he fell in one day, he was rescued by a sailor from Algiers. They became fast friends. He died in a storm a few weeks before I was born but his name lives on in me."

"Sounds like a fair trade-off to me," said Henri.

"I think the man who beat me up was from Marseille. He had your accent."

"I don't have an accent," said Yesim. "It's all these other Frenchmen who talk funny."

"People come to Paris from all over," said Henri.

"You never told me who burned down City Hall," said Max.

"This Great War of yours was not the first time we fought the Germans. In 1871, when I was twenty-one, we suffered a horrible defeat. German soldiers marched down the Champs Élysées and demanded humiliating terms. The government gave them everything they asked. The people of Paris were outraged. When the government sent troops here to Montmartre to safeguard the fortress, fighting broke out. Workers, soldiers and shopkeepers joined forces to form the Commune. We wanted to keep fighting the Germans; we wanted to return to the values of the revolution. Liberty, brotherhood, equality!" As Henri talked, he slowly rose to his feet. He looked past Max as if he could still see the events unfolding. Still hear the cries of his fellow citizens.

"They sent in the national army. They had guns and horses and cannons; we had stones and homemade bombs. We fought them from street to street, from house to house for one long bloody week. In the end, when the cause was lost, we took our vengeance on the mansions on the rue de Rivoli and on City Hall. They took their revenge on our bodies. The Seine ran red. I can still smell the terrible stench of burning bodies. They executed nearly twenty-five thousand Communards and sent twice that many into penal servitude. My father and my brother were both killed. If the records at City Hall hadn't been destroyed, I suppose they would have found and killed me, too. But I escaped."

Henri sank back into his chair like a tent collapsing when its guy ropes are cut. Yesim went to the bar and poured a large tumbler of brandy. He shrugged and poured two more. "No profits for Lachance tonight," he said, setting them on the table. They drank in silence for several minutes.

The hurts of the past make us who we are, thought Max. There is no escape from the cycle of retribution. Germany humiliated France and, in their frustration, they turned on each other. If Germany is humiliated now, will German kill German? And where will that lead? More war? Is that what Hevel is trying to do? Break the cycle and change the path of history?

"When I was young," said Henri, "even after the days of the Commune, I thought the world was like a raisin cake. Don't laugh,

Yesim, I'm serious. The cake was the way people were normally, solid, bland, rational. And the raisins were those little moments of passion and madness that come on us all from time to time. Mostly, they give flavour to life – but you can still choke on one. But, now, after this Great War of yours, I don't know anymore. Maybe what's normal, the cake, is madness and the raisins are those rare moments of kindness and love – ah, listen to me. It's the brandy talking."

"No," said Yesim. "It's a man talking."

"It sounded like the brandy to me," said Minette from the doorway.

"That's because you are young and foolish," said Yesim.

"How is that different than calling you old and stupid?" she snapped back. "Is there any of that brandy left?"

As Minette walked to the bar, Max couldn't keep from following her with his eyes. Yesim was right – she did dress pretty. The click of her high black heels against the hard wooden floor matched the shuddering rhythm of his pulse. Her dress barely reached the middle of her calf and the three overlapping layers of the skirt, in shades of pale yellow, swirled against her legs as she moved, sometimes flaring, sometimes clinging to the outline of her thighs. The top of the dress darkened to gold as it reached past her waist and draped across her small bosom. One shoulder was partly bare while the other was covered in a contrasting blue sleeve that came down to her wrist. Her long white neck was adorned with a single gold chain, from which a yellow stone was suspended. A circle of matching stones graced her bare wrist. She poured a small brandy and turned to lean against the bar, watching them, her eyes glinting with amusement. Her face was perfect, smooth pale skin with a hint of rose on her cheeks, her eyes dark beneath arched brows, her mouth bright red like a cherry ready to be plucked. Her black hair was tight to her head like a cap and glistened in the light.

He realized Henri was watching him watch Minette, a soft nostalgic smile playing on his lips.

"It's time for me to find my bed," Henri said. When Yesim didn't move, he nudged him. "Maybe you should head off, too. We both have work tomorrow."

"I'm not –" Yesim looked from Max to Minette. "Right," he said, yawning. "I should get my sleep."

Then they were alone.

"I should be going," said Max.

"Why?" Minette kicked off her shoes and drifted through the room to sit opposite him. The faint scent of roses wafted across the table. "Are you afraid of me?"

"I'm more afraid of myself."

Minette laughed, a small tinkling sound. She put her elbows on the table and leaned forward, cupping her oval face in her hands. "Am I that beautiful?"

"Yes." He had never felt like this before. It wasn't like the others, forgotten almost as soon as he left their company. Everything he thought about love had been proved wrong in this moment. Now, he knew what love was.

"You're so sweet," said Minette. "Do you want to kiss me?"

"Yes." He had never wanted anything else before in his life. Yet. "Are you sure?"

Minette laughed again. "I'm a woman of Paris. Do you think I've never been kissed?"

"Yes. No. I don't..." It was as if he were rooted to his chair, wanting to move but unable. Then she was leaning over him, her fingers tangled in his hair as she turned his face upwards and pressed her mouth against his. Her lips were soft and slightly parted. He lifted his hands to cup her face and kissed her back. He felt himself stiffen and knew, if he stood, he would embarrass himself. He tried to pull away but she pulled his face closer and slipped her tongue between his lips. For an instant, they hovered like that, his body arching upward, hers leaning down. Minette's teeth grazed his lower lip lightly, then harder, painfully, before she moved away. Max slumped back in the chair, uncertain if he had liked it at the end but knowing he wanted more.

"I think we should stop there," said Minette. "We're drawing a crowd."

Two men, their faces twisted and leering, had pressed their faces against the window. Max jumped to his feet and took several steps toward the door. The men turned and ran.

"I'm sorry. I didn't mean..."

But Minette was gone.

Nine – Monday December 23, to Friday, December 27, 1918

In the afternoon, Max took the Metro to Concorde and then walked along Rivoli to the Hotel Vendôme to meet Buchan. The pain in his back and ribs slowed him but walking was the best medicine. Winter had officially arrived early the day before and, as if in response, the weather had turned markedly colder. A skiff of snow chased pedestrians from shop to shop and the outdoor cafés had been abandoned for restaurants with fireplaces. Max enjoyed the sudden turn; it reminded him of home. Still, he had put his warmest jacket over his suit and had donned a wool scarf and fingerless leather gloves for the walk.

The front desk directed Max to the gentlemen's lounge, separated from the lobby by ornate glass doors and a sense of entitlement. Buchan was ensconced in a forest-green wingback, cigarette in one hand, whiskey glass in the other. He was alone, still in a dark grey day suit but with his tie loosened and his collar unbuttoned.

"Glad you could make it," he drawled. "I like a man who keeps his appointments. Can I get you something?"

Max shook his head and sat in a similar chair opposite Buchan's. He was surprised how comfortable it was. The gentlemen's lounge overlooked the Place Vendôme, a vast stone-clad square, dominated by a column with a spiral of human figures carved from the base to the top. To the left, livery-clad doormen were putting wreathes on the balconies of the Ritz. A few hardy strollers – Canadians like himself, perhaps – were scurrying along the edges of the square. They were well-bundled against the cold. A few were wearing gauze masks over their mouths.

"You look like you've been in a fight," said Buchan.

"A misunderstanding," said Max. The scrape on his face was still red although it no longer hurt much. It probably would look like hell for a week or two but Henri had done a good job and Max doubted it would scar.

"Smoke?" asked Buchan.

"No, thanks, I don't really enjoy it."

"A man who knows what he likes. And I like you more and more all the time."

That didn't make Max feel better. He had come to tell Buchan that he couldn't work for him; to give him his money back. He couldn't serve two masters. But now he wasn't so sure. Shouldn't he be more willing to work for Ginger Buchan than Hevel Barzani? Wasn't he, as Buchan put it, "one of us?" Did that make Hevel "one of them," and so, by definition, the enemy? It didn't feel that way to Max. None of it felt right. Buchan had tried to play on the bonds of patriotism – but he wasn't an American. If he owed allegiance to anyone, it was to the Empire. But he felt nothing for King and Country – not anymore. He had left that in the trenches with the bodies of his friends and comrades. Perhaps Hevel was right – he could only obey his own sense of justice. It was all he had left.

"Is something troubling you?"

Max took the envelope with Buchan's tens out of the jacket pocket. "Here's your money back. I can't work for you."

Buchan didn't reach for the envelope. "Got a better offer, hunh? I figured as much when you didn't take off your coat. I can find more money if that's the sticking point."

"Not a better offer," said Max, though he supposed it was. "A different one."

"Let me guess. From Barzani."

Max hesitated, then nodded. Hevel hadn't paid him to lie; just to remain true.

"That's okay. I've looked into him. He's not a bad sort. His interests don't always lie with those of America but they don't generally go against them, either. Keep the money. If you can do some things for us that don't violate your agreement with Barzani, who does it harm?"

"I don't think so." He held out the envelope again.

Buchan took a drag on his cigarette and leaned back in his chair. "There will be no questions asked," he said. "I'll leave it all to your judgement. If you have something for me, drop a note here at the hotel. I can give you another hundred right now. Call it a retainer."

"I'd have to tell Barzani."

"Fair enough. And if he objects, you can give me back the hundred. Keep the twenty though. I've already claimed for it and the paperwork would be a nightmare."

A hundred dollars was a lot of money. He could live for a month or more at L'Aquilon. But if Hevel objected, he would give it back.

"Alright," he said. He took the bills – ten tens – from Buchan's hand and slipped them in his billfold.

"Now that's the spirit. Like we say at Princeton – in the nation's service and in the service of all nations. In my books, you're now an honorary Princetonian. Take off your jacket and have a drink while I explain what's really going on."

Max slipped off his jacket. Before he could put it over the back his chair, a young boy appeared to take it from his hands and carry it to a carved wooden wardrobe beside the bar. Max settled back into the chair and let Buchan buy him a glass of red wine.

Buchan took a long drag on his cigarette. He blew the smoke up toward the ceiling and looked at Max through the haze that separated them.

The wine arrived and Max could tell by the way the waiter held it and then stood by with a towel draped across his arm that this was a cut above what Yesim served at Le Coq Bleu. Max held it up to the light as Henri had taught him – French culture was as important to the old man as language – and swirled the liquid in the deep bowl of the glass. The wine was clear and glowed a rich ruby colour with glints of a deeper red buried inside. He placed the bowl beneath his nose and swirled the wine again. The smell of fruit dominated but when he breathed deeply, he could detect, as he had been promised by Henri, the faint smell of leather and, even, a hint of earth. He took the first sip, a bare mouthful, which he let run over his tongue. He took a second, fuller, taste. Henri's lessons failed him, fruit yes and berries, then a fuller richer flavour, heavy that lay on his tongue like oil but he had no words to describe it. He swallowed the wine. The after lingered but didn't grow bitter. It was the best thing he had ever tasted. He nodded at the waiter who smiled and left him to his drink.

Buchan had been watching this performance with a faint smile on his face.

"You're really starting to fit into this place, Max," he said. "A regular sophisticate. But why not? Good Americans when they die, go to Paris. And Canadians, too, I guess. You just skipped the dying part."

Max was pleasantly surprised that Buchan remembered his country of origin.

"Have you heard of Wilson's fourteen points?" asked Buchan getting down to business.

Sure," said Max. "I have a framed copy over my desk."

"Really?" Buchan looked doubtful but he shrugged and went on. "Then you know that we, that is, the United States of America, are unequivocally committed to each and every one of them."

"Of course," said Max. He wasn't sure what Buchan has driving at.

"Have you actually read the document you have tacked to your wall?" asked Buchan, his freckles brightening on his face.

Max felt his own face flush. "I'm not an expert on international affairs."

"No, no," said Buchan, making placatory motions with his hands. "Of course, you aren't. I'll give you the short version."

Max sank deeper into his chair and held the bowl of the wine glass under his nose. Short versions were usually lengthy.

"They won't work."

"That's it?" said Max.

"I told you it was the short version," said Buchan, grinning.

"You obviously want to tell me why," said Max.

"Only to the extent that it will help you help me," said Buchan. "Knowing too much is as dangerous as knowing too little."

Max wondered if that was true. Perhaps if he had known more – or less – he could have avoided the beating two nights before.

"In theory, every sovereign nation has equal standing at this conference, but, like I told you before, everybody knows who holds all the cards. What the big four decide, the rest will have to accept." said Buchan. "Russia is a special case and, I'm told by our Asian experts, Japan is, too. But everyone else – whether they came in on our side early or late – is a supplicant. They have their hopes and they'll use every resource they have, but their interests will take a backseat to those of the big four."

"Then why have them attend at all?"

"Excellent question," said Buchan. "Because America, England, France and Italy may have been allies in war but, in peace, they are rivals. Perhaps not bitter ones, but serious ones."

"They each want to increase their own power and influence at the expense of the others," said Max.

"If that was all it was, it would be straightforward. The fact is: each of them has a different theory as to what needs to be done.

Crass interests are a matter of negotiation; theories are the basis for war."

"And what is the American theory?"

"I guess it comes down to three things. Nations should be formed on the basis of national self-determination. All the Poles in Poland; all the Serbs in Serbia and so on. Where peoples aren't ready to govern themselves – the colonies – they should at least have a fair say in how and by whom they are governed. Finally, a League of Nations should be the arbiter and enforcer of international conduct and definitely not the United States. The American people have a limited taste for empire. I'm sure President Wilson wants to see all fourteen points adopted, but I'm pretty sure he would be happy with those three. Of course, I'm an optimist – I think we can get seven or eight."

"Sounds simple enough," said Max, though he didn't really think so. Buchan's talent for making things seem simple when they weren't suggested he was a lot closer to power than he let on.

Buchan snorted. "Don't it just though? It works okay for America and England. Great Britain is separated from everyone else by a channel and the United States only has two borders. But Europe? People are smeared across it without much respect for any dividing lines, current or historic. Where does Poland end and the new Czechoslovakia begin? Is Serbia a single country or do the Croats have the right to self-determination, like my friend Asper wants? You can ask the same question of the Bosnians and Montenegrans for that matter – all likely doomed to come under Belgrade's thumb. So that's what we're up against. And that's what I want your help with."

"What is it you think I can do?" said Max.

"There are people I can see and there are people I can't be seen with – you know, point one of the fourteen, no negotiations conducted in secret," said Buchan. "I might ask you to take a letter to someone. Or go to a party– you'd be surprised how much business is conducted over a tray of hors d'oeuvres – or a meeting, a gathering of Reds or anarchists, or maybe a speech by André Bucard, the new darling of the right. The possibilities are endless. You were an officer in the Canadian army – maybe you know someone who's working in the British delegation, say an old commanding officer."

Max nodded at that. Buchan had been checking up on him, too. Colonel McCallister was in Paris although Max had avoided seeing him since his return.

"And you know Barzani, he's bound to introduce you to people who are in the know. Cultivate those contacts. Nothing may come of it but if you hear something you think might be of interest to me – no matter how trivial – let me know, as long as it doesn't conflict with your other duties. It's all about knowledge, Max. The more we know, the better off the world will be."

Buchan's drink was empty and he signalled the waiter for another. Max declined. He needed to think about what Buchan had told him and about what he had left unsaid. And he needed to find Hevel. He hadn't seen him since leaving the music club Friday night. He wasn't at his hotel and the desk clerk didn't know where he was or when he might return. He wanted to tell Hevel about the attack and now he needed to ask him about his arrangement with Buchan and the Americans. If Havel agreed to Buchan's proposal, perhaps he could talk to Count de la Bois or that general, Lacroix, that he had met at the opera.

After a few minutes he took his leave, with a hundred dollars in his pocket and a letter addressed to Joseph Asper to deliver. He took the long way back to the Metro station, walking along the Quai in the growing dark. He leaned against the railing and looked along the Seine to Notre Dame. The river was the color of steel under the lowering clouds. Ice had formed along the banks in places but he had been told that it seldom froze over. Christmas lights glittered on the dark waters. A few fishermen were hauling their last nets from the river as a solitary barge moved slowly past. Max listened to them calling to each other and laughing but he couldn't make out their words.

§

Christmas came and went without any sign of Hevel. Asper, too, was absent from his rooms; his studies over, he was spending the holiday with friends in Lyons but would return on the 27th. Buchan had asked that the letter be delivered in person and that Max wait for a response.

He finally gave in to the Christmas spirit that seemed to have gripped the city and bought gifts for his brother back home – a wooden model of the Eiffel Tower which, when it finally arrived, he could glue together and keep in his room, if sixteen-year-old boys still did that – and for some of his new friends in Paris, Yesim, Henri and Jean-Marc. For Minette, he found a pair of calfskin gloves in red, personal but not too much so. Despite the kiss, he didn't know how she really felt about him. He gave it to her at the train station as she and Yesim boarded the train for Marseille.

Christmas breakfast was a sombre affair. Marie, the cook's wife, had died of the flu the night before. Jean-Marc did his best to make the morning festive, but his face was drawn and his eyes red. Max went back to his room after eating and returned with two hundred francs to give to Marie's family. Jean-Marc shook his hand formally but resisted kissing him on the cheeks. The fear of the spreading epidemic had begun to affect everyone.

That evening, he dined with Henri at Fouquet's on the Champs Élysées.

"This was where my wife and I ate our first meal together," he said. "It wasn't as fancy then as it is now and not nearly so dear. We came back every year for our anniversary. Since she passed, I have come here each Christmas. My present to myself. It is a pleasure to share it with you."

They exchanged gifts over dessert – for which Max insisted on paying. He had gotten Henri a silver flask with his name engraved on it. "Now you can stay warm on the late shift," he said. Henri gave him a tattered leather volume containing the better-known works of Victor Hugo. "By the time you finish these, no one will be able to criticize your French."

That night, Max had his best sleep since he came to Paris. Perhaps it was the wine or the rich food or, perhaps it was because, for the first time since he was a boy, he felt at home.

§

Early on the afternoon of December 27th, Max crossed the river to Montparnasse where Asper lived in a three room flat with two other students. He still had not heard from Hevel, but he couldn't let that stop him from carrying out Buchan's errand.

The district alternated historic buildings and stately gardens with dingy seven-storey tenements possessing neither central heat nor running water. Residents warmed their rooms with open coal braziers and carried buckets of icy water up rickety staircases from a communal tap on the first floor. The accommodations were neither pretty nor comfortable, but they were remarkably cheap and, by living in them, even students could afford to eat every day in the many small Brasseries that dotted the area or browse for used books in the stalls along the Seine.

Asper was surprised to see him but happy to receive word from Buchan. He seemed embarrassed by his living quarters and hustled Max out almost before he had finished explaining his mission. They walked along Danton to the Boulevard Saint Germain until they reached the Metro station where St. Germain met Bonaparte.

"Let's get a beer," said Asper, indicating a large brasserie on one corner of the square.

"How about lunch?" said Max, adding, when Asper hesitated, "Buchan gave me money for expenses." It wasn't technically true – Buchan had said nothing about how Max was to spend the money he gave him – but it kept the arrangement with Asper strictly business. Besides, he was hungry and Brasserie Lipp was as good a place as any.

It was warm inside the bar, but the beer was crisp and cold and the selection of dried meats and sausages was impressive. Max ordered two large lengths of bratwurst, cooked with small potatoes and onions while Asper had a bowl of goulash with a hunk of rye. After they had satisfied their initial hunger, Max passed Asper the letter from Buchan. He examined the seal critically before opening it. He scanned the contents quickly. His expression was unreadable, and Max couldn't tell if he were pleased or displeased with Buchan's message. Nor did he care.

"Buchan asked me to wait for a reply," said Max.

"Verbal or written?"

"He didn't say. But if it's more than a simple yes or no, you should probably write it down. I'm not sure when I'll see him again and I wouldn't want to get it wrong."

Asper nodded and scribbled a few dozen words onto a sheet torn from a notebook he had carried with him from his rooms. He shoved it back in the same envelope and gave it to Max. He put Buchan's letter into his inside jacket pocket.

"Obviously I can't seal it," said Asper.

"I have no interest in reading it," said Max.

Asper gave him another one of those smiles that only involved his mouth. "Did you have a nice Christmas?"

Max shrugged. He really didn't feel like engaging in small talk with the man. He was not his friend or ever likely to become one. He didn't trust Asper with his half-smiles and furtive manner. He would have left but he hadn't finished his lunch and the food was too good to abandon.

"What about Barzani?"

"I don't think Hevel celebrates Christmas," said Max, being deliberately obtuse.

Asper snorted. Even his laugh was half-hearted. "I mean, have you seen much of him?"

"No."

"I can see why your services are in demand," said Asper. "Are all Canadians this tight-lipped?"

"No," said Max. He was enjoying this game though he didn't know what the stakes were.

"I've heard rumours that place him in Marseille. Others say he's gone to Berlin. I even heard he was in Biarritz. It's where all the catamites go."

Max didn't know that word, but he didn't like the sound of it. "Why are you so interested?"

"Barzani is a player. So am I, though not nearly so well funded. A lot of people would like to know where he gets his money. A lot more would like to know what he gets it for."

"I wouldn't know," said Max.

"And wouldn't tell me if you did," said Asper. "But let me give you some free advice –"

"None of Mr. Asper's advice is ever free, young man." The man who spoke was sitting, alone, at the next table, his back to them. Max couldn't remember if he had been there when they arrived.

Asper turned in his chair. "Captain Gereau. What a coincidence!"

Gereau turned as well. "Life is full of them; some fortunate, others, less so. Shall

I join you?"

Gereau. The police Captain that Barzani had warned him against at the opera.

Asper's smile was even weaker than before. He gestured to the empty chair. It wasn't until Gereau stood that Max appreciated how big he was. Well over six feet, he must have weighed nearly two hundred and fifty pounds, mostly muscle although he had begun to thicken around the middle. He had a strong chin and a broad intelligent brow above large brown eyes. His thinning grey hair was neatly trimmed as was the bristle on his upper lip. He moved deliberately, not like an old man, but like someone who had to keep their strength constantly in check.

"Who's your friend, Joseph?" said Gereau. He was studying Max's face as if trying to place where he might have seen him before.

Asper seemed lost for words to describe their relationship.

"Max Anderson." Max extended his hand. "I'm from Canada."

"Is that where you met? Canada?" Gereau's hand was long and lean with perfectly manicured fingernails. But his handshake was firm.

"No. We have mutual friends."

"That's hardly a recommendation. I know some of Joseph's friends. I am Gereau." No first name, no repetition of the rank Asper had assigned him.

"Captain Gereau is a detective" said Asper, his voice oily. "In the political division of the Prefecture. One of the most powerful men in Paris."

Gereau chuckled deep in his throat. "Nonsense. I'm practically retired. They only assign me to cases that don't really matter."

"I'm gratified to hear that," said Asper.

Gereau's eyes grew narrow and hard. "There are exceptions to every rule. Who do you work for, Mr. Anderson?"

"I don't work for –"

"Don't play games with me. These days, everybody works for someone. Even if they don't get paid. I don't mind really. I just want to know. Information is a hobby of mine."

Max had a feeling that he shouldn't lie to this man. On the other hand, he didn't have to tell him the whole truth. "I was delivering a letter from a member of the American delegation. I'll now take Mr. Asper's reply back to him."

"Oh, well, the Americans," said Gereau. "Everybody loves the Americans these days. If you see Colonel House, tell him Alphonse Gereau said hello. You can go now – I need to have a few words with Joseph. But come see me in the New Year. Sometime after Epiphany." He gave Max his card.

Maybe I should get calling cards, thought Max, *it seems to be the thing to do*. He paid his bill and left. He glanced back at the pair, huddled together at the table. Asper was doing all the talking. His face gleamed with sweat though Max doubted it was caused by the warmth of the bar.

The encounter with Gereau had left Max edgy and alert. Otherwise, he might not have noticed the man who stepped out of an alcove as he passed and followed him down the stairs into the Metro station. The man didn't say anything until they boarded the train. He sat in the seat facing Max and only spoke when the train had left the station, his voice partly muted by the clatter of wheels on track.

"You're Max Anderson."

Max nodded. The car was unusually empty. Three young women in drab coats and, the latest Parisian fashion accessory, gauze masks, talked quietly among themselves at one end and a middle-aged man in some sort of uniform sat at the other.

"I'm Joachim. I'm a friend of Hevel Barzani." Joachim was whippet lean with angular facial features and olive skin. His hair was short and covered in a small cloth cap, black with red stitching along the edge. One of the Jews Max had known in the army had worn a similar cap.

"So you say," said Max.

"Caution is the eldest child of wisdom," said Joachim.

Max had just read that in the book Henri had given him. Victor Hugo. "And the parent of safety. How do you know me?"

"Hevel gave me a very good description," said Joachim. "I was watching Asper's place when you arrived."

"Why?"

"We all watch each other these days. It has become the national pastime – we watch each other, and the police watch us all. Asper is well known to us. He's not a friend but not quite an enemy. But he associates with those who are."

"Enemy to whom?"

"I have grown used to talking in riddles but, as we have only three more stops before we must part company, I'll try to be direct. Do you know what an anti-Semite is?"

Max nodded. He had never met a Jew before he joined the army, but it didn't take long to discover that some people had an irrational hatred of them.

"Now that the war is over, the losers are looking for someone to blame," said Joachim.

"The Germans?"

"Of course, but the White Russians and Hungarians, too. Even those in France who feel aggrieved at how the war was conducted or hate all who are not French, or French enough to meet their standards. They blame the Jews and the bankers – often in the same breath – or the Jews and the Bolsheviks or just the Jews. It is an easy hate with long roots."

The train pulled into St. Michel station. Posters along the wall alternatively advertised the new show at the Folies Bergère and warned of the dangers of gathering in crowds. Two workmen in quilted jackets and a woman loaded down with shopping bags boarded the car. None of them sat near Joachim or Max, whether from fear of influenza or Jews, Max couldn't tell. When the train was under way again, Joachim leaned forward again.

"Hevel is trying to accomplish a great thing: the fair division of the Levant, what the Americans call the Middle East, into autonomous natural states, homelands for Arabs, Jews, Turks and Kurds, whoever is strong enough to deserve one. Of course, he is only one of Faisal's agents but an important one. Faisal is the prince who organized the Arab revolt and helped capture Medina. He has bigger ambitions now. Barzani brokered Faisal's meeting with Weizmann and moves easily between the camps of bitter rivals. They say if 'you don't know Barzani, you aren't worth knowing.'"

"He doesn't claim to be that important," said Max.

"I think that's why he's so successful – he makes sure no one quite takes him seriously. But he has information and he has money and he knows how to use them both to advantage. Of course, the decisions will not be made by people like Hevel or even people like Faisal."

"The big four," interjected Max to save time.

"Exactly, but how will they decide? Whoever speaks to them first will have a powerful impact. And whoever speaks to them last will seal the deal. That is what Hevel – and every other diplomat, national spokesman and fellow traveller – is jostling for. Not one hearing but two and at the most propitious times. And opposing that – competitors like Asper on the one hand and men like André Bucard, on the other."

"Bucard? Heval mentioned him and others, too."

The train had stopped again, and Joachim went silent. The middle-aged man in the uniform walked past them to the exit. It seemed to Max that he was glaring at Joachim.

"He's the coming thing, they say. Nobody really knows his background or even precisely what he looks like – he gives speeches but there's never a photographer around. He's a big man of middle years, short blond hair and a broad face. German looking though they say he was born in Marseille. Some say he has a certain charm; others call him a predator. Founded the Sons of the Republic before the war; got involved in similar groups after the Sons were implicated in some bombings. The current one is called The Black Cross. Bucard is a critic of the current French state but no anarchist. You can find his like in every country in Europe these days – nationalist, anti-socialist, angry and most of all anti-Semitic."

The train began the turn towards Chatelet station. The train was slowing and Joachim stood to leave. Max would continue on to Gare de l'Est but Joachim apparently would not.

"Bucard is rumoured to be in Paris though no one knows what he's here for. Whatever it is, it can't be good for us or for Hevel. You need to warn him. Tell him to meet me at Le Pré aux Clercs any afternoon between 4 and 5. He knows the place."

"Do you know where he is?" yelled Max, as the train doors slid open and Joachim stepped onto the platform. But the doors closed before he could get a response. As the train pulled away, he had one last look at Joachim, standing on the platform, his eyes wide and his face pale from shock. There was a large blonde man standing behind him with his hand on his shoulder. Then the train passed out of the station and was gone. Max watched the lights in the tunnel flash by, then took out his journal and wrote down what Joachim had told him.

§

Max knew there was something wrong even before he entered his room. L'Aquilon was not the warmest of hotels but it wasn't frigid either. Yet, the hallway outside his room was cold and when he placed his hand near the bottom of the door, he could feel a steady rush of air. He never left his window open when he was out but it was clearly open now. Max took out his pocketknife before he unlocked the door. Neither the overhead light nor the lamps on his desk or bedside table were on and the drapes had been pushed back. *The break-in must have occurred while the sun was still up, perhaps right after I left.*

The intruder had come through the window and left the same way. A pane had been broken to reach the latch and glass was scattered on the floor. Some had been ground into the carpet as the room was searched. The bed had been ripped apart and the mattress thrown on the floor; the trunk, emptied and on its side. The money was gone. The desk drawers had been opened and the contents dumped on the floor, but the papers fixed beneath them were still in place. The framed Fourteen Points were undisturbed on the wall beside the desk.

His other hiding places had not proved as useful. The loose floorboard had been pulled out and the papers hidden inside were gone. The armoire had been completely emptied, his clothes and boots in a pile in the middle of the floor. All three jackets had their linings ripped out and their pockets inverted. The thief had also found the documents hidden in the back of the closet.

Max slid out onto the balcony, kneeling as if trying to hide from view. He peered into the alley below and across into the park, lit by a pair of gas lamps at either end of the path that bisected it. He could see no one but that didn't mean there was no one there. Without looking down he cautiously slipped his hand into the planter, digging down with his fingers. The package was still there.

Max moved from one side of the narrow space to the other, staring into the darkness below. Any observer might think he was searching for them.

Max went back inside and turned on the light on the desk. He slumped in the chair and stared at the mess in the middle of the room. His chest felt tight, his mouth, dry. He felt the lethargy that had haunted him since he was wounded began to creep over him. He forced himself to his feet and began to sort through his possessions. Action was the only cure for fear.

Who knew he was working for Barzani? Who might suspect he was holding documents for him? Joachim, Buchan, perhaps Asper and Bonnet, the men who had assaulted him outside the jazz club. There might be others but none came to mind.

It had been a long day. He wanted his bed. But first he'd have to put it back together.

Ten – Tuesday, December 31, 1918 to Tuesday, January 7, 1919

On New Year's Eve, Max found his way back to the music club. He had asked Minette to come with him but she was working for Lachance so he went alone. Jake seemed glad to see him. In fact, he seemed glad to see anyone; the club was less than half full.

"It's this damn flu," he said, as he led Max to a table near the bar. "Everybody's either got it or is afraid of getting it. I heard tell of four women set down to play bridge one night and by the morning three of them were dead. But don't you worry – I got my own special drink to keep the flu away."

"Bring me one of those," said Max, "and some of that lamb stew if you've got it."

"No lamb tonight," said Jake, "but we have a nice little rock hen, stuffed with dates and walnuts and served with a hard orange sauce. Or we have some fresh trout, cooked in white wine and garlic."

Max had never had a rock hen so he ordered that. Jake's drink consisted of orange juice and rum with some gingery spice sprinkled on top. It tasted like something that would keep away the flu.

Max turned his chair so he could watch both the stage and the front door. By turning his head a little, he could also see the entrance to the opium den downstairs. The food was good and the music lively – a full ten-piece orchestra with two singers – and the small crowd made up for their numbers with their enthusiastic dancing. If Minette had been there, he might have danced himself, despite the stiffness of his leg. At midnight, he joined the countdown – dix, neuf, huit – to the start of 1919 which ended in a cheer but only a few awkward kisses among strangers.

He had hoped to see Hevel or even Schmidt but by one it was clear that neither were coming. It had now been ten days since he had seen his friend and he was getting worried.

§

On the day after Epiphany, as Captain Gereau had so politely demanded, Max made his way to the Prefecture of Police, a four-story building on Île de la Cité. It was less imposing than some of the surrounding structures but had a certain authority that made Max reluctant to enter. Even in the bright sunlight, it seemed forbidding. He paused in front of the fifteen-foot-high wooden doors, flanked by striated columns and topped by a formidable balcony. Tall narrow windows, barred on the lower level, flanked the doors and he had the sense that this was a building that was far easier to enter than to leave. Holding Gereau's card firmly in his right hand, he pushed his way into the lobby, where a harried desk sergeant directed him to an office on the fourth floor of the farthest wing.

Gereau was on the telephone, one of the few Max had seen in Paris, but gestured Max through the open door to sit on a hard wooden chair on the opposite side of his desk. The desk looked as old as the building itself. Its broad mahogany top, in the few places it was visible beneath a welter of documents, was scarred and stained. Other than the large arched window that dominated the wall behind Gereau, the only light was an electric desk lamp. The brass base and stand were scratched and in need of polish, while the green glass shade was held together by glue and hope.

"Well, you know what to do, so do it!" Gereau hung up the receiver with a bang. "Do you know what it's like to work with idiots?"

"I was in the army," said Max.

Gereau furrowed his brows. "Ah," he said, after a moment, "the Canadian who works for the Americans. Don't tell me." Gereau stared into space as if consulting an invisible list. "Max. Max Anderson."

Not counting their near encounter at the Opera, Gereau had met Max once, nearly two weeks before and yet he not only remembered his name but what he did. This was not a man to be trifled with.

"What did I want to see you about?" said Gereau.

"I suppose it was because..." Max paused. "I don't know."

Gereau laughed. "You'd be surprised how often that question works. People blurt out whatever they feel most guilty about. What do you feel most guilty about, Mr. Anderson?"

The truth could be a weapon if you knew how to use it, thought Max. A shocking revelation from the past might distract Gereau from more immediate matters. "That I was never able to prove that my uncle murdered my father. And that I left my brother in my uncle's care."

Gereau's eyebrows rose and he pursed his lips. "Those are serious matters. You know, under French law, your uncle could sue you for making remarks like that to the police. Even in jest."

"I'm not joking."

"I could make inquiries. I have friends in both the Royal North West Mounted Police and in The Dominion Police, too."

"There was a coroner's report. Death by misadventure. Not an accident but something like it."

"A suicide?"

"That was the rumour my uncle started. My father, distraught by my mother's death, put himself deliberately at risk. Working alone at night fixing heavy machinery without making sure the safeties were engaged."

"Sounds plausible," said Gereau.

"You didn't know my father," said Max, standing up. "In any case, it was a long time ago. I've resigned myself to it. There's no point in stirring things up. I won't trouble you further."

"No trouble." Gereau half rose and extended his hand. "If there's anything else I can do."

Max felt he had made a lucky escape. He was halfway to the door when Gereau's voice stopped him. "One other thing Mr. Anderson. You work for the Americans?"

"Yes," said Max, without turning.

"And are you also in the employ of Hevel Barzani?"

"Yes."

"Then perhaps you had best be seated again."

Max tried not to let the tension show in his face or back as he resumed his seat in front of Gereau's desk.

Gereau went to the office door and closed it. He rested his hands on the back of Max's chair. His faint reflection in the window seemed to hover like an avenging angel.

"Before we begin," said Gereau. "Were you lying about your father?"

"It's not something men lie about."

"In my experience," said Gereau, "men will lie about anything. But I believe you believe it – so it's a good start for our relationship."

"Do we have a relationship?" asked Max.

"Not yet," said Gereau. "But I'm always hopeful. An enterprising young man like yourself – in Paris for six weeks and already your French is more than passable and you have acquired two jobs. Why not a third?"

"My other jobs pay money." *The way things are going, I'll soon have every job in Paris.*

Gereau laughed. "My resources are more limited – but you may find that having the friendship of a Captain of Police is not nothing."

"Even one who is nearly retired and only assigned the unimportant cases?"

"Even one like that," said Gereau, resuming his seat behind the desk. "What do you do for Hevel Barzani? Come now. My enmity is not nothing, either."

There seemed little point to hold back. Gereau certainly knew the answer to the question before he asked it. Never a bad strategy. "I go places with him. A sort of bodyguard, though not a very good one. He likes to talk – I think he doesn't have a lot of friends, despite the number of people he seems to know."

"I can understand his impulse. You have the kind of face that invokes trust."

"Do you suppose that's why people keep offering me jobs?"

"France had eight million casualties in the war. Talented men – and you are clearly talented – are hard to find. Most English ex-patriates stick to their own kind. You seem to like to mix with others. It's a rare combination of talents."

It was a better explanation than he'd heard from anyone else.

"Now what else do you do for Barzani?"

"I've been holding some documents and money for him but I don't seem to be doing a very good job of that. My room was searched a few days ago. Things were taken."

"Did you report it?"

"I thought I just did," said Max, smiling. "I didn't really know whom I should tell. I only know two police officers and I only trust one of them."

"I'll take that as a vote of confidence. Who's the other one?"

"Sergeant Bonnet."

"François Bonnet? Your mistrust is not ill-placed. Bonnet is not a very good cop but he has friends in the right places – both on and off the force. I can have someone else look into it, if you like."

"No," said Max. "I think the fewer people know about it, the better. At least until I can talk to Hevel."

"You haven't told him yet?"

"I haven't seen him since before Christmas." That was what he really felt most guilty about. Hevel. He had made no real effort to find him. Instead, he had agreed to work for Buchan and, implicitly at least, Gereau. Were these the actions of a man who only answered to his own sense of justice?

Gereau rubbed his hand wearily across his eyes and turned his chair to look out his window. Clouds scudded across the winter sky, throwing shadows across the big man's profile and onto his cluttered desk. Moments dragged into minutes. Max sat silent, unmoving. He had grown patient in the trenches in the long stretches of boredom that separated the hours of terror. Gereau drummed his fingers on the desk, the nails clattering like the sound of distant machinegun fire and Max felt the familiar sick feeling. Someone has died, he thought. He saw the expression on Joachim's face as the train pulled out of the station. He remembered the man with his hand on Joachim's shoulder.

"If something has happened to Barzani," said Gereau, at last. "It didn't happen within the twenty arrondissements. I would have heard."

It didn't take that long to decide to tell me that, thought Max. *I guess my face only creates so much trust.* There are moments that define relationships, questions asked or left unspoken, fears shared or kept private. He wondered if this was such a moment. But then the moment passed. Gereau stood up and once again extended his hand. The interview was over.

"Let me know if Barzani turns up," he said. "I'll worry otherwise. And if I need something from you, I know where you live."

Max had no doubt that Gereau knew exactly where he lived. And that certainty raised all sorts of other doubts.

§

Hevel Barzani was waiting for him in his room when Max got back to L'Aquilon, sitting in the only chair and smiling at the framed copy of the Fourteen Points. Max felt a sudden and unexpected surge of joy to see him.

"Jean-Marc let me in. I hope you don't mind," said Barzani. "That's a clever idea. I would never have thought to hide something in plain sight."

It was only then that Max noticed the fresh bruises on Hevel's face and the white bandage wrapped around his right hand and wrist.

"You've been hurt."

"I had an unfortunate automobile ride. Nothing serious – a few more flaws in a less than perfect visage. The sprained wrist is more of a nuisance but it should be fine in a few weeks. And you? Did you get too fresh with Minette?"

Max blushed and touched the almost healed scrape on his face. He was still uncertain where he stood with Minette. *She* had kissed *him* but then had virtually disappeared from his life. She had stayed behind in Marseille when Yesim returned although he said it was only temporary. Hevel was still looking at him expectantly so Max told him of the attack outside the jazz club and what his attackers had said.

"There is no question they would like to put their hands on the objects I gave you. I'm surprised they haven't tried to search your room. It's what I would do in their place."

Max blushed again. "They did come. Or, at least someone did. The room was thoroughly searched but they only found some of my hiding places."

Barzani gazed at the framed document on the wall. "Tell me what was taken."

After Max described the missing papers, Barzani shook his head. He stood up and began to pace although the room was barely big enough for that. Max noticed that he favored his left leg. He walked from one end of the faded rug to the other and back again several times before speaking.

"Those papers were useful but not the most important. But those who took them might think they have gotten the lot. I think my other possessions are as safe here as anywhere else. Did you report the burglary to the police?"

"Not directly," said Max. He described his interview with Gereau.

"That's all right," said Barzani. "Gereau is a... well, an enigma, really. But not a threat. To me at least, although I prefer to avoid his...gaze. Let's leave things as they are. Now I have business to attend. It may take me out of town for a few days. And, it might be better if no one knows how closely we're working together. Let's meet in a week, next Tuesday at Le Coq Bleu. We can have a drink and catch up. Maybe go someplace nice for supper – as a belated New Year's celebration."

"A lot more happened while you were away. There are things we need to talk about."

"I'm sure it can wait." He picked up his hat from the desk. Max stepped between him and the door. Barzani sighed and put his hat back on the desk and sat in the chair facing Max.

"First of all, why did you choose me as your... whatever I am to you?" Max folded his arms across his chest and leaned against the door.

"We've been through this before. You saved my life. I owed you for that and trusted you because of it."

"That's not true."

"I was there. I should know."

"I don't think so. I saw you talking to one of the men who attacked you – in the train station on the day President Wilson arrived."

Barzani shifted uncomfortably in his chair, glancing around the room as if the answer were hidden with his secret papers. Finally, he sighed and looked Max in the eyes. "It makes no difference."

"It makes all the difference in the world. Our entire... friendship is based on a lie."

"How so?" said Barzani.

"It was staged. Nothing more than another of your games."

"There is no question it was staged – up to a point. I can tell you my cuts and bruises were real. We had to go that far if Marois, the man you saw me with, was to gain the acceptance of the others. I think I mentioned Bucard – those men were connected to him, not directly, but close enough. But it is true I was in no danger of dying. But you didn't know that."

"So?"

"You saw a stranger – a foreigner – being beaten by three men. You could have walked on but you didn't. You could have called for the police but you knew there was no time. Despite your own injuries, you came to my rescue. You risked your own life for me."

"Anybody would have done the same." Max waved his hand dismissively.

"Surely you don't believe that."

Max had no response. Would anyone have done it? What if he hadn't been there – would Bonnet have rescued Hevel? What if he hadn't been able to overcome his fear...?

"Were you ever a lifeguard, Max?"

Max shook his head, confused by the sudden turn in the conversation. "I can't swim."

"I spent three summers working at the British consulate in Tehran. They had a pool they used for exercise and to keep cool in the heat. The heat of a Tehran summer is like nothing you've ever seen. My first summer, I served drinks and snacks, sweating in my formal uniform. It was unheard of that someone like me would be allowed in the pool with Europeans. But after hours, we were allowed to swim. I became quite good at it. When the chef de mission learned of my prowess, he made me the unofficial lifeguard. If a gentleman had one too many drinks on the deck and got into trouble in the pool, my job was to leap in and rescue him. But the first thing the chef told me – 'Save yourself first.' You broke that rule."

"I did what any man would do," Max repeated, more from stubbornness than conviction. He had failed once and the memory of that failure had haunted him and driven him for the rest of the war.

"Did you do it without thinking?"

"I don't know."

"Well, I do," said Barzani. "You didn't simply barrel in, heedless of the risk. You assessed the risk and made a plan. You used every tool you had because you knew you were placing yourself in danger."

"But you weren't in danger." Max hated this. He had hated it during the war – men thinking he was more than he was, simply because he did the right thing when the need was greatest. He could not help but be who he was, though who that was seemed uncertain now.

"You didn't know that. Your act was no less selfless because I was not in danger. If you saw me being attacked again tomorrow, would you stand to one side because it might not be real?"

"No."

"Precisely. In your heart, you believed I was in danger and that you could and should save me. The reality of the situation doesn't change that."

"Then all that counts is what is in your heart?" Max always felt lost in these discussions, like a child looking for vanished parents.

"No. Heart and hand are inextricably linked. Wanting to kill a man is not the same as doing it – just as killing a man by accident is not the same as doing it by intent. But what moves you to act is as important as the act itself."

"You couldn't know what I felt in my heart."

"I was there. I saw you. You put yourself in danger to rescue a stranger. A wog."

"Don't use that word," said Max.

"And that settled the matter," said Barzani. "I saw your face when Bonnet talked to me like that, saw your anger at his casual dismissal of my value as a man. That was the moment that I knew you were the man I could trust."

All of which made it harder to tell Barzani about Buchan. To his surprise, Barzani reacted not with anger but with laughter. He clapped his manicured hands together. "Perfect, perfect," said Barzani.

"You aren't concerned I might betray your interests?"

"Do I need to have a medal forged with the words 'I trust you' engraved on both sides?" said Barzani, still chuckling. "I trust you and I trust your judgment. Besides, I can think of several advantages to having a direct connection to the Americans. There are some things that work best through back channels."

Neither Hevel nor Ginger Buchan had asked him to betray the faith the other had placed in him. And, for some reason, neither expected he would.

"So, I'm useful to you?" Max had hoped for something more.

"That was my first thought," said Barzani. "But in the last few weeks, I've grown fond of you, Max. I had hoped you felt the same."

Max felt his face flush and he looked away. "I…"

Barzani sighed. "I forget how hard it is for English men to express their feelings, especially for other men. Perhaps, you could think of me as a favorite uncle."

"More than that," said Max. "Like a brother."

Barzani smiled softly. "Why not? An older brother. Much older."

Max stuck out his hand and Barzani grasped it in both of his. "Now I should go."

"Not yet," said Max. He told him of his meeting with Joachim and the message he had given him. He finished by telling what he had seen on the platform as the train pulled out and the fearful premonition he had had in Gereau's office.

"I'm sure he will be fine," said Barzani, although the tremor in his voice suggested otherwise. "I'll try to see him today or tomorrow – yet another item on my endless list of things to do. Bucard is a dangerous man. I had hoped he would avoid Paris – and the surveillance of the Prefecture of Police – but he apparently thinks it worth the risk to come. I will take precautions. I suggest you do too."

"I carry my knife with me wherever I go."

"Could you get a gun? Despite the best efforts of the army and police, they are still readily available from the war."

"I... " Max hesitated. During the war, he had used a gun almost every day. He had killed at least five German soldiers – three during the battle that earned him his commission. At the time, it had been necessary but now it seemed somehow dirty. He didn't know why he had kept the revolver. He didn't think he could bring himself to use it again. Not against another human being. But Hevel trusted him with his secrets. "I have a gun but I'm not prepared..." His throat tightened and he couldn't finish the sentence.

Hevel nodded and crossed the room to rest his hand on Max's shoulder. They stood like that for several long moments. "Le Coq Bleu this Saturday at nineteen hundred. Until then, take care, my friend."

Eleven – Saturday, January 11, 1919

Max arrived at Le Coq Bleu shortly after the hour but Hevel wasn't there yet. He took Drebec instead of his usual, gentler, route. The three flights of steep stairs that connected lower Drebec to upper would justify the evening's meal and, perhaps, keep his recent weight gain under control. Max sat at their usual table but, in truth he could have had his pick of seats. There were only two other men in the bar, both sitting as far from each other as they could get.

"It's this damn flu. The doctors say the worst is over but people are still afraid," said Yesim, when he brought Max a glass of Burgundy. "If people ate more garlic and drank more wine, they wouldn't have to worry so much."

Yesim was clearly following his own advice. His pores oozed the pungent aroma and there was a slight sway to his step as he returned to the bar. Halfway there, he spun on his heel and returned to the table. "Almost forgot. Hevel came by earlier and said he wouldn't make it tonight. He had to go out to Poissy and won't get back until late. He'll see you here tomorrow at the same time." He glanced at the two customers nursing their beers along the back wall. "If we're still open."

"Did he say anything else?"

Yesim scratched the stubble on his chin. "He asked if you could meet his friend from the Metro in the next few days. I guess you know what that means."

Hevel didn't see him last week, thought Max. Didn't or couldn't. Or Joachim has something for me from Hevel – that he can't give me directly. Wheels within wheels. Max ordered some bread and olives – more to give Yesim the business than because he was hungry. On the plate with the olives were three peeled cloves of garlic. Yesim stood watching him until Max ate one of them. After the initial sharpness, it was surprisingly good.

He would drink his wine and eat the purple olives, though perhaps one clove of garlic was enough. He had almost finished when Minette came down from upstairs and came to sit with him.

"Aren't you frightened of the flu?" Max asked.

"I'm more frightened of the garlic my uncle keeps pushing at me," she said, daintily plucking one of the olives and putting it in her mouth. "Besides, we all have to die sometime."

"Don't be in a rush. Death will come before you're ready."

Minette laughed. "Sometimes, Max, you sound older than Henri. Come with me tonight. There's a party at Lachance's place."

"A party?" said Max.

"He's desperate to drum up business – it's been dead since Christmas. He's invited some crazy artists to exhibit their work and there will be music and dancing. They say the Americans are coming en masse."

Buchan might be there, thought Max. I need to talk to him. And Minette will be there. That's a lot more important.

"Are you working?"

"Not tonight." Minette pouted. "You've forgotten, haven't you?"

"Forgotten?" There was something Minette had told him about this date. "Of course not. Happy Birthday."

Minette looked doubtful but he hadn't really forgotten. Until just now. He had bought and wrapped a present – a small silver locket. It was in his desk at the hotel.

"What time is the party?"

"It officially starts at nine but no one interesting will be there before ten thirty. Go put on something nice and meet me here at ten."

Max thought he was wearing something nice but apparently a tweed jacket didn't count. At Hevel's insistence, he had spent the afternoon buying three new suits to replace the outfits that had been destroyed by the men who searched his room. Tonight was as good a time as any to wear one, he supposed. He had to go back to the hotel to get Minette's present in any case.

§

Max was back at Le Coq Bleu a few minutes before ten but Minette was still 'gilding the lily' according to Yesim. Henri gave a low whistle when he saw him.

"Yesim," Henri said. "This gentleman seems to have lost his way. Not that this establishment couldn't use a better class of clientele."

"The quality of custom rises every time you go out the door, Henri," replied Yesim. And then to Max. "Would Monsieur like a canapé perhaps? A little paté and a glass of Dom Perignon. It's the best I have I'm afraid."

"You two should take that act on the stage," said Max. "I feel fool enough as it is."

The truth was, Max felt like anything but a fool. But to suggest otherwise would only invite more teasing. The suit – black with a charcoal stripe – draped across his shoulders and back like a second skin and the grey of his top hat matched the stripe perfectly. Beneath, he wore a crisp white shirt with a wing collar and a broad gold silk tie. A matching pocket square was tucked into his breast pocket. He had polished his patent leather shoes until they reflected his image back at him like twin black mirrors. The salesman had persuaded him to buy a cape for the winter cold and he now had it draped over his arm, with a pair of black leather gloves tucked into an interior pocket. He hadn't felt this good since the day he first put on his uniform.

Max sat at the bar and sipped a small *eau de vie* until Minette came down from the upper flat. She, too, was dressed in black, a simple dress that hugged her every curve, although a layer of filmy chiffon provided a hint of modesty, and came just past her knees. A line of symbols, Chineses lettering he thought, was embroidered in a line around her waist. The outfit was accented by a single strand of pearls and tiny pearl earrings. Her hair was feathered around her face and seemed to drift in rhythm to her movements as she swayed toward him on black heels.

Yesim shook his head and shrugged, then gave Max a look that said, "Take care of her. In that outfit she'll need protection."

§

Max hadn't been to La Coquette before and when the taxi pulled up in front he paused to take in its gaudy elegance. Two large doors in gleaming steel and glass were flanked by large brightly lit windows framed by blue velvet drapes tied back with gold rope. The room beyond was large with well-spaced tables, each covered in a crisp linen cloth and adorned with well polished cutlery and crystal glasses. The high-backed chairs had seat cushions in the same blue velvet as the drapes. The tables closest to the windows were already filled with diners but Max could see plenty of empty spaces farther back. Against the far wall was an enormous bar of polished brass and mahogany, its shelves lined with bottles of all shapes, sizes and colors and the racks above filled with glassware for any conceivable drink.

Scattered among the tables were easels and pedestals displaying the work of the "crazy artists" Minette had mentioned. Even from a distance, Max could see they were unlike anything in the galleries and museums he had visited over the last few weeks. The artist himself, a gaunt skeleton of a man with slicked back hair and a long, waxed mustache was flitting from easel to pedestal, making final changes. It was as if the work was never meant to be finished.

Several men competed for the honor of opening the door as Minette approached and then looked on, disappointed, as Max took her arm and led her into the restaurant. Lachance's man, Roget, was standing inside the entrance and glared at Max and Minette as they passed. Max glared back but Minette simply sailed into the room as if she were nobility and not the niece of a bar owner from Marseille. Lachance hustled across the room and kissed Minette on both cheeks; he, at least was unworried by the flu or was determined to appear so. He grasped Max's hand firmly.

"So nice of you to grace La Coquette with your presence," said Lachance. "A handsome couple is better than a billboard."

Lachance waved away the maitre d' and guided them to their table himself, choosing one away from both bar and kitchen but which could easily be seen from either window or the entrance. Max smiled. He had never been an advertisement before. Lachance ordered two flutes of champagne "on the house" then bustled away to greet newly arriving clientele.

Max sipped his drink and let his gaze wander around the bar although it always returned to rest on Minette's face. He could still feel the softness of her lips from the kiss that night in Le Coq Bleu. He hoped it was not the last. He had almost finished the drink when he spotted Buchan's red head. He was with a group of other young men, presumably members of the American delegation. Max stood but sat down again when Buchan looked at him and gave a small shake of his head.

"What is it, Max?" asked Minette.

"Nothing. Let's have another drink."

"I've got a better idea. Let's dance." She gestured to the large space near the back of the restaurant where a dozen couples were dancing. The music, provided by a five-piece orchestra, was much like what he had heard two nights before on New Year's Eve, but more controlled, as if the musicians couldn't risk letting go, here in so much light and glitter.

"I can't dance," said Max. In fact, he could – waltzes, at least – but not the fast jittery dances popular in Paris clubs. Although his leg was fine for walking, even the occasional short run, he didn't trust it for anything more.

Minette pouted. "There are plenty of men here who would love to dance with me."

"I guess that's true. Ask one of them if you like," *But I'd prefer if you didn't,* he added silently. He ordered another drink – red wine for himself and more champagne for Minette – which came with a plate of hors d'oeuvres, buttery crackers with pate de foie gras, sharp cheese and the ever-present olives. Minette picked daintily at the food, her gaze flitting around the restaurant. Her face was flushed with excitement and her lips slightly parted, as if awaiting a kiss. Max resisted the urge to lean across the table and give her one. He tried to think what to say, what words would bring her attention fully on him and only him. Instead, he sat silently and gazed at her, feeling like a school boy among his betters.

"You." The artist was standing at their table. "I will paint you."

Of course, who wouldn't want Minette for their model? The man leaned forward and grasped Max's chin, turning his head roughly from side to side. "Yes. It is a face for the new epoch," he muttered, almost to himself. He dropped a playing card, the Jack of Diamonds, on the table. "Come to my studio, any day after noon."

Before Max could respond, the man turned and strode to another table where he repeated the performance, this time with a woman of sixty. Max picked up the card. An address was painted across the face in thin silver lines almost too fine to read.

"Oh, don't mind him," said Minette. "Jacquard wants to see you with your clothes off. You see his work – it's not as if he actually paints the model in front of him."

Max laughed, though he wasn't sure whether Minette was joking or serious. Another man approached the table, though this time there was no doubt where his interest lay. He was well built but his face was slightly pocked and his teeth seemed too big for his mouth.

His longish hair was swept back from his forehead and plastered to his skull. It made his large grey eyes seem even bigger.

"You're being selfish, buddy," he said in English. "Keeping the prettiest girl in the room to yourself." He bowed in front of Minette and brought her hand to his lips. Switching to flawless French, he said, "David Arnold at your service, miss. May I have the pleasure of this dance?"

Minette smiled and blushed prettily. She glanced at Max. Max looked away, his tongue frozen in his mouth. He heard the swish of her dress and the click of her heels as she walked away from him. He finished his wine and ordered another, while he watched her dance with Arnold. He was replaced by a short balding man in an old-fashioned evening coat. When she moved on to her third partner –impossibly tall, olive-skinned, bearded – who moved her across the floor as if they were sailing on a glass-still lake, he got up and went to the bar. He drank brandy with his back to the dance floor until he no longer cared who she danced with.

The music was wilder now, more rhythmic, more real. The dance floor was packed with gyrating bodies. Men had shed their ties and jackets; women had left their wraps and scarves at their tables. Bare shoulders and arms were gripped by muscular hands and bodies twisted and swayed to the beat of drum and piano, while horns and voices wailed. He couldn't see Minette and he wondered who she had gone with.

Across the bar, Lachance was in a heated discussion with two other men – both taller than him. Max was sure the one wearing a fedora was Marois, the man who had been with Hevel at the train station. He didn't recognize the bigger of the two – broad-faced with dirty blonde hair. Could he be Bucard? Max tried to fit the man to the vague description Joachim had given him. It was true – he did look like a predator. Lachance led them through a door beside the long glass bar. After a minute, with a careful glance around to ensure he was unobserved, Max followed them.

The door led to a dimly lit corridor, which in turn led to a stairwell with narrow stairs leading down and slightly wider ones going up. He had no way of telling which direction the men had gone, no sound of voices came from either stair. Down into darkness or up into light? He chose the light.

The upper floor was quiet, only the faint throb of the music below. He moved along the hallway. Doors led off at short intervals and he tried several before one opened to his touch. It led to an office. Bookshelves, mostly empty, and file cabinets lined two walls while the other was occupied by a large rolltop desk. The desk was open with a scattering of papers covering its scarred surface. More papers hung out of half open drawers or were stuffed in narrow slots. A brass lamp created a pool of light in the otherwise darkened room.

Max stood in the doorway for a moment – it was as if the occupant had stepped out and might return at any moment. A faint wisp of smoke rising from a small ashtray confirmed it. He was about to close the door again when one of the documents caught his eye. He took three quick steps and leaned over the desk, careful not to disturb anything. There was no question – it had been stolen from his room. Hevel had said he could live without it but Max was sure he would like to have it back. *At the very least he will be interested in where I found it*, he thought, as he folded it and slipped it into his jacket.

Max hesitated, looking back at the half-open door. *May as well be hung for a sheep as a lamb*, he thought, echoing his livestock-rustling Yorkshire ancestors. He sat at the desk and rifled through the papers, careful to keep note of their placement and order. Most were invoices and other records of Lachance's business dealings. A great deal of money passed through his hands. A small black book tucked into one of the cubbyholes was in code – a string of six numbers followed by two or three letters and then more numbers, three, four or five depending on the line. Max tried to see a pattern, applying the training in cryptography he had received after being made an officer, but none was obvious. Then he realized the first string of numbers were dates – the earliest ones going back to before the war. Max flipped through until he found the most recent entries. There were three since the documents were taken.

182212 AG 2000, 182812 FRB 10000, 190101 PAM 1200. Max found a pen and scribbled the numbers on a fresh page of his journal. Perhaps they meant nothing but perhaps they were clue to who had searched his room. He shoved the journal in his pocket and put the book back. He replaced the papers he had moved until he was sure the desk looked much as he had found it. *Perhaps it would be better*, he thought, *if no one knows I've been here.* He put the stolen document back on the desk.

As he stood, he heard the sound of footsteps and low voices in the hall. If it were Lachance returning to work – for Max had no doubt this was Lachance's personal office – he was caught dead to rights. He could hardly pretend that he had mistaken it for a bathroom. He stepped into the shadows in a corner of the room.

The door opened a few more inches and then was pulled closed again.

"I told you," said a man's voice. "Lachance didn't come back up here. You should have asked him while he was in the bar."

"I would have," said Minette. "But he came and went too quickly. Who were those men he left with?"

"No one that need concern you. You don't need Lachance. I can fix you up. Do you have any money? Or I can take it in kind if you like."

"You're disgusting, Roget. Lachance gives me what I want for free."

Roget snorted. "You can't really believe that. What do you do for him?"

Minette said a vile word and Roget yelled in pain.

"You little bitch," he said.

"Touch me again and it'll be worse than a scratched face. Eduard will deal with you. Or I will."

"You better watch yourself, Minette," said Roget. "When Lachance tires of you..."

"You know nothing, Roget."

"Don't I? I know why he tolerates your flirtations with that Canadian."

Max leaned forward. The voices outside the door were growing faint as Minette and Roget moved farther down the corridor.

"Max is harmless," said Minette.

"Maybe," said Roget. "But his boyfriend is stirring up a lot of trouble. If he's not careful, he's going to wind up dead."

"Oh, I suppose you'll be the big man who does it."

"No, no, not me." Roget sounded almost embarrassed. "I don't kill people – though I sometimes make them wish they were dead."

Minette said something in response that made Roget laugh. But by then they were too far away for Max to make out the words. He waited until he was sure they were no longer in the corridor, then made his way quickly down the stairs, through the main doors and out into the street. He took a last look through the restaurant windows. Minette was dancing with Roget while the artist, stripped to the waist was painting the body of a nearly naked young woman. In every corner of the room, men and women and sometimes women and women were pressed together, laughing or kissing in disregard of morals or disease. Ginger Buchan, his face flushed and bemused, gestured to Max to come back. This time it was Max who shook his head.

Twelve – Sunday, January 12 to Monday, January 13, 1919

B arzani wasn't at his hotel when Max called the next day. The concierge said he had left early with several 'rough-looking' gentlemen but was expected back in the late afternoon. Max left an urgent message for Hevel to meet him at Le Coq Bleu as soon as he could. He then went back to the hotel to retrieve his revolver. Things had progressed too far for any qualms.

Max had barely replaced the documents in their hiding place and tucked the revolver into the inside pocket of his new leather jacket when he was interrupted by a sharp rap on his door. Sergeant François Bonnet was standing in the hall, shifting from foot to foot.

"Are you alone?" said Bonnet, before pushing his way past a startled Max and shutting the door behind him.

"Not anymore."

Bonnet flashed him a small mirthless smile and appropriated the desk chair. "Sit down. I don't like people standing over me."

Max did as he was told though he didn't like the thought of Bonnet here in his room. He didn't know where he stood with Bonnet. He didn't even know if it mattered. Yesim seemed contemptuous of the man but also fearful. Henri... well, Henri was Henri. Bonnet had shown an interest in Barzani's doings but had not known him before the assault in the graveyard. Perhaps he was trying to figure out where Hevel fit in the scheme of things, although Max doubted it was as simple as that.

"I know you've been holding things for your Arab friend," said Bonnet. "Don't ask me how – the workings of the Prefecture are not your concern. Some of these documents may have been stolen. Some may be state secrets."

"If you know so much," said Max, "then you know they were stolen from this very room a few weeks ago."

"I had heard that," said Bonnet. "What I want to know – are there any more?"

Max resisted looking at the framed Fourteen Points. "No, but feel free to look yourself."

Bonnet grunted but made no move to leave the chair. He rubbed the stubble on his double chin and looked at Max thoughtfully. "Have you thought any more about my offer?"

"Not really. As I told Captain Gereau, I already have –"

"Gereau should tend his own onions." Bonnet laughed. "The old fool doesn't know that things have passed him by. There's a new force within the Force. Once Chiappe is made Prefect –"

"I've no interest in the workings of the Paris police." Surely, thought Max, he isn't serious about me working for him. Maybe it's a cover, an excuse to come to my room. "All I want is to be left alone. I've registered at the Hotel de Ville as required. If there is something else I need do to avoid these little visits, just tell me."

"Don't say I didn't warn you. Things are changing fast and the sooner the anarchists and Bolsheviks and –" He looked pointedly at Max "—their foreign sympathizers figure it out the better off they'll be."

Max had met Bonnet's type in the war, blustering bullies, always full of tough talk and ready to point the finger at traitors or cowards or degenerates or whoever their beady attention had focused on at the moment. Yet they were strangely absent when the bullets started flying.

"I suppose," said Bonnet, rising and straightening his uniform, "that you'll run off and tell your friend Barzani all about our little chat."

"I don't see why he would care," said Max. He was getting sick of Bonnet. He felt the urge to wipe the smug smile off his face but he knew that wouldn't lead to any good result.

"He'd care. I'll do you a little favor. One of my men saw him down at L'Homme Fort on Rue de Rosiers. Do you know the place?" Bonnet was smirking now.

Max shook his head. He stood up and opened the door. Bonnet took the hint but turned back once he was in the hall.

"Well, why don't you head down there now? I'm sure he'll be happy to see you. Then you can see the kind of man you've thrown your lot in with."

§

L'Homme Fort was a discreet establishment in the Marais district. It was marked by a pair of blue painted doors where Rue de Rosiers met Ferdinand Duval, forming a triangular plaza. *So much in Paris happens behind closed doors.* A small garden, consisting mostly of evergreen hedges, formed a tiny oasis across from the doors.

Some boys, dressed in dark suits and black hats, looking too formal for their age, were kicking a ball in the cobbled street but they ran off when Max approached. A small brass plaque over the door knocker – in the form of an athletic man holding a large club in his outstretched hand – was the only indication that this was anything other than a private residence. Beneath the name was inscribed a brief description: A Spa for Discerning Men. It was a bathhouse, though not like the numerous brick and porcelain baths so many Parisians relied on for their weekly showers. A gentleman's private club rather than a public facility.

Max knocked on the door several times but there was no response. When he tried the handle, the door swung open on well-oiled hinges onto a tiled courtyard. An inlaid walk led to a solid oak door, flanked by heavily draped windows. That door was ajar. The well-lit foyer beyond was furnished with large leather chairs and a rack for newspapers. A pitcher of ice water and several glasses stood on a low table. An open newspaper was scattered on the floor beside it. Near the back wall, a low reception desk had a large stack of fluffy towels beside it. No one manned the desk but the remains of a cigarette still smoldered in an ashtray – the pungent tobacco competing with the scent of roses from a large vase on a stand near the only other entrance to the room.

Max took the revolver from his pocket and crept across the room. The hair on the back of his neck rose and a cold stream of sweat ran down his sides. It was the way he had always felt right before going into battle. The back door was closed but not locked. The hallway beyond was white – white tiles on the floor, white walls and ceilings, even the doors that lined its sides were white – and dimly lit by a bulb covered by a white shade halfway down its length. A man's black sock curled outside the only open door was the only mar to the pureness of the space.

Max stood at the entrance straining his ears for any hint of another's presence. The only sound was the faint rush of running water. The air was moist, almost steamy, and was heavy with the musky smell of eau de toilette. Max tried the nearest door but it was locked. He pressed his ear against it but no sound came from the other side. The facing door led to a small room with a sink, with a mirror above it, a tub, a padded bench and a small locker. Several bottles stood in a row on the top of the locker – labels indicated soap, lotion and massage oil. The room was empty and gave no sign of recent occupation. The next two doors led to similar though slightly larger rooms which had showers in addition to a tub and a second padded bench.

A vaguely familiar smell grew stronger as Max approached the final two doors. The one with the sock was wide open; the other, closed but not latched. Another bathing room lay beyond the open door. The locker stood open and there were several damp towels in a puddle on the floor in front of the tub. The basin was still partly full. A tap dripped water onto the surface in an unsteady rhythm. A hairbrush sat abandoned on the sink. There was a feeling of a space just vacated.

Max pushed the other door open. Steam and the oppressive smell of blood fell on him like a cloak. The steam came from the still running shower. The drain must have been blocked; hot water ran over the shower lip and emptied through a hole in the middle of the floor where it mingled with a thin trail of blood. The blood came from a pool gathered around the legs of the padded bench. Max's eyes shied away from what lay atop but he forced himself to step closer, careful not to step into the blood. He wanted no trace of himself here. He put his gun back in his pocket.

He gazed down at the naked body spread across the bench, arms and legs dangling over the sides. The man looked so old and small that for a few moments Max couldn't recognize him. Or perhaps he didn't want to. There was a terrible wound on the man's chest, a deep stab to the heart and around it a series of straight slashes to form a six-pointed star. Despite the loss of blood, the skin of face and arms were reddened. Max looked at the steam still roiling from the shower. *They scalded him*, he thought, *then they cut him, then they killed him.*

He could not bear to look at the wound or the man's face. Max's eyes fixed on a simple silver bracelet on his left wrist. The hand below it was curled, the carefully manicured fingers nearly touching the palm. A jeweled ring adorned the middle finger of the hand. He knew that hand, that bracelet, that ring.

It was Hevel Barzani.

There was no question he was dead but Max checked anyway, resting his fingers against the pulse in his neck. He was surprised how steady his hand was. Inside, he felt his whole being tremble.

I should have seen this coming. If I had gone to the hotel last night instead of this morning, maybe...

There was no point. The past is gone, the future never arrives. What mattered was what he did now.

At least two people had been here when Barzani was attacked, the one at the reception desk and the one across the hall. They had either witnessed the murder, heard it if not seen it, or been warned off by those who did it. Or perhaps one or both were willing accomplices.

Max could feel his limbs stiffen. The smell of blood, the sight of his friend sprawled across the table like the victim of a sacrifice, threatened to plummet him back into the abyss. He needed to move, needed to act. It was the only escape from the silent staring fear. Face your fear, they had told him, when they sent him back. All it had cost him was his men and the use of his leg.

Max shook his head. *The war is over. It's not your responsibility. This is a job for the police, for Gereau or his ilk.* He backed away from the bench until he bumped against the open door. He knew he would be sick soon, would vomit up his pain and fear, but now was not the time. He took a deep slow breath to quiet the thudding of his heart against his chest.

Not surprisingly, no phone was installed in the reception area so Max went back outside. He took out his revolver, wrapped it in his handkerchief and thrust it deep into the thickest of the hedges. He would recover it when he could. Then he went looking for a gendarme.

§

The next twelve hours went by in a blur. He led the police back to the site of Barzani's murder. Soon a half-dozen men arrived, several constables and a weary looking captain named Fontaine as well as two white-coated ambulance attendants. They took photographs and gathered evidence while Max slumped in one of the leather chairs in the reception. A constable asked Max a series of questions; the captain, the same questions an hour later. The owner of the establishment, a thin-lipped older man with coifed hair and an air of faded elegance, arrived, fainted at the sight of the body, was revived and questioned and questioned again.

At last, the body, covered in a sheet, was removed on a stretcher and driven away in the ambulance. The door was locked and sealed and Max and the owner were transported to the nearest station house. They were warned not to speak during the journey and then placed in separate cells. Several hours passed. Max was taken out of his cell for a photograph and to have measurements taken of the main features of his face and body; his fingers inked and pressed onto a card. He was questioned twice – the same set of questions by two different detectives. He explained that he had come looking for Barzani based on the advice of Sergeant Bonnet. The mention of Bonnet's name produced the same response every time – raised eyebrows followed by a grim frown.

By the end of the day, he was exhausted and hungry. He had only had a pint of water since they had brought him in. He determined to ask for Gereau. At the very least, the captain might ask some new questions. When he was ushered into an office rather than the interrogation room, he was somehow unsurprised to see Gereau sitting behind the desk.

"Sit down, Max."

Gereau leaned forward with his elbows on the desk and looked into Max's face for several minutes as if to memorize its every feature.

"They've already taken my photograph," said Max.

"Oh, I'm sure. All part of the Bertillon system of criminal identification. I'm here to release you."

"Then you've caught the men who did this?" asked Max.

"No, though we'll follow up what few leads we have. The doorman was new to the city. From Prague according to his registry, although you never know. The address he gave was false. Frapeur, the owner, was not particularly helpful. His clients," Gereau made no effort to hide the contempt in his voice, "come and go as they please. He has no way of knowing who, if anyone, was there that day. He claims not to know Barzani, but..."

Gereau spread his hands in a gesture that could mean anything or nothing.

"Someone was in the other room. He must know something."

"Maybe," said Gereau, "But he's not likely to come forward, now is he? Paris is noted for its liberality but we do have laws against public indecency. Against homosexuality," he added, in case Max was unsure. "We could examine Frapeur's client list but it is a rather exclusive establishment and we might not like what we find. Reputations must be protected."

"Even if a murder goes unpunished."

"Even so," said Gereau.

"What if it was more than a murder – part of something bigger."

"Do you have any evidence that it was?"

Max still wasn't sure he could trust Gereau, wasn't sure he wanted to trust him. Barzani called him an enigma, a puzzle even his clever brain couldn't fathom.

"That mark carved into his chest. It must mean something."

"If it really is a Star of David and not a coincidence, it means a lot."

"Star of David?"

"A Jewish symbol – but were they accusing him of being a Jew or is some Jewish faction claiming...? Hah! I have to learn not to think out loud. In any case, the *official* theory is it was the result of a particularly nasty lover's quarrel. Crimes of passion are not treated the same as cold-blooded murder."

"It's not true and you know it." Max was innocent but he wasn't naïve. He knew that men were sometimes like that. Unnatural, his

Uncle George would say. Max didn't know. People did what they had to do, what their natures demanded. He might not approve but that didn't change anything. What he did know – in his heart even if his head couldn't prove it – was that Barzani hadn't been killed by a lover. He had been tortured and murdered by monsters. And whether Hevel was or was not what Gereau implied didn't matter. He was his friend and his death was important. To Max if to no one else.

Gereau frowned. "I don't know if I do. But I do know that Barzani was a foreigner. Not even from a French colony. In fact, we aren't even sure he was in Paris legally. It appears that his papers are, let's say, questionable. Even his age – one document says forty-four, another, forty-eight. The official theory is the official stance – you can't expect me to go against the Prefecture."

Max stared at Gereau until the older man looked away.

"Can I go now?"

"You should not judge the Prefecture by a few black sheep. I am thorough, even if Bonnet is not. I wanted every *usable* clue to be found. *My* men and I searched every flower pot, every dustbin, every... hedgerow for a block around. You underestimate us—me—at your peril."

Gereau nodded and stood up. He took Max's revolver, journal and neatly folded handkerchief from the desk drawer and handed them to Max.

"You may want this," said Gereau, nodding at the gun. "Though I trust I will not see it, or you, again."

Max took all three items and shoved them inside his jacket. He stood in the square and looked back up at the windows that hid Gereau's office. He felt the revolver, heavy in his jacket pocket, and wondered why Gereau had given it back. Was he asking him to do something? Or was he giving him permission?

Thirteen – Monday, January 13, 1919, evening

The police released Max too late for him to try to meet Joachim – if indeed he was still faithfully waiting each day after so much time had passed. The winter darkness was compounded by a light drizzle, an apt metaphor for the grayness Max felt inside, although he supposed the grayness would remain even if the sun were shining brightly. He wandered the streets around the Opera, unwilling to return to L'Aquilon or Le Coq Bleu or any of the other familiar haunts on the slopes of Montmartre. Here, among the wandering American tourists or well-established British expats, he could feel alone. That's what he wanted – at least for tonight. To be alone with his thoughts and his guilt.

But life is not like that. The things you most desire or need are always the ones that are farthest from your hand. Ginger Buchan stepped from a café and almost knocked Max down.

"Mind your step, buddy," Buchan grunted. "Oh, it's you."

Max nodded and stepped around the other man. Buchan gripped Max's arm.

"I heard about Barzani. It's a bit of a rum go."

That made Max smile despite himself. An American couldn't spend a week in the company of Brits without adopting half their expressions and a trace of their accent.

"How did you find out?"

"You know how it is," said Buchan. "Bad news has wings. Most of the middle east delegation is staying at my hotel. They're in a bit of flap over it. Upset at the death, of course, but furious because the police will provide no details. Do you know anything about it?"

"I found the body."

"Tough. Though I suppose after four years on the battlefield, you must get used to bodies."

"I guess." Buchan had no idea what it was like to see so much death. It did become routine. The same way pain can become a regular part of life or starvation can diminish the appetite. Yet, he had faced it before. He had been wounded once and returned to do things some men called heroic even if he didn't think of them that way, even after they pinned a medal on his tunic in the hospital after his second, more tangible, wound. He wondered if he would ever fully recover from either hurt.

"Maybe you could come over and give the Arabs the low-down," said Buchan. "Put their minds at rest or at least quiet them down so I can get some sleep tonight."

"Sure," said Max. Breaking bad news was the last thing Max wanted to do, but maybe Hevel's employers could shed some light on the reasons he had been killed or even who might have done it. If only he could only find some additional evidence, perhaps Gereau would be persuaded to launch a more vigorous investigation.

When Max was ushered into the meeting room on the second floor of Buchan's hotel, he knew the details of Barzani's death had already arrived.

"This is Nuri as-Said, Prince Faisal's right-hand man," said Buchan, indicating a slim dark man in a military uniform and a flowing headdress. "And the Prince's secretary, Rustum Haidar."

As-Said was seated at the end of table, glancing at some papers spread out in front of him. His expression was grim, bordering on angry. Haidar, sitting to as-Said's right, dressed in a frock coat with velvet lapels, by contrast, was staring ahead blankly, almost as if he wasn't there. His appearance reminded Max of Barzani, his angular features highlighted by dark eyebrows and mustache.

There was a third man in the room, leaning against a back wall smoking a cigarette. He was blonde with a long sensitive face and wore the uniform of a British officer, although there was another of the headdresses, presumably his, sitting on a pedestal beside him. No one bothered to introduce him.

His duty complete, Buchan fled the room, closing the door firmly behind him. He might be new to diplomacy, but he could clearly see this would not be a pleasant meeting.

Max stood by the entrance and waited. He had learned from his uncle George that silence made an effective question. As-Said had learned the same lesson. He stared at Max for several minutes then stood and slowly circled around him as if he were examining a strange specimen at the zoo.

"So," he said at last, "This is what a *shaz* looks like."

"No need for that, Nuri," the blonde man murmured.

As-Said returned to his seat and shuffled through his papers before speaking again. "What do you know of this death?"

"I found the body," Max said. He was growing tired of saying that.

"And what were you doing in such a notorious place?"

"I was looking for Hevel."

"Then you admit he frequented such spots?"

"Hevel did a lot of things – mostly in service to your Prince."

"Prince Faisal," said Haidar, speaking for the first time, "cannot be associated with a deviant. You will not imply he is."

"Hevel was a lot of things but I do not think he was what you all want to label him." And would it matter if he was? Max didn't know – though he supposed it mattered to these men. "I looked for him there on the advice of a police officer. You can ask Sergeant Bonnet yourself if you doubt my word."

"We have already spoken to Bonnet," said as-Said. "He informed us of the details of the death."

"Why would Bonnet do that?" asked Max.

As-Said shrugged. "As chief investigator, he thought it was his duty."

If Bonnet was in charge, then Gereau was right. Nothing would be done to find Hevel's killers. It would be swept under the rug and forgotten – the official version becoming the only version. Nothing Max learned here would change that. But he had to try.

"Do you know who might have wanted Hevel dead?"

"Every right-thinking man would want him dead," said Haidar. "If you ever come to my country, I will show you how we deal with the likes of you."

Max bristled. The blonde man shifted uncomfortably. "Perhaps you should let Nuri and I handle this, Rustum," he said.

"I will be with Faisal if you have need of me." He bowed slightly to as-Said and left by the rear door.

"Rustum is a good man," said as-Said, "but a little old-fashioned. He's right about one thing, though. No taint of this scandal must touch the Prince. If you go about telling people that this Barzani was his agent, we will have to take measures."

"Are you threatening me?" said Max. That was starting to get old, too.

"With violence? No. With a lawsuit? Most assuredly." As-Said laughed. "We are not barbarians." He began to gather his papers into a pile.

"Then that's it."

"I'm sorry," said the blonde man. "Sometimes, in war, friends are lost and we can do nothing about it."

"But the war is over."

"Not officially," said as-Said. "Besides politics is just war by other means. There is one thing more. Did Barzani entrust you with any letters?"

They weren't going to help Hevel so why should he help them, thought Max. He shook his head. "Some money, that's all."

"Keep it," said as-Said. "Someone needs to pay for the funeral."

§

Buchan was nowhere to be found in the hotel; according to the desk clerk he had left town for a few days. He had left a message for him with the concierge, asking that they have lunch together on Friday. He recommended a café in Montparnasse where a good meal could be had for a few francs and which had the added advantage of being off the diplomatic circuit. They could talk in private without fear of being observed.

It had been a long day but he had no appetite for either food or company so he went back to his hotel. Jean-Marc looked at him sadly but said nothing when he retrieved his key. *Bad news does indeed have wings.*

Max kicked his shoes off and dropped his jacket on the floor. The revolver made a heavy thud and he retrieved it and shoved it in the drawer of the table beside his bed. Max lay in the dark, listening to the patter of rain on his window. He should be doing something. He knew that but he couldn't seem to will himself to rise. *Get up now*, he thought, *get up now or lie here forever.* He pushed himself up to sit on the edge of the bed.

The furnishings of the room were mere shadows but a shaft of light from a street lamp fell on the framed copy of the Fourteen Points. They were too dim and distant to read but Max had stared at them so often, it was as if they glowed in the dark. The words of the preamble seemed to taunt him.

What we demand in this war, therefore, is nothing peculiar to ourselves. It is that the world be made fit and safe to live in; and particularly that it be made safe for every peace-loving nation which, like our own, wishes to live its own life, determine its own institutions, be assured of justice and fair dealing by the other peoples of the world as against force and selfish aggression.

Although the document was meant to establish the relations between nations and peoples, it could, it should, apply equally to each man and woman in the world. A world safe and fit to live in where everyone was assured of justice against aggression. A man's murder should be no less important because he was a foreigner or, even, a deviant. *Thou shalt not kill* was a core tenet of every faith; he who did murder should be punished.

He would not wait until tomorrow to begin. Right now, there were men who thought they were above the law, both man's and God's. They did not hesitate to kill Hevel Barzani and he should not hesitate to find them. He pulled on his boots and turned on the bedside light.

He was debating whether to take his revolver with him when there was a light tap at his door and a soft voice calling his name. When he opened the door, Minette threw her arms around him and wept against his chest. He half carried her to the bed and sat with her pressed against him while she cried.

"I'm so sorry. I'm so sorry," she said.

"It's all right. It wasn't your fault."

"No, I... I knew there were people who wanted to hurt Hevel. I... didn't think they would go so far. You need to be careful, Max, they might come after you if they think you are involved in his...work."

"Do you know who killed Hevel?"

"No, no, not exactly. But Roget said... He said that... someone might hurt him. Maybe even kill him."

"I'll need to talk to Roget."

"Stay away from him, Max. Roget is dangerous, too, and he doesn't like you."

"You mean he's jealous of me. I expect, where you're concerned, he's jealous of everyone. And who can blame him for that?" He lifted Minette's face and was gratified to see a small smile on her lips. He wiped the tears from her face with his thumbs and then leaned forward and kissed her lightly on the lips. She kissed him back but he turned away.

"I can't," he said. "Not now."

"I..." Minette paused. "Max, are you, were you Hevel's boyfriend?"

"What!"

"It's alright, I'd understand. I mean, some of the artists I know are like that. Some like both girls and boys."

"Yesim is right – you are keeping bad company."

"You didn't answer my question."

"I only like girls, Minette," Max said. "In fact, I only like one girl."

Minette smiled again and there was even the hint of blush on her cheeks.

"For what it's worth, I don't think Hevel was like that either. I think they killed him where they did to make sure his own people would turn against him." He told her of his meeting with the Arab delegation.

"Perhaps if those people stayed in their own country, these things wouldn't happen," said Minette. "Jews don't belong in Paris."

"They aren't Jews, Minette, and they're here to *get* their own country. Maybe that's why they won't get involved."

"Then it's hopeless."

"Worse than hopeless – Bonnet is in charge of the investigation."

"Bonnet is not as useless as he appears. Or harmless."

"I don't think of him as harmless. He is a nasty vindictive man. A coward, perhaps, but not harmless."

"I know you feel terribly about Hevel's death but he wouldn't want you to risk your life to avenge him."

Minette was right. Revenge was not part of Hevel's nature. Nor of his. If it were, his uncle would be dead, not enjoying the fruits of his brother's labour. But this wasn't about revenge, it was about justice. If the state would do its duty, find and punish the ones who had done this thing, he would be satisfied. Until then, he had no choice.

"I owe Hevel."

Minette slipped out of his arms and stood up. She crossed the room and stood staring at the poster of the Fourteen Points.

"What does it say? I can't read English."

Max stood behind Minette and put his arms around her. She shuddered and stepped away.

"I should go. Lachance is expecting me."

"Can I see you later?"

"If you like..." She reached up and touched the old scar on his left cheek, then brushed her fingers across the fresher wounds. "I've lost so many people in my life. My parents died in a train wreck – that's why I live with Yesim. Both my brothers in the war. And now this horrible influenza. I don't want to lose you, too, Max."

"I have to do what I have to do."

"Don't be stupid, Max! You only have to do what you *want* to do. What could you possibly owe Hevel that was worth your life?"

"He entrusted me with certain... things. I have a duty..."

"You're not in the army now." Minette's voice was high and harsh. "What things could be so important?"

"Documents – to do with Hevel's work."

"Papers? You would risk your life for a few words on paper? Do you still have these things? Give them to me and I will burn them."

Max hesitated. He didn't care about the treaty. The fate of nations was too big a matter for him. But those words must hold clues to Hevel's death. Dangerous clues.

"No. They were stolen."

"All of them? Every one of them?"

"Yes." There was no one in the world he wanted to keep from harm more than Minette.

She searched his face but finally nodded. "I'm sorry Max. I didn't mean to yell but it's so foolish – to risk your life for documents you don't even have anymore. Promise me you'll leave this alone. Let Bonnet do his job."

She doesn't understand, thought Max. *I don't understand myself.* "I'll let him do his job."

§

There were several people Max desperately wanted to find – Bucard most of all but also Marois and Roget. The former was little more than a name but he knew he had seen Marois with Lachance. Roget, too, was a fixture at La Coquette but he couldn't go there, not tonight. He would have to try when he knew Minette wouldn't be there. He would try to see Joachim and Buchan tomorrow. Who else might be able to tell him something useful? Who else might he find at this time of night?

Asper was asleep when Max banged on the door. "Do you have any idea what time it is?" he grumbled. Despite being roused from his bed he was fully dressed in wool pants and sweater. He had bulky socks on his feet and a scarf wrapped around his neck. It seemed even colder in the apartment than out and Asper's breath puffed white when he spoke.

"Nearly eleven," said Max. "Have you had supper?"

"I ate a little something at six but if you're offering..."

"Name the place."

"Les Deux Magots?" said Asper, hopefully.

Max had heard of the place – one of the more expensive cafés on the Left Bank – though he had never been there. It was said the French poet, Apollinaire, whom Max had begun reading at Henri's suggestion, had lunched there almost every day before his death from the flu last September.

"Why not? Buchan's paying." Max preferred to have Asper think he was on a mission from the American.

"Then I'll order the most expensive thing on the menu. That bastard has done nothing to help our cause – he can at least buy me supper."

Perhaps the worst of the epidemic is over, thought Max. The café was crowded, the babble of laughter and conversation spilling onto the sidewalk when he pushed through the revolving door that formed one corner of an almost square room. High ceilings were supported by three thin columns and a larger central pillar, from which a painting of two seated men, Les Magots, Max presumed, gazed down on the diners.

Asper nudged him and gestured to their left at a padded bench under one of the large windows. A matronly woman with thick dark hair piled in an unruly bun was talking earnestly to a bearded and slightly balding man in wire-rimmed spectacles.

"It's Matisse," whispered Asper, "and that American who buys all his paintings." Max shrugged. He supposed they might be famous if he knew who they were.

The only free table was a small one near the kitchen. The steady stream of traffic assured their conversation would not be overheard except in meaningless snatches. True to his word, Asper ordered foie gras to be followed by a grilled filet of beef in pepper sauce, with Chablis to start and Bordeaux to finish. Max settled on a green salad and herbed grilled trout.

"What does Buchan want?" asked Asper.

"He wanted to know if you've heard further from your contacts." It seemed general enough.

"For that, you had to get me out of bed? Not that I'm complaining," said Asper, savouring a forkful of the liver paste. "My relationship with the official delegation – who have been in town for two weeks already – has, as you may have guessed from my straightened circumstances, soured. I am too much of a Croat for the diplomats to swallow. In any case, Pasic and Trumbic are barely talking to each other, when they need to work together in the face of Italian aggression. The Americans are our only hope but they, despite the bold promise of Point XI, virtually ignore us. Perhaps Buchan has had a change of heart? Even Greater Serbia is better than an Italian protectorate. The news of American help would get me out of that stinking apartment."

"Perhaps he has," said Max.

Asper seemed eager to talk and Max let him describe the intricacies of Balkan politics until it made his head spin. He did learn that the Levantine delegation had been given the first slot at the Conference after it officially opened on January 18th. Asper only wound down when the main course arrived and he could devote himself to the more important business of eating.

When the cheese and pastis had been served, Asper lit a cigarette and leaned back in his chair, a smug smile on his face.

"Did you hear the news about Barzani?" asked Max.

"No, what is the great manipulator up to now?"

"He's dead."

Asper looked genuinely shocked, his eyes wide and his cigarette dangling loosely from his lips. "What happened?"

"He was murdered," said Max. He gave Asper the short version.

"I had heard he was bent," said a pale and shaken Asper. "But it seems a horrible way to die."

"It was," said Max. "Any idea who might have done it?"

"How would I know?" Asper wouldn't meet his eyes.

"You traveled in the same circles. Did the same kind of work. It's all new to me but you've been doing it for years. You must be an expert." Max put five hundred-franc notes on the table.

"I'll tell you what I can," said Asper, reaching for the money.

Max pulled three of them away but let Asper take the other two. "Tell me anything of use – anything at all – and the money's yours."

Asper nodded. His cheeks were flushed and a thin film of sweat formed on his forehead. He licked his lips. "Do you want to ask me questions or should I just talk at random?"

"What do you know about André Bucard?"

"Jesus! Do you think he's involved?" Asper's head jerked up and around as if he expected Bucard to pop out of the kitchen in answer to his name.

"It's possible. Have you heard if he's in Paris?"

"In and out the last month or two. He's wanted for questioning in Marseille so he keeps a low profile. Whatever it is, he's probably guilty but they won't pin it on him. They never do."

"Why not?"

"He's careful not to do anything in an area where the local council and prefecture aren't sympathetic. He'd never try any of his shit in Bobigny. The Reds would lop off his head without thinking about it. But in Marseille and Paris, he has more... latitude."

"Enough latitude to kill someone?"

Asper looked around the restaurant again and lowered his voice.

"Depends on who that someone was. But, yeah, he could do that. If he wasn't caught red-handed, they wouldn't look in his direction. They'd find someone else to look at."

"Who are his associates?"

"The Black Cross is a secret organization. I couldn't tell you for sure who belongs but rumour has it certain officers, some quite high up, in the Prefecture of Police are involved or at least sympathetic."

"Gereau?"

"No, not him. I mean, unless you've heard otherwise." Asper was getting increasingly pale and Max worried he might actually pass out.

He was strangely relieved about Gereau. He still didn't trust the man but at least he wasn't involved with Bucard and his cronies.

"Do you know a man named Schmidt?"

"I know a lot of men named Schmidt," Asper smiled wanly, "but the one you know goes by a variety of names. He's an opium addict and a thief. Beyond that, he's from near the eastern border. A French citizen with German loyalties. Supports the moderates among the German government and is probably working for that faction in peace negotiations – not that it looks like there will be much negotiation for the Germans. Not if Clemenceau gets his way. Le Tigre is determined to make sure they never pose a threat to France again."

"What about a Jew named Joachim?"

"I don't associate with Jews," said Asper, grimly.

"Oh, I thought you were –"

"You thought wrong." He reached out his hand for the money and, after a moment, Max handed it over.

"You didn't come to see me because of Buchan," said Asper, stubbing out his cigarette and standing up. "I don't want to see you again. You wear danger like a cloak."

Fourteen – Tuesday, January 14, 1919

Max slept late, exhausted by the events of the previous day. By the time he awoke it was nearly ten. He finished writing up his notes from his conversation with Asper and then went across the hall to the bathroom to urinate and check the state of the hot water. It was ice cold so he returned to his room to do a stand-up wash at the sink before heading down to the breakfast room.

The buffet – never more than adequate – had been picked through but he found a piece of sugary fried dough and a cup of coffee. It would keep him going until lunch. When he checked his messages at the desk, he found a note from Lachance asking him to come by La Coquette before two. Max wondered if someone had seen him coming out of Lachance's office. There was only one way to find out. At least it settled where he would have lunch.

Lachance's greeting was less effusive than on the night of the party but he didn't seem unhappy to see Max, ushering him to a private booth where a tray of sandwiches and an iced bottle of Sauterne awaited them. After commiserating with him on Barzani's death, Lachance got right down to business.

"I understand Barzani entrusted you with some papers," he said.

"They were stolen." *You should know, since at least one of them wound up on your desk.*

"I heard about that unfortunate incident. But I'm sure there were others."

Max said nothing.

"Come now, Max," said Lachance. "There is a market for such things. One I can access but you can't. Not without risk. Markets run on information. So, I know other documents exist. I even know what some of them are."

"Why would you think I had them?" Had Minette sensed he was lying to her? Had she recognized the framed Fourteen Points for what it was and gone running to Lachance?

"A simple deduction. My sources at the Prefecture tell me nothing of consequence was found in his hotel room or safe. The two banks where he did the most of his business were kind enough to open his safe deposit boxes. Nothing there but money and a most interesting will. You're his sole beneficiary."

Max stared at Lachance, not believing, not wanting to believe what the man had said. It was too painful, too familiar. He lived off the income from his father's death. His father's murder. *I was a boy then*, he thought, *helpless to prove what I knew to be true. But now I have no excuse. Barzani's murder will not pass unpunished. No matter what it costs.*

"So," said Lachance, "you see how honest I am? I'm sure the Prefecture would have told you eventually but perhaps not before all that lovely cash had gone astray. In any case, if there are any more documents – they're yours to do with as you please. I do hope you'll keep me in mind. Now enjoy your lunch. I'm too busy to eat."

"Is Minette here?"

"She was until the early hours but I think Roget took her home this morning. That girl burns her candle at both ends. I wonder where she finds the energy."

§

Minette was asleep when Max arrived at Le Coq Bleu.

"She either can't stop moving," said Yesim, "or she sleeps like she's already dead. I don't know where she gets it from. It's..." Yesim's voice trailed off and his eyes seemed to focus on a distant horizon. "I thought I could protect her from everything, but perhaps it was inevitable..." he mumbled. Then he shook his head and forced a laugh. "I suppose it's the vigour of youth. It's been so long I'm starting to forget."

Max ordered a small beer and sat at the bar with Henri, who gave him a quick lesson on the difference between *depuis* and *pendant*. Neither Yesim or Henri asked him about Barzani's death although Henri, at one point, laid his hand on Max's forearm and squeezed it gently.

"You're a good student, Max," said Henri, as he rose to leave, "but language is like a woman. You have to spend time with her before you can hope to understand. Come to dinner with me tonight and we'll explore the joys of *plus-que-parfait*. I get off at eight."

"I'd like that," said Max. He needed to talk to someone about the murder. Henri may not have gone far in school but he read widely and had observed life from all angles. He could help him see his way through this mess.

It was too early to rendezvous with Joachim so Max ordered another beer and a snack plate – black olives and an assortment of hard cheeses with half a baguette.

"Did they leave a hollow in your leg when they fixed it?" Yesim asked. "You eat enough for two men. And it's starting to show."

"Nervous habit," said Max, though he knew Yesim was right. His pants were getting tight. Still, the olives were firm and sweet and the cheese sharp and smoky. It was hard to resist. He ate them slowly, taking small sips of dark hoppy beer, while he read the newspaper Henri had left him.

The front pages were full of stories of the impending Peace conference. They expressed both optimism and fear. The success of the Bolsheviks in Russia seemed to worry a lot of the commentators and much was made of Clemenceau's desire to create a line of strong states in Eastern Europe to buffer the west against Red expansion. The success of Communists and Socialists in the recent municipal elections, especially in those towns that surrounded Paris, only seemed to add fuel to the fire.

Barzani's murder did not rate a story of its own but was mentioned as an example of the growing crime rate among immigrants. Jean Chiappe, a senior official in the Sûreté and Bonnet's choice for the next Prefect, was quoted as saying "this repulsive crime only underlines the need for better registration and surveillance of deviant groups in Paris." They even spelled Hevel's name wrong.

He was deep into an article on the impact the Spanish Influenza was having on the economy when he was startled by a heavy hand on his shoulder.

"Where's your black armband?" snarled Bonnet in his ear. "I thought for sure you'd be in mourning for your little friend."

"Yes, I did lose a friend yesterday," said Max. "Did you ever have a friend to lose?" He turned on the stool and stood up, forcing Bonnet to step back. He was as broad as the policeman but an inch or two taller. He stepped closer so that their chests were almost touching.

"I choose my friends wisely," said Bonnet, taking another step back. He laid his hand on the white stick hooked to his belt. "I'm more casual about my enemies."

Max wanted to slap him. Bonnet represented everything that was wrong about men in uniform and nothing that was right.

"You're in charge of the investigation," he said.

"One of many that fall under my purview. A trifling case, really. I've a pretty good idea where the finger of guilt points. I expect to have it wrapped up in a day or two."

"Really?" Max was surprised. He had expected that Bonnet would do nothing. Perhaps he had misjudged the man.

"It was obviously a lover's quarrel. One of his boyfriends got jealous and killed him. You know how those types are. Maybe he was jealous of you."

Max turned his back on Bonnet. He sat back at the bar and picked up the newspaper. It was the only way he could keep from knocking Bonnet to the ground. That would do no good. He couldn't solve Barzani's murder from behind bars.

"Civilians should stay out of police matters," said Bonnet. "Tend to your own onions and you won't get hurt."

Bonnet moved farther along the bar and demanded a bottle of beer and a sandwich from Yesim. He left without paying. When he had gone, Max crumpled the newspaper and threw it in the trash. He finished the last inch of beer and dropped a handful of coins on the bar.

"All this time and you still haven't figured out francs," said Yesim. "That's way too much."

"Bonnet didn't pay. That covers it."

"He doesn't deserve your money," said Yesim.

"No, but business is bad. Where would I go if this place closed?"

Yesim broke into a broad smile. "Even if I were reduced to a hole in the wall, you would be welcome to drink there."

§

Le Pré aux Clercs was a small restaurant at the corner of Bonaparte and Jacob, only a short block from the St. Germain metro stop. Double doors flanked by fake Greek columns led to a dim interior. Like most bars in Paris, it was small, not more than a dozen tables spread through the L-shaped space, surrounding the zinc-topped bar. The place was almost empty at this time of day. Near the entry, half a dozen students were arguing loudly about the value of the Peace Conference over several large flagons of cheap wine.

Joachim wasn't there but, at a table in the section farthest from the doors, two men wearing the same kind of cloth cap – *Yarmulkes* he had learned – were huddled in quiet conversation. The eldest, a plump man in his forties with short wiry hair, was doing most of the talking, while the other one, younger and dressed much like the students at the front, nodded and made occasional comments. If they were regulars, they might know Joachim or could point him to someone who did. As he turned the corner of the bar, he realized the men weren't talking in French but in a language that sounded something like German. Max decided to try his luck anyway.

"Pardon me," he said. "I don't mean to interrupt but I'm looking for a man of your... faith."

"There are a lot of Jews in Paris," said the older man. "Do you think we all know each other?"

"No, but Joachim was a regular here. I thought you might know him."

"Joachim ben David?" The older man was frowning. The other started to rise but the older man waved him back to his seat.

"I don't know his last name," said Max. He described the man's appearance. The men nodded in recognition.

"Joachim is dead."

The Metro station. Joachim with a surprised look on his face. The man's hand on his shoulder. The image shimmered across his vision like a pointillist painting. He felt faint and leaned against the back of a chair.

"Help him, Isaac," said the older man. Isaac didn't stir.

"I'm all right," said Max. "When did it happen? Where?"

"And who wants to know?" said Isaac angrily.

"Easy, Isaac," said the older man. "I am Jacob. Sit down and tell us your story. And then we'll tell you ours."

Max took the third seat at the table. The men offered him tea from a large pot. It was sweet and warm and the drink revived him a little.

"My name is Max Anderson. I am... was a friend of a man called Hevel Barzani. Joachim knew him. Perhaps you did, too."

Jacob shrugged and said, "Barzani? Oh, wait. Isn't he that Shabbes goy Weizmann sometimes used as a go-between? In Jerusalem."

"That could be him," said Isaac. "That would explain the connection. Joachim was an active Zionist."

Weizmann, the leader of British Zionism, had been in the newspaper this morning. He was scheduled, along with Prince Faisal, to be among the first to address the Peace Conference. The letters, thought Max, were between two men, initials, F and W. Could they have been between Faisal and Weizmann?

"I think it was," said Max. "He was supposed to meet with Joachim here but he never got the chance."

"Hard to meet with a dead man, except in heaven," said Isaac.

"Then, perhaps they're meeting now. Hevel was murdered two days ago."

"Oy Gevalt!" said Jacob. "A shreklehheh zakh! Terrible thing, terrible."

"Yes, yes it was. I found the body." He briefly described the scene. Both seemed shocked and outraged by the particular mutilation but none could guess at a motive for carving one of the sacred symbols of Judaism onto Barzani's body.

"At least, Joachim didn't suffer such a humiliation," said Isaac.

"How did he die?"

"We don't know exactly when," said Jacob. "His body was discovered in an alcove along the tracks near the St. Germain des-Prés Metro Station on January 6th. He'd been dead at least two days by then, maybe as many as four, given how cold it was that week. I know he hadn't been seen since before New Year's. His throat had been cut. The police said it was a robbery gone wrong but, well, I'm no expert but I don't believe them. I took the body for burial – Joachim is my cousin and he has no closer relatives in the city – and he had been beaten, as well. More than once from the state of the bruises."

Then he hadn't died the day we parted in the Metro, thought Max, but maybe as much as a week later. What had happened in between? Had he been kidnapped? Beaten and then killed and his body dumped? And what did it have to do with Hevel? He had hoped finding Joachim would answer some of his questions but it just seemed to give him more.

"I'll leave you to your tea," he said, rising. He bowed slightly to Jacob. "I'm sorry for your loss."

"And I for yours. Shalom."

"There's one other thing I just remembered," said Isaac. "Joachim was trying to recruit me to the cause, almost a year ago. I'm only a little political so it didn't take. He mentioned this Barzani, I think, as someone who was very helpful. It struck me at the time because... well, Kurds aren't notoriously sympathetic to Zionism. Joachim said something about old loyalties running deep. He didn't explain. Does it mean anything to you?"

"I'm not sure," said Max. "But thanks for telling me. It's good to hear nice things about departed friends."

§

Henri was waiting at Le Coq Bleu when Max arrived. He had already had one glass of wine and they had another while they decided where to eat. Minette was out again. Yesim didn't look happy about it but merely grunted when Max asked what the trouble was.

Max suggested a restaurant noted for its good peasant cuisine and even more for its artistic clientele and cabaret. He had recently attended an exhibition of modern art and wondered what the men who would produce such strange paintings might look like.

"I've been there," said Henri. "We can go if you like but I'd rather try something new. There's a little café not far from here called 'Nouvelle Afrique.' I know the three Algerian sisters who run it."

Max had no idea what Algerian cooking was like but he'd never know if he didn't try it at least once.

The restaurant was tucked into a small street between Clichy and Veron near the Church of St. John the Evangelist. Although its brick clad exterior gave an appearance of modernity, a glance through the open doors, as they passed, showed an interior little different than other gothic churches he had visited.

Nouvelle Afrique occupied the ground floor of an old house. The inside walls had been stripped down to the bare stone and then hung with tapestries and billowing silk sheets. The room was divided by moveable panels of thin wood, painted with geometric shapes. The low tables were surrounded by plump cushions and they sat with their legs tucked under them. The room was warm and filled with the aroma of cooking meat and spices. He recognized cinnamon but the others were elusive.

Henri ordered for both of them and they sipped pale beer from mugs and practiced making hypothetical statements until it arrived. A single dish filled with couscous, a kind of cooked wheat, covered in a thick stew of vegetables and lamb was placed before them but the servers left neither plates nor utensils.

"Are we supposed to eat it with our hands?" whispered Max.

"Your right hand only," said Henri. "The other is considered unclean. I can ask for plates and forks if it bothers you."

"When in Algeria do as the Algerians do."

Henri laughed and scooped up a portion in three curled fingers and transferred it to his mouth without spilling a single grain. Max followed suit, though with slightly less success. Still, by the time, they had begun to slow down, he felt he had mastered the technique – though he wondered how they managed soup.

"Something tells me you had other things to talk about than the finer points of French grammar," said Henri at last.

"If I knew how to express it, I would tell you everything," said Max, smiling, demonstrating that the earlier lesson had not been wasted on him. In truth, his French had progressed to the point he hardly needed further instruction but he liked Henri's company. "Seriously, I need to talk to someone about Barzani's death."

"Why me?" asked Henri. "I only knew him casually. I met him at Yesim's a few times and carried his luggage twice. He was a good tipper and always so polite. And his French! He could have served on the Academy. Isn't Bonnet handling this?"

"Would you trust Bonnet to handle anything?"

Henri laughed. "Maybe a dinner fork – if someone else was providing the dinner. Still, it's dangerous to interfere in police business. They don't take kindly to amateurs, no matter what they say in the popular novels."

"Barzani trusted me. I can't let him down."

"An employment contract ends at death," said Henri.

"It was more than that. He was a good man; someone I considered a real friend. And..." Max was slightly embarrassed to tell Henri about the will. "He left me money – a lot of money. That alone makes me obligated to seek justice for him."

"Justice or revenge. The two aren't the same you know."

"I understand that. I'm not out for an eye for an eye, though it won't break my heart if the killers go to the guillotine. But that is for the courts to decide, not me."

"Fair enough," said Henri. He looked thoughtful for a moment. "Then you don't agree it was the result of a lover's quarrel. That's what Bonnet is telling anyone who will listen."

"No. But it wouldn't change anything if it were. He was still murdered and his killer should be punished."

"In France, the crime of passion," said Henri, "is treated differently. In certain circumstances – finding your wife with a lover, for example – murder is excusable. There have been many husbands, and a few wives, who have walked away scot-free."

"That's not right!"

"Maybe not," Henri shrugged. "But it's the way it is."

"Still, it might explain why the murder took place where it did," said Max. "To keep the police from looking too closely at other motives."

"But what if the police are right? Do you want your name associated with such places? With..." Henri couldn't bring himself to say what he thought. "...men like that."

"Like what? Generous, polite men who were working for the cause of peace? Who were trying to improve the lives of their people?"

"You know what I mean," said Henri, refusing to meet Max's eyes. "I find that behaviour disgusting."

"Given all the other disgusting things we've seen men do, it seems a small thing to me." Only when he said it did Max realize it was true. He had denied, as much to himself as to anyone else, that Barzani might be homosexual, but he now realized that it didn't trouble him if he was. "If it makes you feel better, he asked Minette to marry him."

"They sometimes do that."

"He seemed genuinely hurt when she turned him down," Max said.

"Perhaps," said Henri. "Besides your mind is clearly made up. You'll do what you do. If I can be of any help, I'm glad to do it. What do you know?"

"You know that I rescued Barzani from a beating but he was never in real danger. One of his attackers, Marois, worked with Barzani, though I don't know what their joint interests were. I later saw Marois talking to Lachance and another man. I don't know for sure who the other one was, but he fits the description I have for a man called Bucard. The beating was to help Marois win the trust of Bucard's allies." He described how Barzani had entrusted him with documents, some of which were later stolen. "Lachance came into possession of at least one – though whether he stole it himself or bought it from the person who did is uncertain. I am almost certain that the documents or the information they contain are the reason Barzani was killed but whether the motive was money or something darker, who can say?"

"Who is this Bucard?" asked Henri.

"The head of some right-wing group called The Black Cross. Not simply political, either. Very secretive and not above direct action to get their ways."

"I've heard of such groups," said Henri. "Mostly ex-army officers, not happy with the way things turned out. They're popping up all over France, all over Europe for that matter."

"I've been told he has sympathizers high up in the Prefecture."

"You think they are covering for him?"

"Maybe. Or worse. State-authorized murder isn't unheard of. Even in France."

"Especially in France, if the anarchists are to be believed. Parisians don't forget what happened to the Commune. Or Jaures."

"Then there are all the others jockeying for position at the peace conference. I have no idea who most of them are but Joseph Asper knew Barzani and clearly didn't like him. Even within the Arab delegation, there may have been people who would be happy to see Barzani dead, especially if he really was unnatural."

"You list is getting longer," said Henri.

"I know. Lachance wanted Barzani's papers. Would he have killed the man to get them?"

"How would that help? He couldn't hand them over if he were dead"

"Barzani was tortured before he was killed. Maybe he still wouldn't tell them where they were. Or maybe he did and they had no more use for him after."

Henri grimaced and looked away.

"Then there is Lachance's man, Roget. I think he's in love with Minette. If he thought Barzani was a rival..."

"That would put you more at risk than Hevel," said Henri, smiling. "Anyone else?"

Max blushed. He thought he had kept his feelings for Minette hidden. "If I were to believe the papers, the Reds are behind every dark plot these days, but I have no evidence of their involvement. There is a man called Schmidt who seems to be working to protect German interests." An unpleasant thought had been worming its way through Max's head. "And Ginger Buchan."

"The American you told me about? Surely they are above that."

"Nobody is above anything. Things were done in the war—"

"By all sides," said Henri, "but the war is over."

"As they keep telling me. Buchan is a spy. If he thought Barzani was threatening American interests, he might take action into his own hands. Not only that, he seems to be avoiding me."

"The older I get, the less surprised I am about the perfidy of man. Still, this is a particularly ugly bunch you've gotten yourself involved in. What will you do next?"

"Confront Ginger Buchan."

"You think he's the most likely suspect?"

"Not really. But he seems to me to be... the safest to approach. Frankly, I don't know what I'm doing here. Nothing I've done has prepared me to solve a crime. I'll start with Buchan and, if I don't make a complete fool of myself, I'll tackle the others."

Henri shrugged. "I suppose. Still, he may be the least dangerous of the lot but even a small dog can give a nasty bite. Be careful."

"I will."

"The only faction you haven't mentioned are the anarchists – left, right and sometimes both at the same time, they've certainly shown themselves willing to use violence to achieve their ends. Though I sometimes think the means are more important than the ends to them. They might be worth talking to."

"I wouldn't know an anarchist if I saw one."

"Sure you would," said Henri. "Ask Yesim."

Fifteen – Wednesday, January 15 and Thursday, January 16, 1919

After he finished dinner with Henri, he had gone back to his room and made a list of actions that he hoped would lead him to Barzani's killers. First on the list had been to speak to Buchan – but that had to wait until the American returned to Paris, not until Saturday now, according to the note delivered to L'Aquilon – and the second was to follow up on Henri's suggestion that he seek out and question members of the anarchist movement. Early the next morning, he headed up the hill to see Yesim.

It still seemed odd that anarchists could have an organization but according to Henri they did. They even published several newspapers that were widely read by Parisians. He had picked one up at a newsstand and read it on his way back to l'Aquilon. Like every other newspaper in the city, it had been preoccupied with the opening of the conference on the 18th. Not surprisingly, its editors took a decidedly dyspeptic view of the whole affair. "Yet another farce staged by the moneyed classes to befuddle the people and subvert their urge for freedom." Max had no doubt the anarchists would disrupt the conference if they could but killing Barzani was an unlikely tactic – their approach generally involved the throwing of dynamite.

The morning was clear and dry after nearly three days of overcast and rain. The morning sun sprinkled diamonds in the crevices between the stones of the twisting cobbled street and painted smiles on the faces of people he passed. He was hungry so he stopped at a boulangerie. The smell of fresh bread, stacked in heaps in wrought iron baskets along the stone walls of the old shop, made his mouth water and he bought a large cheese tart and a couple of seed covered rolls to eat on the walk. At the next shop he bought a bottle of beer to drink with breakfast. He needed all the support he could muster.

When he reached Boulevard Rochecourt he turned left on to Clichy. Yesim wouldn't be up this early and Max was in no hurry to wake him. He always liked walking past the music halls and nightclubs that lined the street. This early in the day, they seemed almost church-like with their high stone facades and the intricate carvings over their doorways unless you examined the carvings: the dance hall girl with lifted skirts over the entrance to the Elysee Montmartre or the even more seductive form perched languorously above the entrance to the Theatre Libre. Max hadn't been in a real church since the darkest days of the war but he thought he wouldn't mind worshipping in these houses.

By the time he reached the bar, he was in an almost cheerful mood, his stomach full and his mind concentrated by the light fuzz from the beer. Only the throb in his knee dulled his pleasure. Yesim, ever hopeful that his fortunes were on the verge of turning, was setting out a pair of tables on the sidewalk beneath a small awning. The ever-expanding crowd of conference delegates were always looking for someplace new – and cheap – to eat.

"Is that new?" asked Max, though from its tattered fringe he could see it clearly wasn't.

Yesim grunted. "New to me. I got it in a bankruptcy sale from a café two streets over."

"I hope it brings you more luck than it did them."

"Have you had breakfast yet?" Yesim asked, hopefully.

Why not, thought Max, *it's going to be a long day*. They say breakfast is the most important meal. "Not yet. What do you have?"

"Quiche."

"Sure, and a coffee. American coffee." He didn't think steamed milk would sit well on top of beer. Quiche was unusual. Yesim normally settled for sandwiches from the boulangerie two doors away. It would have been cheaper and fresher for his customers to walk a few steps, but drunks lacked the foresight.

Yesim went back inside and returned a few minutes later with a small pie and a large cup of steaming black coffee. The crust on the tart was flaky and moist and the egg custard thick and full of chopped ham and mushrooms. It was even warm.

"It's good," Max said, after several mouthfuls.

"You sound surprised. I can cook when I have the time." Yesim went back inside and finished setting up for the day. When he returned, he had a large silver coffee pot in hand.

"Things are getting upscale around here," said Max.

"The sale was a good one," said Yesim as he refilled Max's mug. He smiled at a passing couple and Max tried to look like a satisfied customer, but the couple passed without a sideways glance.

"Is Minette up yet?"

Yesim scowled. "How would I know? She didn't come home last night. Do you ever see her? I mean, away from here?"

Yesim probably wouldn't be happy to know that his niece had visited Max in his hotel room. "From time to time. You know, at Lachance's place."

"Maybe you can talk some sense into her head. I know she doesn't listen to me. I don't know why I'm surprised. It runs in the family."

"Sure," said Max, wondering what part of the family Yesim meant. He took another sip of his coffee. "I guess anarchists don't eat breakfast?"

"I'm sure they do. But not here." Yesim looked about warily.

"I heard you could introduce me to someone," said Max.

"Are you working for the police, now that Barzani's gone?"

"No. Henri thinks there are people in the movement who might know something about Hevel's death. He suggested I talk to you."

Yesim frowned. He gestured for Max to wait and ducked back into the café. He was gone long enough that Max thought he might be avoiding the question. When he returned, he scribbled an address on his order pad and gave the folded sheet to Max. "Go to this bar in the 12th arrondissement at five after two tomorrow and ask the moustachioed man behind the bar for Jacques. He will say, 'Jacques Court?' and you reply, in these words exactly, 'No, never him. I want Jacques Grand.' He'll give you further directions. Don't speak to anyone else. Half the people there are police agents."

"That seems like an easy code to crack," said Max.

"Undoubtedly," said Yesim, smiling. "Before you enter the bar buy a flower and put it in the lapel of your jacket. And, as soon as you get there, be sure to order an espresso from the man without the moustache."

"Won't I be followed when I leave?"

"Of course. But if you do as you're told, everything will be fine."

Max shrugged. During the last year of the war, trench codes had been used extensively in communications and sometimes to identify enemy infiltrators. He supposed Yesim's elaborate instructions were some variation on that.

§

Max glanced over his shoulder as he left the bar to which Yesim had sent him. Not one but two men followed him along the wide sidewalk of Rue de Faubourg Saint Antoine, as he wove in and out of the pedestrian traffic, his cane tapping out a brisk rhythm as he walked. The Colonne de Juillet, with its gilded statue of winged liberty, was visible high above the surrounding buildings. His instructions from the moustachioed barman were to cross the square and continue on Beaumarchais to St Sebastian. He was still several blocks from the column, at a spot where the sidewalk widened, when a black limousine pulled up over the curb, scattering pedestrians. Two men leapt out of the front of the car and hustled him into the back compartment before rejoining the driver in the front. The car sped into traffic leaving the pair of police agents gaping futilely on the sidewalk.

The interior of the car was spacious, with two facing benches. The windows were curtained so he couldn't see out. There were two other men, sitting opposite each other – one enormously fat, his dark suit stretched across his belly and a pair of wire rimmed glasses hovering over his face. A greying beard failed to hide his several chins. The other, in a tan double-breasted suit, was so short that his feet didn't reach the floor of the automobile. Max took a seat beside the latter.

"Are you Max Anderson?" said the fat one in an improbably deep voice.

"Yes," said Max.

"Yesim telephoned and said you wanted to meet us. So here we are."

"But I was supposed to go to..."

"Yes, yes," said the short one in a high voice. "Do you think we stayed out of jail so long by being stupid? How many police agents do you think were on your trail?"

"I saw two," said Max.

"That's better than most," said the fat man. "I saw four."

"Five, I think," said the other. He had bright pink cheeks and his eyes sparkled. "There was a woman on a bicycle that I thought I recognized."

"So you see," said the fat man. "We must be careful. I am Court. And my colleague is Grand."

"You look confused, Max," said Grand. "Which was our intent."

"Why such elaborate procedures if you don't use them?"

"The passwords and the flower in the lapel?" said Court, chuckling. "I'm afraid that was Yesim's sense of humour at play. We do use that place sometimes to arrange meetings but not like that.

Yesim was playing a joke – on you or the police or both. He called us and told us what you looked like and where you'd be."

The automobile had made several turns while they talked and now pulled into a large shed. The three men in the front got out, closing the shed door behind them. Neither Court nor Grand made any move to get out of the car.

"So," said Grand. "What did you want to see us for?"

Max explained the circumstances of Barzani's death and his intention to solve the murder.

"One man against the world?" said Court. "That appeals to me."

"I suppose it would," said Max. "Given your political views."

"You confuse anarchism with individualism," said Grand. "My friend is a fan of stories of the American west."

"Have you seen De Mille's The Virginian?" Court mimed a fast draw. "Brilliant."

"I'm not sure what you expect from us," said Grand. "We're not in a position to get involved directly."

"Anarchy, I'm afraid, has fallen on hard times," sighed Court. "We are reduced to a few clandestine cells, producing newspapers in secret locations and distributing them in the dark of night."

"They seem easy enough to buy," said Max.

"You see," said Court. "In the old days we could give away ten thousand copies and now we have to settle for a few sold by bourgeois vendors."

"I'm afraid my friend is a sentimentalist. He still hasn't recovered from the bad name the Bonnot gang gave the movement before the war. Nothing but a bunch of bank robbers in a fast car – but they called themselves anarchists and that lunatic Victor Serge was quick enough to embrace them in l'anarchie. Taking back by individuals was completely legitimate, of course, but illegalism was a step too far. Bakunin would not have approved." Grand folded his arms across his chest and shook his head grimly.

"All dead now of course. Shot or guillotined," added Court.

They sat in silence for several minutes; Court and Grand contemplating the sorry state of their movement while Max wondered what use the two men could possibly be to him.

"I don't need direct assistance," said Max. "Or if I do, I don't know what I'd ask you to do. I was hoping you might have some information."

"Information is a commodity," said Court.

"Property is theft, even intellectual property," said Grand.

"Even revolutionaries have to eat," said Court.

"Some of them more than others," said Grand, pointedly staring at Court's overhanging belly. "Still, I suppose you're right."

"I'd be willing to pay for anything useful," said Max. He took out his billfold and removed twenty ten-franc notes. *Detecting is starting to get expensive*, thought Max. *I should check with the police about my supposed inheritance.* "Maybe you could start with what you know about Barzani. I worked for him but to tell you the truth, I only knew what he told me. For everything useful, I'll put down one bill."

"What did you do for Barzani?" asked Court. He licked his lips and stared hungrily at the money.

"Information, as you say, is a commodity."

"Touché."

Grand gestured for Max to move to the opposite bench, then leapt off the seat and lifted the cushion to reveal several file boxes and a small typewriter. The car was more than transportation; it was a portable office as well. He riffled through a stack of file folders before finding the one he was looking for.

It was only when he moved that Max realized he had been deceived once again, although perhaps only by his own assumptions. Grand was a woman.

"Here we go," she said. "Hevel Barzani. Also known as Hajim Bahrami. Born in 1871 or 72 on a farm near Mahabad but was sent to school in Tehran. A Kurd by birth but he adopted a Persian name and learned to speak Farsi – along with English, French, Italian, Arabic, Hebrew and German. Quite a scholar! He worked as a young man in the British Embassy and used those connections, as well as his obvious intelligence, to gain admittance to Cambridge. He later transferred to Oxford where he received a second. There is a gap in my records, other than a note that says he returned several times to the Middle East and spent some years in America."

Max handed Court a ten. Maybe Buchan had some idea of what Hevel did in America. He might be willing to accept the American wasn't involved but that didn't let all Americans off the hook.

"He next appears," continued Grand, "in 1906 when he accepted a position of junior lecturer in Levantine studies at the University of Manchester."

"Weizmann taught Chemistry there," said Court. "They might have met then."

Max handed Court another ten.

"Indeed," said Grand. "The next year Barzani took a position at a private college in Jerusalem – the same year as Weizmann's first visit there. There is some reference to his later involvement in the Palestinian Land Development Company Weizmann helped found. Then another gap – the next reference has Barzani back in Tehran in 1911, working for the British again – though it doesn't say what he did. However, by the numerous trips he took around the region and back to England, I would guess he was a courier of some sort."

Court looked at Max expectantly. After a moment, he handed over another ten.

"In 1913, he was arrested in Berlin and held for several weeks before being deported. Apparently at some point he had obtained a British passport because he was shipped to London rather than Tehran. Still, a few months later he was asked to leave England as well. That's when he turned up in Paris, where, other than brief journeys in and around Europe and three short and two extended trips to the Middle East, he has lived ever since. He lived at a number of small hotels before moving into his more luxurious accommodations at the Grand last July. That was shortly after his last trip to Jerusalem. A very profitable one it seems. His lifestyle improved dramatically, as did the flow of cash into a lot of interesting hands."

Max reluctantly handed over a fourth note. The information was useful in a general way – it told him who Barzani was likely working for and who might be eliminated from that list. Still, he was no closer to knowing what it was that led to his brutal murder. "I'd like a list of the places and dates Barzani traveled."

Grand shrugged. "I can have one drawn up. It may not be complete. Prefecture records so seldom are. I can send it to Yesim for a small fee."

More material for his notebook. The two anarchists appeared odd and ineffectual but they clearly had their resources, including within the Prefecture of Police. If so, Gereau clearly knew much more than he had been willing to share with Max. Max put two more bills in Court's broad palm.

"It still doesn't tell me who would want to kill Barzani," said Max.

"Well, it wasn't us," said Court. "But the list isn't short."

"That much I already know."

"Start by talking to the Kurds," said Grand. "There are a few in town who might know something. Barzani may have been working for Faisal and Weizmann but he might have had his own agenda, as well. Many would like to see a Kurdish homeland, carved out of Ottoman lands."

"Speaking of carving, there is the curious issue of the Star of David carved on his body," said Court. "Had he gotten in trouble with the Zionists or was it done by the killers to throw suspicion on the Jews? Or did it mean something else entirely?"

"Good questions," said Max. "Do you have any answers?"

"If Barzani was throwing money around trying to grease the wheels for Weizmann and Faisal to get their way at the conference, he could have upset a lot of people on both the left and the right. If he stepped across the line from bribing to blackmail – the man had a reputation – then the field of suspects grows wider." Court paused and closed his eyes. "But it seems to me, that you already know the person who killed Barzani – that is to say, I think you've met him already."

Max considered that. Everyone on his own list was known to him; even Marois had been close enough to touch. There was one exception.

"What about Bucard? I may have seen him but I've never met him."

"That you're aware of – that one goes by a lot of different names and has some skill at changing his appearance. Enough anyway that the police could never lay their hands on him," said Grand. "He'd be at the top of my list if I had one."

"Do you know a man named Marois?" Max was almost certain Barzani's sometime accomplice held the key to the entire mystery.

Court and Grand exchanged glances.

"I know a lot of men named Marois," said Grand. "But none with links to Barzani."

"Our files are not as complete as we would like," added Court. "Can you describe him?"

"I encountered him several times but only saw him unmasked once and that from a distance. He's tall, heavy-set, dark hair with an oval, almost soft-looking face. He was recently cut on his left hand and forearm."

"Could be Phillippe Marois, don't you think?" said Court. "A man with a chequered past. In the old west, he'd be a gun-for-hire."

"Though I think he prefers his fists or a knife to do his work," said Grand. "He could be the man you're looking for."

"Barzani said they staged the attack on him so Marois could gain the trust of the others," said Max. "A way into Bucard's circle."

"It could be," said Court. "Marois has worked for many causes – whichever could pay him the best. Not a stupid man but not a moral one either. He would have no compunction betraying Barzani if he got a better offer. I have a few questions for him myself. If you find him, perhaps you could let Yesim know."

"The police say it was a crime of passion," said Grand, clearing his throat. "Maybe they're right."

"I'm getting sick of that suggestion."

"I'm not suggesting anything. To tell you the truth, I've always thought that Barzani had little interest in love one way or the other. Money and power were his passions. Still, he may have had hidden depths. Was there anyone he seemed interested in?"

"There was a girl. Yesim's niece."

"I always warned Yesim about her," said Court. "It's his weak spot."

"Ah, the glorious Minette," said Grand. "As my friend says, that girl has been causing trouble since she turned fifteen. She is a source of constant worry to Yesim. With good cause, I suspect. It could be someone was jealous of the attention he paid her."

"She didn't take him seriously." Max wondered about Grand's suspicions but didn't pursue it.

"So what? Jealousy is not a rational thing. You know what they say – look for the woman."

§

They drove for nearly twenty minutes but when the car pulled over to the curb and the car door was open, Max found himself less than a block from where he had been picked up. The street sign where they dropped him said: Rue Jacques Coeur, though whether the joke was intentional Max couldn't tell.

Grands's advice seemed good so Max set off in search of the elusive Minette. He supposed she was at La Coquette but he had to pass by the St. Anne's mission on his way there. Yesim would be happy to learn his neice had spent the night caring for veterans in the company of nuns rather than drinking with Lachance.

Minette wasn't at the mission though the Sister in charge told him she had been there for a few hours the night before. "Minette is very kind in her way, although not very skilled as a nurse" said the nun. "She makes them feel alive again in ways the rest of us can't, if you know what I mean. There's something slightly..." The Sister paused and looked out across the ward, a troubled expression on her face.

The ward was lined with beds; a few men were mobile, moving from one end of the room to the other or standing staring out the window, the rest sat hunched on the beds or curled upon them, half asleep. Most had visible wounds, missing limbs and eyes, but others were shattered in other ways, shaking and mumbling from the effects of shell shock. Max didn't realize he was staring until the Sister touched his arm. "I'll tell her you were looking for her if you like."

"That's alright," said Max. He left the mission and caught the Metro to Place de Clichy and then walked along Caulaincourt to La Coquette. He was about to enter the bar when he spotted Minette. She was a few dozen feet farther up the boulevard on the bridge that crossed the cemetery. She was tossing pebbles into the space below. A cat yowled and Minette put her hand to her mouth. Then she threw another stone.

"What are you doing?" he asked, joining her on the bridge. She turned sharply, letting the last of the rocks tumble to the ground.

"Cats," she said. "I hate them. Always slinking around like foreigers looking for a crime to commit."

"You'd hate it more if there were none. They keep the vermin down. We could have used more cats in the trenches."

"I suppose. Yes, you're right. Someone needs to deal with the vermin."

"You're in a funny mood."

Minette leaned on the stone railing and looked across the Cimetière de Montmartre.

"So many famous people – artists and politicians – all dead," said Minette.

"So many only their families know," said Max. "Still dead."

Minette laughed. "I suppose I'l be there someday."

"Better there than in an unmarked grave in northern France," said Max. "I was at the Mission today. They say you're very kind."

"Does that surprise you?"

"That you're kind, no. That you go there – maybe a little."

"I lost my brothers in the war. But they could have ended up like that. When I look at them, at their wounds, their...deformaties...it makes me feel..."

"Yes," said Max, acutely aware of his own wounds. He decided to change the subject. "Have you ever met a man called Andre Bucard?"

"I know who he is," said Minette. "Lachance says he'll be the President of France some day."

"I thought the Prime Minister had all the real power."

"Lachance says Bucard thinks democracy is a failure."

"What do you think?" asked Max.

"I think all politicians are the same. They want into your wallet and my skirts. They talk of the people but they're all – left or right – in league with the industrialists and Jew bankers who have always profited from this." Minette waved her hand to encompass the tangled rows of tombstones.

"You sound like some anarchists I know," said Max. He was slightly shocked by her words, though what bothered him the most, he couldn't say.

"Living in Paris will do that to you," said Minette. Then she laughed. "I don't really care about any of it. I... Max, let's go away, you and I, down to Lyon or Marseille. Someplace we can have fun. Any place but here."

"I can't, Minette. You know that."

"Barzani," said Minette, bitterly. "You have to get over that, Max, before it ruins everything."

Max looked down at the graveyard stretched out beneath the bridge, trying to think of what he could say to make Minette understand. When he looked up, she was walking away, down the street to La Coquette.

Sixteen – Saturday, January 18, 1919

Max had second thoughts about waiting until lunch to see Buchan. He had wasted the previous day going over his notes and trying to make sense of Barzani's documents but he knew he was merely avoiding action. His instincts urged him to go slow, to approach problems in a circuitous way, but he knew that wouldn't work now. The trail would grow cold if he delayed. He dropped by the Hotel Vendôme at seven and found Buchan drinking coffee and smoking in the gentleman's lounge. He appeared to be alone so Max approached the table and sat down opposite him.

"I thought we were on for lunch," said Buchan. He seemed unsurprised by Max's sudden appearance, though not pleased.

"Something came up," said Max. He poured himself a cup of coffee from the silver urn on the table.

"It's probably for the best. The opening ceremonies of the conference are at three p.m. I'm not officially invited but Colonel House has that damn flu so I should be within shouting distance in case my expertise is needed."

"And what is your expertise, Ginger?" asked Max.

"You know, this and that."

"That's how Barzani described his work," said Max.

"Yeah, about that. Asper told me you came to see him and pumped him for information about Barzani. I don't mind what you do on your own time but I don't appreciate having my name dragged into your private affairs. It's not professional."

Max blushed. He didn't like being lectured but he supposed he deserved it. "Sorry," he said. "I'm new to this. I don't know what the protocols are."

"It's all right but don't make a habit of it." Buchan leaned back in his chair and lit another cigarette. He selected a pastry from the plate beside the coffee pot and nibbled it daintily, careful not to get the powdered sugar on his jacket. "The French eat too many sweets at breakfast. Have one if you like."

The breakfast at L'Aquilon was just being set out when he left so Max took a glazed roll and bit into it. The bread was warm and there was a sweet hazelnut paste inside. *I must be turning French; I like sweets at breakfast.*

"What can I do for you Max?" asked Buchan.

"The Paris police are doing nothing to solve Barzani's murder."

"Nothing? They told me they put one of their top men on it."

Max snorted. "You made inquiries?"

"Barzani was in the same line of work as me, more or less. I was curious. Part professional courtesy, part concern for my own safety. Police seem to think politics had nothing to do with it. They said he was queer. You buy that, Max?"

"No."

"Me neither. Know what I think? I think the Bolshies did him."

"The Russians? Why would they kill Barzani? He was working for Faisal and Weizmann to secure better conditions in the Levant – a division of the lands around the Jordan that suited the interests of the people who live there, rather than those of England and France."

"Among other things. Besides, you don't have to go to Russia to find Bolshies. There's a mayor out in Bobigny, one of the Parisian suburbs, who calls himself a socialist but he's as Red as they come. And he's not the only one. They ring this city."

"I still don't understand why the Reds would have any more reason to kill Barzani than, well, you would."

Buchan paused, his cigarette halfway to his lips.

"I'm not sure," said Buchan, "if I appreciate the implication."

"If it makes you feel any better – you're my least likely suspect."

Buchan laughed. "Max," he said, "I'm really starting to like you. What motive could I possibly have for wanting Barzani dead?"

"Everybody has come to Paris looking to have their grievances settled."

"You're telling me. You can't walk down an alleyway without tripping over someone with a beef they want the Big Four to solve for them. I was at a nice little bistro having supper last night and some little guy, Nguyen something, came out of the kitchen and tried to give me an eight-point manifesto on independence for French Indochina. As if that's possible. What's your point?"

"Only some of them can get what they want, right?"

"Naturally." Buchan, despite his earlier protests, picked a jam filled croissant from the tray.

"According to Asper, you made promises to help the Serbs and more specifically the Croats. Though he wasn't impressed with your efforts so far."

"Asper needs to learn patience. We need the Serbs to keep the Bolsheviks in check in Hungary. That means Greater Serbia, not a ragtag bunch of little states. The same way we need a strong Poland in the north."

"America's interests at play."

"Not officially, but there are those in the administration who see it that way. Although that better not get back to me, Max."

"But things might not work out that way if the conference gets bogged down with dealing with the Levant. Time spent settling the division of old Ottoman territory is time not spent dealing with the interests of others."

"No one is that concerned about Arabs and Jews. They've got their own deal worked out and the British and French will settle with them accordingly. It's why they've been scheduled first. Get them out of the way early so we can focus on the more important matters at hand."

"But Barzani was doing everything he could to keep them in the spotlight."

"He was persuasive but diplomacy only takes you so far," Buchan said. He had finished the croissant. He refilled his coffee and started on a berry tart.

"I think persuasion was the least of the tools he was prepared to bring to bear. He had a lot of cash on hand. And he had a large number of documents, too. Bribery. Blackmail. Both seem likely."

"You shouldn't speak ill of the dead."

"I'm not. Hevel believed in a cause. A just cause in his own mind, at least. He was willing to do what it took to see justice done."

"A bit like you."

"I hope so," said Max.

"Then your theory is I killed him to keep him from fulfilling his mission?"

"It's not implausible."

"I think you'd have a hard time proving it in a court of law. Besides..." Buchan took his billfold out of the inside pocket of his jacket and extracted a small gilt-embossed card. He put it on the table in front of Max. "It's not public knowledge but... it's my membership in the Zionist Organization of America."

"But you're a –"

"Red-head from Virginia? The first thing you need to learn in this business, Max, is don't judge a book by its cover. I didn't necessarily agree with all of Barzani's methods but I support the cause he was working for – fair treatment for Arabs and a Jewish homeland in Palestine. I'll do what I can to fulfill his vision. You do what you can to find Barzani's killers. And don't forget the Reds."

Buchan reached his hand across the table and after a moment Max shook it. Max still wasn't sure he trusted Buchan. The man was a spy, after all. But Max didn't think he was a murderer.

§

After breakfast, Max walked along the Quai for several hours, watching the river. All the landmarks were still there but they seemed somehow lifeless without Barzani's quick and clever commentary. Eventually his feet led him to the front doors of La Coquette.

Minette wasn't there, though she was scheduled to work that night. Lachance was away as well and Max was about to give up and head back to his hotel when he spotted Roget coming in through the back door. If anyone would have been driven into a jealous rage by the thoughts of Minette with another man it would be Roget.

"Roget?" he called. "I want to talk to you."

The man still had a faint mark on his cheek where Minette had scratched him. He was rocking slightly on the balls of his feet and his arms hung loosely at his sides. Max had seen the pose before, men standing in the corners of boxing rings, waiting for the bell to sound. Minette said he was dangerous and Max could see it in the set of his shoulders and in the thin lines of scar around his eyes and mouth. Paris was full of dangerous men.

"What do you want, Yankee?" Either Roget had forgotten his nationality or thought he was being insulting.

"Like I said, talk."

"You Americans are all alike. All talk, no action."

"I saw plenty of action in the trenches. What were you doing?"

"Dealing with punks like you."

"More likely beating up men half your size and twice your age."

"What are you driving at?"

"I heard you were making threats against Barzani the day before he was murdered."

"Who told you that? That bitch Minette, I bet. She needs to learn the only time she should open her mouth is when I want to put something in it."

They were standing less than a foot apart, swaying as they barked at each other, like two animals trying to prove which was boss. He was bigger than Roget, taller and broader but the other man was probably quicker; he was certainly more experienced. Max's anger swelled. He sometimes wondered where it came from; today he didn't care, he wanted to let it out to play.

"And you're the so-called man who can teach her."

Roget didn't draw back his hand, didn't even shift his weight. His fist snapped up from his side into Max's belly. He barely had time to twist so the punch landed on his ribs rather than in his solar plexus.

Max grunted and stepped back. Roget closed fast and landed two more hard blows to Max's mid-section. Max lunged forward, wrapped his arms around Roget. He pushed the man hard into the edge of the bar. Roget tried a head butt. Max twisted and avoided the worst of the blow.

Roget dropped, trying to slip from Max's grasp. Max let him and then followed him to the floor. He pressed his knee into Roget's chest, hit him twice, hard, in the mouth. Roget's face went slack.

Max tried to stand but his knee gave out. That saved him when Roget aimed a kick between his legs. The blow caught Max on the thigh. He rolled onto his back. Roget leapt up and grabbed a chair. Max raised his arms to shield his face.

"That's enough, Roget! I said that's enough!"

Roget glared at Lachance but put the chair down.

"This isn't over," said Roget. "Not for you. And not for that little slut." He grabbed his crotch and laughed.

"Go to my office and wait for me," said Lachance. Roget ran his hand through his hair and straightened his tie before heading around the bar and up the stairs.

Lachance offered Max his hand and pulled him to his feet. He found Max's cane and handed it to him.

"Roget was military police during the war. You shouldn't fight with him. He knows too many tricks."

"I gathered that," said Max. He would have bruises on his thigh and ribs to add to the barely healed ones from the last beating he took. Still, he felt he had given as good as he got. Roget had been dabbing blood from his lip when he left the bar.

"I'm sorry for that," said Lachance, though he didn't look sorry. "Stay and have a drink. On the house. Minette should be in later if she remembers. I'm sure she'll be happy to see you."

Max wasn't sure about that. He wasn't sure about anything anymore. "What hold do you have over her?"

"Me?" Lachance laughed. "The same hold I have over everyone who works here. I pay her salary. What she does with the money, with her time, with her body is no concern of mine. As near as I can tell, it's no concern of yours either. Is it? Do you have some special claim on the girl that I don't know about? That she hasn't bothered to mention to me?"

"No," said Max. Minette had promised him nothing though she had offered to run away with him. "No special claim. I don't like the things Roget said."

"Roget is a selfish boy. If he can't have something himself, he wants to ruin it for others. He'll do as I tell him."

Max had seen too many men like Roget – ready to do what others told them, no matter how vile the order was. If Roget was involved in Barzani's death, it was because someone told him to do it. But was Lachance the only one whose orders he followed?

"I think I'll pass on the drink," said Max. "Tell Minette I'd like to talk to her. She knows where to find me."

"I'm sure she does. And Max, don't forget my offer. Barzani's documents have a value now but it won't last. Information is only valuable when it isn't common knowledge."

Seventeen – Sunday, January 19 to Monday, January 20, 1919

The next day, Max could barely get out of bed and didn't even try for most of the morning. The pain in his ribs made it so hard to breathe that he wondered if they were broken. But that was nothing compared to the agony in his thigh and knee – the worst he had felt for weeks. He probed the flesh, his fingers pressing down on the metal plate that held his leg together. The pain didn't increase which he took for a good sign and his knee didn't collapse when he put his weight on it. Still, walking today would be difficult and, if he could avoid it, he would. He poured a packet of headache powder into a glass of water and forced the bitter liquid down. Then he took a shot of brandy to wash away the taste.

He had always thought he could handle himself but, compared to Roget, or the men who had beaten him in the alley, he was an amateur. There wasn't much he could do about it now but he determined to learn the finer points of street fighting before much more time passed. Maybe Yesim or Henri could recommend someone who could teach him.

The right side of his jaw ached from Roget's head butt but at noon he dragged himself to a nearby cafe and compelled himself to eat a hearty lunch, chewing several sandwiches carefully on the left side of his mouth and washing them down with large mugs of black coffee. The pain began to recede – whether from the powder, the brandy or the coffee he couldn't tell – but he was in no hurry to leave the warmth of the café. Several morning papers hung on wooden racks against one wall and Max spent a leisurely hour skimming through them. Given the condition of his body, he doubted he would manage much more that day.

The opening of the conference at the Palace at Versailles the previous afternoon was the focus of all three papers he read. Each editor declared a victory when the original decision of the conference to limit press coverage to official daily communiqués had been reversed. The conference could not "return to the old practice of secret diplomacy and hidden agreements," warned one of the editors, echoing the first of Wilson's fourteen points.

There were sixty-six official delegates representing twenty-nine nations and territories, including the Kingdom of Hedjaz represented by Prince Faisal and Rustum Haidar. Others, such as Weizmann's Zionists, would appear before the conference to present their special cases as the conference progressed.

The conference commenced with trumpet fanfares and military salutes before the French President, Raymond Poincaré, formally opened the conference with a speech that began at three minutes past the hour. Upon the completion of his welcoming speech, the real work began.

Clemenceau, at Wilson's suggestion, was elected permanent president of the conference. He made a brief speech before calling on delegates to submit papers dealing with the special interests of their respective nations. He announced that the League of Nations would be the first order of business at the next Plenary session, scheduled for January 25th, although the determination of the responsibility for the war would rank high for discussion. There was little doubt who Clemenceau intended to blame.

Max was surprised that there would be as much as a week between sessions but then it seemed fitting that a conference aimed at ending the Great War should move as ponderously as the war itself. Undoubtedly, people like Buchan would be plenty busy in the intervening days.

§

Early the next morning, the soreness in his ribs and back had subsided. He knew he had other obligations to Barzani than finding his killers. First, he would deal with the matter of his inheritance. After, there was a funeral to arrange.

Police headquarters seemed less imposing the third time around, maybe because this time he wasn't being held in a cell. The same harried desk officer looked him over sourly before sending him to speak to Sergeant Gilbert, who, he was told, handled claims of lost or stolen property.

Gilbert seemed as small and dusty as the office he occupied, thin with the weary eyes of an old bloodhound, his drooping grey moustache stained yellow by cigarettes and coffee. Even his voice had a faintly dusty quality, low and hoarse with a slight lisp. He flipped through a ledger until he found Barzani's name. He read the entry, carefully screening it from Max's view with a cupped hand.

"Papers," he said.

Max produced his Canadian passport, his residency card provided by the Hôtel de Ville and his discharge papers from the army. Gilbert flipped through the ten-page folder and set it aside.

"It's only in English," he complained. He dropped the discharge papers on top of the passport, probably for the same reason. He perused the residency card with its brief physical description, constantly glancing from it to Max's face to see if it was a match.

"Do you have anything else?" he asked at last.

"I have a letter of introduction from my former commanding officer. In French."

"Let me see it," said Gilbert.

Max took the letter from his jacket and handed it to Gilbert. Folded inside, at Henri's suggestion, was two hundred francs. Gilbert started to unfold the letter but paused when he realized its contents.

He stared at Max with narrowed eyes and Max wondered if Henri had been wrong about the dishonesty of the Paris police.

"I'll need to look at this in better light."

Gilbert went into the hallway. When he returned, he handed Max the letter. The money was gone.

"Everything seems in order," said Gilbert. "Sign here. And here. And here." After Max signed, Gilbert stamped and initialed each signature.

Gilbert went to a metal cage at the back of his officeand came out with a flat metal box, sealed with twisted wire and a glob of blue wax along with an official looking envelope.

"This is an accounting, prepared by a notary and sealed by his hand, of the items found in Mr. Barzani's deposit boxes as well as all taxes, duties, fees and expenses deducted. You will also find letters authorizing you to access his bank accounts and recover all personal effects from the hotel. Finally, there is a certificate of death that will allow you to claim his body from the morgue for burial." Gilbert checked the dates stamped on the envelope. "Please do so in the next forty-eight hours or they will dispose of the body. The address is on the certificate."

Max held the box and envelope in his hands. They seemed heavier than their size warranted. Gilbert stood and held out his hand and Max shook it.

"It was a pleasure doing business with you," said Gilbert. "Sorry for your loss." He might have been talking about the weather for all the feeling in his voice.

Captain Gereau stopped him as he left the building. The big man looked tired, dark circles under his eyes and a slump in his shoulders that Max had not seen before.

When Max commented on it, Gereau said: "It's this damn conference. They have us all working double shifts."

"Has Bonnet made any progress on finding Barzani's killers?"

"Killer," said Gereau. "You know the official theory. Bonnet doesn't report to me. I'm more concerned with the people you're associating yourself with."

"Who exactly? Joseph Asper?"

"Among others. Though I'm more concerned that you were spotted coming out of a notorious Anarchist hangout. What were you doing there?"

It was the way Joachim described it – factions spying on each other while the police watched them all. "I'm a tourist," Max said. "I wanted to see the spot where the people stormed the Bastille."

"Nothing to see there now but a monument," said Gereau.

"As I discovered," said Max. He glanced up at the squat block of police headquarters. "Nothing stands once the people turn against it."

Gereau glared at him but said nothing more.

§

Max stopped first at the Arabs' hotel but was informed by a black servant of the Prince, in halting French, that they had no knowledge of anyone named Barzani and, if they did, could think of no imam or mosque who would take him. Max had watched him depart, wondering at the cruelty of people, when the concierge approached.

"I could not help but overhear. My cousin deals in these matters. In his eyes, the dead are all the same. He can find a plot in one of the civic graveyards if you like. He does a nice job and his rates are fair. I can give you his address."

Max nodded and the concierge wrote out the address in a fine hand. His hand shook as he gave the card to Max and his eyes misted.

"I am truly sorry for your loss. There has been too much loss."

Max offered him a tip but the man refused and so Max shook his hand instead. Every cruelty revealed a kindness.

The morgue was located a few blocks away on l'Archevêché behind the Notre Dame cathedral. Max had heard of its strange reputation even though he hadn't been there himself. Still, the stories had not prepared him for the row of bodies laid out on slabs of black marble behind a large glass window for members of the public to view. The official purpose was to identify the deceased, often pulled from the nearby Seine, naked or in rags, but Max could not believe that was all that drew the line of gawking men, women and children. No ex-soldiers joined the queue; they had seen their fill of unidentified corpses.

The lobby, where the acrid scent of bleach argued with the sickly-sweet odour of formaldehyde, was small and crowded. Most of those who waited on the low benches wore masks over the lower part of their faces but their eyes shared the flat stare of grief. They were not here for the unknown dead. Max presented himself at the desk where a hard looking man in his thirties told him to take a number and wait until he was called.

When his father died, his uncle George had taken him to the town's one funeral parlour to view the body. The casket had been closed below the waist to hide the terrible damage done to the legs but he had stared at his father's face for several long minutes, searching for any sign of the man who, the day before, had rumpled his hair and told him to work hard in school. But the face was not that of his father. It was pale, rather than tanned, with two incongruous patches of pink on his cheeks. The mouth, that, even at the saddest moments, held the hint of a smile, was now turned down. *No*, he thought, *my father has left this world.* As a boy, he thought his father had gone to heaven, but, now, after so many other deaths, he was no longer sure such a place existed. But of the existence of hell, he had no doubt.

At last, his number was called and a stout woman, dressed all in white, gave him a mask to wear and led him to a large room near the back of the building. The room was cold, as cold or colder than the air outside, and filled with several dozen low tables. Every table held a body, each draped in a white cloth. Many of the cloths were stained or patched. Max was not the only one claiming a body. In one corner a young woman sobbed in the arms of an older man, his face drawn and haggard as if he stood on edge of an abyss, waiting to tumble in. Against the far wall, two men, alike enough to be twins, gazed impassively at the body of an old woman.

"I'm sorry you had to wait," said the woman as she pulled back the sheet. "It's this damn flu. They say the worst is over but I'm not sure. Is this him?"

Hevel, too, had left this world. His skin was grey and flaccid and his half-open eyes had a white film across them. Even the chemical smell of the morgue could not mask the fishy stench of decay. Max nodded and the woman replaced the sheet.

"Have you made arrangements to take the body?"

"A Mister Planeur will stop by at four," Max said to the woman.

"Ah, Planeur. He'll do right by your friend."

"Is there anything else I need to do?"

"Sign this," she said, holding out a clipboard. "And here. Ah, I can have the body washed before Mr. Planeur arrives, if you like."

Max nodded, then realized a gratuity was expected. He handed over a hundred francs. "Is that enough?"

The woman's eyes crinkled in a smile and she tucked the notes into her pocket.

Then it was over. Planeur had promised that he could handle all the arrangements. Internment would take place the next day at noon at the Montmartre cemetery near the Tourlaque entrance. An announcement would appear in the best papers, both evening and morning. He offered to find a preacher and arrange for professional mourners but Max declined. The man looked disappointed so Max bought a better casket than he had planned. After all, it was Barzani's money and this was the only way he could take it with him.

§

Max felt dirty after his trip to the morgue but he first stopped at his bank to transfer the contents of Barzani's gift to his safety deposit box. He didn't bother to count the money – a mixture of dollars and pounds and, mostly, francs – but it was clearly more than he could spend in a year, even if he moved into one of the downtown hotels. At the Grand Hotel, he had Barzani's personal effects transferred to L'Aquilon. He enjoyed watching the condescending expression of the front desk manager transform into a cloying smile when he saw the size of the tip Max dropped on the counter.

Back at L'Aquilon, Max indulged in a long bath. There was plenty of hot water at that time of day and it helped relieve the ache in his back and legs. He lay in the tub, reading another of Henri's books, until the water cooled. After, he dressed in one of the new suits he bought on the day before Hevel's death. It was dark green and he chose a pale-yellow shirt and a narrow green and gold tie to go with it. He had learned a great deal in the last few days but he still didn't know what he knew. Tonight, he would go to the jazz bar and listen to the music and let his brain try to digest all he had heard. If he was lucky, he would see no one he knew.

The club had changed since his visit on New Year's Eve. The windows were still painted over but there was a new light over the door and a small sign that read Chez Jacob. Either the basement addition was no longer in operation or Jake had found a better class of gendarme to bribe. A line outside the door was waiting to get in but, when Jake spotted him, he ushered him past it. The stares from the men and women left outside were a mixture of curiosity and resentment. One of the girls – she didn't look more than fifteen – grabbed his sleeve as he passed. "Need a dance partner?" she whispered.

The club was packed but Jake led him to a small table near the stage with a reserved sign propped against the candleholder. A trio was playing the early set, quiet, almost sleepy tunes that inspired few dancers but earned warm applause after every song.

"I always keep a table or two set aside for regulars," said Jake. "And special friends. Hope you'll stay for the second act. Some boys out of Chicago gonna bring the place down."

Max wasn't sure which category he fit into but was glad of the special treatment. He doubted he could have stood in the chill evening for long.

The menu that night offered a choice between blanched veal ragout served with chanterelle mushrooms and rice and a cassoulet – duck stewed with spicy sausages and white beans and served with potatoes. Max ordered the latter with, on the waiter's recommendation, a half-bottle of Syrah.

The trio finished up as Max wiped the last of the stew off his plate with bread. He still had a half glass of wine but he ordered an espresso and a small pastis while he contemplated whether to finish with the chocolat mouse or the crème brûlée. He probably didn't need either but, in his mind, he had decided that this was like the last meal of a holiday – a break before he began the final thrust to solve Barzani's murder. In a week or two, the matter of the Levant would be considered and probably settled by the Conference. Somehow, he knew that Barzani's killers must be caught before then or they never would be. Worse, whatever it was Barzani was doing, and Max now suspected it was far more than mere diplomatic maneuvering, might fail, with disastrous consequences for those involved.

The mousse won out and Max ordered it with second round of liqueur and espresso. It arrived at the same time as the six-piece band from Chicago who launched into a fast rag-time measure that soon had half the bar crowded onto the dance floor. It seemed Paris had gotten over its fear of the Spanish flu, at least for tonight. The music was lively and Max tried to hide within it, letting its jittery rhythms replace his jumbled thoughts.

Max was contemplating a third espresso when Schmidt walked into the bar. He was accompanied by one of the two men from the meeting with Barzani, the tall one who had been downstairs in the opium den. They started for the door that would take them downstairs but Jake headed them off. They were too far away to make out the words but Max could tell Schmidt and Jake were shouting at each other. At one point the man with Schmidt put his hand on Jake's shoulder. Two large men appeared out of nowhere and pulled him away. Schmidt tried to step around Jake but the bar's owner was clearly having none of it. Jake gently turned him around and pointed him to the door. Max gestured to his waiter and paid his bill in time to get up and follow Schmidt and his bodyguard back into the street.

Max let Schmidt get a dozen paces ahead of him before following. He could feel the effects of the alcohol. He felt loose, ready for anything, but he knew it was an illusion. He would need to be careful. He could not take another beating and he was doubtful he was in any condition to prevent it. He opened the clasp knife in his pocket, which he would only use as a last resort. Words needed to be his weapons tonight.

Schmidt hesitated at the corner, perhaps debating if there was another way into the basement of the club. Max caught up to them, stopping about five feet away.

"Herr Schmidt," he said softly. "Could I have a word with you?"

Schmidt started and turned quickly. His bodyguard stepped between them, adopting the same loose limbed pose Roget had used the night before. Max stepped back and raised his hands, palm out, in front of him.

"I don't want to cause any trouble," he said. "I have a few questions, that's all."

"Did Barzani send you?"

Max was surprised. He had expected that Schmidt would know of Barzani's death. Maybe he did and was being careful, distancing himself from the event in case Max was working for the police.

"In a way," he said. It didn't hurt to play along and see where Schmidt stood.

"Why should I answer your questions? Or his, for that matter?"

"Jake's a friend of mine," said Max. "Maybe he could tell me how to reach the Chinaman. That's what you came for."

Schmidt nodded slightly. "All right. Go ask him. I'll wait here."

His bluff called, Max headed back to the bar. He briefly thought of staying there to drink another brandy and listen to the music. But he knew he might not get another chance to talk to Schmidt. He tried to think of an offhand way to ask what Schmidt wanted to know but there wasn't one so he went up to Jake and asked him straight.

"I get that a lot," Jake said. "I sent them packing as part of my new licensing arrangement with Captain Gereau. Mostly, I tell folks to go to hell but, as a last favor to Mr. Barzani, I'll tell you, if you tell me you ain't looking to wash away unpleasant memories."

"I don't even *drink* to forget," said Max.

"Good man," said Jake, laughing. He scribbled an address on a piece of paper and handed it to Max. "Be careful. People who chase the dragon can be dangerous, even when they look like they can't hardly move."

"Thanks," said Max.

"Some of us are coming to the funeral tomorrow, if you don't mind. Mr. Barzani was a good man. Some of the boys want to play him out."

"Hevel would like that."

Schmidt was still standing at the corner, leaning against the lone street lamp. His man had stepped back into the shadows, watching Max as he approached.

Max held out the folded piece of paper. Schmidt reached for it but Max pulled it back.

"Victor could take that from you in a heartbeat."

"Maybe. Maybe not. But people are watching."

Schmidt's eyes glanced past Max. One of Jake's enforcers had followed him out of the bar and was standing halfway between the bar entrance and the corner.

"Very well, Mr..."

"Anderson. Max Anderson."

Well, Max, what questions does Barzani have for me now?"

"None. The questions are all mine. Barzani was murdered four days ago. I would have thought you would have known."

"No. It's a small world but a big city. Compact, perhaps, but thickly layered. But it does explain the silence."

"The silence?"

"People like Barzani, like me, we do a lot of things but mostly we deal in information. A word here, a promise or a threat there. Secrets of all sorts. So, we are constantly listening – trying to hear what others are saying or doing, where they are going. The last few days have been very quiet. People have gone to ground. Something big is about to happen. Barzani's death may be part of that. These things don't happen in isolation."

"Do you know Joachim ben David?"

"Know of him."

"He's dead, too. Killed about two weeks ago and his body hidden in the tunnels near the St. Germaine metro station."

Schmidt looked angry now and a little scared. He said something to Victor who grumbled a reply and took out a small leather-bound book and scribbled a note inside.

"Someone has been very busy," said Schmidt. "Perhaps it is time I went back to Berlin for a few days."

"You think the deaths are connected?"

"Don't you?"

Max nodded. It seemed too much of a coincidence that two men, connected to him only by their relationship to each other, should die such violent deaths – beaten and killed with a knife. There had to be a link. They both had worked for Weizmann but surely the Zionist leader had nothing to do with their deaths.

"Have you heard of a man named Bucard?"

Schmidt's pale skin glistened despite the coolness of the night. He took a handkerchief out of his breast pocket and delicately dabbed at his brow.

"A nasty man. Although I doubt his involvement is direct. He's not the kind to do his own dirty work."

"That seems like a common practice." Max glanced at Victor, hulking in the shadows.

"Oh, well, look at me. I'm hardly capable of much. But Bucard... have you ever seen him?"

"Yes, I think so." The man he had seen with Lachance and Marois. He might have been Bucard. The predator.

"A formidable creature. And a violent one. But so clever and so careful. It's what sets the beasts apart from the monsters. If you suspect Bucard, I have only one thing to tell you. Leave Paris."

"I won't run."

"Well, it's flight or fight. Your choice." He held out his hand. "Are we done here?"

"Not quite. Do you know what Barzani was doing?"

"I know what he was doing for me," said Schmidt. "And judging from recent events, he had at least gotten a start. You were there, you heard what was said."

"He was saying a few words in the right ears to stop Germany from being humiliated."

"To stop it from being *totally* humiliated. Germany is on the verge of revolution. There must be concessions or the government will fall. No, let me be precise, the present government will fall but without concessions, no new government will take its place. No one to sign their precious treaty. And Germany will go to the military madmen who would fight until the last drop of blood is shed or to the workers and their Russian backers. The Allies already fear the Bolshevik presence in Hungary – how will they react to a Communist state on their very borders?"

"I don't care what happens to Germany," said Max.

"You should. But I understand. We are the enemy. But I am not *your* enemy. I was not Barzani's enemy."

"You wouldn't even shake his hand."

Schmidt glanced at Victor. "One must keep up appearances. The French hide their hatreds under slogans of brotherhood. The Germans are not so subtle. They do not like foreigners – especially brown ones. And they hate Jews."

"Every German?"

"Not yet. But there are those who would have it so. Either because they believe the libel or because it is politically expedient to do so. I did my part, too. I whispered what words I could. I even spoke to a young American named Dulles and to some reporters with the Times of London. Something may come of it."

"And Bucard?"

"Bucard is a Frenchman, first and foremost. A nationalist to hear him speak. Appealing to patriotism and national character. Purification. France for the French. That's what they all claim. German, French, Italian, Spanish. The language is different; the sentiment, the same. The West fears the Bolshevik threat but maybe they would be better advised to look at the threat from within."

"The price of freedom is eternal vigilance."

"A Canadian expression?"

Max laughed. Only when he quoted Americans did people think he was Canadian. "A useful one. You say, Barzani was being successful."

"Yes, I think so. None of the eastern countries are happy with the limitations that have been put on them. At least some of their operatives seem to think Faisal and Weizmann, that is, Barzani, is to blame. If Bucard isn't your man, look to the East. The Serbs were particularly pointed in their criticisms. Blackmailer was the nicest of the things they said."

Max couldn't think of any other questions. He glanced at the address Jake had written before handing the paper to Schmidt. If he needed to find him, that was as good a place as any.

Schmidt put the paper in his pocket without looking at it. "I am many things," said Schmidt. "I have my weaknesses – as you have seen. But I am not a bad man, Mr. Anderson. And I am not your enemy. Good luck."

He turned and walked away, Victor following a few paces behind. Max watched them until they disappeared into the night.

Eighteen – Tuesday, January 21, 1919

B arzani's luggage made a formidable pile in Max's room. For the moment, he had little heart for the task of going through it. He could give most of the clothes and the luggage itself to charity but what would he do with the rest, the small personal mementos Barzani had retained in his largely peripatetic life? Barzani had mentioned that his father was dead, but did he have a mother somewhere, back in Tehran, perhaps? Or brothers and sisters? The refusal of the Arab delegation to even acknowledge his existence made it difficult to find out. At least, no wife or children were waiting in some distant home for news of his fate. Barzani had said as much to Minette on the night she mocked his proposal of marriage.

It would have to wait. First, a bath and then breakfast before he made his way to Cimetière de Montmartre, one of three established by Napoleon when he decreed the dead could no longer reside in the centre of the city. Most of the great cemeteries had been emptied, the bones of nobility and commoners alike transported to the catacombs beneath the northern suburbs. Others had been maintained as monuments to the city's past but new interments had been prohibited. The dead had no place in the City of Light.

Max wondered if Planeur's advertisements would draw any mourners. If this were one of the popular crime novels that Henri favored, the murderers themselves would be compelled to appear, their guilt drawing them to see the body laid to rest. *Perhaps*, thought Max with bitter humor, *I should take my revolver just in case*. Still, it was possible that someone might come who knew of Barzani's plans or his enemies. He could only hope.

The surrounding streets pressed against the cemetery so that the windows of the higher apartments looked over the low stone walls unto the tumble of graves crammed together within its borders. The graveyard mimicked the city itself, wide gravel-covered boulevards for strolling mourners, flanked by tenements for the dead. Single graves held generations within their narrow bounds, fresh carved names scrolling beneath older worn ones. And everywhere solitary monuments to the powerful and famous. Max paused before the grave of the composer Berlioz, his profile carved in black stone, before walking on to where Barzani would be buried, against the wall that separated the cemetery from Rue Tourlaque, not far from the Jewish section of the graveyard.

In the end, only Henri and Buchan were beside him at the grave; Jake and four of the musicians from the bar stood in the pathway that ran past it. Planeur and his assistants lowered the casket into the ground, covered it with dirt and laid a stone slab across it.

Hevel Barzani 1871-1919
He Believed in a Better World.

None of them spoke; none knew what to say. But the musicians played, a slow mournful dirge that slowly transformed into a joyous hymn, almost a march. And, perhaps, that was better than words. A few people came onto their small balconies and listened. When it was over, Buchan shook each of their hands and departed through the Tourlaque exit to a chauffeur driven car. The impromptu band played another song as Henri and Max walked out of the cemetery to the La Fourche Metro station, the music echoing faintly as they descended the steps to the station. They took the train, in deference to Max's bruises, to Anvers and then walked to Le Coq Bleu, where they toasted Barzani's memory.

Yesim, who had claimed he couldn't afford to close the bar even for the hour it would take to attend, would not join them in the toast but remained behind the zinc bar, rearranging glasses and bottles and refusing to meet Max's eye. When Max asked him why, Yesim turned and went into the cellar for another case of wine.

"What's with Yesim?" Max asked Henri.

Henri shrugged and held his palms up. "He gets like that sometimes. Moody. Something's bothering him. He'll tell us what it is eventually but until then we'll have to put up with it. Don't let it bother you."

Max couldn't help it; it did bother him. It seemed unnecessarily cruel. Barzani came often enough to the bar to be considered at least a semi-regular and he had always treated Yesim with respect and courtesy. Barzani was beyond caring what Yesim thought or did but he and Henri deserved better.

When Yesim returned, Max asked him what he had for lunch today.

"Nothing," said Yesim, but offered no explanation for his lie. There were two men eating brioche at a table by the door. Max doubted they had brought them with them.

"Fine," he said. "I'll go elsewhere." He turned sharply and walked out the door.

"What's wrong with you, Yesim?" said Henri as Max exited, but if Yesim replied, Max didn't hear what he said.

The meat pie he bought from a boulangerie a few doors down had tasted good when he ate it but now it sat like a sour lump in his stomach. It didn't help that his clothes seemed to have shrunk during the last laundry.

Yesim's behavior was more than a bad mood. He was angry. More specifically, he was angry at Max. And Max had no idea why.

Like everything else in his life, it would have to wait. Barzani was his sole preoccupation now and, he knew that, until he solved the murder or understood once and for all that it couldn't be solved, it would be the sun around which his world would revolve.

When he returned to his hotel, Jean-Marc called him over to the front desk. A dozen or so letters and several telegrams had been forwarded from Barzani's hotel, separately from the luggage. Max took them up to his room and dropped them on his desk. He kicked off his shoes and lay on the bed staring up at the spider web of cracks that covered the ceiling. He could no longer bear the constant drum of anxiety and emotion that had beat upon his mind, waking and sleeping for the last week.

It would be so easy, he thought, *to simply lie here and do nothing.* Today, tomorrow, perhaps for the rest of his life. He had felt this way before. They called it shell shock now; then they called it cowardice. His Colonel had ordered him back to the front, into the heat of battle. The action seemed to have cured him. But sometimes he wasn't sure.

He thought of his father, an inveterate early riser, who had once told him that the reason he got up with the sun was because he was afraid that, if he let himself sleep in, he wouldn't find the will ever to get up again. He pushed his legs off the bed and went to look at the mail.

The telegrams were brief and seemingly inconsequential, confirmations of arrivals and departures of delegates to the conference. None seemed cryptic. The letters were mostly bills from clothing stores and restaurants. Max set those aside to be paid once he got Barzani's money, his money, organized and accounted for. One letter stood out. It had not been mailed – there was no stamp or postmark. The hand-printed address simply said: Hevel Barzani, Hotel Grand. It had been hand delivered. He would need to go back to the hotel to see if anyone knew who had delivered it, though he doubted anyone would, or, if they did, it would lead to anything. But he was learning that detective work mostly consisted of futile inquiries so he supposed he would have to find time to do it.

The letter saved him the trip. It was a single page, written in a neat script, from Joachim ben David, dated December 28th and it read:

Dear Hevel,

As I have not heard from you, I have decided to put in writing the information you asked me to gather. I do not think that I was detected in my efforts but I can no longer be sure. I would prefer to speak to you in person and will not trust this letter to the mail but leave it in the care of my cousin Jacob, to deliver to you and you alone in the event of (here Joachim had written something only to scratch out so thoroughly the paper had been slightly torn) my indisposition. I only hope he doesn't forget – his memory isn't what it used to be. I apologize for being oblique but again, I fear to have this fall into the wrong hands.

You were correct. Several individuals, including the two you named, have arrived in Paris. A conspiracy seems likely although I am not convinced it is what you say it is. Would they dare such a thing when the whole city – the whole world – is watching? Still, you should take precautions to protect his life. These are desperate times and desperate times can produce desperate actions.

Be careful of your own life – men determined to destroy the hopes of a people would not hesitate at simple murder. You put too much faith in Marois to protect you. His loyalties are cheap.

*I have also obtained the Italian codex and I will put it in the
usual place for pick-up. I am sure the decryption will reveal
much of the plans of our enemy.*

*Finally, I think what you seek for yourself is possible but only
if F and W get what they want. Your dreams depend on
theirs. In this, Asper is your deadly enemy. His ambitions
may fail if yours succeed.*

Shalom, chaver

Joachim

Max copied the letter into his leather journal, in case the original
should go astray. The Italian codex had been put in the usual place,
but since both Hevel and Joachim are dead, it might as well be on the
moon. Not that it would have done him much good in any case. Even
decoded, the eight-page document would still be in Italian. Any
attempt at getting it translated might reveal that he still possessed
Barzani's papers.

Still, the letter was valuable in its own right. It confirmed that
Barzani was working for the Arab-Zionist alliance to advance their
claims before the conference but he was also working for his own
goals – a Kurdish homeland perhaps. "In this, Asper is your deadly
enemy." Schmidt had said much the same thing. Barzani's success in
gaining attention to the Levant might be distracting the conference
from the demands of the Balkans. But was that enough to lead to
murder?

Barzani had seemed to trust Marois – sufficiently to take a
beating at his hands – but Joachim didn't share that trust and Max
was inclined to agree. He had seen Marois with Lachance and, he
was certain, Bucard, as well. Two men had come to Paris. One,

presumably, was Bucard. Who was the other and what was his connection to Barzani's death?

He felt like he was running in place. Each piece of the puzzle seemed only to reveal that the puzzle was bigger than he supposed. He needed to find Marois. He needed to confront Bucard. Lachance might know them both but Max doubted he would be a willing informant. Perhaps he could trade some of Barzani's papers for the information but his instincts told him it was the wrong thing to do. If Lachance were sure Max had something to trade, he would be more likely to send Roget to take it than to betray his dangerous friends.

Still, it was the only connection he had. Maybe he couldn't go to Lachance but that didn't mean he couldn't use the bar owner to find the men he wanted. But, first, he wanted to talk to Joachim's cousin, Jacob.

Max waited in Le Pré aux Clercs for nearly two hours, sipping a single beer and picking from a plate of cheese and sausages, before Jacob made an appearance. He and Isaac were chatting amiably as they made their way to what was clearly their usual table. Max hid behind his newspaper until they passed. When they were seated, he followed them and dropped the letter on the table between them.

"Why didn't you tell me you had a letter from Joachim to Barzani?" He tried but failed to keep the anger from his voice. Isaac half rose but Jacob restrained him with a touch.

"I wondered when we would see you again, Max. Sit down."

Max settled into the proffered chair. A waiter brought a pot of tea and two cups and then transferred Max's wine and food from his table.

"Help yourself," he said.

"Thank you, no," said Jacob. "We keep kosher. Part of our religion," he added, in response to Max's raised eyebrows.

"You still haven't answered my question," said Max.

"My cousin – second cousin, actually – Joachim asked me to deliver this letter. It was the last time I saw him alive. He stressed it was to be delivered to Barzani and Barzani alone. To tell you the truth, I completely forgot about it in the shock of Joachim's murder. I only remembered when you came to ask about him. I took it that same day to the hotel."

"You knew he was dead. Why not just give it to me?"

"Well, Max," said Jacob, softly. "Although you seemed like an honest young man, sincerely troubled by the death of your friend, I only had your word you were who you said you were. For all I knew, you killed Joachim and Barzani, too. Perhaps for the contents of this very letter. I thought, if you were sincere, it would wind up in your hands; if not, it might prompt the police to investigate further. I've heard nothing more from the Prefecture, but here you are."

"Yes," said Isaac. "Here he is, bringing danger to us all."

"I'm sure it's not as serious as all that," said Jacob, though it was clear from the look on Jacob's face that he, too, was afraid of sitting with Max.

"This man is connected, somehow, to two murders," said Issac. "When have friends like that ever been good for Jews?"

Jacob shrugged but said nothing.

"We have nothing for you, Mr. Anderson," said Isaac. "And you have nothing for us but trouble. Joachim's family, back in Warsaw, are still in shloshim – the month of mourning – for him. Respect their grief and leave us and ours alone. We have told you all we know of Joachim's business. Go and do not come here again."

Isaac turned his back on Max. Jacob reached across the table and laid his hand on Max's arm.

"If you find the men who did these terrible things, let us know. But, until then, perhaps my young friends are right. We cannot help you and you can bring us nothing but grief. French Jews have had their fill of grief."

Nineteen – Tuesday, January, 21 to Thursday, January 23, 1919

Max had seen Marois at La Coquette; it seemed the logical place to look for him. That evening, he found a shadowed doorway where he had a clear view of the front entrance and squatted there with a wine bottle between his feet and a cigarette dangling from his lips. He had dressed in a heavy wool jacket and wore a cloth cap pulled low over his brow.

By the third night, he had little to show for his vigil but sore buttocks and a slight cough from the cigarette smoke. He spent his days disposing of Barzani's things and hanging around the hotels where most of the delegates were staying. Neither proved profitable but his efforts to contact the Kurds or track down Bolsheviks were even less fruitful so each night he returned to his post outside La Coquette in hopes of spotting Marois or, better yet, the man he now assumed was Bucard.

Instead, he saw Minette come and go, sometimes alone, sometimes on the arm of some well-dressed man. He watched Roget watch her, although they never seemed to speak. He also discovered Bonnet was a regular at the club, though he couldn't imagine Lachance let him get away without paying the way Yesim did. He even saw Jacques Court – if that was his real name – waddle through the door one night, no doubt spending the francs Max had paid him only a few days before.

He supposed it was inevitable that his nightly surveillance would be noticed but he was surprised when a black car pulled up in front of his doorway and Captain Gereau ordered him into the back seat. He told the driver to take them to L'Aquilon.

"Who do you think you are?" asked Gereau. "Vidocq?"

Henri loved to talk about Vidocq, a criminal turned detective who had been the founder of the Sûreté in the days of the Second Republic.

"I'm sure his disguise would have been better."

"It couldn't have been much worse," said Gereau. "I spotted you there last night but decided you deserved to sit in the cold if you were determined to be an ass."

"I'm only doing what you refused to do," said Max, bitterly.

"And what is that? Investigate a crime that has already been solved?"

"You've caught Barzani's killers?"

Gereau glared at him. "Killer. Sergeant Bonnet tracked down the runaway doorman."

"And you have him in custody?" Max didn't ascribe to the police theories about the murder but the doorman must have seen something, maybe enough to identify the real killers.

"He's dead. He hanged himself in a hotel room. There was a note, confessing to the crime."

"How convenient. What did it say?"

"Enough to convince the Prefect of Police that Hevel Barzani was killed by a jealous lover – the aforementioned doorman."

"And you believe this?"

Gereau said nothing for several blocks. "Police work is no place for amateurs. They foul the scene and create no end of trouble for us and themselves. If I catch you at it again, I'll have you arrested."

"You didn't answer me."

Gereau turned his head and looked out the window.

"And what about Joachim ben David? Have his killers been caught as well? Or did the doorman confess to that as well?"

Gereau looked at him sharply. "Corporal, pull the car over and go have a smoke."

Gereau waited until he was well away from the car before turning back to Max.

"What do you know about that?"

Max looked at Gereau. The big man was leaning forward, his eyes hard and glittering but a gentle smile playing on his lips. Max was getting nowhere on his own; would get nowhere without an ally in the Prefecture. He told Gereau of his meeting with Joachim on the train and what he had seen in the Metro station. He pointed out the similarities in the method of their deaths.

"You are sure this Joachim was beaten. There was nothing in the report about it."

"The man who prepared his body for burial swears that he was."

"Does this man have a name?"

"Not one I'd care to share unless absolutely necessary. He fears for his life."

Gereau grunted and stroked his moustache. He leaned back in the car seat and took a deep breath, letting it out slowly in a low whistle. Max took out Joachim's letter and handed it to Gereau. The policeman read it several times before handing it back.

"He refers to two men but does not mention their names."

"I think one of them is André Bucard," said Max.

"I heard that bastard had been spotted around town. And the other?"

"I don't know who the other is. I've heard no other reference to him but I assume he is also part of the Black Cross. I heard they have friends in the Prefecture."

Gereau grunted again. "No doubt, but I'm not one of them. And Marois?"

"Philippe, I think." Max told him about the beating behind the church and how later he saw Barzani and Marois talking in the Lazare train station. "Barzani told me it had been staged to give

Marois an in with 'the others.' Bucard, the Black Cross or some gang connected to them. He wasn't clear."

"Your friend, Hevel, liked to play his cards close to his chest. Too close, it seems. I know this Marois. Not the best of men but not the worst either. Though clearly if Barzani was expecting Marois to protect him, he didn't get what he was paying for."

"I'd like to find out why."

"Is that who you were looking for, outside Lachance's place?"

"I'd seen him there before."

Gereau looked out the window again. The driver had almost finished his cigarette. A light rain had started to fall and the man kept glancing longingly at the car.

"All right. Sit in the rain if you like. But try to blend in better. I can ask the men in my division to ignore you but that's no guarantee that some sparrows won't give you trouble." He tapped on the window and gestured to the driver, who hurried over. "But if you spot either of these men, turn them over to the nearest gendarme. If, as you think, they have killed twice, they would not hesitate at a third." Gereau made no mention of the revolver in Max's room. Either he had forgotten or didn't want to plant the idea in Max's mind. *Too late*, thought Max.

As they pulled up in front of L'Aquilon, Gereau said, "This conspiracy mentioned in the letter. There may be something to it. We've heard rumours of certain men gathering in the city. Anarchists. Have you heard the name Emile Cottin?"

"No."

"If you do hear of him, if you hear anything about anarchists, you need to let me know." Gereau looked at him pointedly.

He suspects I've already heard something, thought Max. The anarchists he had met appeared clownish but Gereau honestly seemed to fear them. But Max didn't want to implicate Yesim.

Despite the man's behaviour, he still thought of him as a friend. He wasn't sure he felt that way about Gereau.

Minette was sitting on his bed when he walked into his room. Her face was pale, even more than usual, and her hair was damp from the rain. Her eyes were slightly red, as if she had been crying. She smiled when she saw him. She crossed the room, her long dress clinging to her slender form, and threw her arms around him. Their lips met and he held her like that for several long moments, their arms wrapped around each other and their mouths kissing hungrily. Her eyes were closed but Max kept his open. He was tense and wary after his talk with Gereau and he had seen her, not an hour before, leave the bar with another man. He broke the embrace before she did.

"What are you doing here?" he asked.

"Isn't it enough that I'm here?"

Max wanted it to be enough but it wasn't. He loved Minette but was unwilling to say so. Not yet, not while the death of Barzani hung over their lives.

"Jean-Marc let me in," she said. "He's a kind man although he's seems sad."

"He has suffered many losses." Jean-Marc had sent a note apologizing for not coming to Barzani's funeral; his nephew, dead from the flu, was being buried the same day.

"Yes. I hate being sad."

"Why are you here Minette? It's not as if you lack for company."

"Don't be cruel, Max." Minette turned away. "Those other men mean nothing to me. I need money and they give it to me."

Max felt his throat tighten so his voice came out almost as a growl. "Do you sleep with them?"

"No. That's why I'm here. The man I went with tonight, tried to force himself on me." She laughed. "I left him regretting the attempt."

"Why come here? Why not go home?"

"You mean that shabby room above the bar? With my garlic-eating uncle who does nothing but criticize me. I'd rather sleep on the street."

"Or here?"

"Yes. Why not? I know you would never make me do anything I didn't want. You're a good man."

"Maybe," said Max. "But I'm not a saint."

"No, not a saint," Minette said. She leaned against him again and he kissed her, long and hard and deep. His hands slid down her back and he pulled her to him. They stumbled to the bed and fell on it, their limbs entangled. He slid her skirt up her legs and until his fingers touched the top of her silk stockings and then moved to the silkiness of her skin.

"No, Max. Not now. Please."

He pulled away, his breath ragged, his face flushed and hot. She put her hands on his chest and he slid off her. Her legs were still bare and he could not help staring at them, at the softness of the flesh so white that a vein showed against it like a blue bruise. Minette tugged her dress down, from shame or something else. Max rolled on his back and lay on the bed, gasping, staring up at the cracks in the ceiling. She stroked his face, kissed him gently and whispered words against his cheek. "Je t'aime."

French may be the language of romance, thought Max, *but why do they use the same word for 'like' and 'love'?*

"I have to go," Minette stood and straightened her skirt. "Lachance expects me. He has some special clients coming by and they will want someone to dance with. All the other girls there have two left feet."

"Are their names Phillippe Marois and André Bucard?"

"The girls?" Minette laughed. "I don't know, Max. They don't always tell me their names. There was a man named Marois who came to the club a few times. But not recently."

"When can I see you again?"

"I'm always at La Coquette. You can see me anytime you like."

"Sure. Maybe I'll come by tomorrow."

"I'd like that." She slipped on a light coat and picked up her purse. "Get some sleep. You look tired."

Max watched her walk out without saying another word. He was tired, more tired than he had been since the worst days of the war. But Minette had left him anything but sleepy. Besides if Marois had come to La Coquette a few times there was always a chance he would come again.

Max changed his clothes, trading the coat for a bulky sweater. With one arm pinned up, he could be mistaken for one of many homeless veterans who wandered the streets of Montmartre, finding comfort where they could. He wrapped a scarf around the lower part of his face. Perhaps it would be enough to hide his identity, even from those who knew him well.

The revolver wasn't buried in the window box. Max felt a moment of panic. He was sure he had returned it to its hiding place. But, no, he only meant to do it. It was, he remembered, still in the drawer of his bedside table.

But it wasn't there either.

Twenty – Thursday, January 23 to Friday, January 24, 1919

The rain had stopped by the time he returned to La Coquette. It was nearly midnight but the party seemed to be barely starting. Music and light spilled onto the street from half opened windows. A line of men, and a few women, waited for admittance, though favoured clients simply breezed past them to the door. To keep the crowd happy, one of the white-clad waiters was distributing demi-glasses of beer and white wine.

Max shambled along the street, sticking out his hand to passers-by. A few pressed coins into his grubby palm but none would meet his eye. No one wanted to be reminded of the war when they were out to celebrate the peace. He would find someone who really needed them later. There was no shortage of hungry men.

He settled into the same doorway – it offered the best view – and placed his cap on the ground in front of him before leaning back into the shadows. It was cold; perhaps it would snow overnight. From time to time, he sipped brandy from the flask in his pocket, though whether for warmth or for courage, he couldn't say.

The missing gun bothered him. Had the thief who took the documents returned or had someone else taken it? Minette, perhaps. Was that the real reason for her visit? But how could she have known he even had a gun? He had been foolish to leave it where it could be found so easily. Anyone could have taken it—Jean-Marc or one of the hotel staff. In the wake of the war, Paris did not lack for guns but a revolver would still have brought a good price on the black market. Or was it something more sinister?

After an hour, a pair of swallows showed up and began yelling at the doorman, something about the noise and licenses. Max thought they might shut the place down but Sergeant Bonnet, in full uniform, suddenly emerged from the bar and took them aside. After a few minutes, they got back on their bikes and slowly peddled away. Bonnet stayed outside, laughing and bragging to whoever would listen, until Lachance came, put his arm around his shoulder and led him back inside.

Nothing much happened after that. People came and went but no one Max recognized. If Minette was there, he didn't see her. At one point, he thought he should try to find her and take her home, but he knew it was no good.

Despite the cold, he fell asleep. The lights were out in La Coquette and the street was empty, save for the tendrils of fog that hung on the corners of buildings. He was cold and stiff and it was an effort to stand. The metro had long ceased to run and there were no taxis to be found. He walked the few dozen blocks back to L'Aquilon and crept up the stairs to his room, unwilling to disturb the other guests by using the lift.

There was no one waiting in his room but his bed was warm and still smelled of Minette. He slept until the noon sun woke him.

§

For a change, Le Coq Bleu was crowded. Yesim was behind the bar pouring drinks and dishing up soup while an older man Max had never seen before delivered them to the crowded tables. Yesim glowered at him when he took a seat at the bar but gave no other indication that he recognized his presence. When the rush died down, Max called to him.

"I'd take a bowl of that soup and a glass of beer, when you've got a chance."

"We're out of soup," said Yesim, filling two bowls and passing them to the waiter.

"What the hell is wrong with you Yesim? Is it Minette?"

"Who?"

"Your niece."

Yesim filled several more bowls with thick steaming soup and slid them along the bar to newly arriving customers.

"That bitch doesn't live here anymore."

"I heard she left," said Max.

"Is that what you heard? I threw her out. I threw her clothes and her things into the street and then I threw her on top of them. Not that it took her long to find somewhere else to go."

"Did she move into La Coquette?" Like most clubs and shops in Paris, Lachance's place probably had a few rooms or apartments on the upper floors.

Yesim slammed a half-filled mug of beer down on the bar, shattering the glass. The pale-yellow beer mingled with blood on the bar top. Yesim swore, a long string of invective that brought a blush to several faces along the bar. He wrapped his hand in a dirty bar cloth and came to stand in front of Max.

"Don't play innocent with me," said Yesim. "I followed her last night to your hotel. I know all about it."

Max's own face flushed and anger tightened his belly. "Minette came to see me last night but she didn't stay."

"She was still there when I left."

"So what if she was? She's an adult. She can go where she wants." Max knew it was the wrong thing to say as soon as the words left his mouth.

"She was just a girl, until you showed up. I don't know what you did to her or why but I swear if you come in my place again, I'll kill you."

"I'm as worried about Minette as you are, Yesim."

"Like hell." Yesim pulled a knife from beneath the bar. His face twisted and his skin darkened. "Get out. Get out and don't come back." The bar was silent now, all faces turned toward the scene playing out at the bar. Max slipped off the stool and stood with his palms out.

"All right, I'll go. But we need to talk. I'll came back when you're calmer."

"That Henri must be a shitty teacher," said Yesim, loudly, playing to the crowd. "This stupid American can't understand the simplest things." He turned back to Max and pointed at him with the knife. "You ruined that girl, you and that dirty Turkish pervert. She was always wild but I kept her safe. But you taught her about..." His voice broke. "Oh, get out, get out, before I do something stupid."

Yesim threw the knife on the bar and went through the door that led to his upstairs rooms. As the door closed behind him, Max thought he heard Yesim begin to sob. Max stared at the door as the bar slowly came back to life. Then he left to look for Minette.

§

Roget blocked the door to la Coquette as Max tried to enter.

"Come back for another beating, Yankee?"

Max fingered the brass knuckles in his pocket. He had seen them in the window of a pawn shop as he walked through Montmartre, too upset to ride the Metro, and bought them on a whim. They didn't replace his missing gun but they would serve if Roget started something.

"Try me." Maybe there was something in his eyes or the tone of his voice, but Roget stepped out of the doorway and let Max pass. His shoulders tensed as he did, half expecting a sudden punch to his kidneys or the back of his head.

"Where's Lachance?"

"Having lunch with friends. He won't want to be—"

"Thanks," Max kept walking. Lachance had a large booth at the back of the restaurant where he held court. Lunch – a large salmon filet surrounded by fresh greens – was being served as Max walked up to the table. Lachance had three guests, two men and a woman. One of the men was François Bonnet; the other, Schmidt. Both Bonnet and Schmidt were wearing expensive dark suits. The woman was blonde and about forty, pretty except for the dark circles under her eyes. She clung to Schmidt as if she were afraid to let him go.

"Max. To what do we owe the pleasure?" He didn't ask him to sit down. Bonnet was smirking but Schmidt wouldn't meet his eyes. The woman looked worried.

"I'm looking for Minette."

"She didn't come back to work last night. I can give you the name of the man she left with, if you like? If you promise to be discreet—he's a good client." Lachance seemed to be enjoying himself.

"I wouldn't be so sure about that. I think Minette may have hurt him."

Lachance frowned. "Sometimes I wonder why I keep that girl around."

"If you're through with her," said Bonnet, "I'd be happy to take her off your hands."

"Careful, François, Max has already taken a swing at poor Roget for insulting Minette."

"Really! I thought he preferred boys." Bonnet sniggered. "Besides, it's one thing to swing at Roget—I'm an officer of the law."

"You're not in uniform now, Francoise." said Max, pronouncing it like a girl's name. Schmidt laughed and the woman nervously joined him. Bonnet's face flushed but he didn't get up.

"Max, I'm going to have to ask you to stop coming here if you insist on picking fights." Lachance was smiling but he didn't look happy. "You seem to know more about Minette's whereabouts than I do. If you see her, tell her the shipment arrived. She'll know what I mean."

"Maybe you can help me with something else," Max said.

"I like to be helpful," said Lachance, "but as the philosopher put it—what's in it for me?"

"I've been considering your offer."

Lachance glanced at his guests. He licked his thick lips and nodded. "Remember what I said about freshness. It would need to be tomorrow at the latest."

"I can do that," said Max though he had no intention of doing so. Lachance nodded again. "Do you know where I can find Philippe Marois? Or André Bucard?"

"What do you want with Bucard?" Bonnet twisted in his seat so he was facing Max. His hand slipped inside his jacket.

"I was going to say it was none of your business – but, on second thought, maybe it is." Max took a step closer and grasped the brass knuckles in his pocket. "Are you a member of the Black Cross?"

Bonnet took out a silver case and turned it over in his hand several times. He removed a cigar, examined it briefly before lighting it. He blew a cloud of smoke in Max's face. "You've been warned – several times I think – to stay out of police business. Don't become tiresome about it."

"I think it's time we left, Ilsa," said Schmidt. "We can conclude our business later, Eduard, when things are a little less – noisy."

"Nonsense, Rudolph. Max was just leaving. I haven't seen Marois for several weeks but he often stays at the Hotel Louvre on Rue St. Honoré. You can try him there." He turned his head away to indicate the conversation was over.

"And Bucard?"

Lachance shrugged. Max would get nothing more from him today. Bucard would have to wait; Marois was Max's target today.

§

Of course, nothing came easily. Marois had been at the hotel but he wasn't there at the moment. Max gave the desk manager fifty francs to send word the minute Marois returned. He gave him another fifty not to tell Marois he had been asking about him. Max stood outside the hotel and stared at the twin fountains in the square. This was where he had met Barzani the first time they went to the jazz club. Had it been a meeting with Marois that delayed Hevel that day?

Max hadn't realized how much time he spent at Le Coq Bleu until he was forbidden to go there. It had been his restaurant of choice, the place he went to think and see his only friends in Paris, unless he counted Buchan and Gereau. Weren't friends the people whose friendship you didn't have to ponder?

He walked over to La Gare du Nord. Henri was working a double shift but he found a few minutes between arrivals to share a coffee from the station café.

"I heard what Yesim did," Henri said. "I'm as shocked as you are."

"What does he think I did?"

"I'm not sure. Other than what two healthy young people often do when they have the chance. Though I can't think that's the problem. Yesim liked you. I don't think he was unhappy that Minette liked you too."

"He's plenty unhappy now. I suppose the loss of his nephews makes him afraid..."

"Nephews? Yesim has no nephews."

"But Minette said..."

"You must have misunderstood. I know she lost some good friends in the war but..."

"Then what is bothering Yesim?"

"He won't talk about it – as if he were embarrassed. He said he found something, something that disgusted him. But then he clammed up. Typical of him. Whatever it was though, he thinks you're connected. You and Barzani. Can you think why?"

Max shook his head. Yesim had said something but it eluded him. He had done nothing to warrant Yesim's anger, not even what healthy young people did when they had a chance.

"Well," said Henri. "Keep your distance. I'll work on him and see what can be done." When Henri went back to the platform, Max headed to L'Aquilon.

He stayed in his room, sorting through Barzani's things. The dozen suits appeared mostly unworn, although that may have only been Barzani's fastidious nature. He could sell them but he didn't need the money. They might fit Henri though he couldn't imagine the elderly porter in such fancy clothes. He hung them in his closet; Jean-Marc might know someone who could use them.

Barzani had an extraordinary collection of cufflinks; Max stopped counting at thirty pair. He set aside four to keep as souvenirs and determined to sell the rest, along with the numerous rings and two of the three watches – he had seen several jewellery shops with offers to buy in their windows. He would donate the proceeds; there were no shortage of charities that could benefit. He looked for the cigar case to include with the other jewellery but it was nowhere to be found.

There were a dozen books including copies of Don Quixote in Spanish, French and English. He added them to the library Henri had started to build for him.

He only went out to pick up half a roast chicken, some salad and a bottle of white wine from the rotisserie next door. He'd had no food since breakfast and he ate quickly but without pleasure. Max corked the bottle before it was half empty. He put it outside his window, as much to avoid temptation as to keep it cool. He needed to keep a clear head to think through the events of the last few days. He decided that the rest of Barzani's things – an assortment of shoes and a few mementos of his travels – could wait for another day.

No doubt Barzani had been involved in more than simple diplomacy. Though he was sure his friend had not been a bad man, he was a complex one—one for whom morality was not black and white and whose actions were determined by their contribution to his ultimate goals. Too many people had suggested that he was not above blackmail to achieve his ends for it not to be true. But, if so, who were his victims and what were they guilty of?

Bonnet's reaction to his mention of Bucard bothered him, too. Was he protecting the man? Had the doorman from L'Homme Fort – nothing now but a nameless refugee – committed suicide or had he, too, been murdered, another loose end tied up to keep a conspiracy from unravelling? Bonnet had sent him looking for Barzani in that club. Did he know what Max would find?

The first time he met Eduard Lachance, the man had nothing but contempt for Bonnet. Now they were eating expensive lunches together. Max retrieved his journal and flipped through it until he came to the page with the numbers and letters from the book in Lachance's office.

182212 AG 2000, 182812 FRB 10000, 190101 PAM 1200. If the first numbers were dates, the letters might be initials. AG could be Alphonse Gereau, FRB, François Bonnet and PAM, Phillippe Marois. The third numbers could be... time? The French used a twenty-four-hour clock but 10000 didn't work in any case. Bribes or payments for services rendered. Of course, he had no way of determining to whom the initials referred but he was willing to bet that Bonnet's middle name started with an R. It would go a long way to explain his newfound friendship with Lachance. Did that mean Gereau was on the take as well? Was that why he was so willing to accept Bonnet's explanation? One by one his friends and potential allies were slipping away.

He had taken this on. He would complete it. Alone if he had to – no matter what the cost. A tremor ran down his leg and Max placed his hand on his thigh to steady it. *No, I will not fail Barzani the way I failed my father. This time my courage will not falter.*

Lachance was the key to it all. Max had examined the eight-page document with the aid of an English-Italian dictionary. It made little sense but it at least confirmed that it was written in that language. It was no use to him without the codex Joachim had mentioned. It would probably be of little use to Lachance either but he was unlikely to know that until he got it translated. But until he figured that out, Lachance's good will might be invaluable in his search for Bucard.

Max read through his notes until nearly midnight, before giving in and drinking the rest of the wine. My reward, he thought, for having one good idea. He told the night desk to wake him if word came from the Hotel Louvre or at eight o'clock in any case. He was paying for breakfast and he thought he might as well eat it for a change.

Twenty-One – Saturday, January 25, 1919

The day dawned clear and unusually cold. Frost had sheeted his window, though the sun was slowly carving a landscape in the ice. His breath came in white clouds when he stuck his head out from beneath the heavy wool blankets. For a moment, he thought he was in his bed on his uncle's farm in Nova Scotia. Remembering that he was in a hotel in Paris, investigating a brutal murder, seemed a relief after that.

The buffet included a hot potato soup in addition to an assortment of breads, sweet pastries and hard cheeses. Max took a steaming bowl to his usual table in the corner. By now, everyone knew he was not worth talking to until his second cup of coffee and staff and guests left him to his thoughts, such as they were.

He stayed in the hotel lobby until past noon, reading the morning papers and waiting for some word of Marois' arrival. He decided to chance a quick trip to see Lachance and deliver the Italian document. He walked past several cabs parked near the hotel, until he spotted a driver who he had used before and whose skills he trusted. At La Coquette, he told the driver to wait for him.

"What is it?" Lachance asked, staring hungrily at the envelope.

"It was Barzani's. It's Italian. Eight pages. It looks formal somehow."

"Interesting. There were rumours of a secret treaty—" Lachance shut up.

Perhaps he's worried about driving up the price, thought Max.

"Of course, it is probably nothing important. The diplomatic equivalent of a laundry list."

"Naturally," said Max. "Why don't you examine it and tell me what you think?"

"You'd trust me?"

"Is there some reason I shouldn't?"

"I could give you a thousand francs—as a show of good faith." Lachance clearly wasn't used to being trusted.

"Sure."

Lachance peeled ten hundred-franc notes from a roll that looked large enough to buy a villa. His hand shook slightly as he handed them over but whether from regret at his offer or anticipation, Max couldn't tell.

"Come back tomorrow and we can settle up—one way or another. Maybe, if you come across anything else the thieves missed, you could bring it then."

Max shrugged noncommittally. After, he sat slumped in the back seat of the taxi and watched the front of La Coquette. Lachance appeared within minutes, bundled against the cold in a long brown leather coat and a dark wool hat. Roget followed and the two of them got in the front seat of a waiting car and headed towards Place du Clichy. Max tapped the driver on the shoulder and he pulled away from the curb and followed at a distance of half a block. The car turned west on Batignolles. At Phalsbourg it turned left, passed through the Parc de Monceau before stopping in front of a three-story stone house surrounded by a high wall. Lachance got out of the car and went into the house. Roget kept driving. Max made a note of the address.

"Do you want me to follow the car?" asked the driver, clearly amused at being conscripted into the detective business.

"No," said Max. "Take me back to where you picked me up."

A bellhop was waiting in the lobby of L'Aquilon when Max arrived. He was clutching a note in one hand and had a determined expression on his face.

"He wouldn't leave the note—said it was for your eyes alone. Like a secret courier!" said Jean-Marc, smiling. The whole city was caught up in the air of intrigue surrounding the treaty negotiations, although Max suspected that expectation of a generous tip had as much to do with the boy's doggedness as anything else.

Max didn't disappoint. The boy clutched the ten-franc bill in his hand and scurried back to his duties at the Hotel Louvre. Marois was back. He had returned to his room and asked not to be disturbed. Max retrieved his knife and brass knuckles from his room.

Marois's room—or rather rooms—were on the third floor of the Louvre. The desk manager had been reluctant to let Max go up alone, despite Max's insistence he was Marois' long-lost cousin from America. Another fifty francs convinced him. Fifty more got a promise of privacy.

The hotel had been recently renovated, its halls carpeted in thick plush and the walls papered in the latest Art Nouveau designs. Max rapped sharply on the door and then stood to one side so Marois couldn't see him through the spy hole. He might not remember the man who cut him on that November night, but Max was taking no chances.

"Who is it?" Marois' voice was surprisingly soft.

"Telegram for Phillippe Marois."

"Who's it from?"

"No name," said Max. "Initials EL."

After a brief hesitation, the locks whispered open and the latch was turned. Max threw his full weight against the door, smashing into the man on the other side and knocking him to the floor. Max stood over Marois, his knife in his right hand and the brass bar settled over his left knuckles.

"What the..."

"Shut up," said Max, pushing the door closed with his foot, never taking his eyes off Marois' chest. Where the chest goes, his hockey coach used to say, the man is sure to follow. "Stay down with your hands where I can see them."

Marois hadn't been expecting company. He was dressed in a singlet and a pair of loose brown trousers, cinched at the waist with a leather belt. His feet were bare and his hair had the rumpled look of sleep, but his eyes were sharp. The wound on his arm had healed although the fresh scar was pink beneath the thick hair that covered his forearm. That seemed to be his distinguishing feature; thick hair sprouted on his arms and shoulders and stuck out in unruly patches from the thin cloth that covered most of his chest. The growth on his face couldn't quite be called a beard but it was only a day or two away. By contrast, his pate gleamed from beneath a wispy layer of dark strands.

Marois had his eyes fixed on Max's face as trying to place him from among the many enemies he had undoubtedly accumulated over the years. Occasionally, they flicked to the sitting room's large sofa. An open valise, its contents mostly scattered on the floor, was splayed open like fish at the market. Max sidled toward it and afforded it a glance. A small revolver nestled among the pile of underwear. Max dropped the knuckles back in his pocket and scooped it up.

"Careful with that," said Marois, coolly. "It has a hair trigger."

"I'll keep that in mind."

"Who are you? A cop?"

"I'll ask the questions," said Max.

Marois shrugged. "Mind if I get more comfortable?"

Max shoved the valise onto the floor and gestured for Marois to sit on the sofa. Through the double doors of the bedroom, the bed was dishevelled but empty. No light shone from the bathroom' open door. Max took a chair against the wall of the sitting room where he could see Marois and both the door to the hall and the double doors that led to the bedroom.

"My smokes are on the table," said Marois. Max put his knife away and tossed them over. If he was nervous having a gun pointed at him it didn't show in his hands. The cigarette was dark, almost black, and the smoke seemed especially acrid.

"Do you know Eduard Lachance?"

"Why should I answer your questions?"

Max decided to see how much privacy fifty francs bought. The little gun made a popping sound and a hole appeared in the cushion beside Marois. The man flinched though it clearly grieved him to do so.

"You make a good argument," he said.

"I can be more pointed if you like," said Max. The anger he had been carrying for nearly two weeks burned hot in him. He felt he could do anything now.

"I'm acquainted with Lachance. I've occasionally done some work for him."

"Does that include breaking into hotel rooms?" Marois's initials—or so Max assumed—had also been in Lachance's book.

"It has. Although not recently. Do you have a particular room in mind?"

"I ask, you answer. Remember."

Marois nodded. He took another long drag on his cigarette.

"What else do you do for him?" When Marois hesitated, Max took out his knife. "I don't have to shoot you. I could cut you again."

"Lachance's secrets aren't worth bleeding for. I brought a package from Marseille around New Year. He paid me 1200 francs. I was fine until I found out what was in it. I told him we were done." Marois' brow furrowed. "Hey, did he send you? Is he worried I'm going to snitch?"

"No. What was in the package?"

"Heroin."

That would explain what Schmidt was doing at Lachance's table. If he couldn't get what he wanted from the Chinaman, maybe Lachance was his new supplier. Or maybe Schmidt was supplying Lachance. It all started to make sense now. Henri had told him that Montmartre had changed during the war, transforming from a village of windmills and art studios into a hideaway for gangsters and drug dealers. The fever in the dozens of new clubs that had opened was fuelled by more than alcohol. There was something else, too. Whatever it was could wait.

"Do you know a man named André Bucard?"

"I've met him a couple of times. In Marseille. And not long ago at a big party at Lachance's club—what's it called?"

"La Coquette." Bucard *was* the man he had seen go off with Lachance and Marois that night. "And later?"

Marois lit a second cigarette from the embers of the first. The air was starting to turn blue. It seemed hot in the room. Sweat run down Max's sides.

"Bucard doesn't take kindly to people digging too deeply into his affairs," said Marois. There was a tremor in his voice. *He's more afraid of an absent Bucard than of the gun I'm holding in my hand.*

"But you have seen him?" When Marois didn't answer, the little revolver popped again and another hole appeared in the sofa, an inch from Marois's leg.

"That's not funny."

"How many bullets does this gun hold?" Max wondered how long he had before someone called the police. The gun wasn't loud but anyone standing the hall would hear it.

"Five. Why?"

"I want to know how many more arguments I can make before I have to kill you. Bucard?"

"I saw him last night. He sent me to Italy a couple of weeks ago. I took a bundle of letters and received a package in return. And no,

I don't know the contents of either of them. But the package was heavy. Guns, maybe."

"Were you still working for Hevel Barzani at the time?"

Marois spent several seconds staring at the glowing end of his cigarette. He took another pull on it before answering. "Now that name I don't know."

"Really?" Max contemplated firing the gun a third time. He let his thoughts show on his face.

"Well, maybe I've heard it. He was a player, right? We never crossed paths."

"I was the one who cut your arm that night," said Max.

"I see," said Marois. "I was hoping to meet you again. Though in different circumstances."

"What did Barzani hire you to do?"

"Ask him."

The gun popped again. Marois jerked and clutched his left bicep. Blood seeped between his fingers.

"You shot me."

"I did. I can again. Twice." Max was more shaken than Marois, though he tried not to let it show. He had meant the bullet for the sofa but had missed. He was lucky the bullet hadn't hit bone. Max had been almost sure that Marois had been involved in Barzani's murder. Now he didn't know. *And what would I do if I was sure?*

"You said Barzani was a player. You must know that he's dead."

"Yes. All right. I thought maybe you were trying to pin it on me. But I didn't do it. We were working on the same side."

"I heard you would work on whatever side paid you."

"True enough," said Marois, almost smiling despite the pain in his arm. "But not this time."

Marois was bleeding slowly but steadily onto the sofa. The manager had promised to keep the maids off the floor for half an hour but someone in the next room might be trying to sleep off a drunk. Max tossed Marois his handkerchief.

"Why should I believe you?" Though, for some reason, he did believe him. Maybe because he thought Gereau and Barzani were better judges of character than the two Jacques. Maybe it was Marois' coolness under fire. Maybe it was the self-deprecating smile. "Tell me what you did for Barzani?"

Marois twisted the handkerchief around his bicep to slow the bleeding. "That's two scars to your credit," he said, though his voice held no rancour.

"Barzani came to me a couple of months ago. Right after the armistice was signed. Everyone knew the treaty conference would be here. France had suffered the most and France deserved the honour of settling the war. People were coming from all over the world. A lot of them carried the animosity of the ages."

"I know all this," said Max. "What did Hevel want?"

"I could tell you that but you wouldn't necessarily understand. Have you ever been out to the banlieues—the suburbs beyond the old fortifications? No? They call them the red belt and not only because of the endless monotony of brick they use to build everything. The twenty arrondissements are old Paris; they are the new. Parisians don't understand that and if they did, they wouldn't like it.

"Old Paris—and it is old, old buildings, old money, even old people—is broken. They cling to the past the way a baby clings to its blanket. But the past is gone and all it represents is gone with it. No one believes the lies of La Belle Epoque. We can't all be happy little consumers; most Parisians never were. They were like urchins with their noses pressed to the window of a restaurant while the privileged few stuffed their faces. The masses no longer believe in the liberal dream. They no longer believe in the protection of the law or the benevolence of the state. If they still believe in democracy, it is not the democracy of reasoned debate. It is the democracy of the clenched fist and the marching parade; the democracy of bullets and barricades. The red belt? They should call it the red noose."

"And which side are you on in this impending revolution?"

Marois laughed. "Whichever side pays me most. Isn't that what they say about me? You think there are only two sides? That would be simple. No, there are dozens of sides—not only the home-grown French ones but all the ones brought here from all over Europe, from our colonies, from the far-flung corners of the world. All hoping to have their dreams fulfilled. Even America has its dreams about Paris."

"Barzani told me the beating was staged."

"True—although I don't think he knew how dangerous it was. The men I was with... it was fortuitous you came by when you did. Have you always been the hero type?"

"Don't call me that." Max didn't think there was anything heroic about pointing a gun at another man—especially an unarmed and now wounded one.

"Suit yourself. His plan worked though. He had heard some rumours. You know he was working for the Zionists."

"I thought he worked for Faisal."

"Him, too, but only as an afterthought. I mean, he was like me, he worked for whoever paid him but he seemed particularly loyal to Weizmann. Sometimes I wondered if he was a secret Jew."

"He was Kurdish."

"The Kurds were converted to Islam in the twelfth century. Before that they had a multitude of faiths—including Judaism. Conversions sometimes don't take."

"Seven centuries is a long time to hide your faith." Maybe this was what had drawn Barzani to Marois; they both had a love of esoteric conspiracies. *In other circumstances*, thought Max, *this man would make an interesting friend.*

"The Jews are a patient people. Who knows? Maybe Barzani simply favoured the underdog. In any case, he heard a rumour of a rumour. An attack on some of the delegates, maybe even some of the leaders. Whether as a political statement or a genuine attempt to stop the conference wasn't clear. He feared Weizmann was the target."

"Was he?"

"Maybe. Something is going to happen but what? I don't know. At least not exactly. And now that Barzani's dead, I don't think I want to know the details."

"I thought this time was different. Doesn't Barzani deserve justice?"

"What does he need me for? He has you. Besides, our goals were shared but not identical. Barzani was complex. He still believed in the future; still believed in the perfectibility of man. I wanted to know what Bucard was planning. If I had to pick between one thing and another, my sympathies would be in the banlieues. Give me a worker's paradise over the jackboot any day."

Max wasn't convinced of the difference. Everyone seemed to think paradise was making other people think the way they did. Religion, politics, family—it was all the same to him.

"And did beating up Barzani get you what you want? Access to Bucard and the Black Cross?"

"Close enough to count. Close enough to learn there is a plan."

"And what is he planning?"

"Nothing as simple as a thrown grenade and a politician gunned down in the street. That will happen but it won't be Bucard. He's playing a longer game. I suspect he wants the conference to succeed, rather than fail. The compromises they'll be forced to make will inevitably make things worse rather than better. Bucard and his friends in Italy—and Germany too—feel they can wait. When it all goes to hell, the people will do what they always do, turn to a strong man to save them. Don't forget, twenty years after the revolution declared the equality of man, the French crowned Napoleon Emperor."

"I thought he crowned himself."

"While the people roared their approval," said Marois.

"You don't think Bucard killed Barzani," said Max.

"I didn't say that. He would kill anyone who got in his way. But the murder itself—it feels wrong. Too elaborate. Too symbolic. The exact kind of murder you would expect from the Black Cross. It's how I would have done it if I wanted to point the finger at Bucard."

"Except it didn't work."

"No, it didn't, did it? Find out why and you might find your killer. I told you I don't know all the details but I do know this. There will be an attack – maybe even two. There's that much turmoil in the city. For myself, I think it will be a bigger target than Weizmann – the American President, maybe – but I'm only guessing. But I do know this much. It will happen between the 10th and 20th of February. Not before or not after. As for me, I'm leaving town until it's all over. That is, if I'm free to go."

Max considered it. Barzani had put his life into Marois' hands. Gereau probably had it right. The man might not have been the servant of justice Hevel claimed to be seeking but he probably wasn't the servant of the devil either.

"You can go. But I'm keeping the gun." He'd rather have his service revolver back but this one would do in a pinch.

"Fine by me. I don't like the things anyway. There's a box of shells in the side pocket of the suitcase."

Max shoved the revolver in his pocket and retrieved the shells. He dropped five hundred francs on the floor. "To pay for the sofa."

Marois lit another cigarette and examined his bandaged arm.

§

After Max left Marois, he went back to L'Aquilon. He felt sick. Feverish. He had shot men before, killed men. But never so coldly. He feared he would have to do worse before he was done. He shivered. This was changing him. But that was a matter for another day. He hid Marois' gun in the old place in the window box and recorded the details of their conversation in his journal.

The conference would start again in the morning. It made sense that the danger would escalate when delegates gathered—although presumably that would be when the police would be most on guard. Still, he should tell Buchan what he had heard.

Max suddenly realized that he was making progress. He knew what was driving Barzani—that alone could help narrow the list of suspects. And he had removed both Buchan and Marois from that list. He wasn't convinced about Bucard but at least Marois had given him a different way of thinking about it. Maybe that was why his head was aching.

Buchan was in his usual spot in the Gentleman's Lounge when Max got to his hotel. He was deep in conversation with two bespectacled young men, who despite the differences in height and hair colour, were twins in the seriousness of their expressions. Buchan waved them away when he saw Max approaching across the bar.

Max was still a few paces away when he suddenly stumbled, black dots dancing across his vision. Buchan leapt up although it seemed he was moving in slow motion. Max's stomach knotted. Bile rose in his throat and then spilled down his shirt.

"Max! Max, are you okay?" His voice sounded like it was coming from the bottom of the ocean.

The carpet was rushing up to meet him. Then nothing.

Twenty-Two – Wednesday, February 5 to Thursday, February 6, 1919

Gentle whorls of plaster floated above his head. The bed was soft, a wide down-filled mattress that cupped his body like a hand holding an egg. The sheets were soft and smelled faintly of roses. The blanket that reached halfway up his pyjama-clad chest was blue. Not a hospital then.

He lay without moving for a long time, simply breathing. It felt good to breathe. He must have slept again because the light had shifted. The sun felt warm against his face. He blinked several times and tried to move his head. After a while, he was able to turn it to the right. Henri was sitting in a chair by the window, reading.

"Henri," Max said. Or, at least, that's what he tried to say. It was enough.

"The sleeper awakes," said Henri. He picked up a glass from the bedside table and held it to Max's lips. It was cool and sweet. Henri fed him a bigger drink. "Slowly. You've been sick with the influenza."

The room was small; the bed, table and window-side chair almost filled it. The walls were covered in floral wallpaper in shades of cream, green and pink. There were half a dozen dolls lined up on the window box.

"This is my house," said Henri. "This was my daughter's room."

"I didn't know you had a daughter." His voice croaked but at least the words were words.

"She died when she was twelve. My wife never would let me change... Well, you're welcome to it now."

"How did I…" Max remembered then. He had been on his way to see Buchan, to warn him of the possible attack on the conference. "What day is it?"

"Wednesday."

"The 29th?"

"The 5th of February," said Henri. "Nearly sixteen hundred."

"What!" Max tried to sit up but the sheets and blankets held him in place.

"Take it easy," said Henri. "You've been very sick. We almost lost you twice."

"I need to see Buchan. And Gereau."

"I know," said Henri. "You called for them many times. You talked a great deal. Most of it made no sense at all. The kind of things people say when they're delirious. And some things you said – about Minette in particular – probably don't bear repeating in polite company. But you were very clear about wanting to see the American and Captain Gereau. They both came several times. As did Minette and Jean-Marc and others from the hotel and even Jake, who came to Barzani's funeral. We took turns watching over you, after the doctors decided you weren't going to die. They released you, a week ago tomorrow, from the American Hospital, where Monsieur Buchan took you when you collapsed."

"I need to warn them."

"You said that over and over – but about what, well, it was all jumbled up. I could never make sense of it, though Gereau took plenty of notes. He told me to contact him as soon as you were sensible again."

Max's face was beaded with sweat but he didn't feel fevered or nauseated. Images came in flashes. Nurses in white gowns and masks, trying to get him to drink. Other faces, Henri and Minette, Buchan and Gereau, their eyes worried above pale gauze. The smell of antiseptic replaced with the odour of rosewater. Soup. Chicken soup.

"I'm hungry," he said.

"I'm not surprised. You could keep down nothing but water for a week and since then, only a little juice and chicken broth."

"I'd have more of that. And maybe a cracker or two."

Henri nodded and turned to go.

"Oh, and Henri," said Max, "You're a good friend."

Max had lost ten days while events whirled around him. *There is so much over which I have no control. The influenza no less than the war, no less than the intrigues of great powers. It's time I took control of the things I can and let the rest go to the devil.*

§

Buchan came first thing in the morning; Gereau was in meetings but promised to visit right after lunch. Max was sitting propped up in bed. He had been able to eat a soft-boiled egg and a piece of toast and drink a small glass of pomegranate juice. He had even walked to the privy in the back yard though he needed Henri's help to get back. He had lost the ten pounds he had gained since moving to Paris and ten more besides, if the fit of his trousers was any indication.

"You gave me quite a turn," said Buchan, perching on the edge of the chair and turning his hat around in his hands. "You fell flat on your face on the carpet and proceeded to empty an entire day's meals on the floor."

"Don't remind me." He was no longer sick but his stomach was still sensitive.

"Sorry," said Buchan. "What was all that about Barzani plotting to kill President Wilson? Or Minette – that's the girl who was here, right? – running off with Prince Faisal? And those were the most sensible of the things you said."

Max blushed, though he could hardly be held to account for the ravings of a fevered mind. He told Buchan of his meeting with Marois and especially of his fears of an attack on Wilson between the 10th and the 20th of February.

"We keep the President under pretty close wraps but I'll warn Colonel House to heighten security. Those dates bother me, though. Faisal presents his views to the Conference Sunday afternoon. The 9th. The Zionists, around the 20th or a few days later. Those dates are also critical for President Wilson although I'm not at liberty to say why."

"Isn't that what Barzani wanted?" Max said. "For the issues of the Levant to have centre stage for as long as possible?"

"I have no idea what Hevel Barzani wanted. Only what you told me," said Buchan. "Officially, I don't care. The United States was never at war with the Ottoman Empire. It will be up to the French and British, and the Italians, if they can hold it together. Settling Europe is our focus now – the Turks will have to wait."

"Faisal and Weizmann were counting on American support – if left to the Europeans, nothing will change."

"The United States has no interest in the Middle East and, unless we can pry the oil concessions in Iran out of British hands, never will. You have to understand, Max, there are forces at home who want to shut the door on the whole world. That's why President Wilson has to go... well, look at the time. I better let you get some rest."

"Sure. Maybe I'll come and see you when I'm up and around. I must owe you something for the hospital stay."

"Yeah. I'd like to say it was covered but my expense account is getting a little stretched. I'll send the bill to your hotel if that's okay. This has to be the last time we talk. And, Max, don't forget about the Reds. They would do anything, kill anyone, to get what they want. Barzani included."

§

Max slept most of the rest of the morning though he woke for a light lunch of chicken salad on a baguette and a few slices of melon. He was determined that he would not fall back into his old eating habits. A detective should be fit, not fat. *Is that what I am now, a detective?* He had coffee for the first time in two weeks and it left him energized though a bit shaky. By the time Gereau arrived, he was dressed and waiting in Henri's small living room.

"You're looking better," said Gereau.

"I understand it would be hard for me to look worse."

Gereau, on the other hand, looked as if he had aged several years. There were dark circles under his eyes and his mouth seemed set in a permanent frown.

"I've seen Marois," said Max.

"So have I."

"Then he told you about the planned attack on the conference."

"He wasn't very talkative." Max felt a sudden chill run up his spine. Gereau was staring at him intently. "Why don't you tell me?"

Max outlined his conversation with Marois, from his political analysis to his predictions about an attack on the American President.

"Did he tell you this before or after you shot him?"

Max blushed. He had hoped that Marois would keep that part of their meeting to himself. "After," he said.

Gereau raised his eyebrows at that. "Then you're a better interrogator than I am."

"I don't understand."

"I saw Marois in the city morgue on the morning of the 25th. He had been shot twice in the head. With two .445 calibre rounds."

Another death. Max shook his head, first in anger then in denial. His gun had been a Webley .445. *Gereau thinks I did it.*

"He was alive when I left him," said Max. "I shot him in the arm."

"That explains why he was shot with two different guns. Where did you get the pea-shooter?"

"I took it from Marois."

"We'll want to see it downtown. At your convenience. More importantly, where is your revolver?"

"I don't know. It was taken from my room a few days, I mean, weeks ago now." He had meant to report it to the police but events had overtaken him. There was no proof that Marois had been shot with his gun. But men had been convicted on less. "Where was the body found?"

"In his room in the Hotel Louvre."

"I didn't kill him. I can't even say why I shot him."

"Given how sick you were a few hours later... you might be forgiven for not being in control. But know this. If I thought you had killed him, we wouldn't be having this discussion in a Montmartre rowhouse. Gunfire was reported shortly before four in the morning on the 25th. The body was still warm when they kicked down the door. Fully dressed with a packed suitcase beside it. By that time, you were fighting for your life in the American Hospital in Neuilly-sur-Seine – not even technically in the city."

Hevel Barzani, Joachim ben David and now Phillippe Marois. One murderer or three? Max found it hard to believe there was no connection but he was hard pressed to see what it was.

"Do you have any suspects?"

"More than usual," Gereau sighed. "As Marois said, the city is full of factions. And now it's also full of firearms and foreigners. I can think of a dozen people who might want to kill Marois – from jealous husbands to political rivals. Marois had a habit of pricking conservatives' balloons but he had plenty of foes on the left, too, some of whom wouldn't have been sorry to see him dead." Gereau paused. "I suppose it doesn't hurt now that he's dead. And you might find it useful in your inquiries – if you haven't given up that foolishness. He was a useful informant on anarchist activity. I never dealt with him personally but he gave the Prefecture several tips that thwarted plots both before and during the war. If that was uncovered..."

Gereau was being generous with his knowledge. Did he want to prove the Prefecture wrong about Barzani's death or did he have a different, less noble, motive? Max didn't care. "What about Lachance? Marois claimed they had a falling out. Over heroin."

"I heard those rumours – I'm not so old that I can't follow a clue. Lachance and his man, Roget, both have alibis for the night. Not iron-clad but good enough to keep them on the streets."

"Especially given his connections," said Max.

"You're a fast learner," said Gereau, grimly.

Max thought of the notation in Lachance's book. 182212 AG 2000. "Have you ever taken money from Lachance?"

Gereau's face flushed and he stood up and stepped forward, towering over Max. Then he sighed and sank back in his chair

"It's been offered often enough. But no, I never have. In that, I'm no different than most of my colleagues."

"But not all?"

"I'd be a fool to say otherwise. What made you ask?"

Max told him about his visit to Lachance's office.

"Well, there are plenty of people with the initials AG in Paris. But I can tell you this – Marois's middle name was Alexandre; Bonnet's, Robert."

Twenty-Three – Saturday, February 8, 1919

By Saturday, Max's appetite had returned and his strength was approaching normal. It would take a few weeks for his muscles to recover their strength but his cuts and bruises had healed. More importantly, his leg felt better than it had since he had been wounded. He moved back to L'Aquilon after one final breakfast – a herb and cheese omelet, firm in his vow to eat more moderately and exercise more. Henri had refused to take any money, despite having missed several shifts at the train station, but Max was determined to find a way to make it up to him.

Barzani's belongings were as he had left them, in three rough piles in the middle of the floor. His hiding places seemed undisturbed. Marois' gun was where he had left it. Max reloaded it and slipped it into his pocket. Until Barzani's killer was caught, he'd want more than a pocketknife for defense.

Gereau had provided him with the names and addresses of several Kurds. Max didn't tell the policeman that anarchists had suggested that line of questioning – he wasn't sure if their developing relationship would stand that particular test. Gereau had made the round of the Arab neighbourhood after Barzani's death – on an "unofficial basis, of course" – but thought Max might get more out of them than he had. "Foreigners had a natural fear of the police, but a Canadian might be different," he had said.

Max wasn't sure where this line of questioning might lead him but until he could track down Bucard and Joseph Asper – who had vacated his old quarters – they would have to do.

The first Kurd refused to open the door more than inch even when Max showed him a fifty. That inch closed rapidly when Max mentioned Barzani's name. The second address wasn't much more helpful though the offered bribe granted him entrance, at least into the front hallway of the small flat. The man who answered the door was short, thick and quite swarthy with dark hair and beard. His face was heavily lined though more from sun and wind than from age. He spoke French with a heavy but understandable accent. No one else was visible in the hall but the low murmur of feminine voices and the laughter of children from another room.

"I knew him – Rahimahulla – though not well," said the man, whose name was Fersad. "I saw him at mosque from time to time though not as often as I should have."

"He travelled a great deal."

"Now he travels with Allah. I have little to say that I didn't already tell the Captain of police."

"Did you know him before you came to Paris?"

Fersad scratched his fingers through his beard. "I was told he came from Tehran. I've never been to Tehran."

"He was born near Mahabad. He was called Hajim Bahrami then."

"Bahrami from Mahabad?" Fersad's thick black brows crawled up his forehead. "Wait a minute." He went into the back of the flat and spoke in a high lilting language. When he returned, he was smiling.

"My second wife – her elder brother married a woman from Mahabad. According to Tatane, my wife, the woman's cousins were called Bahrami. My brother-in-law, Lolo Sayid, also lives in Paris, a very successful rug merchant in the 13th arrondissement. His shop is on La Reine Blanche. He lives over it." Fersad handed Max a scrap of paper where he had written the name, address and the words: Very finest rugs! He refused an offer of more money.

Lolo Sayid was not on the list of names provided by Gereau. Though Barzani never spoke of family or friends. Max thought it worthwhile to check on this possible cousin. The 13th arrondissement had been home to Paris's Arab community for more than a generation and the center of the textile industry for centuries.

Sayid might sell the very finest rugs but the exterior of the shop was, like most of the neighbourhood, run-down and dirty. Soot clung to the stone facade and filmed the windows grey. The only splash of color came from the brightly painted sign over the iron-barred door. The interior, however was sparking clean and lit by numerous electric lights. Carpets of various sizes hung from every wall. Many more were stacked in pyramidal piles on either side of the wide shop. Sayid, a wiry man of about forty-five, was dressed in an expensive suit of the latest style. He was talking to a pair of assistants – a dark-skinned man and a blonde woman – when Max entered. He clapped his hands and they scurried away so their boss could greet the potential customer with a broad smile and extended hand.

Like most of the Kurds he had met, Sayid had a heavy beard and thick eyebrows but his head was completely bald, polished to a shine that competed with his brown leather shoes for brilliance.

"Welcome to Lolo's – very best carpets in Paris. Guaranteed!" Sayid said, pumping Max's hand enthusiastically.

Max hated to disappoint the man but he didn't want to waste his time either. "I'm not really in the market for carpets, Mr. Sayid. At least not today."

Sayid's grin faded. "If you're here from that so-called 'business association,' I'm still not interested."

"Nothing like that," said Max. "It's about your wife."

Sayid bristled. "My wife is not your concern."

"I'm sorry," said Max. "I'm going about this the wrong way. Your brother-in-law, Fersad, sent me to see you. I went to see him to ask about my friend, Hevel Barzani, and he told – "

"My wife's unfortunate second cousin – Rahimahulla – you were his friend?" Sayid looked troubled. "I saw the notice of his funeral in the paper but, given the circumstances, I couldn't be seen."

Even his own family believed the lies. "I have every reason to believe that Hevel was murdered by men determined not only to destroy his life but also his reputation and memory. Your wife's cousin was a very good man."

"With Allah's blessing, I hope so. I have every reason to think so. I certainly do not believe he was a shaz, if that is what troubles you. But what did you want from me? A contribution to the funeral?"

Max was beginning to doubt the value of his trip across the city.

"I don't want money," he said. "I need information. Anything you can tell me might help find his killers."

Sayid searched Max's face for several long moments. He must have found what he was looking for. "What can I do to help?"

"Did Hevel ever visit you? Particularly during the last few months."

"I saw him twice last year," said Sayid. "For the two festivals of Eid. That would be the end of June, Eid-ul-Fitr, and about mid-September, Eid-al-Adha. I remember both very clearly. The former because he had recently returned from a trip to Palestine and was brimming with excitement; the latter because he provided us with a very fine ram for the feast. My wife said he also dropped by on my son's twelfth birthday in November but, unfortunately, I was ill and unable to see him. We did not live in each other's pockets but we were family."

"Did he ever talk about his work?"

"Not often. He was a man who could talk for hours, seeming to unburden his soul but, after, you realized he had told you nothing you didn't already know. I sometimes thought he was too clever by half. Still, once in a while, when the hookah had been passed a few times, he would open up. Not bragging really – 'thinking big thoughts out loud' was how Raman, my son, put it."

"Did he ever mention Faisal or Weizmann?"

"Mention them! He gave a discourse. Told how he helped bring them together and, I remember, this funny story of how Faisal insisted on taking a photograph – with Faisal looking all fierce and warrior-like and Weizmann, dressed as an Arab, barely able to keep a straight face. That was at the end of Ramadan. But later at Eid-al-Adha, things weren't so funny. He was clearly worried but he laughed and joked and handed out gifts to the whole family – and half the neighbours, too. But, late that night, when everyone else had gone to bed, he said to me, 'Lolo, all my family – father, mother, brothers – are gone. Nasik and you and Raman are all I have left.' Then he handed me an envelope and, inside it, Allah be praised, was one hundred thousand francs."

"Did he tell you what it was for?"

"He said it was our inheritance. Something about wanting to do it now when he had the money. Then he said something that chilled me. He told me that he was involved in a dangerous game and that if things went wrong, he would not want anyone to know how much he loved us. He would not name us in his will. I think he felt we could not defend ourselves. I suppose he was right. Those were the circumstances that kept me from his funeral."

"Did he tell you what this game was?"

"Not in detail but he told me there was a plot to kill Faisal and Weizmann before they could present to the conference. And that he had found a way – a back door he called it – to get at the plotters."

Max supposed Barzani had meant Marois. That door was closed now.

"Prince Faisal is scheduled to speak at the Conference tomorrow," said Max. "But Weizmann won't be with him."

Sayid shrugged. "I don't know what else to say. Perhaps if I had seen him in November he would have told me more."

"Thank you for your time," said Max. "I'm glad to know that Hevel had people he loved."

"And who loved him," said Sayid. "But I think we were not the only ones."

"Really? Who else?"

"I have no name for you. It is something my son told me. He's only twelve but he's very smart. Hevel was very... effervescent and Raman asked him if he had a girlfriend. Apparently, Hevel laughed and said no but that maybe it was exactly what he needed. A pretty little French wife."

"That's an interesting way to put it."

"Yes, I thought so. But it was so like him. He was a loving man but not a passionate one. Everything for him was calculated. He never married because he never saw the advantage to do so. If he now sought a wife, it would only be to advance his larger goals."

§

Max took lunch at a small café only a few blocks from Sayid's shop. He was less attracted by the food than the location – right across the street from the opium den whose address he had given Schmidt. The streets between Les Gobeleins textile factories and the Pantheon – home to France's honoured dead – turn on themselves like a nest of snakes. It was here the Chinaman had settled after being pushed out of the cellar of Chez Jacob.

It was too much to hope that Schmidt would make an appearance but he had to eat anyway and his luck today had been good. Sayid had revealed little of Barzani's work but much about the man himself. Barzani had asked Minette to marry him and seemed hurt when she refused. But, if Sayid was right, that may have been an act. Was Minette the pretty French wife Barzani was pursuing and, if so, what advantage did he see in their marriage? Max doubted it was closer ties to Yesim but it was something he would have to ask his former friend.

Luck, both good and bad, often comes in clusters. Max was paying his bill when he spotted Victor, Schmidt's bodyguard. He had his coat collar drawn up and his hat pulled low but those shoulders were hard to miss. He was wary to the point of being furtive, his head moving in quick jerks as he tried to watch everything at once. The street was bright and narrow but the café was dim and Max was sure he couldn't be seen. Victor walked past the den, glanced around one more time and doubled back to the door. Max slipped out of the café and found a doorway where he could see the entrance. He had barely settled into cover when Victor reappeared. He took another look around and then began walking briskly back the way he had come.

Max doubted he was doing a very good job at tailing but it seemed, having accomplished his mission, Victor had lost all sense of caution. He marched along without a single glance back until he reached the Saint Marcel station. Max nearly lost him there, leaping on the train Victor boarded even as the doors slid shut. At each stop, Max stuck his head out the door until he spotted his quarry detrain at Oberkampf. Victor hurried up the stairs and walked briskly for several blocks until he reached the door of the Brasserie Arcand and slipped inside.

Max waited outside for several minutes, as much to catch his breath and rest his leg as to ensure it wasn't simply a way station. After ten minutes, Victor had not emerged so Max crossed the street and went inside. Schmidt, Victor and the third German were sitting together in a booth near the back. Max slipped into the empty seat beside Schmidt.

"Herr Doktor Schmidt. Mind if I join you?"

Schmidt looked sour and Victor started to rise. Schmidt sighed and shook his head. He said something in German and the other two men slipped from the booth. Victor took up a position near the door while the other went outside onto the sidewalk.

"Victor and Luther don't approve of my habits, but they are good boys, nonetheless. Patriots and democrats – a rare combination these days. What can I do for you Max?"

"I have reason to believe that there will be an attempt on the lives of Faisal, Weizmann or both sometime within the next ten days. It may be part of a larger plot to disrupt the Peace conference."

"You shouldn't believe everything you hear."

"The man who told me was killed the same night."

"Marois," said Schmidt, nodding slowly. "And you think that he was killed because he told you about this grand conspiracy."

"There have been three killings, maybe four, in the last few weeks – they look to be connected."

"How?"

"What? Well, if I knew I would have the killer in my hands, wouldn't I?"

"Or he would have you in his? Why do you think they are connected?"

"It's only logical."

"Nonsense," said Schmidt. "Were they killed in the same way, in the same place? Did they all know each other? Did they have the same enemies?"

The same things had occurred to Max but he had no answers.

"I'm not sure," Max said. "Joachim ben David was killed not long after he told me he wanted to meet Barzani. The police say it was a mugging but his relatives don't believe it. The attendant at the place Barzani was murdered hanged himself – an indication of his guilt according to Sergeant Bonnet. Marois was killed after talking to me about Barzani's death. Are you saying they aren't connected?"

"I don't know and neither do you. Although the way you laid it out makes me think I shouldn't have let you sit down. Muggings do go wrong. People kill themselves for many reasons. Gott in Himmel, I know that." Despite the seriousness of his words, Schmidt laughed. "Does thinking they are connected make it easier to solve any one of them? I expect it doesn't. Do you really care who killed all of them?"

"Everyone deserves justice."

"Yes, yes," said Schmidt. "You believe in the rule of law and civil society. Good. The world is painfully short on people who do. But do you care – head, heart and guts – about any one of them?"

"I care about Hevel Barzani."

"Then focus on that. Who killed Hevel Barzani? And why?"

"I don't know."

"Neither do I. But..." Schmidt leaned out from the booth. No one was sitting close but Schmidt leaned forward and whispered anyway. "Go to the club where we first met. Ask Jake why he kicked The Chinaman out of his basement."

"I thought you dealt with Lachance now."

"Lachance demanded too high a price. I'm leaving Paris tonight."

"Berlin?"

"Vienna. There is a doctor there who thinks he can cure me. I'm not so sure. Hence, Victor's errand this afternoon. Everyone should have a back-up plan. Everyone. Good-bye, Mr. Anderson. And good luck."

§

Max arrived at Jake's a few minutes past nine. The club was less than half full but people were arriving in twos and threes in a steady stream. The first set was about to start and Jake was busy making sure everyone who wanted to order did so before the band took the stage. It was a three-piece combo tonight, bass, grand piano and drums, though they promised to have special guests join them as the night wore on. The group might be small but the sound was big enough to get the first few couples out on the dance floor.

He ordered a half carafe of red wine and a small plate of sausages and cheese. His appetite still hadn't fully returned and he supposed he was pushing his stamina even to be here this late, rather than in bed at the hotel. When the waiter brought the food, he asked him to send over Jake when he had a chance. A few minutes later, Jake slid into the chair opposite him. Max leaned across the table and shook his hand and then gestured for him to share in the food.

"I don't mind if I do, Mr. Anderson," he said. "I've been fair run off my feet today."

"Call me Max. Business is good?"

"Steady more than good," said Jake. "But you didn't call me over to talk about my cash flow."

"No," said Max. He didn't really know Jake that well, not even his last name, but he did know that the man had a connection to Hevel Barzani, close enough to mourn at his funeral. "No use in beating around the bush. You know Doktor Schmidt?"

"Know who you mean," Jake frowned. "What about him?"

"He sent me to ask you a question. Why did you throw The Chinaman out of your basement?"

"I don't mean to be rude, Mr. Anderson, but I don't reckon that's any of his business. Or yours neither."

"He seemed to think the answer to that question might help me solve Hevel Barzani's murder."

Jake's expression didn't change. He looked at Max and then down at the stage, where a young black woman had begun to sing about losing her man. When he looked back at Max, his brow was furrowed and his eyes misty.

"How well did you know Mr. Barzani, Max?"

"I only met him a few months ago but we had become friends. He was, I think, a good man."

Jake nodded. He seemed to be listening to the music but Max knew he was thinking about Hevel. He poured himself a small portion of wine from the carafe and took a sip.

"I met Mr. Barzani – Hevel – when I got my discharge last June. I'd had a little wound and then developed pneumonia while I was waiting for it to heal. Still makes it hard to play the trumpet the way I'd like. After I got my papers, I decided I wanted to stay right here in Paris. Lots of black soldiers decided the same thing. Do you know why?"

"I can imagine."

"No, I don't expect you can. You from Canada, right?"

Max nodded.

"I got cousins in Canada. I know it's not perfect but I was born and raised in Georgia. There are so many places in Georgia where a black man can't walk or sit, I'm surprised they can find room to fit us all in. Paris is different. French people got some funny ideas about us but they treat us like men and not boys. It ain't paradise but it'll do." Jake paused again and then he laughed. "But Hevel, he was something else again. The first time I met him, when I was trying to scrape together the cash to open this place, he looked at me and it sent a shiver right down my spine. He looked at me and, for the first time in my life, I knew I was being looked at by someone who could not see the color of my skin. He simply couldn't see it."

Jake's voice caught and he took another sip of the wine. He looked down at the stage. The woman's voice floated high over the soft thrum of the bass, a rising wail of pain and loss that drove into Max like a knife. Jake wiped a tear from his eye. "Crazy Blues, it's a brand-new song but the same old feeling," he said, then continued.

"Hevel helped me out then. A loan and some good advice. He'd show up here nearly every week with a couple or three people in tow. Some of them are still regulars. When he came to ask me to evict The Chinaman – I never knew his real name, I'm not sure anyone did – I wanted to do it. No questions asked. But I couldn't afford it. I actually own this building. I bought it cheap and fixed it up myself. The Chinaman was already downstairs and the rent he paid kept this place afloat some weeks, especially when the flu was keeping everyone at home. Plus, as long as he was here, the police could shake him down and leave me alone.

"Hevel just nodded and asked me how much rent I was talking about. Then he wrote me a cheque for twelve times the monthly rent. When I objected, he asked me what percentage of the club he could buy for that amount. So that's how Hevel Barzani became a ten percent owner of Chez Jacob. Don't know who owns it now."

Max shrugged. "Barzani made me his heir so I guess I do."

Jake laughed and slapped the table. Then he stuck out his hand. "Welcome aboard, partner."

"I don't know anything about running a bar," said Max.

"Neither did Hevel so he didn't even try. But he sure knew how the Paris police worked. Sent me to see a Captain Gereau – said he was the straightest cop in all of France."

"I haven't met that many," said Max, "But he's the straightest one I know."

"He fixed me up – I mean there are real licenses to buy and reports to file but as long as I do that, everything is fine. Any cops show up, I mention his name and they back right down."

"Did Hevel tell you why he wanted you to evict The Chinaman?"

"I don't think he wanted to. He could be like that – as if information was more important to him than money – but I kept at him until he gave a half-assed explanation. He told me he had four reasons but he was only going to tell me three of them – and it was up to me to decide which of them were important. First, he said, The Chinaman had competitors and it was better for all concerned if he moved a little farther away. Second, he told me that he wanted all of his enemies in one place where he could see them, though he wouldn't say where that place was." Jake hesitated.

"You said he gave you three reasons."

"I know," said Jake. "It never made much sense to me so I'll try to tell it to exactly the way he said it. He said – as best as I remember – 'there is no strength in resisting temptation, strength lies in not being tempted in the first place. The man who wants everything for himself is blind to the one who only wants for others. If your enemy is blinded by his good fortune, then he will be blind to his bad.' I tried to get him to explain but he just clammed up."

"Did it mean nothing to you?"

Jake looked down at the band. The singer had left but a couple of players had joined the group and were jazzing on a rag with sax and horn. Jake smiled softly and tapped a counter rhythm on the table with his fingers. Max supposed he'd rather be up there playing himself than talking to his new partner.

"I thought for a while that the first part might be a warning. A lot of the players came out of hard places – the war or their life back home. I know some of them like to chase the dragon but I don't let hopheads work here so they try to stay straight. Having The Chinaman downstairs made it pretty tough. I thought Hevel wanted to take temptation out of their way. But then the second part made no sense at all. I think this was part of one of Hevel's grand stratagems. He was full of them you know. He wanted someone to get over confident or so focused on the prize they don't watch where they're putting their feet."

"Lachance seems to have stepped in to take the place of The Chinaman in Montmartre."

"Tricky guy that Lachance. He puts on quite a show. A real patriot they say – though you know what they say about patriotism. It's the last refuge of a scoundrel."

"I'm not sure about that."

"Hey, I'm as patriotic as the next guy," said Jake. "But I don't use it as a weapon against those who define it differently from me. And I sure don't appreciate it when people wrap themselves in the flag – any flag – to justify why they should have and others shouldn't. Personally, I think the only thing Lachance is loyal to is his own bank account."

"What do you think Hevel's fourth reason was?" asked Max.

"He never did say. But from the way he didn't say, I figured it had to be a woman."

The band was finishing their set and Jack excused himself so he could go take care of "their business." Max finished the wine and picked at the remains of the food, trying to decide whether to stay for the second set or go back to the hotel and get some rest. His decision was made for him when he saw Joseph Asper get up from the bar and head out the front door.

Twenty-Four – Saturday, February 8, 1919

A sper was half a block away by the time Max got to the street. If Asper had chosen a dark coat that night instead of a pale grey one he would have disappeared into the shadows. As it was Max had to hurry not to lose him among the denizens of Saint Denis who were talking advantage of an unseasonably warm evening. Asper showed no interest in the small shops or cafes along Rue de Mont Cenis as he plowed along, head down and hands jammed in his pockets.

Max followed twenty paces behind. Asper's concentration made the job easy, for the man neither slowed nor looked back. The climb up Montmartre was steep and ended in several flights of stairs before reaching the summit. Max's breath came in hard gasps and his knee and hip throbbed from the exertion. Only the thought of Barzani buried a handful of blocks away kept him going. At last, Asper reached his destination, the church of St. Pierre de Montmartre behind Sacre Coeur, a simple Gothic church dating from the twelfth century.

Max stood in the shadows inside the entrance and watched as Asper genuflected and made his way to a pew halfway down the nave and slid in beside a man dressed in a dark coat. Other than a few old women in black kneeling at the altar and an elderly priest moving slowly along the row of chapels that filled the left-hand aisle, the church was empty.

Despite Asper's show of piety, Max had no doubt he had come to the church for this assignation. Max recognized the timbre of Asper's voice while the other man sat silently, merely nodding or shaking his head from time to time. Max slipped along the back of the church, sticking to the shadows and stepping carefully so his heels would not echo off the grey stone flagstones. Four pews behind the two men, he began to make out individual words of Asper's speech, though the content of his sentences escaped him. From this angle, he could see the profile of the other man. It was François Bonnet.

"Well, didn't you? Didn't you!" Asper's voice was high and strained. The priest turned sharply and put a finger to his lips. One of the old women stared at them, a hiss escaping her lips. Asper ducked his head and lowered his voice. Max took advantage of the interruption to step forward and slip into a second pew behind the conspirators. He leaned forward as if praying.

Bonnet finally spoke, his voice low but clear. "What if I did? It's nothing to you. All you have to do –"

"No," said Asper, shaking his head vigorously. "You and your friends have thrown everything into turmoil. Gereau has been asking questions everywhere."

"Gereau is old and old-fashioned. I can handle him."

"You're not the only one with friends in high places."

"Yes," said Bonnet. "But my friends are still rising while his are on the way out. I can handle Gereau."

"The way you handle everyone else?"

Bonnet grunted. "No. Gereau's career has been remarkably clear. If he ever compromised himself, he did a better job than most at concealing it. Now, will you give me what I want or do I need to report your situation to immigration control?"

Asper went still.

"I'm not sure you'll enjoy returning to Zagreb," said Bonnet.

"I was doing my job," said Asper. "No one will hold that against me."

"Perhaps," said Bonnet. "But you have to admit those letters are damning."

"But they don't tell the whole story," said Asper. "There are other documents that show..." His voice trailed off and he leaned his head against the bench in front of him.

"Documents you no longer possess."

"You bastard!" Asper's voice was harsh. The priest had returned to the vestry but the woman hissed again.

"You should be more careful to whom you entrust your luggage." Bonnet laid his hand between Asper's shoulders as if consoling him. Then he put it on the back of his neck. Asper tried to jerk away but Bonnet's grip was firm. He squeezed until Asper coughed.

"Now, listen, you little *bougnoule*, you know what I want. I don't have to send you back to Serbia – there are plenty of people here who would be happy to deal with you. A simple phone call, a delivery of letters into the right hands. You're already in shit with your delegation. What if they thought you were a Boche collaborator?"

"It's a death sentence!"

Bonnet snorted. "Dead spies are all the rage. Everybody's getting in on the act these days."

"Including you?" sneered Asper. Max leaned forward. Was Bonnet going to confess to murdering Barzani? And, if he did, what could Max do about it? Would his word – even Asper's – be enough to send a gendarme to the guillotine?

"I'm always willing to try my hand at something new. But you'll find that Sergeant François Bonnet is always somewhere else when unfortunate things happen."

"Your kind always is. You and Bucard are perfectly matched that way. Have things done but never dirty your own hands."

Bonnet chuckled, low and ugly. When the woman hissed again, he gestured rudely and laughed again. "I'll take that comparison as a compliment. Why take a risk when there are so many tools at hand?"

"One day one of those tools is going to turn and cut you," said Asper.

"Is that a threat, Joseph? You know how I feel about threats."

"No, not me. I'm reliable. I have no ambitions but those of my people. But Lachance?"

"We're as close as collar and shirt," said Bonnet. "Besides wolves don't eat wolves."

"And Roget? And the girl, she's a wild one."

"Roget is a problem but he's Lachance's problem. As for Minette... well, Lachance has her on a string. She'll do what she's told."

"Strings can break," said Asper.

"Not when they're made of heroin. You know what I want. You know where to reach me. Three days. Don't keep me waiting."

Asper nodded and stood up. Max dropped to the floor and watched as Asper and then Bonnet walked down the aisle. He stayed on the floor until the echo of their footsteps had died. He pressed his face against the cool stone and listened to the murmur of the woman praying at the front of the church. Soon, it would be midnight and, he supposed, the priest would return to give a mass. He took no comfort from any of it. God had looked away from him years ago. God had looked away from them all.

He felt tired beyond ways to express it. All life, all hope of happiness had drained out of him at Bonnet's final words. Ah, Minette.

He was no closer to solving Barzani's murder than he had been the day it happened. Bonnet hinted at knowledge but admitted nothing. What had Asper been saying while Max had hung in the shadows? What had he accused Bonnet of doing? "Dead spies are all the rage," Bonnet had said. But which ones? Barzani? Joachim ben David? Marois? And who was killing them? Bucard? Lachance? Gereau's anarchists? Or Buchan's Reds?

And what did it matter anyway? Minette was a slave – not to love, not to excitement, but to heroin. And Yesim thought he was responsible.

Maybe Schmidt was right. Barzani's death was the only one that counted. If he could solve that, he could finally rest. He pulled himself off the floor and sat slumped in the pew. He looked at the altar, at Jesus, hanging wounded from the cross. *Maybe it's time*, he thought, *that I focused on the things that matter.*

§

It was nearly eleven by the time Max got to Le Coq Bleu. The bar was still open though only barely; a few regulars were huddled at one table while Yesim was busily cleaning the others. He looked up when Max entered and scowled.

"I thought I told you never to come back here."

"You did," said Max. "But I don't give up that easily... on my friends."

"Henri's not here," said Yesim.

"What do you think I did to Minette?"

"You ruined her. I don't know how but you did." His voice was low and he wouldn't meet Max's eyes. Yesim went behind the bar as if he wanted to keep a barrier between them. He pretended to scour a stain on the zinc counter top as if any amount of scrubbing would make a difference.

"Did she tell you that? That I was somehow to blame?"

"Minette? She won't even admit there's a problem. Or, if there is one, it's all mine. But I don't know why I'm talking to you – I saw her go to your room and I didn't see her come out."

"Maybe you're talking to me because you're desperate. Yes, you saw Minette at my hotel. It wasn't the first time. either. But she did leave. All we did was kiss a few times. I wanted to do more but she stopped me."

"You expect me to believe that," spat Yesim. "You soldiers are all alike. You come to Paris and think our women are easy. Because they're not like the frozen bitches you left at home. And when they resist you use... force... whatever it takes to make them."

"I don't force myself on anyone," said Max, softly. "I think you know me well enough to know that's true. Minette has changed but I didn't change her."

"Then who?"

"Lachance."

"Don't be stupid! Minette might work for Lachance but she despises him. She would never – "

"Lachance gives her heroin."

"What?" Yesim was motionless, his cloth poised a few inches above the surface of the bar. His mouth opened and closed and opened again but no further sound came out.

"Heroin," said Max. He remembered the bruised vein he had seen on her leg. "Minette injects herself with heroin. Or someone does it for her. I've seen the marks but I didn't know what they were until now."

Yesim stared at Max, his eyes wide and his mouth still open. He made a choking sound deep in his throat and it took Max a few moments to realize he was sobbing. The cloth dropped onto the bar with a sick slap as Yesim raised his hand to his ashen face.

"It's not hopeless. I heard there's a doctor in Vienna who might be able to help."

Yesim waved his hand to encompass the bar. No sounds came from his open mouth save the distant choking but Max understood his meaning: *Viennese doctors cost money.*

"I'll pay, Yesim. Barzani left me some money. I'll pay for the doctor."

Perhaps it was the offer. Perhaps it was the mention of Barzani whose funeral he had so cruelly snubbed. Or perhaps, he remembered the wholehearted sorrow of an injured child but Yesim's body shook and a cry tore from his throat so piercing and painful that even the drunks looked up from their wine. Tears poured down his face.

"Not that," he said. "I wanted anything but that. You must be wrong. You have to be."

Max moved around the bar and put his arm around Yesim. The man didn't resist as Max guided him to a table. Max left him there, his face buried in his arms, while he turned out the remaining patrons with an offer to cover their bill. He locked the door before returning to sit beside Yesim.

"I'm not wrong. I overhead Bonnet talking about it. He didn't know I was there and he had no reason to lie. But it's not hopeless. I know. There were men at the hospital where they fixed my leg, men who had become addicted while in the hospital. But they stopped once they were away from the war. If we get Minette away from Lachance, away from the life he's forcing her into, she can stop, too. We can send her to a doctor and – "

"No, you don't understand." Yesim didn't raise his head from his arms and his voice was low and muffled. Max had to lean forward to hear his words. "I should have known but I refused to see the evidence even when it was shoved in my face. I preferred to think she had become a whore."

"Minette isn't a... that," said Max. He believed it was true. Or perhaps he, too, simply refused to know.

"It doesn't... Minette's parents are dead. Did you know that?"

"In a train crash."

"No. She was eight and it was easier to tell her that," said Yesim. Max knew he didn't want to hear what came next but there was no way to stop Yesim now. "We couldn't show her the bodies. A train crash gave us that excuse. Minette's mother was murdered. My brother committed suicide with a shotgun."

"He killed her?"

"No. Raoul was a weak man but not a bad one. He was an addict, too. He fell into debt and his suppliers killed her as a warning. To him, to others, I don't know. I lived four doors away and I knew nothing of this until the police told me. How can you love someone and not see what is killing them?"

"Maybe it's because you do love them," said Max.

"What are we going to do?"

"We're going to bring her home."

"Here? She'll never come."

"Who said anything about asking her?" Max stood up. Yesim lifted his head and gazed into his eyes.

"I'm sorry, Max. I needed someone to blame other than myself."

"What are friends for?" He patted Yesim on the shoulder and headed for La Coquette, the comforting slap of Marois' revolver against his side to keep him company.

§

La Coquette was still crowded but there was no line and the muscular man at the front, masquerading as a waiter, let him in without a second glance. There was an eight-piece band occupying the stage but the music seemed almost old-fashioned after the jazz at Chez Jacob, though perhaps that was only the pride of ownership talking.

Roget was sitting at the bar, smoking a thin cigar. He glared at Max but didn't get up when he approached.

"Where's Minette?"

"Do I look like her keeper?" snarled Roget. "I saw her with some Russian count an hour ago. Find him and you'll find her."

Max suspected Roget was lying. All they ever did was lie to him so why should it be different tonight? He knew she was here, probably in one of the private suites Lachance kept upstairs.

"You are Lachance's keeper. Is he here?"

"I'm really getting tired of your attitude, Yankee," said Roget. He shifted on the barstool until one foot was planted on the ground. The opposite hand gripped the edge of the bar. His whole body tensed.

Max slipped his hand in his pocket and pressed the .32 against the cloth of the jacket. Roget jerked and then settled back on his chair.

"That the gun you used to kill Marois?" Roget's grin was hard, feral.

"No," said Max. "This is the gun I took from him." *Is he bluffing? If Lachance wanted Marois dead, isn't Roget the one he'd send to do it?*

"I have a rule," said Roget. "No loaded guns around my charge."

"So, he is here."

Roget jerked his head to the door behind the bar. "He's doing inventory."

Max started for the door. Roget popped off the stool and blocked his way. He held out his hand for the gun.

"I'm not stupid enough to give you my gun."

"If you want to go through that door, either give me the gun or use it."

Roget grinned and rocked on the balls of his feet, his arms hanging loose and ready. Whatever else he might think of Roget, Max had to grant he didn't lack courage. Gereau might excuse the wounding of Marois as an act of delirium but shooting Roget in cold blood would be, at best, assault and, at worst, murder. Max couldn't do murder but he couldn't leave without Minette either. He handed the gun to Roget.

"I'll want that back."

Roget flipped open the chamber and emptied the bullets into his palm. He dropped them into a glass and put it behind the bar. He handed the gun back to Max.

"I don't like guns," said Roget. "You can have the bullets back after Lachance is done with you."

Max smiled, reached into his pocket, and dropped a handful of shells onto the bar.

Roget led Max down a long flight of stairs into a cavernous stone cellar. Lachance, spectacles balanced delicately on his broad nose, was reviewing a lengthy ledger while two nervous-looking men in starched white shirts looked on.

"You've got company," said Roget.

Lachance looked up and frowned. He handed the list to one of the men. "We'll continue this later, Eric, and I'll expect a better explanation than 'spillage' for these discrepancies." He waved them away. Eric nodded and retreated with his colleague to the farthest reaches of the room.

"What do you want, Anderson? I'm a busy man and don't appreciate these unannounced interruptions." He glared at Roget.

Roget shrugged. "He has a gun. I thought it might be important." He laughed at the expression on Lachance's face. "Don't worry – I have the bullets."

"Very amusing."

Interesting. Maybe Roget is not as much Lachance's man as I thought. "I'm looking for someone," he said.

"Bucard?" asked Lachance. "So you can administer your rough justice – the way you did with Marois?"

"I wouldn't mind laying my hands on Bucard but I didn't kill Marois."

"Really?" said Lachance, raising his eyebrows. "Surely you don't think I had anything to do with it, do you?"

"I understand you and Roget vouched for each other to Gereau."

"Oh, he wouldn't take our word for it," said Lachance. "But a couple of young ladies were present."

"Minette?" From what Max knew of the drug, an addict would do almost anything to preserve her supply. Providing an alibi would be the least of it.

"So that's it," said Lachance. "You came for the girl. Heroic types are all the same."

"Is she here?" Max asked. He was getting tired of sparring with Lachance.

"How should I know? She's a free agent – she does what she wants." Lachance made a rude gesture, suggesting what Minette might want to do.

"A free agent?" Max was angry now. Angry at the callousness of Lachance's gesture, at his sheer indifference to another person's life. "She's tied to you with bonds as strong as love. I know what you've done to her, what you've given her."

"What I gave her, she took of her own accord. This girl is no innocent – no matter what she or her fool uncle may have told you. There's something..." Lachance shook his head. "If you want her, she's upstairs. Roget will show you the way. Be prepared to carry her. I doubt you can wake her. And I doubt you can keep her away from here."

Twenty-Five – Sunday, February 9, 1919

Lachance's words proved prophetic. Minette slept like the dead, even when Max, with Roget's unexpected assistance, carried her down the stairs to the cab.

Yesim hadn't moved from the table but he jumped up when the cab stopped in front of Le Coq Bleu and ran to help Max haul the still insensate Minette from the back seat and up the narrow stairs to her room. Raw emotions, from tearful relief to raging anger, danced across Yesim's face and he alternately muttered endearments and curses as they labored with the dead weight of her unconscious body.

"I'm getting too old for this," Yesim said as they lowered Minette onto her bed. He placed a pillow under her head and covered her with a quilt while Max watched from the doorway. Yesim locked the door behind them and then fetched pillows and blankets from his own room. He arranged them into a nest in front of the door and declared he would not budge until Max returned in the morning. "We can discuss that doctor – and who will pay for him – then."

Max contemplated spending his night in the hall with Yesim but his recent illness still weighed on him. He was tired and sore and morning would be hard enough to face without sleeping on the floor.

A cold wind had swept in from the west and the cobbles were slick from the fog that wreathed and clung to the ancient stone facades of the buildings. The streets were nearly empty as he walked back to his hotel – even the prostitutes had given up for the night.

Things were coming to a head. Max could feel it deep within his aching bones. In the next few days, he would discover who had killed Hevel Barzani – discover him and bring him to justice.

Either that or he would join him in a Parisian grave.

§

When Max returned at eleven the next morning, Minette was gone, her window broken and the fire escape ladder lowered into the alley behind the bar.

"I heard the glass break," said Yesim, "but by the time I got the door unlocked, she was gone. I've already been to Lachance but he says he hasn't seen her. The lying bastard."

"What did Roget say?" asked Max. For some reason, he felt Lachance's bodyguard might be willing to help them – or, at least, help Minette.

"I didn't see him," said Yesim. "There was someone else occupying his usual place at the bar."

"I saw him," said Henri from *his* usual place at the bar. "He was getting on a train for Lyon, this morning at six."

There has been a break between Lachance and Roget, thought Max. *I wonder what the cause of it was. Maybe Gereau can talk to his counterpart in Lyon.*

"I wish I had never let him buy into my business," said Yesim. "The government claimed there was never any rationing during the war – to keep morale up. Somehow though, I could never keep my shelves stocked. No rationing maybe but plenty of corruption. Lachance had supplies – men like him always did – and he passed them on in exchange for a piece of Le Coq Bleu. And now he's taken Minette."

"We'll get Minette back. Somehow. But..." Max hesitated. He didn't want to offend Yesim again. "I have some money. How much would it take to get Lachance off your back?"

Yesim stiffened. "I can't take your money."

"Not as a gift maybe," said Max. "But you're a businessman. Wouldn't I be a better partner than Lachance?" *I'm already a partner in one club*, he thought, *why not two?*

"He couldn't be any worse," said Henri, laughing.

"Of course, you would have to run the business your own way. I'd be a silent partner."

Yesim frowned. He shook his head. Then, he named a figure. Max nodded. It was less than he feared, though it would use up half the francs Barzani had left him. Still, counting the other currencies, it still left him well off and, if worse came to worst, he would always have places to eat and drink. "I'll get it for you Monday."

Yesim wiped a tear from the corner of his eye and blew his nose on a bar rag. "After the way I treated you..."

"You were afraid for Minette," said Max. "I would have done the same." He stuck out his hand and Yesim shook on the deal.

"Didn't I tell you not to be foolish?" said Henri.

"Yes, yes," said Yesim. "In future, I'll listen more closely to your criticisms. But what do we do about Minette?"

"I think you're right, Yesim," said Max. "Minette probably went straight to La Coquette. I suspect Lachance only let me take her to prove how strong his hold on her was. I doubt he will be so cooperative again."

"No," said Yesim. "The whole time I was talking to him, he was flanked by two brutes that made Roget look like a school boy. They practically threw me in the street when Bonnet showed up."

"Bonnet was there again?" asked Max.

"From the way he was swaggering, you would think he owns the place. He stopped at the bar to pour himself a drink and then marched over to where we were talking. Lachance put on a big smile but I could tell he wasn't happy. He and Bonnet went off to a private booth where a couple of men were already sitting."

"Was one of them German-looking? Big with a broad face and dirty blonde hair?"

"I think so."

"Bucard," said Max. "He's been hovering in the background for weeks but whenever I look for him, he's gone. Maybe this time I can lay my hands on him." Max stood up. Yesim gave him a stricken look. "I think Minette is safe – at least as safe as she has been these last few weeks. I'll figure out how to find her and, next time, we'll make sure she stays."

"Be careful," said Henri. "These are dangerous men."

"Let me come with you," said Yesim. "I'm good in a fight."

"I've no doubt," said Max. "But I need you to do something for me. I need to talk to your anarchist friends again. Only this time, I want to be the one to surprise them. Can you get an address for me?"

"I wouldn't do that for anyone," said Yesim, glowering. "Except, of course, my new partner."

§

Bonnet and Lachance were alone when Max arrived. Lachance was sipping a small espresso while Bonnet crammed the last of a Croque Monsieur down his gullet.

"Where is Bucard? I know he was here."

"And you came to worship at the great man's feet," said Bonnet between bites.

"Idiot," said Lachance. "He had no idea –"

"What do I care what he knows?" said Bonnet. "He staggers all over Paris looking for who killed his boyfriend when the answer is right in front of him. It's a lovely display of loyalty, I guess, but stupid."

"What do you mean?" said Max. Was Bonnet admitting that he had something to do with Hevel's death. Or did he mean Lachance?

"I mean the case is closed. That Hungarian doorman did it."

"I don't suppose you have any proof?" said Max.

"He was there. He ran away. He killed himself. What more proof do you need?"

"Did he have a motive? I don't mean some dirty minded speculation but an actual provable reason. Did you find a weapon? Or even any of Barzani's possessions? I found the body, remember? Someone had taken the money from his billfold. Someone had taken his silver cigar case. Did the Hungarian have them?"

Bonnet flushed even redder than usual. Then he laughed and waved his hand in dismissal. "You're as bad as Gereau. The Hungarian did it. Case closed."

"Until I find the real murderer."

"I blame it on the novelists," said Bonnet to Lachance. "Everyone thinks they can be a detective."

"Still," said Lachance. "I admire the determination. The loyalty. It's hard to find, you know."

"Yes, loyalty is a fine thing," said Bonnet. "If it's not misplaced. Of course, it helps to have a little insurance."

Lachance frowned but said nothing. Bonnet finished his lunch and wiped his face with his napkin. He looked up at Max.

"Are you still here?" Bonnet took out a silver case and extracted a cigar. Max couldn't be sure but he thought it looked like Barzani's. And he had first seen it in Bonnet's hand days after Barzani's death. "I really don't understand your persistence. You've made an honest, if misguided, effort to find Barzani's killer. But you're meddling in things you don't understand. The world is changing and you need to change along with it. You came here looking for Bucard. But what for? To make wild accusations of murder? Don't be foolish. André Bucard is a man of consequence. Men like that don't sully their hands."

"No," said Max. "They get other people to do it for them."

"Like an officer commanding his troops, Lieutenant?"

"The war is over."

Bonnet laughed. "The war has just begun. And you need to know which side you're on. Men like Bucard are the future. He could use someone with your determination, your well-developed sense of loyalty. If not here, then back in Canada."

"Thanks for the lecture but I think I'll decline."

"Suit yourself," said Bonnet. He clipped the end of the cigar and lit it, exhaling a cloud of harsh smoke in Max's direction.

"Where did you get that case?" Max asked.

"It was a gift. Why do you ask?"

"It looks like Barzani's."

Bonnet took another pull on the cigar and made a show of examining the case. "Really? I'm sure you're mistaken. It's not an uncommon design."

"Then you won't mind telling me who gave it to you," said Max.

"And feed your delusion? This was the gift of a grateful citizen. I won't repay their gratitude by sending you to harass them. Now if you'll excuse us, Lachance and I have business to discuss."

"Sure," said Max. "Is Minette here?"

"I think," said Lachance, sneering, "that Minette has made it clear it is none of your business where she is."

Max had nothing to say to that, so he turned on his heel and walked away with as much dignity as he could muster. The revolver slapped against his side like an insistent question that would soon demand an answer.

§

When Max got back to Le Coq Bleu, Yesim looked at him sadly but said nothing about Minette. He handed Max a slip of paper with an address scribbled on it. "They have a safe house on the second floor. You can only reach it from the back. The password today is 'green tea.' Don't underestimate them. No matter what they look like – Les Deux Jacques can be dangerous."

Two trains and three buses later Max was walking along a trash-strewn street in the northern banlieu of Bobigny. It had taken more than two hours to reach the address and the sandwich Yesim had pressed into his hand as he left the bar was nothing but a distant memory. Number forty-four was nondescript; the fourth in a series of brick row houses built to house workers expelled from the city core during Haussmann's urban restoration. Far from the heart of commerce, they had rapidly deteriorated into tenements for immigrant workers. They also formed the beating heart of the Red Belt that circled the city and made men like Buchan so afraid.

Faces in windows watched him as Max strolled past the house, perhaps trying to determine if he was a bill collector, a police agent or a tourist who had lost his way. Two men, neither more than twenty, stepped off a rickety porch to block his way, their faces sullen and their eyes hard. Max met their gaze, standing loosely the way he had seen Roget. The men must have thought him not worth the risk, despite the obvious quality of his clothes. They stepped back and he walked past them. He refused to glance back even though his shoulders buzzed with the anticipation of a blow or a blade. None came and Max maintained a steady pace until he reached the end of the block and turned the corner.

The alley way that separated the rows of houses was more decrepit than the street. The smell of human waste hung heavily in the air and Max held a handkerchief over his mouth as he picked his way through the unidentifiable refuse scattered across the dirt roadway. He went all the way to the end and then walked back to make sure he was approaching the right house. The back door was boarded over but a set of stairs – newer-looking than the rest led to a narrow landing.

Max checked his jacket pockets. Marois' gun nestled in the right one while the left held the brass knuckles and clasp knife that completed his arsenal. He didn't think he'd need any of them but he wasn't taking any chances. Not anymore. He mounted the steps and rapped on the door three times as Yesim had instructed.

The door opened a crack. "What you selling?" The owner of the voice was above average in both height and girth but he looked unhealthy, his narrow face sallow under a thin beard. His hair was lank and clung to his head like a skullcap.

"Green tea," said Max. The man peered at him but opened the door wide enough for Max to enter. He reached out to pat Max's jacket but Max slapped his hands away and growled a profanity.

"You know better than that," Max said, trying to sound tougher than he felt. It was enough; the man stepped aside to let Max out of the vestibule before resuming his seat by the door. From outside, the house looked abandoned but the interior was clean and well-lit, with electric lights spaced in glass-sconces down the central hall. It continued to the front of the house where it ended in a sort of sunroom – though heavy curtains over the large windows prevented any actual sun from entering. The rug that ran the length of the hall – a zigzag pattern in primary colours – was new and the two doorways on each side of the hall were framed in polished oak.

The first two, sleeping quarters with four bunks to a room were empty, as was the small kitchen. The final and largest room was furnished with two comfortable couches and twice as many chairs, all in a half-circle around a large fireplace, where several logs were burning merrily. A thick rug with geometric patterns covered the floor and the pale blue walls were hung with several paintings like the ones he had seen at La Coquette. Les Deux Jacques were modern, if nothing else.

None of the five in the room, including the two Jacques, stood as Max entered and he was able to take up a position with his back to the wall before anyone reacted to his presence. Jacques Grand leapt from her seat as did two of the men. Jacques Court merely swiveled in his place on the farthest coach and glared at Max sourly. One of the men took a couple steps toward Max but stopped when Max showed him the gun in his hand.

"Why don't you all sit down and we can have a little chat?" said Max.

"What makes you think we have anything to say to you?" asked Court.

"I know where you are – I'm sure there are others who would be happy to have that information."

Grand snorted. "Not persuasive. This place is useless to us now."

"Pity," said Court. "This divan is divine."

"Then perhaps this is reason enough." Max lifted the gun higher.

Grand snorted again. "Don't be silly. That model holds five shots. Even if you could kill us all, which I doubt, there is still our friend by the door."

"He doesn't look well," said Max. "I think I can take him."

Grand frowned and looked thoughtful. The man who had remained seated glanced nervously at Court, as if seeking instruction, but the other two were appraising Max, judging their chances. At least one of them was armed, the bulge of holster showing clearly under his arm. *The rest probably have guns, as well,* thought Max. He didn't much like his chances in a firefight. He could feel the cold sweat run down his sides and the inside of his legs and he hoped his fear didn't show on his face.

"I suppose we have Yesim to thank for this," said Court. There was no mistaking the threat in his voice. "We don't have much use for traitors."

"Is that why you killed Marois? Because he betrayed you?"

"But you said no one –" the nervous man began.

"Shut up!" said Court and the man cringed back in his seat.

If Max had any doubts about who was in charge, he no longer did. The others were all looking at the fat man now, waiting for a sign of how this would all unfold. The face he had once thought jolly, even clown-like, had hardened and Max had no doubt that his life and, perhaps that of Yesim, as well, would depend on how he handled the next few minutes.

"It wasn't Yesim's idea to tell me where you were," said Max.

"But a little money, a few threats, and he gave us up?"

Yesim knew the danger he was creating for himself when he handed me that address, thought Max, *and I never even gave it a thought. I can't solve one murder at the risk of causing another.*

"Not even then," he said, thinking furiously. "But when I slapped his niece a few times, he had no choice."

"Minette – I always did say she was Yesim's weak spot," said Court.

"You did. You did," said Grand. "Mr. Anderson, you've changed. Grown harder somehow. You even look more chiseled. Like a cowboy, don't you think?"

Court grunted.

"What is it you want from us?" said Grand.

The game had somehow shifted. Or perhaps no one was fully in charge. They were anarchists after all. "The same as always," said Max. "Information."

"Same terms as before?" asked Court.

"No," said Max. "I think the terms have changed a bit."

"You do have the trump card," said Court, nodding at the gun. "Perhaps we can come to an accommodation. Our friends will leave. The hour is late and they have a long way to go. You may have noticed the buses are not reliable in these neighborhoods. When they are gone, we can sit down over a nice bottle of wine and discuss matters."

"What's to stop them coming back with reinforcements?"

"Why would they bother? We are your willing hostages. I have no doubt you would shoot us if pressed but not out of hand."

"I might – if I thought you had killed Barzani. Or ordered it done."

"But," said Grand, "we know we didn't. And I think you do, too."

"All right," Max nodded. "We'll do it your way."

Max continued standing with his back to the wall until the others had left and Grand returned from the kitchen with a tray carrying a bottle of wine and three glasses.

She put the tray on a small table in front of the fire and filled the glasses. "I'd offer you some food but our provisions are low. This is nothing but a way station."

Max doubted that was true. Someone had gone to considerable trouble on the décor and the living room at least had the feel of frequent usage. Still, he suspected Captain Gereau would find nothing if he were to come here tomorrow. Max took a seat in one of the chairs across from where the two Jacques perched together on the coach. The chair was comfortable with a deep seat and high arms and Max resisted the urge to relax into it. Instead, he sat on the edge of the cushion with his feet planted firmly on the floor.

"You can put away the gun, Mr. Anderson," said Court. "The men of action have all left."

Max nodded and slipped the gun back into his jacket pocket. Sitting the way he was, it would be easy to pull it out again.

"What are you planning between now and the 20th?" Max asked.

"So much for conviviality," said Grand.

"My time isn't unlimited," said Max. "Neither is my patience."

"Why don't you shoot us now and save our colleagues the trouble of doing it later," said Court. "I told you how we feel about betrayal."

"I told you what happened with Yesim," said Max.

"And you were very convincing, wasn't he, Court?"

Court giggled. It wasn't attractive. Max felt a chill run down his spine. He had met the enemy before – across the barbed wire and face to face – but he had always thought that in different circumstances – freed from the burdens of duty and constraints of patriotism – his foes might be his friends. He didn't think that of these two.

"What can I do to... I have money," said Max.

"Money," Court said the word like it was a curse. "There are some things that can't be bought."

"That's not been my experience," said Max.

"How much would you take to forget Hevel Barzani?" asked Grand.

They were right. Some things couldn't be bought. He knew there was a difference between his loyalty to a friend and theirs to a cause but, at the moment, he couldn't say what it was.

Court waved his hand. "Yesim is safe for now – if only because it's not worth wasting a man to kill him. That could change. And the only warning you'll have is the tinkle of glass that precedes the arrival of the bomb in your lap."

"But why concern ourselves with events that may never happen?" said Grand, smiling. She raised her glass. "To absent friends."

Max didn't join in the toast. He couldn't imagine how Grand might have poisoned his glass and not her own but he was no longer willing to take any chances with these people.

"We seem to be at an impasse," he said. "I want to know things and you want to keep secrets. I suppose I could shoot one of you and see if the other would talk."

"Shoot Grand," said Court. "She has less blood in her. Blood is so hard to get out of carpets."

"Very nice," said Grand.

"I thought material things didn't matter to anarchists," said Max.

"Don't be foolish. The material world is all there is and everyone wants a part of it. Money is the problem. When one group of people has all of it and the rest have none, revolution is not only necessary it is inevitable."

"Like in Russia?" Maybe if I just keep them talking, thought Max, they'll tell me what I want to know. People like this – who plot while others act – love to talk.

"One tyranny replacing another," said Grand. "The natural state of man is equality. Everything that interferes with that state – wealth, politics, religion – is unnatural and must be eliminated. Sadly, that can seldom be done without the use of the bomb or the assassin's bullet."

"Who are you planning to kill?"

Grand opened his mouth and then closed it.

"You were right, Grand. He has changed. Grown crafty."

Grand leaned back in the couch and laughed. She waggled her finger at Max. "Very good. Very good. If I had someone in mind, I might have said so."

"If you won't tell me, let me guess. You plan to kill Prince Faisal and Chaim Weizmann."

Court and Grand went still. They exchanged glances. Then they laughed.

"What do we care about wogs or kikes?" said Court. "What do we care about anything but our own backyard? All politics is local. Someday even the communists will figure that out."

"Then Barzani was wrong. There is no plot to kill them when they speak to the Conference."

"None that involves us or anyone we know. Anarchists are, by their nature, prone to individual action. The idea of a grand anarchist organization can only be believed by those who have never met anarchists. Still, I'm sure we would have heard something."

"Let us be clear," said Grand. "We don't plan to kill anyone. Not at the moment. What we have done in the past or may do in the future is not your concern. Now is all that matters. Our cell – the men you saw here today – is focused on other tactics. We think the people can be moved by other means – propaganda, sabotage, street demonstrations. Make no mistake, there will be disruptions. There may even be violence but we – the two Jacques – will not be behind it. I cannot speak for others in the movement."

"That's probably enough," said Court. "I will tell you this. Anarchists are not the real enemy. We never have been. We are the bogeymen who justify the police crackdowns, the endless surveillance of workers and foreigners, the political deals on left and right that keep real change from happening. That is how it has been in France for fifty years. Little improvements here and there while the status quo of wealth and power is maintained and strengthened. But the social contract was shattered by the war. The individual is nothing but a cog in a machine now. Anarchism is a dream. Communism and fascism – as the Italians call their peculiar blend of nationalism and hate – are the coming nightmare. Movements not men. They might well take aim at Arabs and Jews – if only to excite the passions of the masses."

"Then we are back to Bucard," said Max.

"Perhaps," said Grand. "I wouldn't discount radicals on the left but... they have no allies at the prefecture. The central arrondissements are dangerous ground for them. Bucard and his friends come and go as they please."

"Faisal was scheduled to present his case today," said Court. "If he is still alive tomorrow, I suggest you keep your eyes on Weizmann. Now, as pleasant as this has been, we really need to be on our way."

"One more thing," said Max. "Did you kill Marois?"

"Why would we do that?" said Court.

"He was a police informant."

"Yes, he was, wasn't he?" said Grand.

Then they both shut up and said not another word until Max got up to leave.

"There are a few places Bucard is known to frequent," said Court. He mentioned the church where Max had overheard Bonnet and

Asper. "He also prays at Saint-Germain-l'Auxerrois – the priest there is an old friend – and drinks at La Tour de Montlhéry. He's not there often but it is probably worth a try."

"Good bye, Mr. Anderson. We won't meet again," said Grand. "And guard yourself. Once bullets start to fly, they seldom care where they land."

Twenty-Six – Monday, February 20, to Tuesday, February 21, 1919

As soon as the banks were open Monday morning, Max arranged to transfer the funds to Yesim. He suspected it would be better if his friend dealt with Lachance directly. He was beginning to feel distinctly unwelcome at La Coquette.

After, he walked along the Quai des Tuileries with the Seine to his right and the Louvre, ancient fortress and now the greatest art museum in France, perhaps in the entire world, on his left. Saint-Germain-l'Auxerrois was less than a block from the museum on the quiet side street, Rue de L'Arbre. It had been the parish church of the kings of France when they resided at La Louvre. It was a short walk from the west entrance of the palace, across a small garden, to the main entrance of the church, with its three high arched doorways. To the left was a tower whose bells had heralded the St. Bartholomew's Day massacre in 1572 when three thousand French Protestants were slaughtered in the streets. Sometimes, Max thought that Paris should be called the 'City of Blood,' rather than the 'City of Lights.'

Like most churches in Europe, this one had been built over a span of centuries and the different styles overlapped in its towers and arches. It was less gaudy than Notre Dame or the Basilica atop Montmartre, but it was impressive nonetheless, if only for its central role in the history of France. Max suspected Bucard worshipped there for reasons other than his friendship with the priest.

The main aisle, or nave, was stunningly high and long but narrow. Huge stone columns supported a series of gothic domes, peaked in the center. Stained glass windows high in the walls filled the church with misty light. Chapels to the patron saints of France lined the left aisle while the graves of kings marked the right. A smaller, more intimate chapel stood near the right entrance, separated from the nave by dark wood panels.

According to the vicar who assisted him, Father Beaudoin was hearing confessions when Max arrived. He waited on a small bench near the entrance, feeling the weight of history and a thousand years of prayer weigh on him. When Beaudoin emerged, Max took a few minutes to observe him before making his approach.

The man was tall, although not excessively so, and lean. He looked to be in his forties, his wavy black hair tinged with grey at the temples. His long narrow face was unlined, save for creases that framed his mouth and several lines across his brow. It was not a face given to smiling and his thin lips were turned down as he watched Max advance.

"Pardon me, Father, for interrupting your work but I am looking for André Bucard. I understand he worships here when he's in town."

"André is a very devout son of the church. I am proud to have him under my care. Are you a friend of his or a... business associate?"

"A friend of a friend might be closer," said Max, trying not to lie more than he must. He was no longer certain of his own beliefs but he saw no need to insult others. Or to take unnecessary chances on the afterlife if there was one. "I was hoping Mr. Bucard could tell me something about what happened to him."

"Your friend is missing?"

"My friend is dead," said Max.

"And you think André knows something about it?" The priest's frown was deeper now and his eyes narrowed as he peered into Max's face, perhaps trying to discern precisely what it was Max was looking for.

"I don't know," said Max. "But it has been suggested by several people that he might."

"What people?"

"People who know him."

"I see," said Beaudoin. "André was at mass yesterday. He took communion but other than that I didn't speak to him. I don't know where he's staying. Sometimes he stays with friends, sometimes at hotels but he has no particular favorite. He sometimes comes to the evening mass. I can tell him you're looking for him if you give me your name."

"My name is Max Anderson and he can reach me at Hotel L'Aquilon in Montmartre. My friend's name was Hevel Barzani."

Beaudoin nodded. If he recognized the name, it didn't show on his face.

§

La Tour de Montlhéry had been a coach inn in the eighteenth century. Its interior walls were still lined with stone and the remains of a horse post stood beside its narrow door. Snuggled between the Haussmanns that towered over it on either side, it seemed archaic. However, the interior had been updated with modern fixtures including electric lights and a tile floor of repeating squares. The long bar had panels of dark carved wood along its length but across the polished zinc top bottles lined glass shelves and goblets and wineglasses hung from stainless steel rails.

According to the barman, Bucard and several friends had enjoyed a leisurely lunch after mass the previous day but he wasn't there now. It was as good a place as any to eat and Max had a hearty beef stew and a glass of burgundy while he contemplated his next moves.

He still felt that Bucard held the key to unlocking the puzzle box that had sprung up around Barzani's life and death. Yet, until he could actually talk to the man, all he had were rumors. Some seemed to think he was the architect of a coming revolution; others dismissed him as a nothing more than a member of the lunatic fringe.

Barzani had called him dangerous, but hadn't seemed concerned about him except as an interference to be dealt with. Marois, too, had doubted his involvement in either Barzani's death or the plot he was trying to prevent. But they were now both dead. Had Bucard fooled them and then struck while they were looking the other way?

Four men were dead – Barzani and three others who were, in small ways or large, connected to him. The bathhouse attendant, on the surface, seemed the most direct link to the murder. Even discounting Bonnet's theory – which Max did – he might have been a witness. He could have been killed to cover up the crime. That was Max's theory but was there another one? Maybe he had other reasons to kill himself. He was, after all, an immigrant, probably without proper documentation and now without a job. How had he come to work in such a place anyway? Was he a homosexual? Max had heard of men driven to self-murder by the revelation of their sexual behavior.

If he had been a direct witness, wouldn't the killers—Max was sure there was more than one—have dealt with him on the spot and not several days later in a distant part of the city? He had been there and fled but it might have been before the murder and for different reasons – say, the risk of exposure by a policeman or someone posing as one. Gereau said the suicide note had been enough to persuade the Prefecture that the man had killed Barzani, but how little was "enough?"

He had no way now of investigating the attendant's death – the body was gone and evidence locked away or discarded. If the death of the attendant was suicide, but unconnected to Barzani's death, it made things simpler.

What about Joachim ben David? He had been looking into the same things as Hevel. Joachim had talked about two men coming to Paris, come to carry out a plot of some sort, according to Hevel, though Joachim had expressed his doubts. Bucard and his unnamed associate were likely those men. Joachim, and later Marois, had warned that if they were planning an assassination or worse, they would not hesitate to kill anyone who got in their way. If the same people who killed ben David killed Barzani, it was almost certainly Bucard or someone associated with him. But if Joachim ben David had died at the hands of a thief as the police had said, then who killed Barzani?

Gereau had seemed troubled when Max suggested that the two murders were connected. Perhaps he had looked deeper into the case. He had to see Gereau in any case to tell him about his meeting with the anarchists. He owed him that much. And it wouldn't hurt to let him know about Bonnet's close associations with a known criminal, either. And he wanted to ask him about tracking down Roget in Lyon.

That left Marois. Certainly, there were plenty of suspects – including the two Jacques – but in Max's mind Marois' death seemed inextricably connected to Hevel's. That, too, pointed to Bucard. Marois had certainly been afraid of the right-wing leader. And it eliminated two of Max's earlier suspects. Roget might have killed Barzani out of jealousy but he had an alibi for Marois' death. The same alibi as Lachance, who, now that Max thought of it, had wanted to obtain documents in Barzani's possession.

It had to be Bucard. And yet... Marois thought it a set up and everyone else claimed Bucard was not a man to get his own hands dirty. At the most he had ordered it done but someone else had committed the murders. But would Marois have opened his door to Bucard? Or to one of his associates?

Joseph Asper? He had been named by Joachim as Hevel's deadly enemy. Was that more than hyperbole? The anarchists, too, had suggested an eastern European connection. Asper fit the bill. He knew both Marois and ben David – but was that sufficient to indicate murder? Asper seemed too much of a coward to take direct action alone.

There was no other suspect than Bucard. Max wiped the last of the stew from his bowl with a piece of bread. He paused with the bread halfway to his mouth.

The attendant frightened off by someone in authority. A police officer knocking on a hotel door at four in the morning demanding entry. A man who, according to the entries in Lachance's ledger, had been paid a large sum of money after Max's room had been burglarized. A braggart and a bully who admired Bucard and hated wogs and Jews.

François Bonnet.

Max pushed the remains of his meal away. His stomach knotted in anger; he no longer had an appetite. Not for food.

His anger only took him as far as the street. Bonnet was despicable and he's certainly corrupt but could he really have committed, not one, but as many as four murders? As far as Max knew, no connection existed between Bonnet and ben David. Although Bonnet sympathized with the Black Cross, would that be enough to drive him to the random murder of a Jew?

If Barzani's death and that of Joachim ben David were linked, Bucard and his retinue remained Max's primary suspect. Bonnet must know something of the murders, but he was too small a man to have been the driving force behind them.

Going to La Coquette in what might prove a futile search for Bonnet might make it impossible to return to the church in time to catch Bucard at mass. A better use of his time was to contact Gereau at police headquarters, only a short walk away on the Île de la Cité. If he were lucky, he might find Bonnet there, though what he would do then was uncertain.

Neither man was at the Prefecture. Gereau had been called home to Brittany for a family emergency and was not due to return until

Thursday the thirteenth. Max made an appointment to see him at nine that morning.

With time to kill before the service, Max decided to explore part of the city he had up until then avoided. He stood for several minutes on the Pont au Change, staring down at the muddy waters of the Seine as it flowed around the island. Small boats and barges made their way slowly along the river. It was a pleasant day for mid-February, but despite the unseasonable temperatures and the growing warmth of the sun, few pedestrians were about. The Spanish flu, which had seemed to run its course a month ago, had returned with a vengeance. Those who did venture out, at least here in the bourgeois centre of the city, avoided company and, more often than not, protected themselves with scarves or gauze masks. For the first time in weeks, he wondered about his friends and family back in Nova Scotia. Had the epidemic spread there, too? Had he suffered losses of which he was not even aware?

Leaving the bridge, he walked slowly around the column at La Place du Châtelet, gazing up from the circle of sphinxes, water spouting from their mouths, to the guardian angel, arms raised in victory, who stood vigil at the top of the column. He stopped at the artful display of cakes in the windows of the Cador André. On impulse, he went inside and bought a dozen meringues to share with Henri and Yesim that evening. A half dozen blocks brought him to the entrance to the Louvre. It was as good a place as any to while away a few hours. He browsed through the galleries, stopping from time to time in front of a particularly striking painting or sculpture. He spent several long minutes gazing at the Death of the Virgin by the Italian artist Carravagio, strangely moved by the exhibition of silent grief of the mourners gathered around Mary's body.

The Mona Lisa also captured his attention. He was surprised at how small it was, though he supposed it explained how it had been stolen one night in 1911. The French poet Apollinaire had been suspected and he had implicated the painter Picasso before it was finally recovered, two years later, when the thief, an Italian named Peruggia, tried to sell it to the Uffizi museum in Florence. Several senior police officers had seen their reputations ruined and careers ended over the scandal. *And yet good men can be murdered, and no one loses sleep over it let alone their jobs.*

On one level, the Mass was another disappointment in a disappointing day. If Bucard needed religious solace this evening, he sought it elsewhere. Yet, Max was glad he had come. It had been many years since he attended a service of any kind; he had never sat through a Catholic Mass. The elaborate robes worn by the priest and his assistants, the smell of incense that filled the air, the haunting sounds of the Latin phrases, the ethereal chanting, the call and response, ran over and through him and gave him a sense of peace he had not experienced since boyhood. His own faith was shaky but here, at least, he could understand what faith was and why it existed.

§

Max returned to Le Coq Bleu after the service. Henri and Yesim were plotting how to rescue Minette from the clutches of Lachance. Max wasn't sure she wanted to be rescued but he was too tired to argue. After a light supper he pleaded exhaustion and returned to L'Aquilon to make an early night of it, leaving the meringues for the two older men to enjoy. By the time he was settled in bed, a heavy lassitude enveloped him. The sun was past its zenith when he woke. He tried getting dressed but the effort seemed too much. He pushed himself from the bed and hauled on the clothes he had left scattered on the floor the night before.

The kitchen was closed but Jean-Marc found some bread and a piece of hard cheese and Max broke his fast on that and a cup of luke-warm tea.

"You don't look well," said Jean-Marc. "You're not having a relapse, are you?"

Max shook his head. He was tired and his leg was hurting again but otherwise he felt well. "I think I tried to do too much too soon."

"You should go easy on yourself," said Jean-Marc.

"I'll try," said Max. Despite his exhaustion, Max determined he had to make some progress. Marois' deadline was fast approaching and he still had no idea what was planned. He finished the tea and took a cab to La Coquette.

Lachance bustled over as soon as he spotted Max. He had apparently had enough of Max's unannounced visits disturbing his custom.

"Minette is indisposed," said Lachance, "and as far as you and her Uncle are concerned, she is likely to remain so."

"I'm looking for Bonnet," said Max.

"He's not here," said Lachance. "He was kind enough to go on an errand for me, out of the city. He'll return Thursday. I'm sure he'll be overjoyed to see you then."

Max wondered if Bonnet had assumed Marois' role as courier or if the task Lachance had set him fell more within his official line of work. Max didn't bother asking.

"I suppose I have you to thank for Yesim's sudden fortune. I hope your investment brings you more pleasure than mine ever did."

Max shrugged and turned away. He really didn't like Lachance.

He checked in with Yesim, who was happy to be out of his obligations to Lachance but still worried about his niece. He had had no word from Minette, though according to those of her friends that he knew, she was still in Paris and still working for Lachance, though none of them had seen her for several days. He went over to St. Anne's but Minette hadn't been there in more than a week. He drifted along Clichy for a couple of hours but she was in none of her usual haunts.

Max finally gave up and returned to L'Aquilon and, after an early supper crawled into bed. He picked up Dumas' Three Musketeers, another of Henri's gifts and started in where he had left off, right after D'Artagnan and Constance had delivered the Queen's jewels to the Duke of Buckingham.

He awoke late Wednesday morning with the bedside light still burning and the book weighing on his chest. An early lunch invigorated him and, after scanning the papers for any news that might offer a clue to coming events, he headed to Saint-Germain-l'Auxerrois for the first service though he didn't go inside. The Mass had been moving and yet disturbing, too. It had not changed in a thousand years. The Great War that had changed everything had not touched it. That seemed wrong somehow. Max stood across the street and watched the celebrants come and then go. Bucard was not among them.

Nor was he at La Tour de Montlhéry, although he had been in the previous night. Max was beginning to feel like a cat chasing a particularly elusive mouse. *Though, perhaps, I'm the mouse. A particularly suicidal one.*

He knew he should return to Le Coq Bleu but the menu there was limited at the best of times and, with Yesim preoccupied with Minette's disappearance, Max knew he would receive neither a decent meal nor the privacy he needed to think his way through this puzzle. Instead, he headed for Chez Jacob. If he was going to pay for a meal, he might as well profit from it. The music was anything but ethereal but it seemed to stimulate his thinking. He needed all the help he could get.

The bar was surprisingly full despite the renewed fears over the flu. Perhaps jazz connoisseurs were natural risk takers, thought Max. An eight-piece band was playing a lively fox trot, the clarinet leading and two trumpeters scratching out a response through the bell-shaped mutes on their horns. The doorman, a small man with a thin mustache, greeted him by name and introduced himself as André. He led Max to a table well away from the kitchen and bar and close enough to the stage that he could watch the action without being overwhelmed by the music or jostled by the dancers. A waiter arrived seconds later with a plate of cheese and olives and a basket of bread.

"This table will always be available for you, Mr. Anderson" said André. "Jake is busy in the kitchen but he asked to be told if you came in. He'll drop by as soon as he's free. In the meantime, can I recommend the roast chicken? Perhaps with a nice glass of sauterne?"

Max nodded and the waiter rushed off to fill the order. There were three cheeses – peppered brie, a slightly acidic bleu and a goat cheese flavored with thyme and rosemary – and both black and green olives on the plate and Max had sampled all of them by the time Jake came to his table.

"Business seems good," said Max.

"Knock on wood," said Jake, tapping lightly on the table top in perfect synchronization with the band. "Been hard to keep the kitchen staffed with this new outbreak but it doesn't seem to have affected the clients much. Though you notice the band doesn't bother playing waltzes. Even these folks ain't that keen to dance cheek-to-cheek."

The waiter arrived with the chicken but hesitated to serve before Jake gave him the go ahead. "I'm not staying," he said. "No point in letting it get cold."

When the waiter had retreated, Jake pulled a sealed envelope out of his jacket and laid it on the table beside Max's plate. "Schmidt's man, Victor, dropped by yesterday. His French is none too good and my German is worse but I got the impression that this was important but not urgent. Still, if you hadn't come in tonight, I'd have dropped by your hotel in the morning."

"Is Schmidt back in Paris?" asked Max.

"Victor said something about Vienna, so I guess not."

"Good," said Max. If Schmidt were still in Austria, it meant his treatment was working. There might still be hope for Minette if they could ever wrest her from Lachance's grasp. The next time, she would not escape.

Jake left him to his meal. The chicken was moist and flavored with oregano and a dusting of finely ground pepper. Tiny wedges of roast potato melted in his mouth and, though wilted and over-cooked, the greens were rescued by the delicate butter and garlic sauce that lightly coated them. The sauterne, sweet and cold, was the perfect match. When he had finished and coffee had been brought, Max opened the envelope and removed the single sheet of heavy white paper folded within.

The handwriting was blocky but the message was clear. Jake was wrong – the letter was both important and urgent.

M. Anderson,

Although I have left Paris, perhaps for good, my agents have remained active. I have information that will aid your inquiries. I seek no reward. I have reasons of my own for despising Bucard and his ilk. Their bile will lead us back to war or worse. I cannot bear to see Europe burn in the fires they are lighting.

Bucard will leave Paris on the twenty-first. Until then, he is staying at the Hotel Meurice on Rue de Rivoli. He is a man of regular habits. You will find him in the hotel bar between twenty-two hundred and midnight every night. He will be occupied with his associates and may refuse to speak to you. But he will be there.

Schmidt.

It was already nearly eleven-thirty. He might be able to reach the Meurice before midnight but, if he did, he would be at a disadvantage, in a strange place, facing an unknown foe. It would be better to wait. Tomorrow, after seeing Gereau, he could go to the Hotel for lunch, scout out the terrain and plan his line of attack. He would return well before ten and watch as Bucard and his accomplices entered. When the moment was right, he would strike.

Twenty-Seven – Thursday, February 13, 1919

Gereau was at his desk when Max arrived. He didn't get up when Max entered, barely acknowledged his presence when Max took the chair opposite him. His face was haggard and drawn; he seemed to have aged ten years in the last week. Max waited in silence until Gereau lifted his eyes from his desk and met his.

"A week ago, I had two brothers; today I have one. I had two sisters-in-law and now I have none. I had three nephews and a niece; only the girl survived. This sickness is worse than the war. At least then we had an enemy to hate. How can you hate something you can't even see or touch?"

Max had no answer for that. Gereau shuddered and shook his great head. He moved a piece of paper from one side of his desk to the other and then moved it back again. He took a great gulping breath and for a moment, Max thought he would break down. Gereau looked down at his hands spread on his desk. When he looked up his face was calm and his eyes clear.

"You're lucky to have caught me. The funerals are tomorrow and I have to catch the late train to Rennes. What can I do for you Max?"

Max told him about his meetings with the anarchists and what they had revealed about the planned demonstrations that should rock the city in the next few days. He repeated their claims that violence was not part of their plan.

"Violence is always part of their plans," said Gereau. "I'll have some men go to this address, though I'm sure it will be empty and picked clean by now. Still, some of the neighbors might know something. Not that they'll talk to the 'dirty flics.'" Gereau chuckled and shook his head. "I've heard of this pair, or at least those you described. They change their names so often it's hard to keep track."

Gereau took a photograph from a drawer and shoved it across the desk. It was grainy and taken from a distance but the man in the centre looked like one of those in the safe house.

"He's trimmed his beard but I'm pretty sure he was one of the men I met."

"Emile Cottin," said Gereau. "If he was there, I think we can count on there being violence. It's only a matter of what kind. What else do you have?"

Max recounted the conversation he had overheard between Asper and Bonnet and described the apparent close relationship the gendarme had developed with Lachance. He kept his suspicions to himself. Nor did he mention his planned confrontation with André Bucard. Gereau had enough on his mind. Besides, that was something Max needed to do for himself.

"Bonnet thinks he can handle me, does he? Maybe it's time he learned that Captains still outrank Sergeants. Don't worry about Bonnet, I'll deal with him when I return."

Max nodded. If all went well, by the time Gereau returned, he would be able to hand him Barzani's murderer.

"I have some news for you, too," said Gereau. "You thought Joachim ben David's death was related to Barzani. We caught his killers yesterday. Brothers from Poland, big burly blonds who were making their living robbing people in the Metro. They specialized in Jews, Algerians and undocumented immigrants – people who might be reluctant to report it to the police. Generally, they took their money and let them go, though anyone who resisted got a beating for their trouble. Ben David apparently took the beating but not the vow of silence. He tracked them down and threatened to report them to the Prefecture if they didn't leave the city. They panicked, cut his throat and shoved him in that tunnel. We caught them in the act of robbing another victim and, when we searched their rooms, we found ben David's wallet and identification papers. The younger one broke under questioning and blamed his brother for the whole thing. They'll both go to the guillotine, of course."

"Have you told his family?" Max felt stunned. This changed everything.

"Not yet," said Gereau. "It's on the list. I'll do it as soon as I get back."

§

Max found himself once again on la Pont de Chance, staring at the waters of the Seine, slate grey now under a lowering sky. Everything had changed, though Max couldn't quite make out how the landscape had shifted. If Joachim's death was not part of the pattern, was Bucard still his primary suspect or had he been supplanted by Bonnet?

No matter, Bonnet wasn't due back in town until late. He could see Bucard and, if need be, go to La Coquette to find Bonnet. He was bound to be there until closing.

§

The restaurant at the Meurice was wood paneled and low ceilinged. A cluster of tables stood near the entrance and beyond the long mahogany and steel bar, a row of booths with leather covered benches lined the wall. Several of the booths had shutters to allow for more privacy and Max hoped Bucard wouldn't pick one of those. It would make approaching him more difficult. Besides the brass-fitted entry off the lobby, a door behind the bar probably led to the wine cellar; another swinging door, farther back, led to the kitchen. Max had checked after lunch and discovered an exit from the kitchen into a side street. An escape route if he needed one.

Max was sitting at the bar, nursing a beer and reading the broadsheet, Paris-Soir, when a broad-shouldered man in an expensive suit walked in at precisely ten o'clock. It was the man

Max had seen with Lachance and Marois all those weeks ago in La Coquette. It was the first time Max had seen him up close and he watched him over the edge of the paper as he made his way through the bar, stopping to greet other patrons, with a few words or a smile, like a veteran politician. Two men, one holding a leather valise, followed him closely but did not join in the glad-handing. Bucard was the leader; the others, merely followers.

Bucard was handsome, his features chiseled and his teeth even and white. His smile radiated sincerity. Even his eyes played along, blue and twinkling, with just enough crinkle around them to signify maturity rather than age. He was well over six-feet and as fit as a man approaching fifty could be. His hair was blonde and if it were streaked with grey it didn't show in this light. His hands were outsized – swallowing those of other men in his grip. Yet they also seemed gentle. He wore a silver ring on his right hand. It bore an insignia of the black cross.

Max glanced at the other two men. They wore the same rings. The larger man, bald and clean-shaven but with what looked to be a perpetual shadow on his chin, was beefy rather than muscular. His hands were pale and thick-fingered with tufts of black hair between the knuckles. Max was prepared to bet that he spoke with a rasp. The other man was small, not more than an inch or two over five feet, with a thin black mustache and curly black hair. He was the youngest of the three, built like a whippet, all sinew and grace. Max was sure it was Bucard's men who had assaulted him the first night he had been at Jake's place.

Bucard glanced at him, caught and held his gaze over the newspaper's edge. Max felt he had been assessed and found wanting. It was the way he used to feel when his Uncle George looked at him when they were getting ready for church.

It took Bucard and his men nearly ten minutes to complete their perambulation. By then the barman had descended into the cellar and returned with a dusty bottle of red wine and delivered it to their booth. It was not one of the shuttered ones. Bucard intended to see and be seen.

Max waited to see if anyone else would join them before folding his paper and walking over to stand at the end of the table.

"André Bucard," he said.

"Who wants to know?" rasped the larger of Bucard's companions. His eyes were narrowed and he had slipped his hand into his jacket pocket. Max could feel the weight of his own gun at his side.

Bucard put his hand on the man's arms. "Easy, Michel, the Americans are our friends." His voice was deep and resonant, suited to bombast as well as gentle persuasion.

"Canadian, actually," said Max.

Bucard shrugged and smiled. "Brothers in arms, all. What can I do for you?"

"My name as Max Anderson."

Bucard raised his eyebrows quizzically. The smaller man said, "Hevel Barzani's friend."

"Thank you, David. I would like to speak to this man." When the other two didn't move, he added. "In private."

Michel and David slid from their seats and sat at the bar. Bucard motioned to the barman and he brought another glass. Bucard poured a measure of ruby into the deep bowl and slid it across the table.

Max held the wine to the light. Diamonds swam in a crystal pool of deepest crimson. The bouquet, after he swirled the wine and held the bowl to his nose, was earthy, with the faintest hint of leather and berry. The leather was more pronounced on his tongue, farther back, blackberry and smoke. The finish was smooth and fruity and lasted without bitterness.

"Excellent vintage," Max said.

"You have sophisticated tastes," said Bucard. "For a Canadian of what, twenty-five years?"

Max felt himself flush. "I'll be twenty-six in May."

"A glorious age," said Bucard. "Old enough to know what it means to be alive, young enough not to believe in death."

"I believe in death," said Max.

Bucard looked at him thoughtfully. "Yes, I suppose, young men do believe in death, now. I was being nostalgic for an age that no longer exists."

"Do you believe in death?"

"I understand it," said Bucard, his voice low and gentle. He leaned forward, the bulk of his shoulders looming large. His pale blue eyes fixed on Max's face. There was no one else in the room; there was no room, only Bucard and Max.

"Hevel Barzani was my friend," said Max. "He was murdered. It was not a pleasant death."

"And you think I had something to do with it." Bucard didn't make it a question.

"Did you?"

"Perhaps. Although not directly."

"I'm not interested in semantics," said Max. "If you ordered it done, you may as well have carried the knife yourself."

Bucard leaned back, the intimacy gone as if a light had snapped off. "Have you ever heard of Thomas Becket?"

"No."

"He was Archbishop of Canterbury under the English King Henry the Second. He angered his king, as men of faith often do. In a fit of rage, Henry was heard to cry: 'Will no one rid me of this vexatious priest?' Two knights took his words as a command and killed Becket in his own cathedral. The king repudiated his followers in a great show of remorse and the Pope made Becket a saint. The Archbishop had the last laugh, albeit from heaven."

"You're Henry the second and Michel and David are the knights. Does that make Barzani a saint?"

"Metaphors have their limits. My men don't try to guess my intent. If I want something done, I tell them. My other supporters are not always so astute. It is possible that someone heard me speak against the flood of immigrants that are polluting the land and blood of France. They might have interpreted that as a call to action. I cannot take responsibility for the actions of extremists."

"It seems that no one ever can. But why would your supporters kill Barzani unless you mentioned him by name?"

"An excellent question. I knew of Barzani, of course. It's a small city for all that and men who work on the international stage often rub against each other. Frictions develop. But Barzani was at most a minor irritant. For the most part, I found him a figure of bathos. Like Don Quixote, tilting against windmills."

"That would make me Sancho Panza, I suppose."

"Excellent, Max. I had almost despaired of your education."

"What was quixotic about Hevel's ambitions?"

"Men make history and are made by it. Barzani understood the first part of that equation but not the second. History has its own impulses; it rises and falls like the tide. Men may sail with the tide and achieve great things. But no one can sail against the tide. Barzani could see the shape of things to come as well as I but he thought he could change them. The liberal dream died in the trenches of Europe. No one – certainly not someone like Hevel Barzani – can revive it."

"Your defense, then, is that Barzani wasn't worth killing?"

"My defense is that I didn't do it. Or order it done. Did a supporter of mine do it? Perhaps. I have many supporters. More every day. Did they do it for political reasons? Perhaps, although if so, the benefits are obscure. Barzani was a trader in information and other dangerous things. He did it for principles; others do it for money. Most murders are committed for money or love."

"Speaking of money, I've seen you with Eduard Lachance."

Bucard raised an eyebrow. "You do get around. I've had a drink or two at La Coquette. I've spoken to the owner but that's the limit of it."

The waiter appeared with a small plate of paté and small pieces of toasted bread. Bucard spread the meat thinly on a square of bread with a small silver knife, the motions of his large hands surprisingly delicate. Bucard was completely focused on the task and Max realized the conversation was over. He took one final sip of his wine and stood up.

"Hevel Barzani believed in justice. He believed in the rights of people. He was kind and he was fair. If that is tilting at windmills, then hand me my lance and lead me to my horse."

Bucard laughed. It was a genuine laugh and, in other circumstances, Max would call it a good laugh.

"Good luck, Mr. Anderson. I hope you solve your little mystery." Bucard's face grew hard. "If you try to stand against the tide of history, you will be swept away. Not a threat. Merely a prediction."

Twenty-Eight – Friday, February 14 to Sunday, February 16, 1919

Max perched on a stool at Le Coq Bleu, nursing his beer and idly drawing figures in the moisture pooled on the zinc bar. The metal plate in his left leg throbbed, a reminder of the wound that had ended his war six months earlier. He had thought himself well out of it. No more violence, no more senseless death. But now memories of the war threatened to overwhelm him.

The August sun sent shimmers of heat off the churned earth of the French countryside. They had been fighting for days in the endless struggle to take Amiens. His unit, the 246th Battalion CEF – the Nova Scotia Highlanders as they were known – had been in the thick of the battle and had taken heavy casualties. Less than ten days had passed since his promotion to the field rank of Lieutenant, when Michael Whittington, a twenty-two-year-old boy from Amherst, had taken a sniper's bullet to the brain. The new brass "pips" on his shoulders seemed like a weight on his back and he lived in constant dread that he would falter at the moment of crisis.

He had proven himself in the trenches of northern France and had the medals to show for it. But still, the nagging doubt had plagued his mind. Did he have what it took? The doubt plagued him still.

He had done what they asked – removed his sergeant's stripes and traded his faithful .303 Lee Enfield for an officer's sidearm. The Webley .445 calibre revolver, inherited from Whittington, who himself had bought it from a British officer on the Somme in 1916, had served him well. And now, all these months later, the revolver was missing.

Max shook his head, trying to clear it of the memories of that August day. He could still hear the sporadic rattle of small arms fire as the battle started again. And then the terrifying howl of an incoming artillery shell. A week later he had recovered consciousness in a field hospital with his femur shattered and his leg in a cast from hip to ankle. Lucky to be alive, the doctors said, luckier still to have a chance at walking again. *Lucky to be out of it*, Max thought.

The Armistice on November 11th was supposed to end the killing. But, it seemed, no one had told the people of Paris.

At a table near the back, Henri was already well into his second brandy, though it wasn't yet noon. Yesim had decided to close the bar for a few days, until the latest outbreak of flu subsided, but he always made exceptions for "special customers."

"Hey, Max, it says in Le Matin," said Henri, pointing at the paper spread out in front of him, "that someone shot Bonnet."

"A surprise that's no surprise," said Yesim, stacking almost clean glasses on a shelf. "The man had more enemies than friends."

True enough, thought Max. Bonnet was the kind of gendarme who wore his uniform with arrogance rather than pride, who took more pleasure in enforcing the law than upholding it.

"I heard on the street it was an execution," said Yesim. "A single bullet to the back of the head. Payback for what he didn't do in the war."

"Must have been a different Bonnet," said Henri. "Le Matin says he was shot three times. Twice in the belly and once in the back as he tried to get away. There are no suspects."

Not officially, thought Max, *or not yet*. It was only a matter of time before they found a likely candidate.

"Hah! Journalists! What do they know?" Yesim came from behind the bar and sat down in the chair opposite Henri. "What else does it say?"

"Why don't you read it to him, Max? You said you wanted to master the passé simple." Henri held out the paper. Max's French was now more than passable, thanks in part to Henri's encouragement and regular instruction.

"Does it say what the police think?" asked Henri. "The police always have a theory."

"Let me see," said Max. The formal prose of the better French papers was not his usual fare. "Captain Fontaine of the Sûreté refused to speculate on the reason for the murder but other sources within the department noted that anarchists were known to be active in the area."

"Anarchists!" Yesim spat on the floor. "Whenever the flics are clueless they blame the anarchists."

"Where did it happen?" asked Henri.

"Behind the Hotel Fournet. In an alleyway. His body was buried in refuse when they found it this morning."

"A fitting tomb," said Yesim. "That hotel's where the girls at Les Follies stay. Bonnet was trying to get a peek and one of their pimps killed him."

"I thought they were dancers," said Henri.

"All the same to me." Yesim came around the bar with three coupes and a bottle of cheap champagne.

"What's that for?" asked Henri. "You only drink on special occasions."

"He was a dirty flic and no friend of mine," said Yesim. "But he was a regular. That makes it special."

"He was a regular who never paid his tab," said Henri. "But I'll miss insulting him."

Max threw twenty francs on the table. He despised Bonnet and all he stood for but even the devil deserved a proper send-off. "If we're going to do this, let's have something drinkable. And in proper glasses."

Yesim scooped up the crumpled banknote and retrieved a bottle of Cliqot from the ice chest under the bar. He unlocked a cabinet against the back wall and took down three flutes. The crystal glinted in the weak morning sun that filtered through the blinds

"To François Bonnet," said Henri, lifting the glass of sparkling wine in the air.

"To Bonnet," echoed Yesim. They touched glasses and drank. Max refilled the flutes. He had no doubt that Bonnet's death was linked to another. No matter what the police thought.

"And to Hevel Barzani," Max said, raising his glass again. Henri stared at him, his eyes more watery than ever. Yesim shook his head and turned away. Neither man lifted their drink from the table.

"To Hevel Barzani," Max said again. He lifted the glass to his lips and drank. "I'll toast him even if you won't."

"It's not that I won't." said Yesim. "I still feel ashamed I didn't go to his funeral. I'm reminded every time I look at that table." He gestured to the place beneath the flickering neon sign.

"All the more reason to toast him now," said Max. Yesim nodded and the three touched glasses again.

"You still won't accept the official story," said Yesim. "That he was... you know."

"When do you believe what the Prefecture says?" Henri snorted his derision.

"Barzani was a man," said Max. "A man whose death was unavenged."

"Maybe so," said Yesim. "But what good is it? You're no closer to solving it than you were the day it happened."

"Bonnet knew more than he claimed," said Max, glancing down at the paper that had brought the news. "Somehow he was connected to Hevel's death. And this is the proof of it."

Henri shook his head sadly. "Nothing good can come of this, Max. You have to leave it to the police."

"I wanted to leave Hevel's death to the police and you saw what came of that."

"But this is one of their own. The flics never rest when it's one of the brotherhood," said Yesim.

"Maybe," said Max. "But Bonnet had as many enemies as friends at the Prefecture. They'll round up the usual suspects and find someone to pin it on. An anarchist, if they can find one. A foreigner, if they can't."

Yesim gathered up the champagne flutes and took them back to the bar. As he returned for the bottle, there was a furious banging on the door.

"Can't you read?" yelled Yesim through the drawn blind. "We're closed due to the flu."

"Open the door," a hoarse voice bellowed. "Open in the name of the law. Open for Captain Fontaine of the Sûreté."

Yesim peeked around the blind and then unlocked the door. A short burly man in the uniform of a Captain of police pushed past him. Two swallows, their white sticks held at the ready, followed him.

"Maxwell Anderson," said Fontaine, his small close-set eyes squinting at Max's face as if he could read the name printed there. "You are under arrest."

"On what charge?" blurted Henri.

"On the charge of murder in the death of Sergeant François Bonnet." Fontaine gestured and the two constables hauled Max from the chair and dragged him to a waiting van.

§

The wheels of justice turned quickly in France, especially when the death of a policeman was involved. Max was brought before a magistrate as soon as the courts opened and was back in his cell a few minutes later, formally charged with murder. His trial was scheduled for the following Tuesday and the judge and attending officers made it clear from their tone and the looks they gave him that they had no doubt of the outcome. He had not been interrogated and no evidence had been presented so Max could only guess why he had been arrested. So far, his guesses had come up short.

Guilty until proven innocent despite what the Declaration of the Rights of Man and the Citizen might proclaim, thought Max. Still, the judge had asked if Max had a lawyer and offered to appoint one if he couldn't afford it, which was probably more consideration than he would have received in Canada.

The problem was, Max didn't know any lawyers, not in Paris anyway and had no way of finding one, locked in a jail cell. He had had no visitors – which probably meant he wasn't being allowed any. Supper, a thin stew served with a wedge of black bread, had come and gone before a guard came to his cell and announced a visitor.

They took him to an ill-lit room with grey walls and shabby furniture – a narrow table that ran the length of the room with hard-backed chairs lined up on either side. The prisoners – three were there when Max was thrust through the door – sat on one side and their visitors on the other. Inadequate screens separated each pair and two guards stood at each entrance, only a few feet from where their charges and the visitors sat, talking. Privacy was not a consideration.

The screen was high enough that Max couldn't see who had come for him until he was right in front of Minette. She looked paler and thinner than the last time he had seen her but it might only be the light and his memory playing tricks on him. Her eyes were red-rimmed but whether from lack of sleep or tears he couldn't say. Her face showed no emotion save for a small smile she gave him when he sat down.

"Five minutes," said the guard.

"Are they treating you alright, Max?"

"I've been fed and I haven't been beaten," Max said. He was rewarded with a slightly larger smile. "I... I'm glad to see you."

"But surprised."

"A little. I thought you didn't want to see me again."

"It's my uncle I don't want to see. You're part of the package."

"Yesim only wants what's best for you."

"Can we not talk about him?" Minette's face still showed no emotion but there was a tremor in her voice.

"Alright," said Max. "Do you know why I'm here?"

Minette bit her lip and looked away. Her voice was very small. "Because you killed François Bonnet."

"Do you think that's true?"

"I don't know," she said. "Lachance said you threatened him."

Had he? Max wasn't sure anymore. Bonnet had often made him angry and Max had come to suspect he might have had more to do with Barzani's murder than just sweeping it under the carpet. But what had he said that might lead Lachance to say that?

"What do you know about it?"

"Me? What do you mean?" Minette glanced nervously at the guards. Max supposed a drug user had reason to fear the police.

"I know where Bonnet was killed and that he was shot but the morning papers had few other details. Have you heard anything?"

"The police came to see Lachance this morning. You know Bonnet has been spending a lot of time at La Coquette. I saw him there myself last night at about nine. He was killed sometime after that but I don't know when."

"They talked to Lachance this morning and then arrested me at noon. Because Lachance claimed I had threatened Bonnet." Max was increasingly sure that he hadn't, not directly at least. "Did he say anything else?"

"I don't know. They talked to us separately." Minette bit her lip again. She leaned forward and lowered her voice. "I know that it was

Bonnet who broke into your room and stole those papers. I didn't tell the police but Lachance might have."

"What kind of gun was Bonnet killed with?"

"The papers said it was a revolver but no weapon was found."

"Someone took my revolver," said Max.

Minette smiled softly but didn't meet his eyes. "Maybe Bonnet took it when he stole those papers."

The guard appeared behind Minette. "Time's up," he said and led her away. A few seconds later, they escorted him back to his cell.

§

Max slept poorly. The narrow cot was hard and, when they didn't keep him awake, the cries and groans of the other prisoners filled his dreams with shadowed alleyways and bloody bodies. The cell had no window and morning was announced not by light but by clanging bells and a tray shoved through the slot at the bottom of the door. Max picked at the greasy eggs and soggy toast before pushing it aside. The coffee was weak and black but at least it was hot and he sat on the bed, clutching the mug with icy fingers, waiting for what fresh torment the day would bring.

It was late afternoon before the cell door banged open and Max was summoned to an interrogation room. Captain Fontaine was sitting at the table along with a stenographer. The gendarme who had fetched him stood inside the door, staring at nothing. Fontaine offered him a cigarette.

"I don't smoke," said Max.

"Good," said Fontaine, lighting up. "It's a filthy habit." He laughed at his own joke but stopped abruptly when Max didn't join in. "Have you been fed?"

Max nodded. "I'd like to see a lawyer."

"Innocent men don't need lawyers."

"I suspect they need them more than guilty ones," said Max.

Fontaine shrugged.

"You're a Canadian? I have cousins in Montreal. I don't suppose..."

Max shook his head. "It's a big country."

"I've heard that," said Fontaine. "You visited Phillipe Marois the night he was shot. Am I correct?"

"What does that have to do with Bonnet's death?"

"I'll ask the questions for now. Were you—?"

"Yes. But it's already been established that I didn't shoot him."

"I was under the impression that you did. With this." He held up the .32 revolver. "I can have the bullets compared."

"I didn't kill Marois."

"And Bonnet?"

"I didn't kill him either."

"But you threatened him."

"Maybe. I don't remember. Bonnet was an easy man to dislike. I imagine a lot of people threatened him."

"You reported a stolen gun to Captain Gereau. A .445 caliber service revolver."

"Yes. A British Webley. Has it been found?"

"No. Marois was shot with a .445. So was François Bonnet. Would you be surprised to learn that it was the same gun?"

So that was it. Marois and Bonnet were killed with the same gun, probably his gun. He had been at the scene of Marois' murder. He had even shot him. He had threatened Bonnet. And he had a motive. Bonnet had stolen things from his room. It wasn't much but it might be enough to convict him. Of course, he had an alibi for Marois's murder. Supposedly he had been in a hospital bed on the outskirts of the city. But, at four in the morning, who could confirm he was actually there?

"When was Bonnet shot?"

"Don't be tiresome. Thursday night."

"But what time?"

"I think it would be more helpful if you told me where you were Thursday night. From twenty-one hundred hours until midnight."

"I'm not sure of the first thirty minutes. Walking along the Quai des Tuileries, I guess. I arrived at the Hotel Meurice at half past the hour and drank a beer at the bar until the man I was waiting for arrived. From ten past ten until, maybe, ten thirty, we sat together and talked. Then, I left and returned to my hotel in Montmartre. I took a taxi from the Meurice to L'Aquilon. You can probably find the driver. I retrieved my key from the night clerk at about eleven and went to bed. Alone."

"I see. Can anyone confirm this?"

"The hotel bar was half full. I think the man I spoke to will remember me."

"Does this man have a name?"

"André Bucard."

Fontaine started at the mention of Bucard. He frowned. "Strike that name from the record." He looked at Max coldly. "What would a man of Monsieur Bucard's stature have to say to riff-raff like you?"

Another of Bucard's admirers.

"Riff-raff like me helped keep the Germans out of Paris. It was a private conversation." Max didn't think it would help his cause to bring up yet another murder. "You can ask him yourself. He'll be at the same table tonight."

"Take him back to his cell," said Fontaine. "If I find you've been lying to me, it will go very hard on you."

Twenty-Nine – Monday, February 17 to Tuesday, February 18, 1919

Henri came to see him Sunday afternoon and promised to find a good lawyer to work on his defense. As it turned out, it wasn't necessary. Although Bonnet's body hadn't been found until morning, the coroner ruled he had been shot the previous night between twenty-one hundred and midnight. Shots – three of them – had been heard by over a dozen witnesses at about twenty past ten. Once Bucard confirmed Max's alibi, the police had no choice but to release him. They even returned Marois' .32 to him as show of good will.

It was nearly noon on Monday by the time he returned to L'Aquilon, tired, sore and in desperate need of a hot bath to wash off the stink of three days in a filthy jail cell. As he lay in the steaming water, he wondered what the death of Bonnet did to his careful calculations of guilt or innocence. He was as much Bucard's alibi as the politician was his. Moreover, neither of Bucard's men had left the bar during the critical half hour when Bonnet met his death behind a hotel at the base of Montmartre. Bonnet was killed with the same gun as Marois, which meant he had not been involved in that shooting, either. Did Bucard have other agents in Paris? If he did, Max had no evidence for it. Certainly, Michel and David had been the men who had accosted him the night he and Barzani had met Schmidt. And Bucard had been alone on the night he saw him with Lachance and Marois.

If none of them were involved in the deaths of Marois or Bonnet, and the death of ben David was at the hands of Polish robbers, who was left from his list of suspects? Lachance – and Roget –

were still possibilities. They served as each other's alibis for Marois'
death, though, apparently there were some women present as well.
Lachance must have been at La Coquette when Bonnet was shot –
else the police would have been more aggressive in their questioning
– but Roget was supposedly in Lyons. He might have returned at
Lachance's bidding to remove Bonnet from the scene. Or acted on
his own to remove a rival. He had no idea why Lachance would want
Bonnet dead but when thieves fall out, anything is possible.

Joseph Asper was being blackmailed by Bonnet – his very life
endangered by the information the Sergeant threatened to reveal.
What about Barzani and Marois? National ambitions had cost the
world eight million dead in the last few years. Max had no doubt
that the desire for a homeland would be enough to make a man kill
two more if the stakes were high enough. He had lost track of Asper
weeks ago and had no idea where he was living now. Time was of
the essence – only three days remained in the window Marois had
identified – and he could not rely on chance to help him find Asper
now. If anyone knew where Joseph Asper was, it would be Ginger
Buchan.

Max made his way to Buchan's hotel where, with obvious
reluctance, Buchan agreed to have a drink with him in the
gentleman's lounge. If any of the staff remembered Max's last visit
to the place and the mess he had made of the carpet, they gave no
sign. The service, as always was prompt and proper, and soon he and
Buchan were facing each other over a pair of brandy snifters.

"I'm not happy to see you, Max."

"I'm surprised you agreed."

"I take it you're no longer suspected of Sergeant Bonnet's death."

"You heard about that?" asked Max.

"Heard about it?" growled Buchan. "I'm still trying to explain
to Colonel House why I was taken from the French Ministry of

Foreign Affairs by two armed members of the Prefecture of Police and questioned about my relationship with a suspected killer."

"I'm sorry I embarrassed you."

"I'm lucky to still be employed. If it weren't for my expertise on the Balkans, I doubt I would be. I appreciate the effort to come down here and apologize, but this really does have to be the last time I see you."

"And it will be, Ginger," said Max, "if you can tell me where I can find Joseph Asper."

Buchan's face turned nearly as red as his hair. "That's blackmail."

"I guess you could call it that. I understand it's a standard tool of diplomacy."

Buchan grinned at that. "Fair enough. I don't know where Asper is living these days, but he can be found most days at the reading room of the National Library on Rue de Richelieu, doing research for the Serbian delegation – all in the interest of Croatian independence, I'm sure."

"Thanks, Ginger."

"Guess it's the least I can do. I got you started in this mess. But no more questions, okay?"

They finished their drinks in companionable silence and parted company as friends.

§

The National Library occupied a city block and looked like a prison with its walls of flat unadorned stone and high barred windows. There were even turrets where guards might look down on approaching patrons. The entrance off Vivienne was somewhat more inviting, a twenty-foot iron fence with two massive gates opening onto a flag-stoned courtyard. The carved profiles of intellectuals ringed the third floor, gathered as if for a symposium. But the rows of windows, grey in the morning light, stared down at him like accusing eyes. He knew he was close to finding the answer and yet it eluded him.

The interior of the library was as light and airy as the exterior had been heavy and stolid. The reading room was vast, row after row of desks, surrounded by towering shelves of books. Metal and glass cupolas were supported by iron pillars so delicate that the roof seemed to float above the heads of the hundreds of patrons. Light flowed across the wooden fixtures and lent warmth to the room that belied the chilly morning outside.

Max spent a frustrating hour searching the carrels and stacks for Asper. He was about to leave when he finally spotted a familiar face, not the sharp dark features of Joseph Asper but the pale, sensual face of the British officer who had been a silent observer during his meeting with Faisal's delegation.

"Excuse me, Colonel..." Max realized he didn't know the man's name.

"Lieutenant-Colonel," the officer corrected him. "Lawrence." His blue eyes were like agates shining out of his face. "I remember you. The American friend of Barzani."

"Yes," said Max, not bothering to correct him.

"Did they ever find who killed him?"

"No, not yet."

"Too bad. I always thought he was a decent chap. What can I do for you?"

"I understand that Prince Faisal made his presentation to the conference a few days ago."

"On the ninth, yes."

"I thought that he and Weizmann were to make a joint presentation."

"That was the idea but the Big Four had other plans. Weizmann, along with other Zionist leaders, will appear on the twentieth."

"I see. Will the Prince attend?"

Lawrence stared at him for several long moments as if trying to pierce his deepest thoughts. "Yes. Prince Faisal will return to the city for the speech."

"He has left Paris?"

Lawrence looked away. "There were... well, he thought it best to get away for a few days. The city can be a little unwelcoming to strangers."

"I've noticed that myself."

"But he will return on the twentieth for Weizmann's speech. He owes him that much at least."

Lawrence glanced back at the large tome he had been reading when Max approached. Max got the hint and took his leave. He made one more circuit of the library but Asper wasn't there.

Max felt a vague sense of relief as he walked back to his hotel though it took several minutes to understand why. If Barzani was right, Faisal and Weizmann were joint targets of a plot. If Faisal was away from the city, then Weizmann should be safe. That gave Max three more days to find Barzani's killer and, perhaps, foil the plot against the two leaders' lives.

§

Max felt less certain the next morning when he returned to the library. Monday had deteriorated into a series of pointless trips and futile searches. Gereau had not returned from Rennes as planned and he could find neither Lachance nor Minette at LaCoquette – or, at least, they avoided being found.

He spotted Asper almost as soon as he entered the library. He was at the reference desk arguing with a weedy looking man about access to one of the private collections. The librarian's face was flushed and he looked on the verge of calling a guard when Max approached Asper from behind and laid his hand on his shoulder. Asper jumped as if he had been bitten and turned on Max with a snarl.

"Take your hand – oh, it's you."

"Morning, Joseph. I've been looking for you."

"I've been around. What do you want?"

"To talk."

"I told you all I know about Barzani," said Asper.

"I thought we could talk about François Bonnet, instead."

"W-who?"

"The man who was blackmailing you."

"I don't know what you're –"

"Don't waste my time, Joseph, it's too precious to me. Let's go someplace we can talk."

Asper looked like he would raise further objection. Max didn't want to show the revolver here but he had decided before he came that he would do whatever necessary to secure Asper's compliance. By the time the police arrived, they would be long gone. Asper must have read the determination in Max's face. His shoulders slumped.

"Alright," he said, glaring at the librarian as if he were the source of all his troubles. "I'm getting no help here, anyway."

He led the way out of the library to a small café across the street that, from the shabby appearance of its clientele, catered to students or vagabonds.

Max ordered a café au lait. He looked at Asper's glum expression and said, "Go ahead, Joseph, I'm treating."

"You're a credit to your nation," said Asper sarcastically, but he ordered a large mug of hot chocolate.

"Did you kill Bonnet?"

Asper blanched and raised his hands in protest. "Could you lower your voice? People know me here."

Max glanced around but no one seemed to have taken much notice of his question. They might know Asper but they weren't much interested in him.

"I'll be as silent as a mouse if you're straight with me."

"Alright," said Asper. "Of course, I didn't kill him."

"Why should I believe that? You don't radiate rectitude."

"I was a pacifist before the war; an objector during it. If I wouldn't kill Hungarians, why would I kill Bonnet?"

"Because he threatened to expose you as a collaborator."

Asper paled. People were looking now. Collaborator was a filthy term.

"I wasn't." His voice was barely audible. "I was a spy. There are letters that show–"

"But they're gone now."

"How do you know that?"

"I was in the church when you and Bonnet met. I followed you there from Chez Jacob."

Asper's mouth twisted in an ugly imitation of a smile. His body tensed and Max thought he might bolt. He took the gun out of his pocket and held it in his palm so only Asper could see it. His eyes fixed on the gun and all color drained from his face.

"I thought I was free when Bonnet was killed – but now you're here with the same threat. I have no money left – Bonnet took it all. Or will you make me run your errands, too? Like a slave?"

"You ran errands for Bonnet?"

"Bonnet. Lachance. I did what I was told. But I didn't kill anyone."

"Bonnet was killed with the same gun as Phillipe Marois," said Max. "That links their deaths."

"Barzani was stabbed."

"That doesn't mean he wasn't killed by the same man."

"Maybe," said Asper. "But you can't prove it. So, you come here and harass me. Maybe Bonnet was right – Barzani was killed by his lover. There is no link to Marois or Bonnet."

"I don't believe that."

"I don't believe in Vladimir Lenin. That doesn't mean he doesn't exist."

Asper took a silver cigar case out of his jacket and removed a cigar.

"That's a pretty fancy case for someone who has no money," said Max. "Where did you get it?"

Asper hesitated and Max put his hand back in his pocket.

"You wouldn't shoot me here. Not in front of witnesses."

"I found you once," said Max.

"La – Lachance gave it to me."

"The gift of a grateful citizen."

Asper furrowed his brow. "I think it belonged to Bonnet. He was always forgetting things at LaCoquette. Look, it has his initials on it."

Asper turned over the case. The letters, inlaid with thin gold wire, were cursive with extra loops and flourishes. Max took the case and stared at the initials.

"I guess you could mistake that H for an F."

"What?"

"These initials are HB not FB. Hevel Barzani not François Bonnet."

Asper grabbed the case and stared at the back. He took a pince nez from his vest and, with shaking hands, fixed them to his nose. After a moment, he handed the case back.

"HB," he said.

"Hevel's killer took this from his body and gave it to Bonnet. Now, Lachance has given it to you."

"And I'm giving it to you."

Max slipped it into his inside jacket pocket. "You've been a big help, Joseph."

"Doesn't it bother you to know the last two people who owned that were killed."

"Maybe." Max dropped a few francs on the saucer and stood up. Asper looked relieved that the conversation was over. "Does it bother you that a man, who might be a killer, gave it to you? What do you suppose Lachance meant by that?"

§

The cigar case was the evidence linking the murder of Barzani to that of Bonnet and, because Marois had been killed with the same gun, to his killing as well. That link ran through Lachance. He had given the case to Asper; it was almost certain he was the 'grateful citizen' who gave it to Bonnet as well. Yet, what did that really prove? Lachance himself might have been given the case by Barzani's actual killer. Before he could persuade the courts, he needed something more substantial. The only place to find it was LaCoquette. That was where LaChance had his office. It was where he lived. If the evidence wasn't in La Coquette, Max didn't know where it would be.

Yet, he couldn't simply walk in and accuse Lachance in the hope he would break down and confess. Things like that might occur in the pulp novels, but Max doubted it happened in real life. At best, Lachance would laugh in his face; at worst, he would send someone to kill him in his sleep.

"It's simple," said Yesim, when Max explained his predicament. "Break in after the bar closes."

"I thought of that," said Max. "But Lachance has an apartment upstairs. He's not there every night, but when he's not, there is always someone on guard."

"Lachance, and his bodyguards, could be a problem," said Henri, "but I know the night watchman. If he's not asleep an hour after the bar closes, I'll eat my shoes."

"I have an idea," said Yesim. "I did a final accounting of Lachance's share of the receipts. I could go tonight to give it to him. He wouldn't avoid me – there's money involved. At least, I can let you know if he's there."

"I guess," said Max. "But I have another problem about breaking into the bar."

"Moral qualms?" asked Henri.

"Not exactly," said Max. "I don't have the first idea how to do it."

Yesim cleared his throat. "I could probably help you with that, too."

"How?"

"You don't think he left Marseille," said Henri, laughing, "to fulfill a life-long dream of owning Le Coq Bleu, do you? Our friend has more than anarchy in his past."

§

Yesim was in LaCoquette less than five minutes.

"Lachance wasn't there. And there was no sign of the gorillas who replaced Roget. Even if Lachance was upstairs, one of them would have been in the bar to guard the stairs. Lachance has become a lot more cautious since he became a patriot."

"What do we do now?" asked Henri, who had insisted on accompanying them.

"We wait until everyone goes to sleep," said Yesim.

The wait wasn't long. Wednesday night crowds were sparse at the best of times; in the midst of a flu outbreak, they were almost nonexistent. By midnight, the bouncers were ushering the few remaining patrons into the street, while waiters piled the chairs onto tables and shuttered the windows.

Max, Yesim and Henri, all of them dressed in black for the occasion, stood in a shadowed alcove for another hour until the bar was dark and the street empty. Finally, Yesim gave the signal and led them around the corner to a small pawnshop, its door covered in a metal grill. The store, along with several others, shared an inner courtyard with La Coquette. Yesim had chosen this entrance because it was farthest from any of the widely-spaced streetlamps. And the locks, he had said, would be easier than those on the delivery gate.

It took several minutes for their eyes to adjust to the dim light. Yesim knelt in front of the lock.

"I'm worried," said Henri, gesturing at the station entrance half a block away. "It's so close to the Metro."

"It's closed," said Max.

"Yeah, but the Americans don't know that – they think Paris never turns off its lights."

"Pretend you're drunk," muttered Yesim. "You'll fit right in."

A few seconds later, Max heard the 'snick' of the yielding latch. The door swung open with the faintest of squeals.

Henri stepped forward but Max put his hand on his shoulder.

"No," he said, "this is my job."

"What if you run into trouble?"

"Then, I won't want to worry about hitting either of you when the shooting starts. Besides we need someone to keep watch on our escape route."

"If you need me, I'll be here," said Henri.

Max and Yesim hesitated inside the entrance. The owner almost certainly lived above the shop and, although the place was dark and quiet, he might have a dog. Hearing nothing, they passed through the shop and into the courtyard. Yesim made short work of the lock on the back entrance to La Coquette.

"Here," said Yesim, handing Max a screwdriver and a small pry bar. "If the hinges are on the outside of the office door you can pry out the pins with this. It's slower but quiet. Otherwise use the pry. Get as close to the lock as you can and give it a sharp pull. Hold on to the handle so the door doesn't hit the wall."

"Thanks. I'll be fine. Keep Henri company – I worry for his nerves." Max put the tools in a small leather satchel. He carried it in one hand and the .32 in the other. The door led to a short hall that ended in another door. It was unlocked and opened into the main saloon. He would have to walk past the bar to get to the stairs leading to Lachance's office and apartment. The door behind the bar was open and light spilled from the opening, making it easier to avoid running into the furniture. The faint sound of off-key singing drifted up. Henri's friend wasn't sleeping – not yet at least. At least, it explains where Lachance's missing wine is going.

The upper hallway was pitch-black. Max put away his gun and took a pocket-sized flashlight from his satchel. The door opened inward. Max inserted the pry as Yesim had instructed. The lock held but the door frame cracked with a muffled snap. Max held his breath but there was no answering sound of footfalls.

Max pushed the door shut behind him to stifle further noise. The office had not changed since his last visit, although the desk top had been rolled down and locked. All the outer drawers were firmly closed. Most were unlocked but held nothing more interesting than stationery and office supplies. A large file drawer was locked. Max checked the file cabinets. One was unlocked. It was crammed full of invoices and papers, all of which, on cursory inspection, seemed to relate to the operations of the bar. The other was locked.

There was no way of guessing what, if anything, he might find to incriminate Lachance in Barzani's murder, nor of where he might find it. The desk was wooden; the filing cabinet, wood but with its frame reinforced with steel. A metal bar ran through a set of rings bolted to the drawers and was secured with heavy padlocks at top and bottom. He'd begin with the desk.

The lock on the rolltop was flimsy and he was soon rifling through the slots and small drawers. He found Lachance's black book and slipped it into his pocket. There was a ring in one of the drawers, marked with the insignia of the black cross. A link to Bucard, despite what the politician claimed. It joined the book in his pocket. Nothing else seemed useful.

The desk drawer proved sturdier than the top. In the end Max had to break off the front panel when the lock refused to yield.

Max held his breath but the sharp crack went unanswered from the bar below. The effort proved worth it. One file folder contained a number of the documents stolen from his room. Max dumped all the folders into the satchel for later examination. He could only hope they contained something incriminating.

The locked file cabinet might prove to be another treasure trove but it resisted Max's efforts to break it open. The screwdriver did nothing but scratch the locks. He inserted the pry bar between the metal rod and the cabinet and slowly exerted force but to no effect.

Every minute increased the chances the watchman would finish pilfering wine from Lachance's cellar and make his rounds. Worse yet, Lachance might return. And how long could Henri and Yesim wait in the pawnshop entrance without being spotted by passersby or patrolling swallows? Max examined the cabinet more closely with his light. The front and sides were heavily reinforced but the back was constructed of lighter materials. *If I can move it away from the wall, I might be able to get into it that way.*

Max put his full strength into pulling the heavy cabinet along the floor, only too conscious of the noise it made. When it tipped, he was in no position to stop its fall as it bounced off the desk and settled on its side on the floor. A shout echoed the crash. The side of the cabinet was damaged and a few files had spilled from one drawer. In the moments that remained to him, Max shoved papers and tools into his satchel.

The lights in the bar were ablaze. Max reached the stairs as the watchman came around the corner onto the landing. Max lowered his shoulder, the way he used to when he played defense on his school's hockey team and hit the man square in the sternum. There was a satisfying woof of expelled breath as he careened into the wall and fell at Max's feet. Max avoided his grasping hands and stumbled down the stairs.

"Go, go!" he yelled as he burst through the pawnshop and tore down the street. Henri and Yesim were hard on his heels and none of them stopped until they were several blocks from La Coquette. They ducked through an archway and up a flight of stairs before stopping. Max leaned against a stone wall, his teeth gritted against the pain in his leg. Yesim was bent over, gasping and retching from the unaccustomed exertion. Henri, only slightly winded, stood on the landing, watching for signs of pursuit.

"Did you get what you came for?" Henri asked when the others had recovered.

"I hope so," said Max. He nudged the satchel. "Lachance thought these papers were worth keeping under lock and key. Even if they don't prove he's guilty of murder, there may be enough about his illegal activities to lock him away for a long time."

"What will you do with them now?" asked Yesim.

"We can't very well drop them off at the local police station – who knows how deep Lachance's claws dig? I'll give them to Gereau as soon as he returns. He'll know what to do with them. In the meantime, we need to keep them someplace safe. L'Aquilon and Le Coq Bleu are the first places he'd look."

"I'll take them," said Henri. "I doubt if Lachance knows where I live."

"It could be dangerous," said Max.

"Life is dangerous, it's what makes it worth living," said Henri. Max didn't think he had ever seen the old man happier. He shoved the book and the ring in the satchel and handed it to Henri.

"Very well," he said. "I'll go get a few things from my room and then find another place to rest my head. I suggest you do the same, Yesim. We'll meet at Gereau's office at two."

On impulse, he stuck out his hand, palm down. Henri recognized the gesture immediately and placed his hand over Max's; Yesim followed suit.

"One for all," said Max.

"And all for one," Henri completed the oath.

Thirty – Tuesday, February 18th to Wednesday, February 19, 1919

Jean-Marc was asleep in his chair when Max returned to L'Aquilon. He had been working double shifts due to the flu, so Max didn't wake him as he recovered his key.

As soon as he opened the door to his room, he knew somebody was there. He slipped his hand in his pocket and clasped the revolver but didn't draw it.

"It's me, Max."

Minette.

Minette was stretched out on his bed, her bare skin pale in the faint light from the window. She was on her side, the curve of her shoulder, the indent of her waist, the rise of her hip like a desert landscape. She raised her white arm and beckoned him, her fingers curling slowly. His breath caught at the sight of her small firm breast, the dark nipple, her taut belly, the dark triangle between her legs. His own clothing fell as if of its own accord, his unconscious fingers finding fastenings that his waking hands would have fumbled.

Then, he was beside her on the narrow bed, lips pressed together, hands entwined, then releasing to find their own places. Mouths, lips, tongues, fingers seeking and finding, caressing, touching, entering. Bodies moving.

Max found himself staring down into this face, these lips barely parted, eyes wide, then closed, eyelids fluttering, as he rose and fell above her. Bodies shifting. Her above him, head thrown back, breasts outlined against light as he lifted and fell.

No sight but her pale cheek, no taste but her dark hair in his mouth, no sound but their names whispered over and over, no smell but musk and apple and spice, no touch but the deepest one.

It took a moment; it took forever. Then, it was over and they were two people again. Two people, hands entwined, hips and shoulders pressed together, damp skin cooling in the night air, hearts and breath shaking their bodies. No words to say other than the secrets they had already told.

And later. Again. Slower and longer. Then sleep.

When Max woke, he was cold. And alone. Minette had slipped away, as silent as a ghost. He sat up, but she was not in the room. He tried to remember what it had been like to lie beside her, the taste and feel of her, but it was like a dream. For a moment, he wondered if that was all it was. But the smell of her perfume lingered. And she lingered in him. It was, he realized, his first real time. And no matter what came next, this would remain.

He turned on the bedside light and sat on the edge of the bed, his bare feet on the cool floor. He had known someone was in the room. He had seen it without observing. Sensation transformed immediately into knowledge. Things had been moved. Things were missing. The framed Fourteen Points was gone. He knew without looking that all his secret places had been found and emptied. He was glad he had left the evidence of LaChance's guilt with Henri. He could picture the man's rage when he found out.

Lachance had sent Minette to finish the job Bonnet had started. The rest had been a consolation for what was lost. *Or a distraction*, he thought bitterly.

What had tasted sweet as honey, now lay on his tongue like ashes and gall. Max dropped his head into his hands and wept, as he had not done for his father or for Barzani. He wept for himself. And he wept for Minette.

He dressed but then didn't have the heart to pursue her. After, he fell back on the bed. He stared at the cracked ceiling, uncaring if Lachance or Satan himself came for him, until sleep relieved him.

§

The sun was pouring through his window, when he was awakened by pounding on the door and a harsh call. "Anderson, let me in, Anderson."

He knew the voice yet, in his befuddled state, couldn't place it. He dragged on his pants and threw a shirt over his shoulders.

The pounding stopped.

"No, don't please," the same voice, higher now. Desperate.

Two shots. Loud in the closed space of the hallway. Something – a body – slamming against the outside wall. A cry of pain.

Max leapt to the door. A third shot, smashing through the door, splinters flying at his chest and face; the window opposite shattering. Max fell back and pawed for his jacket, found the gun in the pocket and crawled back toward the door. A clatter. The sound of feet running.

Max eased the door open and leaned through the opening, gun first. Roget slumped against the wall, two holes in his chest leaking blood onto the faded carpet. Jean-Marc tore up the stairs, a ball peen hammer in his upraised arm, courageous and foolish in a single gesture. He froze at the sight of the crumpled body and Max on his hands and knees, gun in his hand.

"Did you see him? On the stairs?" asked Max.

"What? No, I..." Jean-Marc was still staring at the gun in Max's hand.

"Not me," said Max, pointing at the revolver lying abandoned in the middle of the hall. His revolver. Left by the killer to be found in his hotel beside its third victim. Even Gereau couldn't protect him from that.

He reached Roget's body. He could hear the breath rattling in the man's chest. Still alive, though for how long, Max couldn't tell. He pulled away the man's shirt. One wound was low on his left side, the second higher up on the right. The bullets had missed his heart and his liver, but it was hard to say what damage they had caused inside.

"They must have taken the back stairs," he said. "Get a doctor. And the police."

"I'll try," said Jean-Marc. "But it may be hard to find a flic."

"Why?" Max took off his shirt and pressed it against Roget's chest. The bleeding wasn't bad but it was steady and the sound of his breathing had grown more ragged.

"The whole city's in an uproar. Clemenceau was shot today. An anarchist attack, they say."

Max shook his head in wonder. Gereau had been right – it had been the anarchists all along. He stood up. He needed to make sure Lachance had really left. Roget grabbed his wrist.

"Wait," his voice was a bare whisper. Max knelt and put his ear close to Roget's mouth.

"Save your strength. There's a doctor coming."

"I came to warn you," said Roget.

"And they tried to kill you," said Max.

"Tried," Roget laughed. Blood bubbled on his lips. "Succeeded."

Lachance had come to kill Roget before he could tell Max something, maybe about the papers he had stolen.

"Rest," he said. "It's fine."

"Need to..." Roget coughed and blood sprayed onto Max's face. "Lachance killed Barzani. I was there but... left. I'm not a killer, Max."

The proof he needed but only if Roget lived. His hand still gripped Max's arm and Max put his own over it and squeezed gently.

"I left... funny, a guy like me... it was for Minette. I couldn't stand what Lachance was turning her into..."

"It's all right, Roget. I'll look after Minette. I'll save her."

Roget coughed again. More blood but no more words.

"Proof, Roget. I need proof," Max said. He wished he hadn't sent Jean-Marc away. He wasn't sure that Roget's death-bed confession would count for much if he was the one reporting it.

Roget said nothing. His grip was loosening and Max thought he was gone. Then his eyes opened and his mouth curled down. Max didn't think he had ever seen such sadness on a man's face before.

"Bucard," he said. "Bucard knows."

Then his eyes closed and his body slumped.

Jean-Marc returned a few moments later. He had a doctor and a very young-looking police officer in tow. The doctor shoved Max out of the way and bent over Roget's body.

"He's still alive," he said. "But he won't be for long if we don't get him to a hospital."

The gendarme looked around helplessly then left to find an ambulance, pausing only to pick up the revolver, wrapping it in his handkerchief to preserve fingerprints. Max went into his room and washed the blood from his face and chest. He dressed slowly in his new suit. For some reason he wanted to look good when he saw Bucard. He slipped Marois's gun into his pocket and headed for the Hotel Meurice.

§

Max bought a newspaper at the kiosk across the street to read during the short taxi ride to Bucard's hotel. The headline blared the news of the attack on Clemenceau. The picture below was of Emile Cottin, now beardless, but still recognizable from his thick wavy hair and intense stare. He looked far too young to be a "dangerous anarchist." He had been rescued from a lynch mob by police who arrested him minutes after he emptied his revolver into Clemenceau's car as it drove past. Only one bullet had struck the man inside and the wound was described as serious but not life threatening.

The door to the bar in the Meurice was closed. A burly young man, his arms crossed, sat on a stool in front of it, glowering at the cluster of waiters who stood in the lobby, smoking and chatting nervously. He stood as Max approached and moved to block the way. He was several inches taller than Max and twenty pounds heavier but, when Max shoved the gun under his chin, he had a change of heart. He let Max through, then headed for the exit.

Bucard was sitting in the same booth as before, flanked by David and Michel. Six other men stood in a semi-circle in front of Bucard. One of them was talking as Max rounded the end of the bar.

"Those damn anarchists have ruined everything. The conference has been postponed. How can we proceed with..."

"Shut up," said David, when he spotted Max.

Max stepped forward, his arm extended and the gun pointed at the middle of Bucard's chest.

"Nobody moves and nobody gets hurt," he said, feeling slightly foolish but meaning every word.

"There's no need for that, Max," said Bucard, smiling. "We're all friends here."

"I doubt that," said Max. Bucard was the only one smiling. The other eight faces now turned toward him, their expressions a mixture of anger and hate. "Are these the men you brought to Paris to kill Weizmann and Faisal?"

One of the men shifted his weight, his hand snaking behind his back for a hidden gun.

"Don't move. Unless you want a dead leader."

"Dramatic but unnecessary," said Bucard. "It's true these men did intend to disrupt the conference but killing was not part of their plan. They are frustrated with the slowness of proceedings. The Conference should focus on Germany not waste its time with trivialities. Jerusalem will always be there but Europe needs peace now. I asked them to come here so I could persuade them of the futility of such protests. They have agreed to leave Paris tonight, isn't that right?"

The men clearly didn't have a clue what Bucard was talking about. But David nodded and Michel followed. Soon they were all bobbing their heads like pigeons picking grain off the sidewalk.

Max made a show of studying each man's face as if memorizing his features for a report to the police. "I'd be happy to have them go," he said. "I'd even be happy to forget they were ever here if you would answer a few questions for me."

David scowled and looked like he had something to say, probably a death threat, but Bucard put his hand on his arm and the words remained unspoken.

Bucard frowned then shrugged expansively. "Why not? David, see to their packing. Michel, stay with me, in case Mr. Anderson needs something else."

When the other men had left the bar, Max slid into the booth opposite the other two men. He rested the gun on the table but kept its muzzle pointed in Bucard's direction.

"You know who killed Hevel Barzani," said Max.

"We've been through this before. I'm afraid the death of your friend remains a mystery."

"Eduard Lachance killed him. Roget says you can prove it." Max saw no need to tell Bucard that Roget was probably dead.

"I see," said Bucard. "It's true. Lachance did kill Barzani. Proof, however, is problematic."

"How so?"

"There is no physical evidence to link Lachance to the crime. The murder weapon is sitting at the bottom of the Seine. Nothing was taken that definitively links the two men."

"I have Barzani's cigar case. Lachance gave it to Bonnet."

"A tenuous link at best. There were witnesses, of course, but they are all dead or compromised."

"Then what did Roget mean?"

"He meant *I* am the evidence. Lachance confessed, no, boasted of killing Barzani. He told me. Michel was there as well. It would be enough to convict, I think."

"Why would Lachance do that?"

"Because he is an idiot. He wanted to prove to me how tough he was and how much a supporter of my cause. As if I would believe he hadn't killed the man for his own sordid reasons. Lachance offered me a great sum of money to assist my work. I suppose he thought he could buy a way into a position of prominence. No matter what you think of me, Mr. Anderson, I am a man of strong moral principles. Do you think I would associate myself with a drug dealer and a whore monger?"

"Then you'll testify."

"No," said Bucard. "I will not, cannot, be linked to this man even as a witness at his trial."

"Is that why you kept silent?"

Bucard smiled. It was not a pretty thing. "I kept silent because I didn't care. Barzani – his whole race – I wouldn't cross the street to save them all."

"We seem to be at an impasse," said Max. "I need to see Lachance punished. Neither of us is going anywhere until I'm satisfied."

"You are a stubborn man. Very well. There might be a compromise," said Bucard, removing a notebook and a gold fountain pen from his jacket pocket. "I could write a testament. Michel could witness it. I can write it in a way that does not implicate me in any of this."

Bucard tore a sheet from the notebook. His handwriting was compact and flowing.

"I doubt this will be needed in court. When Lachance hears that I have turned on him, I suspect he will confess."

"Why would he do that? A confession will send him straight to the guillotine. At least with a trial he would have a chance."

"I made my sentiments clear to Lachance when I rejected his offer. He will not want to anger me. Even a man like Lachance has people he loves, people he will want to protect. A brother in Picardy, an aged mother in Nice. I'm sure I could find others."

It was only then that Max had the true measure of the man. Not for the first time, or the last, he wondered how evil could wear such a pleasant face.

"I understand," he said. "But I have one more question."

"Very well. Although I suspect you will find it one too many."

A chill ran down Max's back. Maybe Bucard is right, thought Max, maybe I should leave it alone.

"Marois and Bonnet. I'm sure their deaths are linked to that of Barzani but Lachance has an alibi for both of them."

Bucard smiled again. "What do you think he keeps that woman around for?"

It was as if Bucard had leaned across the table and slipped a knife between his ribs. Max's breath caught in his throat.

"Minette," he said. He shook his head but he knew it was true.

"She lured Barzani to that filthy establishment with promises of who knows what. Lachance and Roget tried to beat what they wanted out of him. She suggested immersing him in scalding water. I understand Roget left in disgust. Lachance killed him but it was Minette who mutilated his body. When Marois and Bonnet became problems, the former for threatening Lachance's supply lines, the latter, because of a crude attempt at blackmail, she shot them."

And this morning, Max thought, *she came to my hotel and shot Roget.* Then it hit him. *She couldn't have known Roget would be there.* She *came to kill* me. *To stop me from pursuing LaChance. From pursuing her.*

Bucard finished his affidavit and signed it. He handed the pen to Michel who added his signature under Bucard's. Bucard folded and slid it across the table to Max. He put it in his pocket without reading it. Bucard tore another scrap of paper from the book and scribbled an address on it.

"This is Lachance's bolt hole. I'm sure you'll find them both there as cozy as rats in their nest."

The cold in his guts threatened to engulf him. Max looked at the gun in his hand and then at the address again. He shook his head and put them both in his pocket for Gereau.

"I suppose one night, one of these," he said, nodding at Michel, "will come for me."

Bucard laughed. "You are an intelligent young man of good breeding. Moreover, you are brave and resourceful. A good leader does not waste resources. Someday, whether you like it or not, you will prove useful to me. Until then, good bye, Mr. Anderson."

Epilogue

Bucard's predictions proved true. Lachance and Minette were found in a well-furnished apartment in the fifth arrondissement.

Minette denied everything at first but when Lachance learned that Bucard had turned on him, he confessed freely to Barzani's murder, though he claimed it had been Minette's idea and he only did it at her urgings. After that, they turned on each other like animals.

Minette blamed Lachance and the drugs he gave her; she blamed the tragic death of her parents when she was a girl; she even blamed Yesim for not watching over her as an uncle should. She blamed everything and everyone but herself.

Lachance was sentenced to die on the 14th of March, the same day Emile Cottin was condemned. The anarchist press campaigned successfully to have Cottin's sentence commuted but no one spoke up for Eduard Lachance.

In the witness box, Minette wept as she told of her part in Barzani's death. She sobbed as she recounted how she flirted with Marois so, when she came to his door in the middle of the night, he opened it willingly. When he turned to enter the bedroom, she shot him in the head. She cried, too, as she described luring Bonnet to the alley way with promises of sex and more evidence to use against Lachance. She greeted him with two bullets in the stomach and then finished him as he staggered away from her. She spat on his body and covered it with garbage. He was a coward and a blackmailer and deserved nothing better. The righteous anger in her voice sounded almost real.

She broke down when she told how she had come to L'Aquilon to end Max's pain – from the war and Barzani's death – but had shot Roget instead, fleeing before she could be discovered. Roget, recovered from his wounds, sat in the front row of the courtroom everyday of her trial, holding a bouquet of roses but she never acknowledged his presence.

Perhaps it was the tears, perhaps her youth and tragic past, perhaps her pretty face, but Minette was sentenced to fifteen years in prison for her crimes.

Max sat in the back of the court and watched her weep. But he shed no tears. When they took her away, she stared into Max's face. But he would not meet her eyes. She was more than dead to him; it was as if she had never lived.

§

On June 28th, the day the Germans signed the treaty, Max met Henri and Yesim at Le Coq Bleu to toast the peace.

Max hadn't seen them since the trial had ended. He had travelled to the south of Spain and walked the dusty hills and lain in the sun next to the turquoise sea. He had eaten carefully and exercised and read the books Henri had given him. He had spoken French to Spaniards and Americans and drunk large quantities of cheap red wine. He needed to purge himself of darkness: the war, Barzani's death, Minette's betrayal. When he felt healed in body and mind, he had returned to Paris. His home.

"To the peace," he said, touching his glass to theirs. The wine was cold and crisp.

"You look well," said Henri. He stared long and hard into Max's face before he spoke again. "Have you seen Minette?"

Max grew very still.

"You haven't told him?" he asked at last, looking at Yesim. The other man turned away.

"Him?" said Henri. "He's like a clam. He never speaks of her. He didn't even go to her trial. I don't think it's healthy."

"Every man must bear his own burdens," Max said. "She was barely settled in her cell when she caught the flu. I'm told she didn't suffer long."

"To the end of suffering," said Henri and they touched glasses again. After a moment, Yesim, his face strained and his eyes red, joined them in the toast. "Let it end," he whispered.

Wasn't that what was supposed to happen now? The end of suffering. A time for the world to have peace after the war to end them all. And President Wilson's League to preserve it.

Max had his doubts. He didn't see an end to suffering. Not with men like Bucard stalking the French countryside. Or the Italian demagogues calling for racial purity and the rebirth of the Roman Empire. And the German.

He didn't care. The future would bring what it would bring. For now, he had his friends and the memory of friends to comfort him. And he had Justice. She was a harsh mistress but she would never betray him.

Don't miss out!

Visit the website below and you can sign up to receive emails whenever Hayden Trenholm publishes a new book. There's no charge and no obligation.

https://books2read.com/r/B-A-ZSKO-YJCOB

BOOKS 2 READ

Connecting independent readers to independent writers.

About the Author

Hayden Trenholm is an award-winning playwright, novelist and short story writer. His short fiction has appeared in many magazines, including Analog Science Fiction and Fact, and anthologies such as The Sum of Us and Strangers Among Us, and on CBC radio. His first novel, <u>A Circle of Birds</u>, won the 3-Day Novel Writing competition in 1993; it was recently translated and published in French. His trilogy, *The Steele Chronicles*, were each nominated for an Aurora Award. <u>Stealing Home</u>, the third book, was a finalist for the Sunburst Award. Hayden has won five Aurora Awards – three times for short fiction and twice for editing anthologies. He purchased Bundoran Press in 2012 and was its managing editor until the press closed in 2020. He lives with his wife and fellow writer, Liz Westbrook-Trenholm, in Ottawa, having retired in 2017 after 15 years as a policy adviser to the Senator for the Northwest Territories.

Read more at https://www.haydentrenholm.com/.

About the Publisher

House of Straw is an Ottawa based publisher of mysteries and other genre books.